TO THE
GREAT DEEÞ
THE DEATH OF ARTHUR

PRAISE FOR JAY RUUD AND THE MERLIN MYSTERIES:

"Like Merlin in his clever series,
Jay Ruud works his own special kind of magic."
—TRENTON LEE STEWART, *New York Times* bestselling
author of *The Mysterious Benedict Society*

"Once again Ruud skillfully weaves medieval literature
into a modern mystery rife with jealousy, betrayal, and murder."
—JOSEPHINE KOSTER, author of *Teaching in Progress*,
on *The Knight of the Cart*

"I could not put the book down!"
—CELESTE FORSLUND for NetGalley
on *The Knight of the Cart*

"Who knew a book so smart could be so entertaining?
Jay Ruud's *Lost in the Quagmire* is ... brilliantly light
and expertly well-plotted."
—JOHN VANDERSLICE,
author of *The Last Days of Oscar Wilde*

"[*Lost in the Quagmire* is] A Red Ribbon Winner
and highly recommended."
—THE WISHING SHELF BOOK AWARDS

"*Lost in the Quagmire*... takes us into the world of King Arthur...
in a remarkably fresh new look at age-old themes of honor and
redemption, love and valor, and power and destiny."
—NANCY ALLEN,
author of *A Down Home Twelve Days of Christmas*

TO THE GREAT DEEP

THE DEATH OF ARTHUR

A MERLIN MYSTERY

JAY RUUD

To Margi... I hope you like it!

[signature]

Encircle Publications, LLC
Farmington, Maine U.S.A.

TO THE GREAT DEEP Copyright © 2020 Jay Ruud

Paperback ISBN 13: 978-1-64599-090-1
E-book ISBN 13: 978-1-64599-091-8
Kindle ISBN 13: 978-1-64599-092-5

Library of Congress Control Number: 2020941508

Editor: Cynthia Brackett-Vincent
Book design: Eddie Vincent
Cover design and digital illustration: Deirdre Wait, High Pines Creative
Cover images: © Getty Images

Published by: Encircle Publications, LLC
PO Box 187
Farmington, ME 04938

Visit: http://encirclepub.com

Printed in U.S.A.

DEDICATION

For all the students

ACKNOWLEDGMENTS

King Arthur's death (and his status as the "once and future king," destined to return to save Britain when he is needed most) is first told in Geoffrey of Monmouth's early twelfth-century Latin *Historia Regum Britanniae* ("History of the Kings of Britain") and is further elaborated in other poetic chronicles, including Wace's mid-twelfth century *Roman de Brut* (in Norman French) and Layamon's very early thirteenth-century *Brut* (in early Middle English).

What might be considered the "full" story of Arthur's downfall, complete with the roles of Lancelot, Agravain, Gareth and Gawain in the story, is told first in an early thirteenth-century prose romance that is part of a huge cycle of romances called the Lancelot-Grail Cycle, or sometimes the Vulgate Cycle, since the tales were written in vernacular French prose. There are two fourteenth-century English poetic romances, the much admired *Alliterative Morte D'Arthur* (whose source is the chronicle tradition, particularly Layamon) and the less acclaimed *Stanzaic Morte D'Arthur*, which tells much the same story as the Vulgate romance. Sir Thomas Malory, in his authoritative compendium of Arthurian legend from the late fifteenth century, also retold the story, using what he called the "French book," though he was clearly also familiar with both the *Alliterative* and the *Stanzaic* treatments in English. Since Malory, the story has been told and retold countless times, most effectively, to my thinking, by Alfred, Lord Tennyson (in his *Idylls of the King*) and T. H. White (in *The Once and Future King*), and my version here makes use of all of these antecedents. I have added a bit of a mystery, of course, to give my Merlin and Gildas something to

vii

do—though Gildas does find plenty to do here on his own.

Gildas is the name of a sixth-century monk who wrote a book called *De Excidio et Conquestu Britanniae* ("On the Ruin and Conquest of Britain"), which gives us the first descriptions of Arthurian-era battles in written European history. Gildas's fellow monk at the (fictional) Saint Dunstan's Abbey, Nennius, was historically a Welsh monk whose *Historia Brittonum* is the first text to refer to Arthur by name as the British leader in their battles against the Saxons. I should note, however, that the historical Nennius lived in the ninth century and was not a contemporary of the sixth-century historical Gildas.

As always, I need to say a few things about canonical hours, by which time is referred to in the novel. Before the development of accurate clocks, medieval people often thought of the day as broken up into the established times for divine office as set by monastic communities. There were eight of these hours or offices, and the bells of churches, monasteries, and convents rang out to call their members to sing the holy offices at those times. Assuming a day in spring or fall, with approximately equal twelve-hour periods of day and night, the office of *prime* would occur around sunrise, about six A.M. according to modern notions of time. The next office, *terce*, would be sung around nine A.M., *sext* would be around noon, *none* at about three P.M., *vespers* at six P.M., *compline* about nine P.M., *matins* at midnight and *lauds* around three A.M. These are the approximate times for events in the novel.

Again let me state my usual caveat that the novels in this series are not intended to be "historical" in the sense of presenting an accurate picture of the "real" King Arthur (whatever that may mean) in the sixth century, as so many modern writers do. Instead, they are intended to conjure the imagined world of the early Arthurian romances, a somewhat glamorized twelfth to thirteenth century— and to further make connections with contemporary lives, with the implication that these are people not unlike ourselves. So do not be surprised at the occasional deliberate anachronism.

I have made chess a favorite pastime of Merlin's, though I must note here that the chess played in the twelfth and thirteenth centuries was not precisely the same as our modern version: the queen, for example, could not move an unlimited number of spaces, and there are other differences as well. However, to make the game comprehensible to modern readers without long digressions on the old rules of the game that would have detracted from the story, I've allowed Merlin and Gildas to play by modern rules. The chess match depicted here in chapter two is, as in previous books, elaborated from the web site "Best Chess Games of All Time." This one happens to be based on the match between Karol Pinkas and Gizelak, which took place in Poland in 1973, and can be found at http://www.chessgames.com/perl/chessgame?gid=1229026.

But when that moan had past for evermore,
The stillness of the dead world's winter dawn
Amazed him, and he groan'd, "The King is gone."
And therewithal came on him the weird rhyme,
"From the great deep to the great deep he goes."

—Alfred, Lord Tennyson, *Idylls of the King*

CHAPTER ONE

AGRAVAIN THE OPEN-MOUTHED

"The queen is Lancelot's whore, and everybody knows it! Now what are we going to do about it?" Sir Agravain exploded, bursting in the door to the chambers he shared with his brothers, his face fiery crimson as his flowing hair.

The mercurial Agravain was often exercised over some minor matter or other.

"What's disturbing you now, brother?" asked Sir Mordred, his dark eyes flicking up ironically in Agravain's direction. "Did Guinevere fail to praise your new surcoat again?"

"I'm serious, you little maggot!" Agravain answered him. "I'm talking about the queen. I've just seen her batting her eyelashes at Sir Lancelot again in some secret corner when she thought nobody was looking. It's unconscionable. I could swear she is cuckolding our uncle day and night with his own chief knight, and nobody will approach the king about it! It's a vile dishonor to the greatest king in Christendom to have his queen whoring after his own vassal! And we are his close kin—this is shame to us as well. And greater shame if we continue to allow it!"

By now Sir Gawain was rising from his seat at the head of his table, his brows lowered in anger and his face competing for redness with Agravain's own. "Enough brother! We have guests, in case you haven't noticed. We'll discuss this as a family matter at another time…"

"It's a court matter, not a family matter, and we should discuss

1

it now!" Agravain was insistent. Always the most passionate of the Orkney brothers, Agravain resembled in that his oldest brother, Gawain. The green eyes and red hair that affirmed their Celtic heritage at the same time reflected the heat of their passions. Sir Gaheris and Sir Gareth, on the other hand, tended to be the calmer and more peaceable of the brothers—except for that one uncomfortable incident in Gaheris's past that we won't go into just now—and resembled each other with their matching blond hair and blue eyes. And then there was Mordred. The baby of the family. And he didn't resemble any of his brothers.

The entire Orkney clan was there in the rooms when Agravain entered. So were several of their closest supporters in the court—people like myself, former squire to Sir Gareth and now a full-fledged knight of the Round Table. We were gathered for an impromptu banquet Sir Gawain had decided to arrange in these rooms, chiefly to discuss what Gawain and Gareth were beginning to perceive as a coming crisis in the realm: the fact that King Arthur, having for more than thirty years served as King of Logres and now Emperor of Scotland, Ireland, Wales, Norway, Brittany and Gaul, and de facto heir to Imperial Rome itself, had no legitimate heir of his own body to pass this inheritance on to. Perhaps, indeed, the king would reign for another twenty years or more, but given the uncertainties of this transient world, the Orkneys believed it was only prudent for the king to declare his choice to inherit his throne, and to do it soon. As far as the Orkneys were concerned, the king's oldest nephew was the heir apparent. And that was Gawain himself. At least, *most* of the Orkney clan felt that way.

We had been in the midst of these serious discussions when Agravain burst in, and our faces registered shock and confusion after his initial explosion. Sir Ywain, the Orkneys' devoted cousin, finally spoke up, growling and shaking his great brown mane of hair. "Where is this coming from, Agravain? I thought you were one of the queen's own knights. Why have you suddenly turned on her like this?"

"It's not so sudden," the vile Sir Mordred intoned again, the sardonic edge he loved so much punctuating his voice as he leaned back and put his cheek on his hand, looking almost bored. "Agravain

2

has been muttering about this same topic for weeks now, at least to me."

"Yes, I'm one of the Queen's Knights!" Agravain shot back at Ywain as if Mordred had not spoken. "And so I've been around her constantly. Every day for months part of my duty has been to attend on the queen. And I've followed her when she was not aware of it, as well, just to keep her safe—at least that was my intention at first. But not now. I've seen her meet secretly with Lancelot on more than one occasion. Now I understand. Why else would Lancelot defend her against any and all of her accusers as he has in the past? Why else does he spurn the attentions of any other lady in Camelot or in all of Logres? He slakes his vile lust on our uncle's queen, and it is treason, I tell you!"

"How can you say that?" Gawain exploded in frustration. "Have you actual proof that anything is going on!"

"Let me tell you, brother," Agravain continued, lowering his voice as if confiding something to Gawain though the entire room could still hear him. "I had a dream last night in which I watched as Lancelot entered the queen's bedchamber and she invited him into her bed where he tupped her repeatedly—I tell you it was a sign that my suspicions were all true!"

Gawain sputtered, too angry to speak, and Sir Gaheris exchanged bewildered looks with his former squire, Sir Hectimere, and so, it seemed, it was up to Sir Gareth to speak for the Orkney brothers against these wild accusations. My former master stood up deliberately, looking gravely at his brother, and spoke with a calm authority. "I will hear no more of this insolent prattle. This dream is nothing but your own lurid imaginings. Whatever you have seen, you must now admit you were mistaken. Look," he added, suddenly turning his gaze directly at me. "We have Sir Gildas of Cornwall here with us—Gildas who was once the queen's own page, closer to her than you will ever be, Agravain. And like you one of the Queen's Knights as well. If what you are claiming about the queen and Sir Lancelot has any merit at all, Gildas would know. And yet he has never witnessed anything untoward in all of his long association with Her Majesty Queen Guinevere that he felt obliged to mention to me, or, indeed, to anyone else in Camelot. Isn't that true, Sir Gildas?"

Now I knew full well that Lancelot had been the queen's lover for more than twenty years—longer, that is, than I'd been alive. I knew it because the queen had told me so in no uncertain terms back when I'd been her trusted page. And I knew it because I had been in the next chamber that night in Gorre when Lancelot had broken into Guinevere's rooms, at her own invitation, to bed her after he'd crossed the Sword Bridge to rescue her. And what's more, knew that Sir Gareth was fully aware that I knew these things, because when I had been his squire I had kept nothing secret from him, just as he had told me things about his own family—about Mordred's secret parentage, for example—that were not common knowledge among the court at Camelot. So I knew for certain that what Sir Gareth wanted from me now, what he hoped I would contribute to the current conversation, was a bald-faced lie. One, indeed, that would defuse the situation, keep the peace, and preserve the reputation of the queen and the honor of the Great Knight, Sir Lancelot du Lac. Not solely for their own sakes, but for the sake of the fragile bonds of loyalty and allegiance that held together the Order of the Round Table and the peaceful chivalric empire of the good King Arthur of Logres. Bereft of his queen and his chief knight, Arthur would fall and the Round Table would break to pieces. And so, of course, I lied.

"Sir Agravain, I put no stock in dreams. But I can understand why you might become suspicious. I know that the queen will often meet with Lancelot in private. I've even known her to invite him to her private rooms in the castle—always with her ladies-in-waiting present, mind you. But generally this is to touch base with him on matters of state—to get his views on, uh, political matters that may come before the king, so that she, um, might better advise Arthur in these matters when she speaks with the king in private. Besides that, Sir Lancelot has been the queen's defender on numerous occasions—in the matter of the death of Sir Patrise, for instance, and just recently with regard to the accusations of Sir Meliagaunt—a situation you yourself were involved in, you remember—that sometimes she will single him out for some special gift or something, which she would prefer to give him apart from the rest of the court precisely to avoid evil rumors of the sort you seem to have been listening to, my lord Agravain. But truly, I swear on my sister's honor, there is nothing disreputable in these liaisons between Lancelot and the queen." I was glad at that point that I was an only child. By now Gareth's eyes were rolling at me.

But Ywain and his former squire Sir Thomas, as well as Sir Gaheris, the newly knighted Sir Hectimere, and Gawain's son Sir Lovell all looked at me with a kind of grim satisfaction. Only Agravain's former squire, Sir Baldwin, looked skeptical. As did, of course, the vile Mordred, with whom I was observing a shaky unspoken truce while attending his brother's little banquet. Being Mordred, he felt that he had to respond in some sort of contrary manner.

"Hah!" he scoffed, dismissing my defense out of hand. "Guinevere's ladies-in-waiting? That's a laugh. Nothing but a gaggle of shameless sluts themselves, from all I've heard. And I'm willing to say that applies to my own hussy of a wife as well." Now it was my turn to grow scarlet-faced as I thought of my dearest love, the lady Rosemounde of Brittany, miserably married to this foul-mouthed Mordred. But I endured the barb as best I could, for this was not the time or place to address it, and it would only derail my defense of the queen—which was no doubt Mordred's goal anyway.

"That kind of licentiousness flows down from the top," the mocking voice continued. "If the heart is rotten, the limbs will be too." Now Hectimere and Gaheris began to glance at each other, somewhat swayed by Mordred's comments. It was his own wife he was discussing now, wasn't it? Surely he must know what he was talking about in that regard. "Women are nothing but slaves to their lusts. If you ask me, this queen's as guilty as Agravain is saying."

"Well nobody asked you," Sir Gawain pronounced definitively, trying to regain authority at his own banquet. "And I want nothing to do with this foolish notion of yours, Agravain. What are you trying to do, break up the Table and ignite a war with Sir Lancelot? If that happens half the table will side with the Great Knight, count on it. For heaven's sake, Lancelot has saved my life on more than one occasion. For that matter, you know full well he saved your own life, Agravain, and yours too, Mordred, when you were being held prisoner by Sir Tarquin. Now you're going to turn against him?"

"I'm going to the king," was all Agravain replied.

"With baseless rumors and adolescent dreams?" Sir Gareth put in. "I want no part of this. Sir Gawain is the head of this family, and he's telling you to drop it."

Now Gaheris, finally swayed by Gareth's vehemence, threw his weight to his favorite brother's side. "I agree with Gareth. This is idiocy. Drop it and let it go. You have nothing but rumors to go to the king with. You'll make our family look like fools. Or worse, like traitors."

"I know it's true! I don't need anything but what I've seen with my own eyes and what I feel in my heart. I'm going."

"No, Agravain, wait." It was Mordred, to my surprise. "They're right. You won't get anywhere with the king if you just come to him with rumors and innuendos. You need to find some solid proof that the queen and old Lancelot are making the Beast with Two Backs. You should set a trap of some kind, maybe even catch 'em in the act, *in flagrante delicto* as our dear theologians might say..."

"Now you go too far!" Sir Gawain shouted, bringing his fist down on the banquet board so hard it shook the entire meat course. "And I'll no longer stay in the same room with you to hear any sort of treacherous plotting against Her Royal Majesty. I will no longer be of your council!" And with that he stormed out of his own rooms.

"Nor will I," my old master Gareth agreed, and left as well.

"I stand with my brother," Gaheris added, following close on his heels. Sir Lovell and Sir Thomas, murmuring a kind of garbled agreement, also left the room, and Sir Ywain, whose loyalties were never in question, gave a low growl before he exited: "Consider well what you are doing, you little villains. I'm close kin but I'm not of Orkney, and I would have no qualms in sending either of you little bastards to meet your maker."

"Oooh," Sir Mordred sneered at Ywain's disappearing back. "I've been called bastard before, but for me it's something to be proud of. You know who *I'm* close kin too, don't you?"

I gave King Arthur's illegitimate offspring a withering look before following the others. I waited long enough to realize that Sir Baldwin and Sir Hectimere had decided to stay in the room, and, therefore, to side with Sir Agravain and Sir Mordred. At the time, I figured they were just wrong-headed. And I thought nothing would come of this plot born of malice, spleen, and lurid dreams.

Sometimes I could be a complete dunce.

CHAPTER TWO

A GAME OF CHESS

"Well, Gildas, you Cornish dunce, let's find out if you've learned anything yet from the dozens of times I've beaten you over the past few years. White or black?"

I hadn't really come to Merlin's cave for a game of chess, but it looked like that's what I was going to get tonight. I was still worrying over the charges that Agravain had made at Gawain's dinner three nights before. Not that I expected anything to come of Agravain's ranting, but Mordred was a sinister force who, once he'd got his twisted mind around something, could cause untold harm. I had a feeling we had not yet seen the merest tithe of the damage he was capable of inflicting. But when I had mentioned it to the old necromancer, all he had done was move to his chessboard and stare at me expectantly from under the dense shade of his shaggy eyebrows.

But of course I knew Merlin, and I knew that when he wanted to ponder something, he often did so over a chessboard, and I had seen him work many other things out while working out how to attack my queen. The one on the board, I mean, not Guinevere herself.

And he had a nice fire going to take the chilly edge off the cool October night, so as I sat in one of his simple wooden chairs at the small round table where his chess board was permanently set up, I felt pretty comfortable in the old man's den. I looked around at the large, warm tapestries that lined his walls, and mused on how at home I had always felt here in the mage's cave, away from the turmoil and constant pressures of life in the castle. Merlin had moved here after the nymph Nimue had rejected him, calling it a prison, but in truth it was a haven. At least I had always found it so.

"All right," I told him, "I'll play your little game. But remember it's *Sir* Gildas now, and I still want to pick your brain while we're playing."

"Well before we get started, tell me one thing, boy," Merlin said as I settled in for the battle of wits I was always prepared to lose. "What on earth were you and Sir Mordred doing in the same room together?"

"Oh, that," I scoffed. "It was Gawain's doing. He wanted to have a fancy banquet in his rooms where he gathered together everyone he could call solidly in the Orkney faction at court, so he could have a discussion over dinner about the state of the nation without an official heir proclaimed. He and Gaheris put a lot of pressure on Mordred to be on his best behavior, and Gareth talked to me before the dinner to get me to swear not to provoke Mordred in any way. So I ignored him as best I could. At least until that last crazy development with Sir Agravain. Pawn to king four."

"Yes, I'll do the same," the old man countered, moving his black king's pawn two spaces ahead. "That was a bad business with Agravain. A rumor here or there we could deal with, as long as there was no dissension among the king's closest advisers. But if one of his own nephews begins to spread those rumors, there's no telling what the repercussions could be."

"You're telling me! Gawain and Gareth may have been able to contain it if it had only been Agravain letting off steam. But once Mordred joined him, it turned a lot more serious. Sir Baldwin would have always supported Agravain, but Mordred's endorsement swayed Sir Hectimere over to their party as well. I tell you, it's Mordred who really worries me. He talked about setting a trap. And you know as well as I do what a sneaking, conniving little bastard he is. Who knows what kind of devious plot he might be hatching."

"Who knows indeed?" Merlin echoed. "Has anyone thought to warn the queen to be on her guard? Or Sir Lancelot either?"

I blushed, feeling a hollow thud in the middle of my stomach. "Well, I...hmmph. I thought I'd talk to you about it before I did

9

anything. And Gareth said he might talk to Lancelot the next time he saw him…"

"God's kneecaps," Merlin swore. "Make your move, you Cornish knothead. But you need to talk to the queen at your earliest opportunity. Sir Mordred is not going to be sitting back and waiting for opportunity to drop into his lap. He will seize it."

"Yes, uh…queen's knight to queen's bishop three," I responded. It was a pretty conventional move, and one I didn't have to think about much. "But Lancelot and Guinevere have been carrying on this affair for a quarter of a century. I think they're accustomed to being discreet by now, don't you?"

"Perhaps," the mage mused. "Or perhaps they've grown so accustomed that they've become negligent. King's knight to king's bishop three."

"Right. Well, you've made your point. I'll see the queen at my first opportunity. So, king's bishop's pawn to king's bishop four."

"Queen's pawn to queen four," Merlin countered.

"The absurd thing about all of this fuss is that Agravain is mainly reacting to a dream that he had—some crazy sex dream where he saw the queen with Lancelot. Isn't it just insane that he'd get this worked up over a dream? I guess he's one of these people that thinks dreams are prophesies or some such silliness."

Merlin humphed. "Well, you know, my lad, there are a number of instances in your Bible of dreams proving to be prophetic. You know the story of Joseph interpreting the dreams of Pharaoh in ancient Egypt, right? And Daniel, doesn't he interpret dreams too, something about writing on a wall?"

I knew I recalled something about that, so I answered tentatively, "Yes, I suppose…"

"And doesn't the other Joseph have some sort of dream that warns him to scoot out of Nazareth and head south to get his new baby out of Herod's clutches?"

I couldn't deny that this example was well-known and more or less a pillar of my own faith, if not Merlin's. "Yes, of course," I answered him, "but these are special cases, aren't they? Cases where God Himself had something to do with sending the dreams.

You can't claim that all dreams, or even most dreams, are like that."

Merlin seemed lost in contemplating the chess board for a moment. "Queen's pawn to queen four," he said. "No, you can't claim that. Why, just the other day I was dozing over a book and dreamed that I was stepping off a cliff. It woke me up with a start, I can tell you, but I don't expect it to come true any time soon. But speaking of books, it might interest you to know that a lot of people, serious scholars included, think that dreams can often be very significant. In fact..." and with this the old man got up and bustled over to the pile of manuscripts he always had next to his bed, for he never went off to sleep without spending some time with his books if he possibly could. He extracted a manuscript from the center of the pile, leaving the tower to lean rather precariously, and brought it back over to the chess table.

"Take a look at this!" he said, shoving the weighty tome into my hands. I put it in my lap and opened the unremarkable cover to the first page of the manuscript. "*Commentarii in Somnium Scipionis*," I read aloud, uncertainly pronouncing each word. "By Macrobius Ambrosius Theodosius. So...I haven't had much opportunity to work on my Latin, but even I can figure out that this work is a 'Commentary on the Dream of Scipio.' I'll bite: Who is this Scipio, and why is this Macrobius fellow commenting on his dreams?"

Merlin rolled his eyes at my abysmal ignorance, and said, "Make your move you uneducated churl, and I'll tell you."

I turned my attention back to the board for the moment, and said, "I suppose I'll just take that pawn. Bishop's pawn to king five, and you're one pawn down."

"I'll return the favor," Merlin said. "King's knight to king five taking *your* pawn. Now listen: Scipio was a Roman general who fought the Carthaginians and helped pave the way for the Roman Empire. The Roman statesman Cicero tells the story of this Scipio having a dream about his grandfather Africanus, who was another commander who had beaten the great Carthaginian general Hannibal."

All of this seemed irrelevant to me. "King's knight to king's bishop three," I said, thinking to get him back to the subject by getting his mind back in the game. "What's all this got to do with Agravain and his dreams?"

"I only mean to say," Merlin replied, a bit miffed, "that Macrobius here argues that there are several types of dreams. Two of them are meaningless—those are what he calls a *visum* or apparition, where you see something frightening or ghostly in the dream but it dissipates—actually I think my dream of slipping on the cliff was of that order; and the *insomnium* or nightmare, which is a bad dream that is caused by indigestion perhaps, or by worrying about something so much that you dream about it at night."

"So Agravain's dream about Lancelot and Guinevere might be that kind of a dream, an *insomnium*, that he dreamt because he was obsessing over the queen having a lover so much while he was awake?"

Merlin shrugged and pursed his lips. "There's a chance that might be it," he said. "But Macrobius also claims that there are three different kinds of dreams that really *are* meaningful. One of these is the *oraculum*, which is what Scipio's dream was. It's when an important figure like an ancestor or a great man of the past comes to you in a dream and just tells you what's going to happen or gives you important advice. Africanus in Scipio's dream shows him the fate of the good in the afterlife, the good being those who contribute to the 'common profit' in Cicero's way of thinking. The highest kind of meaningful dream, according to this Macrobius, is the *somnium*, which is an enigmatic dream made up of strange symbols or events that must be looked at and interpreted before anything can be made of it."

"If you can't figure out what it means, why is that the highest category?" I asked. Reasonably, I thought.

"Just the sort of question an illiterate simpleton like yourself would ask," Merlin said, only half in jest. "This Macrobius is a scholar, remember. Of course, the dream that requires the musings of a scholar to decode is going to be the highest form. It's certainly the most interesting to *him*. But look, there's one last kind of meaningful dream called the *visio*, where you just dream something that actually comes true. I think that you and I could agree, knowing what we know, that it is possible to interpret Agravain's dream as an actual *visio*—since what he dreamed is in fact the truth. And while you digest that, I'm moving my queen's bishop's pawn to queen's bishop three."

I did think about it. Part of my mind noticed that my knight was in danger. Slowly I moved my own king's bishop to queen three, and then finally responded to Merlin's long exposition on dreams: "I still don't buy it. I don't care how many books this Macrobius has written or how good his Latin is. My own experience tells me that dreams come from our own heads and what's in them, not from some secret message sent by God or the devil or bloody Apollo or anybody else."

Merlin raised one of those ponderous eyebrows at me for a few seconds and then broke into a low chuckle. "Precisely my own opinion, young Gildas," he said, picking up the manuscript of Macrobius and returning it to the pile next to his bedside table. "With one caveat: I happen to think there is something to be said for the concept of the *somnium*, the enigmatic but prophetic dream. Now don't start arguing before you hear me out," he said, motioning me to calm down as I had started to rise with an emphatic "no."

"I don't say that the *somnium* is a message sent by some supernatural power. Only that there are times that our own minds send us signals in dreams that we don't understand at the time. King's knight to king's bishop six, by the way, taking your knight."

"Well then, queen's pawn to queen's bishop three, taking your *own* knight. But as for what you say about symbolic dreams, I still don't know. Show me why you think they're real."

"How else do you explain my own famous power as a seer or prophet? You know I have that reputation and you know how bogus it all is. You know when I have one of my 'spells' that I have visions. It's some odd quirk about the way my own brain works—but think about it. What are those visions but virtual waking dreams? Isn't it so?"

I shrugged. "If you say so."

"I do say so! And what kind of dream do they resemble most?"

"You're going to tell me they're like the symbolic, *somnium* dream, I suppose," I answered. "Because…"

13

"Because, as you know yourself, there is no clear message in them. Only a symbolic suggestion that must be interpreted. The green tree, which turns out to be an heraldic emblem. The dog turning on its master, which describes the faithful servant murdering her mistress. The widow who triumphs, which is, well, a widow taking revenge for her murdered husband. You remember the vague suggestiveness of those visions. Or should I say those *somnia*. So... king's bishop to king two."

"Yes, all right," I said thoughtfully. "I'm going to castle now."

"And I'll do the same," the old man responded, moving his king over to his king's rook and flipping the rook to the other side of his king.

I saw an opening here and took it. "King's bishop to king's rook seven," I said. "Check."

That got his attention, and while he pondered the situation for the moment, I got back to the thing that was really bothering me. "But surely you're not saying that this dream of Agravain's is prophetic in the same way."

"King to king's rook two," Merlin said, "taking your bishop. Certainly not in any sense that our friend Macrobius has in mind. But yes, Agravain's dream is prophetic in that, like my own visions, it is the result of his mind exercising on a particular matter and suggesting solutions. Agravain pondering the relationship between the queen and Lancelot has hit upon what is, in fact, the correct solution in the form of a dream."

That was surely not what I had hoped to hear from the old necromancer. "Knight to king's knight five. And check again." I had the advantage in the game, I thought, and moved to pursue it. In real life, however, I was feeling not at all in control. "So what do we do?"

"King's bishop to king's knight four, taking your knight," Merlin followed up. He was looking curiously at the board, as if he was either surprised by my aggressive attack in the game or confused by Agravain's accusations. Either way I sensed that he was unsure about his next move.

"Queen to king's rook five," I said. "Check. Agravain is a pest. But as I said before, Mordred is truly sinister."

"Agravain cannot be taken lightly," Merlin said, his eyes closing as he tried to keep himself calm. "His mouth will spread the rumor of his own dream throughout the castle. I do not know what the king will do if confronted with it. But if both Agravain and Mordred are focused on finding proof of the queen's affair with Lancelot, they can keep a permanent watch on either Lancelot or Guinevere and, if anything indiscreet occurs between the two, be the first to know. King's bishop to king's rook three."

"King's rook to king's bishop six. What do we do?"

"Do? About Agravain and Mordred?" Merlin twisted his mouth to the side in an emblem of frustration. "Nothing much we *can* do. Warn Lancelot and Guinevere that they are being watched. Spread rumors that Agravain and Mordred are untrustworthy and not to be believed. Try to get Gawain and Gareth, and Gaheris too, to exert some pressure on them to give up this quest—try to convince them that the only possible outcome of this witch hunt is the breaking of the Round Table and the end of Arthur's reign. And that is something Agravain for one could not possibly want to bring about. Ah… queen's knight to queen two."

"King's rook to king's rook six," I said, pondering Merlin's words. "Taking your bishop."

"Hmph. I didn't think you'd make that sacrifice," the old man said. "King's knight's pawn to king's rook three, taking your rook."

"Sacrifice. Yes," I said. "Agravain wouldn't make the sacrifice of Arthur's kingdom for vengeance on Lancelot, but Mordred, I'm afraid, has no qualms whatever. He doesn't care for Guinevere and he doesn't care for Lancelot. But Arthur he hates with a white-hot passion. He'd stop at nothing to bring down the father who refuses to acknowledge him and who tried to kill him as a baby, and then pick up the pieces and start all over with his own little kingdom. Queen's bishop to king's rook six, taking your pawn—which is all Agravain is, by the way, Mordred's little pawn, and he's got no qualms about sacrificing *him* either."

"King's rook to king one." Now the old man bit his lower lip. "God's eyelids, Gildas! I'm afraid you're right. Mordred wants to tear it all down. He's just been waiting for his chance, and proving an

15

affair between the queen and the Great Knight would give him just that chance. But he's a devious scoundrel. Whatever he does will be underhanded. It will probably take him some time to put together a foolproof plan..."

"Bishop to king's knight five, attacking your queen. And check, by the way."

Merlin glanced at the board with some surprise. "I must be losing my touch," he commented. "Or this Mordred business has got me more perturbed than I'm used to. Of course, this is exactly what Mordred intends: to threaten our queen and thereby to set our king up for the *coup d'état*. Uh, king to king's knight one."

"Bishop to king's bishop six," I countered. "Maybe you're right about Mordred needing time to put a plan together—unless he already has one. Think about it. He may have been plotting some way to bring down the king for years."

Merlin nodded his assent. "Mordred almost certainly has suspected Guinevere for a long time but did not want to be the one to bring the affair up before the king. He knows how often it is the messenger who suffers for the message. But if he could get someone else—like a dim-witted Agravain—to bear the message, then the jaws of the trap could snap. And he wouldn't be blamed. And by the way, why aren't you taking my queen? Have you got some trap of your own ready to snap on me? Knight takes bishop, attacking *your* queen."

"Queen to king's knight six. Check, again, by the way. So what you're saying means that it may even be too late to warn Guinevere and Lancelot—that the only thing to do is to stop Mordred before he can spring his trap, and the only way to do that is to, what? Have him arrested?"

"On what charge? The king is just to simply make a preemptory arrest, because we think Mordred *may* do something later? King to king's rook one."

"How else do we get rid of him? Can we think of some quest the king might send him on immediately? But he's never had any compunction about not doing what the king asks. Of course, if it were in the form of a royal command, he wouldn't be able to turn it down, without being arrested! Maybe *that's* the solution. And speaking of solutions, pawn to king's bishop six, taking your knight."

Merlin glanced down at the board casually, and then did a double take. His eyes bulged wide and his mouth hung open. "And mate in one move!" He exclaimed. "Hmm—my only move is to sacrifice my queen, but that would only postpone the inevitable. Or I could put you in check and just lose my rook and it still would be checkmate on your next move. Same thing. The only thing I can do is... resign. Gildas, you blithering Cornish dolt, you've beaten me!"

Now it was my turn to stare in disbelief at the pieces on the board, as Merlin knocked over his king in a gesture of surrender. In all my years playing against the old necromancer, I had never once beaten him. I'd come close a few times, or at least thought I was coming close, but he had always pulled something out at the last minute and snatched the game away from me. And that's what I thought was going to happen this time. But I'd actually won. I didn't know whether I had simply gotten that much better, or the old man was slipping.

But I'd definitely won fair and square, and for a moment had actually forgotten about the crisis posed by Agravain and Mordred, but when I turned toward Merlin I got another shock: One of his eyes was still bulging out, but the other seemed contracted and he'd closed it. He was also slowly reeling about as if off balance, and holding his hands to his temples, where I knew he was feeling a good deal of pain. I didn't have to question what was going on—I'd seen it often enough to recognize that one of Merlin's periodic spells was coming on. I rushed to him and helped to steady him, guiding him over to his bed where I knew he would curl up and sleep for at least twelve hours.

"Listen!" The old man murmured as I laid him down. "The maiden rises again! The look that kills strikes from behind."

"Right..." I said, pondering that one. But I knew it would only become clear after long contemplation—maybe even after it would do us no good at all. It was another one of Merlin's famous "visions."

"So," I whispered to myself. "Looks like we've got a *somnium* here."

CHAPTER THREE

MY LADY'S CHAMBER

"Who goes there? Answer in the name of the king!"
The harsh challenge from the barbican jolted me out of my reverie as I approached the front gate of the castle. I'd been musing on the position of my beloved, the lady Rosemounde, if anything were to happen to her sovereign lady, the queen, as a result of the current crisis initiated by Sir Agravain's accusations. Married to a violent beast of a husband—that is, the brutal Sir Mordred—my Rosemounde was safe as long as she remained one of the queen's chief ladies-in-waiting, since Mordred could not touch her, wife or no wife, in that haven of the queen's protection. But take that shield away, burst that protective bubble, and there was little the law could do to prevent the beatings that had caused Rosemounde to seek shelter back with the queen in the first place. Little the law could do, but as long as I could swing a sword there was actually plenty I could do if it came to that.

But coming to the gates of Camelot, I found that the drawbridge was raised—unheard of at this time of the morning, when every farmer and tradesman from the city of Caerleon and the surrounding villages was due to arrive carrying carts full of produce and goods for the king's kitchens and for the knights and ladies within the walls. Not only that, but I was greeted by this commanding and unfamiliar voice from above the gate, calling out this challenge to me. To me, a knight of Arthur's Round Table and one of the Queen's own Knights—not, to be sure, as well known on sight as Gawain or Lancelot or Bors or

Gareth, but certainly easily recognizable to any veteran member of
the King's Guard. I decided this must be some inexperienced new
recruit on duty and thought to smooth things over with a little charm,
and a bit of name dropping.

"You don't recognize me in there, eh? Look, I'm one of the Queen's
Knights! I've only been gone overnight, not on a year-long quest.
Who is that? Is Robin Kempe with you up there? He can vouch for
me. It's just Gildas of Cornwall, the queen's favorite ex-page here.
Lower that drawbridge quickly now, boy, before Guinevere finds out
and has you demoted to counting chickens in the castle kitchen!"

"Stay right there!" the disembodied voice ordered with an even
sharper edge of authority. And at that word five officers of the king's
guard came out to stand on the fortress atop the barbican and, before
my unbelieving eyes, notched arrows in the tight strings of their
longbows and pointed them unambiguously in my direction.

"What the...hey! What is this about? What's going on? Listen, you
men," I called to the archers on the parapet. "You're not going to want
to be part of this once the queen finds out. Put those bows down!"

But I'd have been better off just talking to the castle wall itself, for
those guardsmen never made a move to lower their weapons, and I
realized with a sinking feeling that the drawbridge was now opening,
and that a troop of five more guards was waiting within to arrest me.
At that point I regretted having walked to Merlin's cave rather than
ridden my gallant destrier Achilles, since I'd have avoided capture
with ease if I'd been on *his* back. But it was only a mile's walk to
Merlin's den and it had been a pleasant night. Now, unarmed, I had
little choice but to put my hands above my head in a sign of surrender.
With a queasy stomach I wondered, what was going on? Had the
castle fallen to hostile forces overnight? But no, these men were all
in the green uniform of King Arthur's palace guard. Something else
was happening—something that I had a feeling I wasn't going to like
at all.

"Keep your hands behind your head and follow me," the company's
apparent commander ordered. I strode over the drawbridge directly
behind the strutting popinjay, flanked by two well-armed guards
marching on either side of me. They could be walking me to my

execution for all I knew, and I called to their leader in a voice I hoped
had some gravitas behind it. "Look you, sergeant or whatever you are,
I'm not following you any farther until I get some answers. What's
going on here? And just where are you taking me?"

He spun on his heel and gazed back at me, and for the first time
I saw a kind of disoriented panic in his pale grey eyes. He ran his
right hand through an unkempt swirl of long brown hair and his lips
quavered for a brief moment before he spoke. I realized that he didn't
know what he was doing any more than I did. Fear and confusion
were the order of the day here, and I had just stepped innocently into
it. "Castle's under martial law," the young sergeant said, as if that
was an explanation. "We're taking you to the officer in charge of the
battlements." And with that he spun back around and marched on,
and I followed behind with my green-garbed escort.

We moved at a quick march across the bailey and toward the base
of the castle keep, that great stone tower intended for the stronghold's
final defense in case of siege. There I saw the chain-mail-clad back
of a tall knight with long tawny hair, pointing to the battlements on
the castle walls and barking out orders to another group of a dozen or
so men, wearing the same green forester-like uniforms of the king's
guard.

As we approached, the knight turned in our direction and I
recognized the tan-bearded countenance of Sir Ywain, the Knight of
the Lion.

"Gildas!" He cried as he saw me being brought to him in custody.
"What have they arrested *you* for?"

"Uh…my lord," the young sergeant began to stammer, somewhat
abashed that I should receive so friendly a welcome from the knight
in charge. "We apprehended this fellow as he approached the gate.
He'd clearly been out of the castle overnight, and he twice invoked
the name of the queen in his defense. We thought it best to detain him
and bring him to your honor to determine what to do with him."

"Yes, yes," Ywain nodded benevolently but with a bit of impatience.
"But Sir Gildas is beyond suspicion. He is Sir Gareth's former squire,
and so one of Gawain's own men. But you did well to question him. I
will take charge of him now. Stay vigilant at the barbican!"

"Yes sir!" The sergeant shot back and gave Sir Ywain a stiff salute before turning and marching his men back to the gate. I turned to Ywain with my face twisted in confusion, but he gave me a quick and subtle shake of his tawny locks, shifting his eyes as if to say, "We can't talk right here, not right now," and then he shouted to the guards around him, "Carry on, then, and see that those battlements remain manned at all times! If I am needed, I will be in the throne room, reporting to the king with Sir Gildas here." With that he strode off purposefully, and, taking my cue, I skipped along beside him, now giving rein to my frustrations.

"Ywain!" I cried. "I've just returned from Merlin's cave. What in the name of all that's holy is happening here? I've been gone *one night*!"

"And you picked the wrong night to go hobnobbing with wizards!" Ywain told me, in a much quieter voice. "Now keep your voice down while we talk. As you can see, all hell has broken loose here."

"But why on earth would they arrest me, just for coming back to the castle?"

"Two reasons," Ywain explained in a low growl. "First, you apparently tried to impress them by claiming to be a favorite of the queen. Bad mistake in the current climate. Secondly, you were away from the castle during the night. That looked suspicious, because it suggested you might be one of those who escaped from the castle overnight. With Lancelot."

And now things began to come into focus for me. I felt a deathly cold tingling in the back of my neck, and a sudden weakness in my limbs. I had to stop walking and hold Ywain's arm for support. "No…" I murmured. "It hasn't come to that…has it?"

The leonine knight put his hand on my left shoulder and hung his head down as we walked slowly toward the throne room. He shook his tawny mane and spoke low, with a quiver in his voice. "There's nothing for it. Mordred and Agravain must have had spies watching the queen ever since they came to Gawain's dinner that night, just hoping to catch Lancelot in her chamber. And last night they did."

"Well, so, what does that prove? *I've* been in the queen's chamber. That doesn't prove anything was going on there. She might have asked him to come to discuss some matter of court. They could have been talking about the weather, for all we know..."

Ywain looked up at the sky and growled his dissent. "Agh, no, it's gone way beyond that, Gildas. Agravain and Mordred had a gang of ten other knights with them and tried to storm into the queen's quarters to arrest Lancelot."

I whistled. "That could not have turned out well," I said, as neutrally as I could, waiting for Ywain to let drop the other shoe. Something irreversible must have occurred. Something that would permanently change things in Camelot. "And?" I encouraged Ywain.

"And Lancelot killed Sir Agravain. And the other ten knights as well. Mordred is the only one to escape. And he went straight to the king, as soon as he was able."

My heart sank within me, and then a sudden rush of panic shot it back into my throat. "Wait...what about the queen's ladies-in-waiting? Lady Anne and Lady Mary and...the others. Weren't they in the middle chamber of the queen's suite? Were they injured? What happened to them?" I knew my voice was nearly screeching in panic but I couldn't help it. My dearest Rosemounde, in the midst of carnage like that—sometimes in a melee the innocent could be badly hurt unintentionally.

"It's all right," Ywain patted my arm, sensing where my thoughts had gone. "The queen had sent them to sleep in other quarters for the night. She must have wanted some privacy for the evening. Only Gawain's squire, her former page, Peter, was there."

"Thank God for her foresight," I said, breathing a sigh of relief. "But what happened to Peter?" I asked with some concern. Peter, after all, had been my replacement as the queen's page, and I had a good deal of fellow feeling for him.

"He did not fare so well. He tried to stand between the armed knights and the queen's door, and Sir Mordred cut him down with his sword. He lives, but he's badly wounded."

"Bastard!" I said, finding even more reason to hate Mordred.

We had reached the steps to the throne room. Ywain shrugged. "Lancelot fled the queen's quarters and stopped briefly at his own to tell Bors what had happened. They got their armor, went to the stables for their horses, and left the castle. Bors and Lancelot, Ector and Blamor de Ganys, along with Sir Bleoberis, Sir Brandiles, and those new fellows, Sir Lavayne and Sir Urry. Maybe one or two more. But they cleared out fast, while Mordred was trying to raise a hue and cry. The king had been off hunting with Sir Gawain and Sir Gareth, and so didn't know anything until he got back, and the damage was already done. The whole castle's on high alert now. But listen: I really am going into the throne room here. But you—" he paused and his eyes flicked in both directions to assure himself that he could not be overheard— "you should go to the queen. Do it, boy. If she ever needed a friend, it's now."

With that he turned to mount the steps that led into the throne room. I turned to a separate staircase, which would lead me up to the queen's royal chambers in the same building, but off the great hall and the throne room. I could only imagine what I would find.

***

In the queen's outer chamber, before the curtains that separated the queen's inner chamber from the corridor that ran the length of the second floor of the castle, to my slight surprise I found Sir Gareth and Sir Gaheris guarding the entry. They were in full mail armor and coif and were equipped with short arming swords hanging at their sides. When they saw me, there was visible relief on their strained faces. Gaheris actually broke his usual stoic silence with a sighed, "Thank God," at my approach.

"Ah, Gildas, my lad," Sir Gareth said, reaching out to grasp my arm in heartfelt welcome. "We had feared the worst!"

"The worst?" I queried. "What do you mean? You thought I was dead?"

Gaheris shrugged. "There's many a good knight who *is* this morning, I'm afraid."

"But no, no," Gareth was quick to add. "We knew you could not have been in…Agravain's party," and with that he swallowed hard, and I saw by the red rims of his eyes that he had been weeping sorely overnight. He had never had a great deal of affection for his prickly

23

brother, but family is family, and Gareth was always a soft-hearted bloke. "No, what we feared was that you were one of those who had fled the castle with Lancelot. He and his party are gone, and there is no chance they will ever be a part of Camelot again."

"I spent the night in Merlin's cave," I told them. They looked at each other with manifest relief.

"The Table has broken," Gaheris stated with grim composure. "This may mean civil war. We all will remain loyal to the king, but it remains to be seen whether Arthur can stand without Lancelot. There are certainly knights here this morning who are considering where their truest loyalties lie. Arthur is liege lord to most knights here, but many of them owe Lancelot their lives because of his past deeds."

All of this may have been true, but the Orkney brothers' concerns had sent me into an alarmed anxiety. "But tell me," I interrupted. "Who all has been killed?"

Gareth and Gaheris looked at each other and then down at the floor as if they were ashamed to list the newly dead. "Agravain, of course," Sir Gaheris began. "And Sir Baldwin his former squire."

"Sir Mador de la Porte," Gareth added. He shrugged. "He's never had much love for Lancelot after being bested by him in the queen's first trial. And then Sir Degore, who had some grudge against the Great Knight after the death of his brother-in-law, Sir Meliagaunt."

"Then there were some other hangers on, young knights whose minds Mordred had been poisoning against Sir Lancelot and against the queen—even against Gawain, in the hope of generating support for himself as heir to the throne. People like, oh, Sir Cursesalyne, Sir Meliot de Logres, Sir Petipace of Winchelsee, Sir Galleron of Galway. No big names except…well, who am I forgetting, brother?"

Gareth knitted up his brow and counted on his fingers. "Sir Melyon of the Mountain," he added, "Sir Ascamore, Sir Gromerson Erioure—knights from Scotland who knew Agravain of old. And then…" he paused and looked at Gaheris. His brother shrugged and nodded back at Gareth. Neither of them seemed willing to give me the last name, but ultimately it seemed to have fallen to Gareth.

"The last knight killed was Sir Lovell," my former master told me. "Sir Gawain's own son."

My heart sank, and I let out a breath as if I had been punched in the stomach. Sir Agravain was, one might say, an acceptable loss for the Orkney clan. He had been warned not to pursue this dangerous path and to let things remain as they were, and he had paid the price for his brash interference. But Lovell was Gawain's treasure. How could he absorb that kind of blow?

"Lovell?" I cried, uncomprehending. "How did he become a part of that plot? Didn't he leave Gawain's room with the rest of us that night Agravain and Mordred started hatching their plot?'

"We don't know when he changed his mind, or why," Sir Gaheris said.

"But we can make a pretty good guess," Gareth added. "We know Mordred, with his serpent's tongue, has a way of making the most ridiculous notions seem reasonable. My guess is he convinced poor Lovell that Lancelot was replacing his father in the king's affections, or some such charge. Led the poor boy straight to his death."

I sighed heavily but could think of nothing else to say at the moment. I was still trying to digest the enormity of the last night's developments. I switched subjects. "And the queen?" I asked. "How is she holding up under all of this?"

Sir Gaheris rolled his eyes. Gareth said, "We were told to guard the queen. By Gawain, who I assume is acting under Arthur's orders, though nobody's seen Arthur since this started. And when I say guard the queen, I don't know whether we're supposed to be guarding her to see that she doesn't escape or guarding her from anyone that wants to do her harm."

"So we're doing both," Gaheris said.

"You, though, my friend," Sir Gareth smiled wanly in my direction, "are certainly not here to harm her. Nor do I expect you'll be trying to smuggle her out to safety." And in a low voice he added, "Go give her what comfort you can."

Within the curtain, in the queen's inner chamber, six of her ladies-in-waiting sat in a small circle in the middle of a room some twenty feet square. It was a somber gathering. Usually when I entered this space, there was some lively chatter going on as the ladies worked on their embroidery or on some other kind of needlework. Or perhaps

25

they were absorbed in some French romance set in ancient Rome or Troy. But today I heard only soft weeping and consoling whispers, the ladies all holding hands or touching one another's arms or shoulders. Lady Anne, usually the leader of the group, was in no condition to lead them anywhere as I saw her sobbing into her hands, and Lady Vivien, the lover of romances, could do nothing now but pat Lady Anne's elbow. Lady Barbara and Lady Alison, the queen's newer ladies, looked like frightened mice, heads together whispering quiet comforts to each other. Lady Mary, the youngest and most full of silly banter, was speechless now as Lady Rosemounde laid her arm around Mary's shoulders, whispering soothing words in her ear.

When she saw me enter, Rosemounde sprang up, rushed over to me and, without a thought, flung her arms around me, crying, "Oh Gildas! I was so afraid you were caught up in this tragedy somehow and were wounded or dead or had ridden off with Sir Lancelot and his party!" I was quite happy to receive the embrace, but even I knew that such a familiar display was unwise, even in the security of the queen's chamber, for it could only cause trouble if word of it got back to her churlish husband.

Keeping that in mind, I did not return the embrace but inclined my head slightly and said, "My lady, your concern is heartening to me. I assure you I am completely intact, as you see." When my eyes glanced up at her, however, she could read the gratitude and delight in them at her bold display, and she returned my look with her characteristic smirk, then seized me by the hand and pulled me toward the door that led to the queen's private closet.

"She will want to see you," the lady Rosemounde insisted. "You may be the one person that can cheer her." And with that she opened the door a crack, pushed her face into the room, and said softly, "Your Majesty, Sir Gildas has come to see you." I heard a low whimper from behind the door, then a hoarse reply. I could make out none of the words, but plainly they were approving, as Rosemounde immediately opened the door for me and followed me in. "My lady," she said formally. "Sir Gildas of Cornwall."

The queen's closet was a small room without windows and some fifteen feet square. Guinevere's bed was against the wall to the left of the door. The walls were covered with tapestries, except the one to the right of the door, where the fireplace stood. I noticed immediately that something was missing: On previous occasions when I had entered this room, a sword and shield hung over the fireplace as part of the room's furnishings. They were gone now.

But chiefly when I entered my eyes focused on the queen herself. I had not been prepared for this. In a disheveled nightgown streaked with stains of blood she lay writhing on the bed, whose curtains were thrust aside and were torn and apparently slashed in places. Her blonde hair was unkempt, even barbaric as a wild tangled bush, and her face was flushed crimson with emotion, wet with tears. In places her cheeks were streaked with thin lines of blood where she had apparently scratched herself in wild hysteria. Her eyes were swollen, red, and rimmed with dark circles. Objectively, I had always known that she had been Arthur's queen for nearly thirty years by now. But this was the first time I had ever seen her as an old woman.

Perhaps it was my years of devoted service as the queen's own page. Perhaps it was my veneration of her as the beautiful symbol of the peace and splendor of King Arthur's golden reign. Perhaps it was only the very basic and visceral response to another human being in severe mental and spiritual anguish. But without any conscious thought I stepped forward to the edge of her bed and got down on one knee. I reached out tenderly and took her frail hand in mine, like a little bundle of twigs and—tempted to bow my head as protocol would demand, but compelled somehow instead to look directly into her eyes—spoke from my heart:

"My sovereign Lady," I began. "You are the living soul of this kingdom, and without you there is no Camelot and no Round Table. But even if all the kingdoms of the earth should fall, you will still have one devoted servant. I pledge to you my sword, my love, and my life. I will take up your cause against all the armies of hell and will die defending you if I must. I pledge to you my absolute fidelity."

She looked at me astonished for a moment, then something softened in those black-ringed eyes. "Oh Gildas," she murmured. "You're the only person I can stand."

27

Jay Ruud

***

There was a small table at the side of the queen's bed, on which was hastily placed an open Book of Hours. Guinevere had, apparently, been trying to find some solace in prayer before we had arrived. A glass of wine had also stood on that table, but it was now in the queen's hands as she sat with Rosemounde on the bed, sipping it to calm her nerves. She'd insisted that Rosemounde stay with us, and I leaned against the fireplace, listening to her give her account of the traumatic events of last night.

"The king, we knew, was to be off hunting overnight with his nephews…or at least, with some of them." It seemed she had forgotten momentarily that Agravain had also been nephew to the king—as, for that matter, was Mordred, as far as the rest of the court knew. "Sir Lancelot had sent me word through poor Peter," at the boy's name she broke down for a moment, recalling how he had been struck down in the melee. "Word that he wished to visit me that evening. I did not know the purpose of his visit, but naturally gave him permission, knowing it could be for no illicit purpose." I glanced at Rosemounde and raised my eyebrows questioningly, and she rolled her eyes a bit. I can't speak for Rosemounde, but I had the feeling Guinevere was trying out her story on us, preparing her testimony for when she was brought before the court on charges of adultery and treason. I studied the great tapestry that covered the entire wall behind her bed—a weaving that depicted the ancient Israelite Judith, whose smooth tongue had enticed the Assyrian general Holofernes, enabling her to behead him in his own tent and thereby save her city of Bethulia from annihilation. In the arras, Judith was holding the severed head of the warrior in her left hand, while her right hand held high the bloody sword with which she had done the deed. I wondered as I studied the image whether Queen Guinevere could, like the biblical Judith, even now manage to beguile her own accusers and ultimately prevail over those who sought to destroy her.

"After Peter had left to inform Sir Lancelot of my approval," she continued, "I told my ladies that they were to sleep in another chamber for the night, and I did the same with my clerk Master Holly,

28

as well as my new page, Lucas. They both usually sleep there in the outer chamber."

"Thus assuring that no one would see Lancelot enter your chambers," I added.

"And also that you were completely unguarded, so there was no one to stop Agravain and my...and his cohort from sneaking into your chamber and taking you by surprise," Rosemounde added.

"And what would you ladies have done to protect me? Or the aged Master Holly? Or the boy Lucas? No, it was a blessing, not a curse, to have you all gone when the fighting started."

Rosemounde shrugged, not completely accepting the wisdom of that. "We could have raised a hue and cry that roused the rest of the castle, that there were armed men approaching the queen's undefended bedchamber. Perhaps there'd have been no fighting at all. Perhaps there'd have been no discovery of Sir Lancelot in your closet, and so no need for our defense."

The queen hung her head. Even she could see the sense of what Rosemounde said. Then she sighed. "It is much easier to decide what should have been done after the fact, than it is to consider what should be done concerning what's *about* to happen. At any rate Sir Lancelot had been in my closet for no more than five minutes when we heard a great ruckus. It was Peter—he'd seen Agravain and his thugs gathering in the great hall and guessed what they were about. The poor boy had grabbed a sword and rushed back here to head them off before they broke in upon us unawares."

"How would he have known what they were about when he saw them?" I asked, puzzled at Peter's foresight.

Guinevere closed her eyes and waved her right hand up and down as if frustrated with herself. "I'm not telling this in the best order," she apologized. "Sir Lancelot had asked for this meeting with me in order to tell me that Agravain and Mordred were planning to set a trap to try to expose us and have me dishonored. He had just learned of the plot from Peter himself, in fact. Sir Gawain had sent his squire with a confidential message to Lancelot to warn him of his younger brothers' conspiracy." Just as Merlin had advised, I thought. Just a day too late.

"And so Lancelot had come straight to you, after using the same go-between to warn you he was coming," I concluded. "Peter knew just what he was seeing when he saw the conspirators gathering in the great hall."

"We barred the door when we heard the commotion," Guinevere went on. "Someone had certainly been watching Sir Lancelot, skulking in the shadows, and had watched him enter my chambers. As a result, they knew he was here and they knew he had come unarmed. So they were armed to the teeth. Twelve well-armed knights against one defenseless victim."

I looked at the tapestry filling the wall to the right of the queen's bed. It depicted Saint Agnes, the young virgin martyr. Her virginity had been preserved even as she was kept in a brothel, as God struck blind anyone who attempted to take her virtue. The queen, it struck me, had in Lancelot a defender who made things even worse for those who had made any attempt on her. Glancing above me, I looked at the empty place on the wall where the queen's decorative sword and shield had been. "But Lancelot wasn't defenseless, was he?" I interjected then. "You have always had a sword and shield right here, and he made heavy use of it last night, didn't he?"

"Thank heaven for my foresight!" she cried at that. "They pounded on the door, shouting horrible things. 'Traitor knight, leave your whore and face your death!' Things like that. I heard Agravain himself calling, 'Sir Lancelot and Queen Guinevere, we arrest you in the name of the king! Submit quietly and we will not harm you!' But I told Sir Lancelot not to believe them. They were men without honor, weaving plots in the darkness. There was no truth in them."

"If my husband had anything to say about it," Rosemounde agreed, "they would have killed you both before you were ever brought before the court. Lancelot could have demanded a trial by combat, and no one could have stood before him. The only way to get the desired result—to have Lancelot out of the way and the Table in turmoil, giving Mordred the opportunity to seize power— would be to kill you both."

I nodded my assent, thinking how well Rosemounde understood the politics of this situation. And how well she understood her contemptible husband's villainous character.

"But Lancelot still had no armor," I noted. "How did he manage to escape unscathed? Or did he?"

Guinevere closed her eyes again, as if wishing to expunge the memory of the scene from her inward eyes. "They kept shouting, calling him a traitor, and Lancelot wanted most of all to cut short those cries, but he had no armor, and I broke down in tears at the thought of dying at the stake. But he took me in his arms and told me not to worry on that score. 'If I die here,' he told me, 'Sir Bors will never let you burn. Appeal to him for my sake.' And he took up the sword and went to unbar the door. I screamed for him not to do it, and he just looked back at me with that grim smile of his and said, 'If I'm killed, pray for my soul. But I'm taking the fight to them. They're going to know it was Lancelot they challenged.'

"He unbarred the door and opened it a crack. Outside, they had gotten ahold of a bench, and were lining up to have a go with it at the door, to break it down. But they were so surprised when the door opened they didn't move at first, and Lancelot grabbed the first knight he could—it was Sir Baldwin, Agravain's old squire—and pulled him into the closet, shouting at me to bar the door again. Which I did, before anyone had the chance to kick it back open. By himself, though fortified in his armor, Baldwin was no match for Lancelot, even fighting in this tiny space. Their swords flashed around the bed curtains—that's how, you see, they were cut and torn—and within seconds Lancelot had given Baldwin such a buffet on the helmet that he was stunned, and that was long enough for Lancelot to shove his sword up under Baldwin's unprotected chin and drive it into his head. He fell choking on his life—" with that she paused, dealing with an unsuppressed gagging reflex. "I suppose this is his blood you see here on my nightgown.

"Well, with my help, Lancelot quickly stripped Baldwin of his mail coat, his coif, and his helmet, and I assisted him in pulling them onto his own body. All the while those beasts were banging at the door with that heavy bench. The door had begun to crack visibly, and could not have taken many more blows, when Sir Lancelot pulled it open quite suddenly. There were five of them holding the bench who were thrown off balance when Lancelot opened the door, and he leapt out, armed and gripping his sword and shield. He kicked the bench to the side and those five knights tumbled away with it. The other six came on to attack him together and at once, but now he had set himself in his borrowed armor, he could not be overcome."

"There is no better fighter than Sir Lancelot," I agreed.

"They came at him in a rush, but he felled the first knight, I think it was Sir Mador, with a single blow to the side of the head, and Sir Degore, who followed him, Lancelot dispatched with a sword thrust into the neck. The other four were lesser knights, and when three of them assailed him together, he whirled about like a lethal top and felled all three before they could even lay a sword on his shield. The last of those knights was Mordred. He took one look at the carnage Lancelot had wrought, turned, and ran from the chamber."

I gritted my teeth and muttered, "Typical. He thought they'd attack a defenseless knight with twelve armed warriors. When the odds were down to six to one against an actual fully-equipped fighter, he fled like the cowardly bastard he is."

Rosemounde sighed. "My husband is treacherous and contemptible, but not such a coward as all that. When pressed, he will fight boldly. But not against an armed Lancelot."

"The five knights who had been stunned and thrown to the side after seeking to batter down the door had recovered by now, and the first to come at Lancelot was Sir Agravain himself. He came on like a madman, screaming insults all the while, calling Lancelot a traitor and recreant knight, and a *defiler of ladies*. Can you imagine?" There was an irony in the queen's voice that seemed out of place, and I cocked my head at her. She seemed to be recovering her balance in the telling of the story, as if relating her lover's prowess emboldened her, and remembering—and, I suspected, anticipating—the judgment of others on her affair filled her with a haughty contempt. She was, in any case, moving far from the abject figure I had met on entering her chamber.

"So ferocious was Agravain's assault that he neglected his own defense, and Lancelot nearly decapitated him with a single blow," Guinevere continued. "He had a more difficult time against the next three knights, the Scottish ones, who came at him more deliberately. They had him backed up against the wall, but in his armor, with his shield, they could not break his defense, and one by one finally fell by his sword."

I dreaded what she must relate next. "And...Sir Lovell?" I prompted. "He had stayed out of it till the last?"

There were now tears welling in the queen's eyes. And her voice turned softer and far less audacious than it had grown earlier. She knew what I knew: that the death of Lovell was a blow Sir Gawain would have grave difficulty overcoming, though he had supported Sir Lancelot to this point. "Lancelot looked around and saw Sir Lovell standing alone," she began. He had to be having second thoughts, I reasoned. What knight, even if Lovell had been as doughty and experienced as his father, would dare face Sir Lancelot in single combat? Why, even in tournaments no one would meet the Great Knight either in joust or in the melee. Lancelot had to attend tournaments in disguise just to get somebody to spar with him. And here was someone my own age, with just a score of summers behind him, a knight of but one year's standing, daring to stand toe-to-toe with the most efficient killing machine the world of chivalry had ever seen.

"Sir Lancelot at first merely played a defensive game with the boy," the queen explained. "He knew him by his shield and his manner, knew that this was Sir Gawain's own youngest son. He had no desire to incur Gawain's enmity, any more than he may already have done by slaying his brother Agravain. Lovell continued to attack, and Lancelot parried every assault with ease. The young man punctuated each blow with some curse or insult, charging Lancelot with trying to steal his father's place as the king's right hand and his heir. This had gone on for several minutes, until we could hear Mordred raising a hue and cry in the great hall and could hear knights and squires beginning to stir and to come to Mordred's call. Lancelot could delay no longer."

I looked at the last tapestry in the queen's closet. It depicted the passion of Saint Ursula, the virgin martyr from our own land of Logres, whose pilgrimage to Rome to avoid marrying an unbaptized husband drew ten thousand virgin supporters to travel with her, all of whom were martyred with her by pagan Huns in the city of Cologne. The tapestry showed the slain companions all around her as Ursula, preserving her purity to the end, stood defiant before the final arrow that would take her life. I couldn't help but think of Lovell in that light, unflinching before the inevitable.

Guinevere continued: "When he knew he must flee or face the entire castle, Lancelot turned to me and implored me to come with him. But I told him I would only slow him down, and that it would make the king even more likely to make war on him if I was with him. 'If they condemn me,' I told him, 'ride to my rescue. But for now save yourself. No harm will come to me without a trial.' And with that he nodded and made for the door. But Sir Lovell would not yield nor give up his attack, and he blocked Lancelot's way into the corridor. With a final blow of his sword against Lovell's side—and he used the flat of his sword for the blow, not the edge—Lancelot sent him flying, and fled down the corridor toward his own rooms, where he gathered Bors and Ector and the others and rushed to leave the castle. But as ill luck would have it, Sir Lovell had been shoved against the fallen bench that he had helped to carry to hammer on my door, and he flipped over it so that he came down head first against the stone floor, and at an ungainly angle. He fell and did not move. After Lancelot had charged out, I rushed to Lovell's side to help him. But the fall had broken his neck. He was dead. As were all the others."

I nodded. It was just about as bad as it could possibly be. The queen would find little sympathy among the knights in this court, not after so many of their colleagues had been killed in the fracas surrounding her discovery and Lancelot's escape.

"Lancelot, Bors, Ector, a few others, they all got to their horses quickly and fled the castle," Rosemounde concluded. "The king and his companions did not return until hours later. By then, the knights were on high alert, thanks to my husband's quick alarm."

A thought had struck me as I listened to this last remark. "But…if the castle had been roused, then how were Lancelot and his followers able to get out? Shouldn't the drawbridge have been pulled up, and the portcullis down? If this happened in the middle of the night, then the front gate would have been shut in any case. Who opened it?"

Rosemounde paused for a moment, knowing I would not like the answer. "It...it appears," she began, visibly trying to form her words, "that the captain of the king's guard, Robin Kempe, deliberately let down the drawbridge to allow Lancelot and his men to escape. He... he's in the dungeon right now."

Now that was a blow I didn't see coming.

CHAPTER FOUR

THE QUEEN ON TRIAL

A rthur's throne room was consciously designed to inspire awe in the hearts of visiting dignitaries and lowly subjects alike. Somber and formal, it was the one place in the castle dignified enough to house the most important trial in Camelot's history, at which Arthur's own queen was to be brought before her husband and monarch to face charges of adultery and treason.

The king himself, in a royal blue cloak trimmed with ermine fur, sat high on a dais on the north wall of the room on his cushioned, ornamented throne. His hands gripped the carved armrests that were shaped into dragons, which referenced the lineage of his father, King Uther Pendragon. Three more rampant golden dragons on a red field decorated the banner that hung on the wall behind the throne as well, the banner of his father that had gone before Arthur's armies in dozens of battles. The high back of the gilt cherrywood throne towered over his heavy imperial crown of state, and engraved on that heavy wood was the king's own coat of arms: three crowns, each here encrusted with inlaid gems, whose untold value could have built the king another Camelot, and purchased another Guinevere. In his hands the king held the orb and scepter, recognized symbols of his royal and imperial power and of his authority as the final arbiter of justice in the realm.

At Arthur's right hand stood Sir Gawain, his Heir Apparent, clad in a green tunic over which he wore a great cloak of bright Orkney plaid. At the king's left stood Sir Bedivere, oldest of the Round Table knights and acting as Arthur's bailiff, who was dressed conservatively in grey tunic and cloak and holding a long, heavy staff of office, with which he now thumped heavily on the dais to call the large and very vocal crowd of litigants and spectators to order.

I was in the front row of the throng of knights before the dais, standing next to my old master Sir Gareth on my right and our close friend Sir Palomides, the Moorish knight, on my left. Behind us were Sir Ywain, Sir Gaheris, and Sir Thomas, my contemporary and peer. We formed a solid group of Guinevere's supporters, hoping to sway the court's opinions if we possibly could. But all around us, voices seemed to be clamoring for the queen's blood. Lancelot had killed too many of their friends for the majority of the knights to let things go on as before. And his flight, with a great number of his own retainers, had left the queen with little protection in that castle.

For in front of us, directly under the king's gaze, stood Sir Mordred on the left side, flanked by several supporters, including some of the queen's own knights whose heads had been turned by Agravain and by their chagrin at the number of their friends dead by Lancelot's hand: These included Sir Hectimere, Gaheris's own former squire, as well as Sir Pelleas, the young and handsome Scottish knight known as "the Lover," whom Mordred had won over along with some of the other Scots of the Table. With them stood Sir Geraint, one of the petty kings who owed allegiance to Arthur, but one who had gone so far as to be admitted to the Order of the Round Table. These were all knights for whom I held a great deal of respect and even admiration, and it struck me then that Mordred's skill in speech must be prodigious indeed if he could convince knights of this caliber to stand with him before the court in his condemnation of the queen.

Guinevere, as the accused, stood on the right-hand side. I admit to being initially quite shocked at her appearance. She looked essentially as I had seen her the day before in her private closet: haggard, abject, clad not in the royal finery in which the court was so accustomed to seeing her but rather in a simple white shift, without cloak or any other accoutrements. Her feet were bare, as if she came to the throne as a pilgrim suppliant. Her hair hung loose and without adornment of any kind, and her face was untouched by paint or cosmetic, her red eyes starkly visible in her pale face that showed every care and wrinkle of her more than forty-five years in this vale of tears. But I got over my shock fairly quickly. I knew that the queen had regained some of her old confidence by the time I had left her yesterday, and that this face she was presenting to the king and to his court was the calculated exhibition of humility and contrition, two qualities she hoped would go far in taking the sting out of the charges Mordred was preparing to bring against her. At the queen's side, dressed in their simplest gowns themselves, were my beloved Lady Rosemounde and the queen's longest serving attendants, Lady Anne and Lady Vivien.

Sir Bedivere gave the dais another sound thumping, before declaiming in a thunderous voice, "Whoever has any business before the king's court of justice come forward now and state your case!"

Sir Mordred, at this cue, stepped up to present his charges. Having been apprised of his dear brother Agravain's suspicions of the queen and Sir Lancelot, and concerned to protect the honor of their uncle the king, which such a treasonous liaison could only besmirch, he and Agravain had gathered a group of like-minded patriots intent on discovering whether these rumors swirling about Lancelot and the queen had any truth in them.

"And when we had come upon these vile adulterers," he continued, "catching them *in flagrante delicto* in the queen's own closet, though shocked and saddened at their betrayal, my poor brother Agravain urged restraint on us, and called to the couple, arresting them in the king's name. We pleaded with them to surrender quietly and to submit without violence, promising a fair trial before Your Majesty and this court. But when Agravain's former squire Sir Baldwin sought to enter the closet and peacefully lead them from it, Sir Lancelot treacherously seized hold of him and slew him without mercy, blocking the door until he could strip this knight in Your Majesty's own service of his armor, after which he burst through the door and without warning attacked Your Majesty's knights mercilessly, though I daresay many of them had come unarmed, thinking only to investigate the aforesaid rumors without thought of violence. And I alone, as his servant told the ruined Job, am escaped to tell thee."

It was more like the serpent in Eden, I thought at the time, but the murmurs from the court made it clear that the majority there were convinced by Mordred's words. As for me, the choler rose in my heart so hot that I could no longer contain myself. "And I say you lie in your teeth, coward and villain!" I cried, stepping forward despite Sir Gareth's hand on my shoulder. I had meant what I had said in the queen's chamber, about championing her before the whole world if need be, and I was not about to let this bully and batterer of women spew his vile venom in the queen's face. "You brought a fully armed company of knights with the deliberate purpose of attacking an unarmed couple, and you can have no knowledge of what they were doing in that room. And you yourself ran like a faint-hearted poltroon rather than face an actual knight in a fair fight. Well you can't run now. I declare before this court that you lie, that the queen is innocent of these charges, as is my lord Lancelot. And I stand ready to prove it on your craven body if you dare to try me."

There was a buzz of disapproval from the ranks behind me. Glancing up, I saw the brow of the king lower like a thundercloud. My actions seemed to be angering him, but I wasn't sure if that was because he had hoped the queen's name could be cleared without any resort to violence—perhaps he was thinking of the grim death of Sir Meliagaunt after that knight's charges against the queen were defeated by Lancelot's sword. Or perhaps he had hoped that a more seasoned knight of the Table would have been moved to step up in the queen's defense. That at least was the way that Sir Palomides seemed to interpret the situation, for he stepped between me and the king immediately, laying a hand on my chest and whispering, "Sir Gildas, I do not doubt your courage or your skill, but Sir Mordred is a doughty knight and you are essentially untested. Sir Gareth here can hardly be expected to do battle against his own brother. So may I request that you yield to *me* the honor of defending the queen..." His dark features were twisted into a kind of grimace, for he sincerely feared for me, I was certain, as well as for the fate of the queen should I prove unable to best the bastard Mordred.

I shook my head and glared at the haughty figure of that smug adversary, who had been standing with his arms folded at his chest and a maddening sneer on his arrogant face. Now he uncoiled at me, waving a hand in my direction and addressing the king once more. "Is it not a sign of your queen's moral degeneracy that no one in this court dares to offer a defense for her crimes but this lowly puffed up squire, who only rose to knighthood by mischance when so many of Your Majesty's good knights were killed in the catastrophe of the Grail quest? But I accept this pitiful challenge if Your Majesty wills it, since it will surely be easier to establish the queen's guilt by brushing away this pesky gnat than by allowing her to testify, and by her tears perhaps sway the emotions of some in this court," and with that Mordred looked up at the king with a sideways glance, making sure his words had struck home.

Behind Mordred, on the west wall of the throne room, hung a great tapestry depicting Arthur's victory over the Roman legions of the emperor Lucius, a magnificent celebration of the greatest victory of the king's early reign. I was struck by how starkly the young Arthur's glow of triumph in that artist's depiction contrasted with the worried, almost anguished face of the king who now sat on that throne, searching for an answer to Sir Mordred's barbs that would not anger the rest of the court, which seemed to relish the queen's humiliation.

Into that hubbub, without warning, a ball of fire came from the back of the room, whizzed through the air, and struck with a mighty crash. Every voice ceased, and shock and awe appeared on every face in the hall. Except mine. I laughed out loud. I knew Merlin's calling card when I saw it.

***

"Trial by combat is out of the question, my Lord!" The old necromancer's voice sounded like a clarion from the rear of the hall. The crowd parted like the Red Sea as our contemporary Moses, white beard flowing and his hand grasping a long staff, strode to the front of the room to stand, tall and imposing, before the throne raised on that dais.

"If I may be allowed to address the court, Your Majesty?" Merlin queried, knowing it was just a formality. King Arthur, suppressing a smile as wide as my own, nodded his permission to the mage, and

Merlin whirled around to face the crowd. "The only just employment of a trial by combat," he began, his fiery eyes glaring at Mordred from under his substantial eyebrows as he spoke, "is when an examination of the evidence provides no immediately obvious solution. Wouldn't you agree that this is so, Sir Mordred?"

Even Mordred's confident swagger could not stand up for long against the inexorable glare of the old man's eyes. "Well, I..." he stammered, "er...that seems to make sense..."

"Precisely!" Merlin pushed on. "Then let us examine the facts in evidence as we have them, shall we?" He looked around the room. The queen's head was now raised and her eyes showed a glint of hope that these proceedings might not end disastrously after all. Behind her head, on the east wall of the room, hung another great tapestry, this one depicting the fifteen-year-old King Arthur, brandishing his sword Excalibur as he stood in triumph after his unexpected defeat of King Lot of Orkney, the father of Gawain, Gareth, and the slaughtered Agravain as well. Guinevere was beginning to anticipate a triumph over this other son of Orkney, this bastard Mordred, if Merlin could be allowed to work his verbal magic.

"The facts as we have them are these," the old man continued. "First, we have the character of Sir Lancelot. Lancelot has been the king's chief supporter and defender for more than twenty-five years in this court. He has helped the king win battles on numerous fronts, most notably against the Roman forces in the battle with the emperor Lucius," and at this Merlin gestured at the tapestry behind Mordred's head. "Lancelot has been the chief example of chivalry for this court, and is responsible for the rescue of many knights in this very chamber, including forty at one time when he defeated the recreant knight Sir Tarquin." Merlin looked around and saw the chagrinned faces of several of the knights, now hanging their heads rather than murmuring in support of Mordred's charge. "Among these I do not exempt the king's own heir apparent, Sir Gawain, who owes his own life and liberty to Sir Lancelot's efforts." Gawain, standing at the king's side in mute support of his uncle in this time of need, nodded a dignified assent to Merlin's harangue.

"And let us remember, finally, the case of Sir Urry, just witnessed

41

in this court a few months ago. Recall that every knight in this room was asked, at that time, to search the wounds of the Hungarian knight, for it was claimed that he could only be healed by the greatest knight in the world. Not one of you was able to heal that knight's hurts, but Sir Lancelot did so, only by touching them. Does this not prove him beyond question the most chivalrous knight in the world, and if the most chivalrous, then by definition the truest? And this is the knight we are being asked, against all evidence, to proclaim a traitor to the king?"

I could feel the tide turning in that room, as the court, convinced by Merlin's litany of praise, was finding it difficult to maintain their negative image of the Great Knight, he who had so convincingly healed the incurable wounds of Sir Urry. I knew, of course, that it was Merlin himself who had provided Lancelot with a salve that had started the Hungarian on his road to recovery, but nobody else needed to know that. And besides, the healing was only the manifestation of what we all already knew: Lancelot was without peer in the field of chivalry. But Merlin was continuing his presentation:

"What other facts do we know? We have Queen Guinevere, accused as well of infidelity and of treason. These kinds of imputations are nothing new, and I can only attribute them to envy. For look at the past history of the queen: She, too, has been at King Arthur's side for nearly thirty years. She, too, has supported him in all of his campaigns and has been the jewel in his crown at all state occasions in peacetime. Yet she was accused, you will recall, of treachery in the untimely death of Sir Patrise—a charge that I had some part in ultimately proving completely fallacious. She was falsely accused, as well, of an adulterous liaison with Sir Kay, the king's own foster brother, a completely unfounded accusation that Sir Lancelot himself put a stop to and restored the reputation of the queen as well as that invaluable knight, Sir Kay."

With that the old man gestured toward Kay, who stood near the rear of the hall, his yellow teeth protruding in a kind of grimace from his thin lips. He nodded his round head humbly, letting his greasy hair fall in clumps like rat tails before his face. Kay stood as a prime example of one who owed his very life to Sir Lancelot, and as a living reminder of the futility of the last accusation that had been made against the queen. Of course, I knew better than anybody in that room how the queen's innocence in the face of Sir Meliagaunt's accusations had been only technical: She was completely innocent of any wrongdoing with Sir Kay because of course she had been with Sir Lancelot at the time. But nobody needed to know that.

Looking at the south wall behind Sir Kay, I could see a tapestry commemorating King Arthur's victory over the Irish King Rience, who had demanded Arthur's beard to trim his cloak. In the weaving Arthur could be seen leading a cavalry charge against Rience, while in the background Merlin himself was depicted, enchanting the Giants' Ring of great stones in order to transport them back to Salisbury Plain in Logres, there to be renamed Stonehenge. I couldn't help thinking that Merlin now was weaving a tapestry of words, with which to charm the court and finally move them precisely where he wanted them.

"And who in this court has not benefited from the queen's great munificence?" the old man continued. "Her generosity is a byword of Camelot. Sir Agravain himself—and Sir Pelleas and Geraint as well—she made her own 'Queen's Knights,' and lavished gifts upon them—though now they stand there with Sir Mordred accusing her of treason." At that the two young knights looked abashed, or I suppose that could have been my imagination, but I swear I did see their eyes glance downward if only for a moment. The queen, at least, raised her chin up a little higher as the mage wove his spell.

"Given her penchant for generous gifts, why should it come as a surprise that she at times rewarded her husband's greatest ally, and her own staunchest defender, with the occasional gift? And given the rumors of her misdeeds, rumors begun by the late Sir Agravain himself in his mad fervor to discredit his benefactress, why should it have come as a surprise that she might meet secretly with that same staunch defender in her private chamber to warn him of this plot aimed at discrediting him as well? I ask you, gentlemen…and ladies of this great court," he nodded to Rosemounde, Anne and Vivien at the queen's side, "do these litigants have even *one shred* of actual evidence that this charge is true? Do they?" He glared at Mordred and his toadies, the full force of those imposing eyebrows pointing straight in their direction.

"Everybody *knows* it's true!" Sir Hectimere burst forth, and at my back I heard the gasp of disappointment from Sir Gaheris at the perfidy of his own former squire, and heard him whisper under his breath, "traitorous ingrate."

"Knows it you say? *Knows* it? Do you even know what it *is* to know, young Sir Hectimere? You *know* things when you have the testimony of your own eyes and ears. You know things when you can prove they are true. You know things that you have *evidence* for. What do you have here?" Merlin looked at Hectimere, then looked around the room. "You have a closed door. You have evidence of nothing."

Sir Pelleas cleared his throat and attempted to defend Sir Hectimere's claim, though with a bit of uncertainty, since Merlin seemed to be having it all his own way. "I think that most people would agree that a closed door is evidence of *something*. I mean, I have the evidence of my own experience, if it comes to that," and with that Pelleas "the Lover" flashed a sly hint of a smile, drawing himself up to his full height and stepping back as if having scored a point.

"And for that, the rest of us have only the evidence of your own mouth," Merlin shot back, raising a few snickers from the assembled crowd, despite the seriousness of the occasion. "Which is all the evidence anyone has ever had of the queen's infidelity. God's bunions, you young dunces, King Arthur's sister Morgan le Fay visited the castle last week and spent some time in the king's private chamber—behind closed doors—in discussions with him. Are you implying that we should assume the king was bedding his own sister at the time?"

A collective gasp filled the room. Merlin's history with Arthur was such that he could say things to the king that no one else would dare to, but even I thought Merlin had gone too far this time. It wasn't just the shocking suggestion of Merlin's words regarding the most powerful monarch in Christendom, and in the king's own presence at that. It was also the dark family secret (known to the Orkney brothers themselves, and to Merlin and me, but to few others) that the king had in fact unwittingly sired the bastard Mordred on his own sister, Queen Margause of Orkney, before his own parentage was known. At the suggestion, Sir Mordred actually looked uncomfortable and turned a deep shade of red, and the king himself was stirring with a face like thunder, and made as if to rise from his throne. But Sir Bedivere laid a hand lightly on Arthur's shoulder and the king, desiring to keep what decorum he could under the circumstances, settled back down as Bedivere did his speaking for him.

"My lord Merlin," Sir Bedivere cautioned. "You forget yourself. Even to suggest such a thing of the king is out of place here—or anywhere else, for that matter!" The old knight quickly corrected himself as Arthur's glare now turned in *his* direction. "Some may even consider your words tantamount to treason!"

"Why?" Merlin drew back in mock surprise. "How is it that my suggestion that the king could have been sporting with his half-sister Lady Morgan can be thought treasonous, but the accusation that Queen Guinevere might be doing the same with Sir Lancelot, her husband's own brother in arms, is to be taken seriously? Which is actual treason: the analogy made in jest, or the serious allegation against a royal personage?"

"Now you are accusing *us* of treason, you old windbag?" It was Sir Geraint this time. The young Geraint was petty king of Arthur's province of Dumnonia, bordering my own home of Cornwall, but as a vassal of Arthur's he was knight of the Round Table. "If you were a knight, and about a hundred years younger, I would throw you my gauntlet and see you in the lists."

"Enough!" The king exploded and now rose to his feet. "This bickering is unseemly in my court and I will not have it! Now Sir Mordred, do you have any evidence of your charges at all? Because all I have heard from your side is innuendo and hearsay. If you have nothing else, I see no reason to continue this charade, and am prepared to clear my queen of all charges against her." With that he allowed himself to glance at the queen, who was standing much taller now, her hands on her hips and a defiant glint in her grey eyes.

"But Your Majesty," Pelleas objected. "We haven't even touched on Sir Lancelot's murder of your good knights in his escape from the queen's chamber! There is ample evidence of that: eleven dead bodies lying unavenged!" At that the whole hall began to buzz with an approving murmur as knights, ladies and squires turned to one another in excitement, judging that Pelleas had indeed raised a telling point and gotten to the gist of the question.

But Merlin, not about to let his opponents score a point against him, quickly shouted above the hubbub, "My Lord Arthur, if I may speak?" When the king had nodded to him, he continued: "Your Highness, Sir Lancelot is not on trial here. Whether he is guilty in the deaths of these knights or was merely defending his own life and therefore guilty of nothing but dealing blows in self-defense, is not the question before this court at this time. If Lancelot were ever to stand here in the dock, these gentlemen may bring the appropriate charge against him then. But it is the queen who is on trial here, and she is not implicated in these deaths." Another murmur of agreement, this time in Merlin's favor, spread through the crowd.

Now it was Mordred's turn to bring the focus back to his cause. "Your Majesty! We do have one more piece of irrefutable evidence to present!" And at this he nodded to Sir Hectimere, who darted as quickly as he could for the rear doors of the throne room. As Hectimere wove his way back through the crowd, Mordred explained. "Your Grace, we have a witness to this outrage, whose testimony will resolve this matter once and for all."

"Unless it is someone actually present in the room with Lancelot and the queen, I don't see how that is possible," Merlin said.

The king, now seating himself back on his throne, set down his orb and scepter and folded his arms across his chest. He, too, sounded skeptical when he warned, "We will hear this witness of yours Sir Mordred, but if he provides no new information, then this trial will be at an end and we will release the queen. Proceed."

With that Sir Hectimere reappeared at the rear door followed closely by two armed soldiers of the king's guard, and between them, his arms shackled in chains before him, strode Robin Kempe.

Robin looked none the worse for wear, and I could imagine

that as captain of the king's guard, he was not likely to have been subject to rough treatment or aggressive questioning by those who, until yesterday, had been under his own command—especially when, for all they knew, he would once more be their commander tomorrow. Thus he'd been handled, as it were, with kid gloves. Now he marched in solemnly, looking neither to the right or the left, until Hectimere and his guards had brought him directly before the king. There he stood next to Merlin, who looked down at Robin with his left eyebrow raised quizzically. Robin looked down at the floor.

"Robin of Kempe," Sir Mordred began. "You were…"

"Robin Kempe, sir," came a loud, clear voice from Robin's bowed head.

"What's that?" said Mordred.

"I say it's just plain 'Robin Kempe,' sir. No hifalutin Robin *of* Kempe. I mean, I ain't no nobleman you see, sir, just good yeoman stock on both sides of my family."

"All right," Mordred said, annoyed by now at his own witness. "Robin Kempe, then, you were…"

"I'm pretty sure there isn't a place called 'Kempe' neither," Robin went on. "So I couldn't possibly be *from* there, ya see, couldn't be Robin of Kempe, 'cause there's no 'Kempe' to be 'of,' if you get my meaning sir."

"That is not what I'm asking you…"

"The name means 'coarse hair,' you know?" Robin reached up and ran his fingers through his own thick brown mop. "Runs in the family it does. So, like I say, not a place, but a quality."

By now the king was standing again and glowering in exasperation. Whether he was more irritated with Sir Mordred or with Robin himself I could not tell, but he was definitely angry. "Sir Mordred," he barked. "Your witness had better say something pertinent to this case or I'll have him put on the rack!" It was an empty threat. Merlin had told me that Arthur *had* no rack or other instruments of torture. He believed that men were reasonable beings and could be convinced by reason to tell the truth. It was just one of the many ways in which his idealism did not match the real world.

With a chance to address the king directly, Robin dropped his evasive insolence. "Your Imperial Highness," he began. "These men arrested me the night before last, while I was in the midst of doing my duty. I was stationed in the barbican, as I often am in the late evening, when Sir Lancelot, Sir Bors, and a dozen other mounted knights, came galloping up to the front gate of the castle. They called up to me that they were in great haste to be off on an errand of vital importance, and so I ordered the portcullis to be raised and the drawbridge lowered as quickly as possible."

"You didn't find it odd that a group of knights would be in such a rush to leave the castle in the middle of the night?" Sir Geraint asked, with some sarcasm in his voice.

"It was Lancelot," Robin shot back. "One does not question the word of Lancelot in Camelot. He's the king's right-hand man, the most chivalrous of all the knights, not to mention the fact that he can knock anyone out of the saddle and cut off their sword arm in less time than it takes to say it. So no, I didn't think anything other than 'do what the man says.'"

"This adds nothing to our knowledge," the king said, throwing his arms up with frustration. "If there is nothing else…"

"This is not all, Your Grace," Mordred cried. "Ask him what Lancelot said to him when the gate was being lowered. Ask him."

Robin's eyes went first to Mordred then back to the king, and he shook his head. "I don't remember him saying anything. Don't know what you're talking about."

"It's difficult to hold a private conversation with somebody in the barbican when you're down below seated on a horse," Mordred sneered. "Two of your men also heard what Sir Lancelot said…"

"Then call them as witnesses, why don't you?" Robin snapped back. "I didn't hear nothing…"

Now the king stepped in once more. "Robin Kempe, we have been patient. But if you give false witness here, if you perjure yourself, our laws require that you be stripped of all your possessions and scourged in the public square. Now for the last time, tell this court precisely what Sir Lancelot said to you before escaping through the gate that you opened for him!"

Robin looked at Mordred with hatred, then swiveled to look

at Merlin and then to the queen with an apologetic air. Then he answered: "Lancelot said, 'Robin, I've got to fly. Those bastards laid a trap and finally proved the queen to be my paramour.'"

At that the room erupted into pandemonium. My own heart sank in my chest and I looked to the queen, who appeared to have crumpled into the arms of Rosemounde and the lady Anne. A glance at the king showed him collapsed back onto his throne, and though he tried to maintain his veneer of objectivity, I noticed the scepter quivering in his hand. And Merlin was caught staring, his mouth open, with nothing left to say. As the assembled crowd rumbled in indignation, Sir Mordred could be heard shouting above the clamor, "Condemned by his own mouth! This is treason! The queen must die!"

The thud of Sir Bedivere's staff on the king's dais finally grew loud enough to quiet the tumultuous mob, and when they had ceased their noise the king stood. His voice was loud but it quavered as he began to speak. At his side Sir Gawain looked sick and pale, anticipating what must be the king's verdict.

"This court has no choice but to find Queen Guinevere guilty, as charged, of adultery and of treason against our person." Arthur could not look at Guinevere, and in trying to find somewhere else to fix his stare, against all odds fixed it on me. As the queen remained prostrate, I looked directly into Arthur's dark brooding eyes as he pronounced, "The law provides only one punishment for the crime of treason: death by fire. Accordingly, Guinevere, Queen of Logres, Princess of Cameliard, I hereby declare that at the hour of prime two days hence, you will be brought to the lawn before the great cathedral in Caerleon, and there before the witness of this court, you will be..." now the king choked as he tried to force out the words. After a moment to collect himself, he continued, "you will be burned at the stake until you are dead. May God have mercy on your soul."

There was another explosion in the room. Mordred looked inordinately pleased with himself, but most of the others in the room, even those who supported the king's sentence, looked broken or chagrined. The queen I could not see. I turned to see tears on the

49

faces of Gareth, of Palomides, of Ywain and Gaheris. Then I slowly tried to wend my way out of that room. I suddenly needed fresh air, and needed it quickly, for I was feeling sick and faint.

Approaching the south wall of the throne room, I looked up to see the final tapestry that decorated the hall. This was a depiction of the Battle of Mount Badon, where Arthur, bearing an image of the Virgin Mary on his shield, was said to have slain nine hundred Saxons in a cavalry charge up the slope of the hill. Excalibur was drawn and bloody in the king's hand, and his mouth was open in a berserker's war cry. Seeing that image, I could think of only one thing: What bloody carnage lay in wait for Arthur's knights two days hence on the cathedral lawn, if Lancelot rode to the queen's rescue?

CHAPTER FIVE

THE TALE OF SIR GARETH

We met in Sir Gawain's rooms again the following night, on the eve of the queen's scheduled execution, just a small group of the queen's supporters—perhaps the only ones left in Camelot. I had come with Merlin, and we were gathered there with Sir Ywain, Sir Palomides, and Sir Thomas, along with Gareth, Gaheris, and Gawain of course. After the death of his son Lovell, Gawain was circumspect about his feelings toward Lancelot, but to the queen he remained unwavering in his dedication, as did the rest of us gathered in that room.

It had been a strange day, one I felt I had stumbled through as if half asleep. I'd not been allowed to visit the queen, and since Rosemounde had remained at Guinevere's side in her chambers all day, I had not had an opportunity to see her either, or to learn anything about the queen's state of mind in the wake of the astounding reversal in the throne room. It was also apparent that a trickle of Lancelot's friends, who had stayed in court after his escape in order to plead his case, had stolen away one by one over the course of the day.

It had begun with Robin Kempe, who, guarded by his friend Alan of Winchester, had in the early morning hours slipped his prison and, with Alan in tow, stole from the castle unnoticed until the kitchen sent his breakfast hours later. We believed that they had escaped by hiding in the cart driven by the dwarf Thorvald, another devotee of Sir Lancelot, for the cart was seen leaving the castle before dawn. It was good bet that Alan and Robin, and Thorvald as well, were

51

all supping with Sir Lancelot even now. In that they were probably joined by another handful of knights, including Sir Breunor le Noir, Sir Caradoc, Sir Helyan le Blanc, and, most disturbing, the king's loyal butler Sir Lucan, all of whom had reportedly left Camelot to hunt in the woods, but never joined the hunting party and were not seen again. These were knights who, torn between support of the king and of Lancelot, had seen the condemnation of the queen as the last straw, and could no longer stay in Camelot as it now was. Whether they, too, had gone to join Lancelot, we did not know. But it was a good bet. This situation had every knight of the Table searching his soul, torn in their loyalties and making the best choices they could.

Our choice was to stay with the king. We could not help Guinevere by leaving, but the king would not hear any plea for her either.

And how could he? A king that blinked at his queen's infidelity and his vassal's betrayal was a king that would never command loyalty again. But he was a king who had lost his greatest friend and supporter in Lancelot, and the love of his life in Guinevere, and he was a king who must send that same love to die in flames the next morning. We were a glum lot there in Gawain's chamber. Everyone sat with head down, and Merlin was curled in a corner, his head buried in his arms. I feared he might be sinking into one of his black moods. Sir Palomides tried to soothe us by regaling us with a song he had written that day, singing it to the accompaniment of his psaltery:

"I usually want my music to bring joy, or at least to praise love, even if that love is unrequited," the Moorish knight said in a subdued voice. "But music partakes of all human emotions, and comforts us or sustains us in every one of our moods. I wrote this song after the queen was condemned. I will sing it for you now:

> *Queen of my heart, a name not lightly given,*
> *But one you've earned through years of gentle grace.*
> *Your golden hair, the glories of your face,*
> *These we'll not see again this side of heaven.*
>
> *Your generosity to every soul,*
> *To knight or page or to your ladies fair,*

Your gentleness and poise, they have no peer,
And losing them, we are no longer whole.

Our hearts from out our bodies fly
To find you in the heavenly spheres,
Where floating on a flood of tears,
We seek your essence in the sky.

He ceased, breathing heavily, a tear tracing the contours of his dark brown cheek. "That is all I have written," he said as we all sat in compete silence as the last echoes of his instrument hung in the air. "I do not know if it is done, but I cannot bring myself to write any more of it."

It was some time before anyone spoke again, and it was Sir Ywain who finally broke the silence. "Is there nothing that can be done? Is there no one the king will listen to?"

"If he will not listen to Merlin, it's hard to imagine there is *anyone* he'll listen to," I said. "What about his sister? What about Morgan?"

Ywain raised his tawny eyebrows. "Mother?" he said. Again I had forgotten that Ywain was the king's nephew as well, son of his troublesome sister Morgan le Fay and her deceased husband King Uriens. "She's had too many run-ins with him in the past for him to listen to her now. Besides, she's never been on friendly terms with Guinevere. Remember that whole business of the Green Knight?"

"We tried talking to him," Sir Gawain said in a low defeated voice, his shoulders up around his ears as he slouched dejectedly on a stool against the wall of his chamber. "He would hear nothing in the queen's favor. In fact, he all but ordered me to guard the queen tomorrow, and walk her to the stake at dawn. Told me it would show that we are of one mind, he and I. That the whole house of Orkney is behind this action."

"What did you do?" Ywain demanded.

Gawain straightened up and said with some pride. "I told him under no circumstances would I be a party to this travesty. And I walked out of his chamber."

That drew a smile from Ywain and from Thomas, but Sir Gaheris was quick to follow up with the bad news. "He didn't give *us* a choice," he said gloomily. "He ordered Gareth and me to escort the queen tomorrow. He would brook no defiance. I tell you, if it were not for Sir Gawain's position here, I might have considered following Lancelot out of here myself, as my squire Sir Lowell urged me to do. As it is, I wouldn't be surprised if he left by himself."

Lowell, father of Lady Mary and the murdered Lady Elizabeth, was an impoverished knight whom Gaheris had welcomed as his squire when Hectimere was promoted to Knight of the Table. "I would miss Lowell," Palomides said, "But I cannot fault his conscience."

"We will show our own defiance in any case," Gareth said. "Gaheris and I have refused to bear arms when we accompany the queen. We will wear no armor and will carry no weapons. We will not be guarding the queen but accompanying her in sympathy. That is how we will obey the letter of the king's command but defy it in spirit."

"Will the king stand for that?" Thomas asked innocently.

"He will have to," Gaheris declared. "Or find someone else to do his bidding."

There were several nods and grunts of agreement around the room, until finally Merlin unwound himself and stood up, glaring down at the rest of us. "God's molars, I'm in a room full of dunces. Do you seriously think that the king wants to go through with this atrocity? Think about it. Where is he holding this projected burning? Is he holding it here in the castle, where the walls can keep out anyone who might want to stop the execution? Not a bit of it! He is holding it in the wide open field in front of Saint David's Cathedral in Caerleon—a place completely undefended in case an armed force comes galloping in at the last minute to stop the execution. Is he asking Sir Mordred or Sir Pelleas or Sir Geraint to guard the queen as she goes to her stake? No—he is asking Lancelot's own dearest friends." At that Sir Gawain scowled and turned away, his face flushing as red as his hair. But Merlin, apparently oblivious, continued. "Sir Gareth and Sir Gaheris are the least likely knights in Camelot to fight to keep Lancelot and Bors and Ector from snatching the queen away from her doom. Can you not see that the king cannot pass a lenient sentence on the queen, but he can stage the execution in a way that guarantees its failure? Why do you think he eased up on the close guard that was being kept on the castle, allowing Robin Kempe and Sir Lucan and others to sneak off? He expects them to tell Lancelot exactly the time and place of the queen's ordeal. Mark my words, this will not happen tomorrow as Mordred wants it to. We can only pray that the result is not a complete bloodbath that dooms Arthur's entire reign."

Sir Gawain gave a low growl and stood up, stretching his shoulders and neck, stiff from sitting slumped on that stool so long. "Well, I hope you're right, old man. I think it may well be as you say. And for the queen's sake I must wish Lancelot success in the morning. For myself, I will refuse to be anywhere near the site of the queen's proposed execution. I will not watch that, and I do not wish to see Sir Lancelot of the Lake ever again. I have owed him a great deal, but I think the life of my son is enough to pay. Pardon me if I do not stay to sing his praise." With that he started toward the door, head bowed, muttering something about needing some fresh air. Sir Ywain popped up immediately, grunting, "I don't like the mood he's in right now. I think he needs some company."

And as Ywain went out the door after his cousin, Sir Gaheris rose and, glancing at Gareth, said, "I'm going to help keep an eye on our brother. Stay here, will you? There ought to be *some* Orkney brother left to entertain our visitors." And he left as well.

"Well, old man, you certainly know how to kill a party," I muttered to Merlin, tongue in cheek.

"It wasn't a lot of fun to begin with," Merlin replied, *sotto voce*.

"Well what do you suppose *that's* all about?" Sir Thomas wondered aloud. He was the one here least familiar with the Orkney brothers and their various moods.

Sir Gareth stood, hands on his hips, looking after the departed Gawain and the rest of his family, and pursed his lips. Without looking at Thomas, he answered slowly, "I think it's just as Gawain said. Agravain dug his own grave with his irresponsible mouth, but Lovell was young and easily swayed. He followed his uncles out of family loyalty, not out of malice or even a clear conviction that the queen was guilty. Remember he left these rooms with us when Agravain first raised the issue. None of us was there, but it seems likely that Lancelot could have simply disarmed the lad and left him—was there truly any need to kill him? Gawain is deeply troubled by this. He will certainly never forget it, and I cannot imagine he will ever forgive the man who killed his son."

Thomas nodded. "He says he never wants to see Lancelot again," he said. "Is there a chance...do you think he might...I don't know, try to stop Lancelot from rescuing the queen? I mean, is Gawain vengeful in that way?"

Gareth looked at Thomas's innocent blue eyes beneath his close-cropped sandy hair, and apparently decided that the young man was sincere in his question, a question I already knew the answer to. Sir Gareth sighed and sat down on the stool Gawain had evacuated, then put his head back, his mouth opened slightly and his eyes looking at the ceiling, as if he were reviewing a long story that he was about to begin. "Sir Gawain said that he will not attend the queen's proposed execution tomorrow. He will not go back on his word, so he will not try to avenge himself on Lancelot, at least not tomorrow. He has said that he does not wish to see Lancelot ever again. I believe that is true as well. Given that fact, I have to say that he is not contemplating vengeance at this point. But is Sir Gawain a vengeful person, you ask? Let me tell you the story of Sir Lamorak. After you've heard it, young Thomas, you can judge better whether or not Gawain can be regarded as a vengeful man."

My own ears pricked up at that. I had heard Lamorak's death alluded to many times, but I had never heard the full story of exactly how it had occurred. And I leaned forward, fascinated to hear the full account from the lips of the one Orkney brother who had not been at the scene. Sir Palomides leaned his head on his psaltery, ready to listen but no doubt already familiar with the story. Merlin closed his eyes and looked anguished. He knew the story well, I was sure, and it was a story he never found pleasant to rehash.

"The story really begins with King Pellinore," Sir Gareth began. "He was petty king of Anglesey, an island off north Wales, and after initially resisting King Arthur's hegemony, eventually became his vassal and supported the young Arthur in his early wars, including his first war against my father, King Lot, and the other barons who refused to recognize a fifteen-year-old king of doubtful parentage. Even when Lot pledged Arthur his loyalty, Pellinore never trusted him, and there was never any love lost between them. Then, when Arthur tried to have Mordred killed right after he was born, Lot reneged on his loyalty oath."

"Wait...what?" Thomas started up. Apparently, he hadn't heard that story either.

But Palomides put his hand on Thomas's shoulder and cooed, "Not now, youngster. That's another story and you'll have to hear it another time. Let's focus on one tale at a time."

"Be that as it may," Gareth continued, pouring himself a glass of Sir Gawain's private stock of Claret while he was at it, and passing the pitcher around as Palomides grabbed a few cups from a shelf. "My father allied himself with the Irish King Rience when he challenged Arthur, and it was in the Battle of Tarabel that he met his end. Pellinore was a huge man—I remember seeing him once when I was a lad, when I came to Camelot with my mother and brothers. Hmmph," Gareth paused a moment. "That must have been when Mordred was conceived, when my mother seduced the young king..."

"Wait. What?" Sir Thomas interjected again.

"Not now!" Palomides waved at him again, and Thomas shrugged.

"In that battle, Pellinore met my father one-on-one, and I am told that with one swing of his long sword, he beheaded Lot's horse on the battlefield. Lot tumbled from the saddle and, when he was sprawled in the dirt, Pellinore brought his sword down on Lot's helmet and split his skull asunder." At that Thomas gagged and turned away, and Gareth followed his movement with his keen blue eyes, a grim smile on his face. "Yes," he said. "It seemed an unchivalrous way to kill a man. And Gawain never forgot how our father died. From his first moment at Arthur's Table, he looked for an opportunity to settle things with King Pellinore."

"But they were both members of the Round Table," Thomas reasoned. "Wouldn't the king have put a stop to that?"

"The king discouraged any bad feeling as best he could, and Gawain held his temper for ten years. If Gawain were more devious—if he was, say, our loving brother Mordred—you could say he was waiting for Pellinore to get older and lose some of his edge, while he himself grew stronger and honed his knightly skills. But it wasn't like that. Gawain was never one for plots or schemes. He leads with his heart," Gareth said, hanging his head as he thought. "It's passion, not reason, that guides my older brothers. And so it was at a dinner one evening some ten years after our father's demise, when Pellinore was at the same banquet as Gawain and several others. The old man was in his cups, remembering his greatest victories and bragging about them so the whole table could hear. And he had the bad judgment to mention his defeat of King Lot at the Battle of Tarabel within Gawain's hearing.

"Well Gawain wasn't about to let that pass, and he called Pellinore out, told him how striking my father like that, after he'd fallen from his horse, was a coward's act and none but a recreant knight would have done so low a deed. Pellinore says if Gawain wasn't the king's nephew, he'd be picking his teeth up off the ground right now, and Gawain says 'You and what army?' or some such thing—I don't know, I wasn't there, but that was the gist of it. The upshot is they met in the lists the following day, man to man, and had it out with sword and shield. It was a long bout, but Pellinore was past his prime and Gawain wore him down, and then *beat* him down. Pellinore wouldn't ask for quarter, and Gawain was fine with that—he ended by driving his sword through Pellinore's unprotected throat, and that was it. Gawain didn't gloat visibly, but that victory sure made him feel validated, I'll tell you that."

"So, you're saying that Sir Gawain *is* a vengeful knight, though it seems he takes his vengeance in his own time, and only when he is greatly moved..." Thomas said.

"Just wait," Gareth told him. "*That* wasn't vengeance. That was *honor*. It was when Pellinore's son, Lamorak, came to Camelot that the fires were lit in Gawain's belly."

"Ah," Thomas perked up at that. "I've heard that Sir Lamorak was one of the three greatest knights of Arthur's realm, right up there with Sir Tristram and Lancelot himself."

Sir Gareth rolled his eyes at that, his blond hair falling to the side as he jerked his head back. "That's what everybody says about Lamorak. It's what Lamorak always said about himself, much to Gawain's displeasure. It was as if Lamorak liked to trumpet his prowess in Gawain's presence whenever he could, as if to say 'Hey, King Pellinore's son is mentioned in the same breath at Lancelot and Tristram. And King Lot's son? Who's he?' Even though Gawain had beaten Lamorak's own doughty father, and everybody knew that if men talked about the four greatest knights of Arthur's realm, they'd have to include Gawain. Or perhaps I should say, they might include Sir Palomides," with that Gareth nodded to the Moorish knight, who gave him a little half smile, as if he knew what had just come into Gareth's mind. "Because I remember one joust I was told of when Palomides unhorsed both Sir Tristram and Sir Lamorak on the same occasion. But anyway, Lamorak made his reputation on the jousting field and in tournaments, not in battle where Gawain had won his renown. In Arthur's war with the Gauls, Lamorak was still a boy. When Gawain fought the Emperor Lucius, where was Lamorak?

"Well, there was a rivalry growing, a pretty strong one, and one day Arthur held a tournament at Camelot, one at which Sir Gawain won the prize on the first day. But the second day Lamorak overthrew Gawain and then went on to unhorse Gaheris and Agravain as well. They were all pretty miffed at that, and Gawain thought of it as a personal affront. But it wasn't as much of an affront as what happened right after that tournament.

"Apparently my mother, who was never any better than she should have been, had seduced the young Lamorak when he had just arrived in Camelot. She'd been here visiting her sons—I think it was when I was still working incognito in the kitchen, which appalled her as much as I hoped it would. But she took up with the randy boy Lamorak in secret. It was easy enough to seduce him: She was still trim and beautiful, even after five children. Maybe she really was a witch as some people said. But she enticed the boy. I don't know why. Maybe it was a kind of victory she felt she was gaining over the man that had killed her husband, that she would cause his son to dote on her. But Gawain and Gaheris especially felt it was the starkest dishonor to our father's memory.

"Well, Gawain had brought Margause here to live in a small castle he owned not far from Caerleon, and Lamorak had begun visiting her there. My brother Gaheris had got wind of this and one night, when he knew Lamorak had gone to her in that castle, he armed himself and stole into the castle under cover of darkness, and slipped into mother's bedchamber. Lamorak was naked in the bed, and Gaheris had his sword drawn when he arrived, just as the two were making the beast with two backs. Gaheris pulled the bed-curtain open, grabbed Margause by that long blonde hair she shared with him, and with one stroke cut her head clean off."

Sir Thomas's jaw fell halfway to his knees, and he managed to cry out once more, "Wait! What?" But this time Palomides simply raised his eyebrows at him as a caution, and Thomas closed his mouth and continued to listen.

"Now some of this I had from Gaheris, and some of it from Hectimere, who was quite young and his squire at the time, and who witnessed much of this. I can tell you he never forgot it. Sir Lamorak, of course, leaped out of the bed in horror, clothed only in gouts of his paramour's blood. He was trembling, Gaheris said later, but whether with shock, or cold, or fear I can't say. Gaheris had the sword pointed straight at him, and called him a defiler of chaste women, which let me tell you was pretty far-fetched—but Lamorak threw it back at him, calling Gaheris a matricide—which was pure truth. But some resilient belated notion of chivalry stayed Gaheris's hand, and he told Lamorak to get his clothes and begone, for he refused to kill an unarmed knight."

"Too bad for Margause that he wasn't feeling particularly chivalrous a little earlier," Merlin commented dryly from his corner of the room.

Gareth shrugged and went on as if nothing had been said. "Gawain told Gaheris that he approved of his actions. Mother had to die for the honor of the family. But it would have been dishonorable to have slain an unarmed man."

"Was Margause armed?" Merlin whispered.

Sir Gareth pursed his lips. "I do not say that I approve of Gaheris's deed," he continued. "I am not really sure that Gawain did, but he said what he said to try to ease Gaheris's remorse, which was deep.

He felt remorse for killing mother in the heat of the moment, and he also felt some remorse for sparing Lamorak. But it was only a matter of time. Gawain was incensed, and there must be a confrontation.

"The catalyst was a dream, as it turned out. Just two days after the incident at his castle, Gawain dreamed that King Lot visited him in his sleep to chide him for allowing this defiler of his own wife to continue to breathe. Gawain awoke with a cold determination to finish the job."

I looked to Merlin at that, and he nodded to me with a grim smile. Another dream. This one being what his book had called an *oracular* one, in which the dreamer is visited by an oracle from his own family, like Scipio with his grandfather Africanus—and here used as an excuse for murder.

"Gawain took the dream to heart, and he convinced Gaheris, Agravain and Mordred, a youngster at the time, to uphold the family honor by ambushing Lamorak. I'd like to think they did not include me because they knew I would refuse, but I can't say that in certainty. I was away from Camelot at the time, though I swear on my father's bones I would have had nothing to do with the deed. They hid, armed and mounted, in the clearing in the woods north of Camelot on a day they knew Lamorak would come riding through. And when his horse ambled into the clearing they burst out of the trees, attacking him from four sides. He fought valiantly, Gaheris told me later, and Lamorak got in some telling blows before it was through, but in the end he could not fight four at once, and I am told that it was Mordred who finally dealt the death blow—from behind, you may be sure."

All was quiet in the room then. Merlin broke the silence with his signature exasperation. "God's whiskers, boy, this code of vengeance that lives on from your pagan ancestors on this isle adds nothing but chaos to your society. It's the one trait I tried so hard with Arthur, in those early years, to eliminate. The code of chivalry, the Pentecost Vow that all knights of the Table take, is designed specifically to guard against this kind of thing. Yet the poison persists, it persists even in the king's own family."

"I do not understand this pagan code either," Sir Palomides lamented. "You kill one of ours, we kill one of yours. It goes on

61

and on till no one is left alive. When I became a Christian, I did so because it does not allow such things. Turn the other cheek, Christ said. He nullified the 'eye for an eye' morality. Yet men in Arthur's court, men who sought the Grail itself, act thus."

"Maybe it's the old gods who are really still in control," Merlin said, though I knew he had no more real faith in them than he had in any other god.

"Gaheris believed in vengeance at that time, and though he justified it then and continues to do so today, his conscience is not at peace about it. Gawain's, however, is. So…you asked if Gawain believed in revenge. I think it's fairly clear that the answer to that is yes."

Sir Thomas let out a sigh. "So it seems. But it does seem that he will not act on it until he feels things are unbearable, or unless things are done before his face…"

"And so he is determined never to see Lancelot more. But I tell you, if the death of his son is not enough to push him over the edge, I cannot imagine what could be worse." And with that Gareth left off, and I nodded. But we would soon learn that there could indeed be something worse.

***

Sir Palomides swallowed hard as he stepped out of Caerleon's Cathedral of Saint David into the dim pre-dawn light that marked the approach of prime, the hour of the queen's execution. Thomas and I followed him out. Like Sir Gawain, Merlin had chosen not to attend the proceedings, saying he could see nothing good that could possibly come from them. But we were eager to be as close as possible to the queen when she made that terrible walk across the lawn to the stake, already in place and piled high with straw and branches that would catch fire quickly. I felt faint when I saw it, my breath sinking into my roiling stomach, my heart beating loudly enough, I was sure, to be heard by my companions. Even though I felt certain—well, fairly certain, or at least hopeful—that Sir Lancelot would be riding in to rescue her and hold her safe from any harm, no matter the cost, I still felt anxious, not knowing what that cost might be. As it turned out, that cost was too high, and it continued to bleed Arthur's kingdom dry, in body and spirit, until the very end. It was a morning that would haunt my soul for decades, so that even now, looking down the long span of years, I cannot remember that day without tears.

All of Camelot had awakened that morning at lauds, to ensure that all was in readiness for the queen's ordeal at prime. Knights armed themselves as if for war, knowing that they could well be embroiled in battle before the morning was through. I myself had pulled on the precious mail coat and coif my father the armor-maker had sent me at my investiture as knight of the Round Table, and the sword Almace that my old master, Sir Gareth, had given me on that same occasion, though I did not expect to be needing them, having no intention of battling Lancelot and his retinue when they rode in to stand between Guinevere and the fire. But it was a matter of caution—it did not seem wise to stand unarmed in a place where swords may be wielded in anger.

Palomides and Thomas were similarly armed as, I noted, were Sir Mordred and his own cortege of Hectimere, Pelleas, and Geraint, who stepped from the cathedral directly behind us to stand nearby the church's western portal to await the procession of the queen and her guard. As I looked at that door behind me, the Last Judgment tympanum above the portal took on a grimmer significance as I pondered the relief. There sat Christ in glory as the Son of Man, the naked souls to his right being led by angels into the paradise prepared for them from the beginning of time, some of them carried to the lap of the seated patriarch Abraham, to spend eternity in his bosom; while at his left still more naked souls were being seized and carried by hideous demons into the great, gaping, monstrous jaws of hell, there to spend eternity in the endless fires of everlasting damnation. Even if the queen escaped the fire this morning, were she and Lancelot destined to spend eternity in those inescapable eternal fires in the end? Was their love a damnable offense? Was my own? For I myself had committed adultery with my beloved Lady Rosemounde, call it what we would and excuse it as we might by her husband's vicious treatment of her and by our own professed love. Or were those flames reserved for the likes of Mordred, the scheming, bullying climber who cared nothing for anyone else and would do anything to avenge himself on his father for having spurned him, and on the world itself for not providing him what he demanded as his due. Or were we all destined for that gaping mouth in the end, all but the truly good—Sir Palomides, perhaps, or Sir Bors, or almost certainly Sir Gareth, that paragon of honor and truth and generosity and good fellowship.

Now the sun had broken blood-red above the eastern horizon, exposing the cloudless, naked blue sky to the revealing light of dawn, and the king, clad in the purple robes of state and his heavy imperial crown, came from the cathedral door and mounted a dais built to the right of the portal, seating himself on a portable throne set up for the occasion. He was followed by Archbishop William of Glastonbury, in full ecclesiastical regalia, who sat on the king's right hand in order to give the appearance of the Church's approval and orthodox blessing of the day's planned proceedings. Guinevere's execution was sanctioned by both civil and canon law, such was the unspoken message of that spectacle. And it was the mitered archbishop who ultimately gave the order to proceed with the execution.

By then all the knights currently in Camelot had come onto the lawn, armed and standing in two rows, between which the queen was expected to be brought from the church's door to the prepared stake. Across from me, from the coats of arms on their surcoats, I could recognize Sir Ywain, Sir Kay, Sir Griflet, Sir Cliges and other veteran knights. At the archbishop's word, some forty green-clad members of the King's Guard, armed with longbows and quivers of arrows, marched out and stood, surrounding the stake toward which the queen would walk. Then accompanied by the slow beat of a drum played by one of the watch, Sir Bedivere as king's herald marched out, his sword drawn and held before him as if pointing the way. Finally, dressed only in a light shift, her hair wild and her face contorted with anguish, Guinevere stumbled out, barely able to stand but held up on either side by Sir Gareth and Sir Gaheris. True to their vow, they were not armed, but wore their own best tunics, covered by matching green Orkney plaid cloaks. They made their way slowly between the rows of knights, steadying the queen in as supportive a manner as they felt they could get away with, resisting as best they could the inevitability of that drumbeat. Behind them, Mordred and his toadies had fallen into step, as if they had the right to follow closely in order to see their version of justice carried out. Sir Ywain from one side and Sir Palomides from the other fell into step behind Mordred and his crew, as if to keep an eye on them, and I followed with Thomas and several other knights as the march to the stake became a procession.

That was when I heard another beat, at first a kind of murmur under the rhythm of the drum, but building to a crescendo that ultimately drowned out the drum completely. And what occurred next I witnessed as if in a dream. Everything took on a hazy quality as if time had slowed down and it was all happening through a fog, so that nothing I could do could stop or change it.

With the thunder of hoof beats at least two dozen galloping knights in full armor crashed into the assembled crowd on the church lawn. I recognized Lancelot by the three golden fleur-de-lys of his coat of arms on the azure background of his shield. I recognized Sir Bors and Sir Ector and a dozen others by their own shields, and all came with couched lances to strike down whoever stood between them and the queen.

The knights in the yard, though most had expected something of this sort, were taken aback by the speed and violence of the onslaught, and many were barely able to unsheathe their swords before they were mown down by the heavily armed shock attack of Lancelot's cavalry charge. After the initial jolt, Lancelot and several others reined their horses around and began to strike about them indiscriminately with drawn swords, until none of Arthur's original troops were left standing anywhere near the trembling queen. Then, with Bors, Ector, Urry and Lavyne guarding him, Lancelot leapt down from his saddle with a kirtle and gown that he threw over the queen—an act purely intended to erase the shame of her humiliating walk in her shift—and boosted her up into his saddle, then climbed back on the horse with Guinevere behind him.

And with that they all galloped off as quickly as they could, without giving Arthur's troops any chance to regroup. Obviously speed and shock had been Lancelot's calculated weapons, and he had used them with great success. Neither I nor any of my companions had made a move to prevent Lancelot's taking the queen—we had been caught so flat-footed there was no time, and when it came down to it we had no desire to do so in any case. But in the aftermath, I wandered about that bloody lawn in a daze, finding to my chagrin a number of friends among the wounded knights, including Sir Kay, Sir Pelleas, Sir Bedivere, and others. Worse, there were several dead—anyone, in fact, who had put up more than a token resistance: many of the guard, but also Sir Tor, Sir Priamus, Sir Griflet, Sir Aglovale, and Sir Bellias le Orgulous, to name a few.

And then I heard a loud unearthly scream from close to the stake where the queen had been led. Through the dust that still lingered in the air after the galloping horses had departed, I could make out the red hair on the kneeling figure of Sir Gawain. He had heard the hooves and had come running from the castle, realizing immediately what that noise had portended. He had arrived too late to have offered any help in the battle, but just in time to view the carnage left in its wake. And as I drew closer to where he knelt, I could see what he held in his arms, what he grasped with what I could only call hysterical panic. With the dead body of Sir Gaheris at his right side, Gawain was holding the head of another, its blond hair darkened by the blood and brains that had gushed from the great sword wound that had split its unprotected skull. With Sir Gareth's crimson life's blood soaking into his green Orkney plaid cloak, Sir Gawain wept in a kind of frenzy, without shame or constraint. His world had just come crashing down, and my own was left shaken to its foundations.

CHAPTER SIX
WAR

I should add that Merlin had also arrived on the scene within minutes of the massacre. He moved far slower than Sir Gawain, and was leaning more heavily on his staff than when I first knew him. But unlike Sir Gawain, or unlike me, he had his wits about him, and could be seen moving from body to body, directing those figures standing about to bring this or that fallen knight into the cathedral to have wounds attended to. A physician from Caerleon was sent for, and Merlin had bade a page to run to the nearby convent of Saint Mary Magdalene in order to bring the sisters' infirmarian out to the field to help patch up wounded bodies. When he came to those who were past hope, knights like Sir Priamus and Merlin's own old friend Sir Griflet, the mage shook his head and clicked his tongue, mumbling curses and blasphemies, some of which only he actually knew the meaning of. I began following him around for lack of anything I could think to do myself, and if I couldn't be any help, at least I could join him in his curses.

He started a bit, I noticed, when he came to the bodies of Sir Aglovale and Sir Tor, lying together, and bent down to examine their bodies more closely. When he stood up again he was rubbing his nose thoughtfully. Moving on across the battlefield, we came upon Sir Pelleas, who had taken a buffet on the helmet that had stunned him, and a vicious sword swipe across his shoulder that had put his right arm out of service for the foreseeable future.

"Here," Merlin said to Pelleas as he helped him into a sitting posture. "Are you able to walk, lad?"

"I think so," the young knight said, holding his right arm in his left and shaking his head a bit to knock the cobwebs out of it. "So, old man, what do you think of your precious Lancelot now?" He breathed deeply and glanced around. "Has he left a knight of the Table standing?"

The old necromancer growled deep in his throat, and I helped Pelleas to his feet and pointed him in the direction of the cathedral doors. "They're tending the wounded in there," I told him, giving him a gentle nudge as he wobbled his way toward the church's west works.

When I turned to rejoin the mage he muttered to me, "What did they expect, the simpletons? That Lancelot would come on a gentle palfrey and ask politely if he might ride off with the queen? This bloody work was set in motion as soon as they condemned the queen. Nay, long before—it was inevitable from the moment Agravain and Mordred hatched their scheme to take Lancelot in the queen's chamber. Don't they understand that actions have consequences? Bloody fools. Why do I bother, Gildas? I'm an old man. No one has ever listened to half of my warnings—they just carry on and then they get surprised when life smacks them in the face. And now the king is going to want a war council. I'm going to advise a peaceful solution and do you think anyone will listen? Not bloody likely."

I looked toward Sir Gawain, to where he groveled in the dust, still clasping Sir Gareth's lifeless body to his breast, and said, "In the face of the revenge that man is going to want? No. Your talk of peace is going to have as much chance as an unarmed Gareth against a full-on cavalry charge."

Merlin sighed as he nodded. "A feather in the wind."

When we came up to Sir Gawain, Merlin laid a gentle hand on his shoulder. The prince had ceased his wailing and now emitted only muffled groans. His grip on Gareth's body was so tight I did not think he could be pried loose, and I lowered my eyes, tears coming again and streaking down my cheeks. Merlin squatted down to put his face at the same level as Gawain's and asked in a soothing voice if he might be allowed to examine Gareth's body. I was not sure why

Merlin wanted to do this—there was no question that my old master was dead. Gawain nodded—a good sign, I thought, since it indicated that he was in his right senses. Still, he did not loosen his grip on the body and Merlin poked around those parts of Gareth's corpse that were not clutched to Gawain's breast. Merlin spent some time poking about a particularly bloody patch of Gareth's back. Then, thanking Gawain, the old man knelt down next to Sir Gaheris's body, finding an equally bloody area on the older Orkney brother's back.

Merlin rose from his examination of the bodies and once more touched their grieving brother's shoulder, murmuring in soothing tones, "My Lord, though I intend to ask for at least a day so that heads may cool, the king is sure to demand a council of war quite soon. Perhaps it would be best if you were to make your way back to the castle, compose yourself, perhaps get yourself cleaned up so as to take the leadership role you will no doubt be expected to assume in that council."

"Cooler heads?" Gawain hissed through gritted teeth. "Council? There is only one council: Revenge. I will have his heart to burn on Gareth's grave."

"Well," I said, raising my eyebrows in Merlin's direction. "Not much ambiguity there, then, is there Old Man?"

***

The next time I saw Gawain was the following afternoon. Merlin had at least been successful in keeping Arthur from summoning his barons into the cathedral in the immediate aftermath of the slaughter on the church grounds and launching a holy war then and there. Instead, we were meeting in the king's private chambers, around a table where the situation could be discussed rationally. At least in theory.

Gawain was dressed in a fine blue tunic covered with a new brown cloak he had borrowed from Sir Ywain, since his own cloak of green Orkney plaid had been ruined by the stains from Gareth's bloody corpse. But Gawain looked lordly sitting on the king's right, his flowing red hair lying in perfect waves around his florid face. He sat next to his cousin Ywain, second in line to the throne, who had come out of the fracas of the previous day with only a few superficial scratches, having, like my friends and me, no real desire to stop Lancelot's rescue of the queen. On his left sat the king's only other surviving nephew, Sir Mordred, smirking at having finally been invited into the inner chamber where he could help make policy for the entire kingdom.

On the other side of the table sat, of all people, Morgan le Fay, the king's on-again off-again estranged sister, who had been visiting Arthur, as Merlin had mentioned, a few days before and had been staying at the nearby castle that had formerly belonged to Gawain— the site, I realized with a chill, of her sister Margause's demise. Arthur had called in Morgan, a renowned herbalist and healer, to help tend the wounded, and now had invited her, as his only other living kin aside from his three nephews, to this war council. She wore a black gown with a black cloak the better to live up to her popular image as a witch, though if her son Ywain was to be believed, it was all an act. Also on this side of the table sat Merlin, the king's oldest advisor, both in age and time served. He looked haggard and I remember thinking that he was probably right: There was nobody at this table who as going to have thoughts of peace. And what was I doing at that table, you may well ask? I was a buffer, as far as I could tell. Merlin must have requested that I attend as his personal assistant, but mainly I think I was there to sit between him and Morgan, so that neither would have to be in the direct line of fire from the other.

The king sat at the head of the table, but not in luxurious robes of state or his great imperial crown. He was dressed fairly simply in a purple tunic and blue hose, with a small gold circlet over his brow, just to remind us, I suppose, that he was still king. These were the clothes he wore to meet with his closest advisors, to do the real work of governing. There would be no posturing here, not by the king and not by anyone else. The members of the council would say what they intended without flattery or subterfuge. At least that is what I assumed. Then I remembered Mordred was in the group.

The king called us to order with no preamble. "You all know why we're here," he said. "Sir Lancelot and my queen betrayed me. Because such a betrayal involves the possible pollution of the royal line, such adultery is not only a sin in the eyes of the church, but the crime of treason according to the laws of the state."

I glanced around. Everyone was letting that go, even though as a woman beyond the age of forty-five, Guinevere was hardly likely to be giving birth to a royal heir any time soon. The law was, after all, the law, even if its protections were now unnecessary.

"The consequence of that affair coming to light was the queen's death sentence," he continued, and I noticed he blamed not the affair itself but its discovery. "You all know how that turned out. Yesterday morning, Sir Lancelot and a company of knights, most of them former knights of the Round Table who have therefore also broken their sworn oaths to me, swept into the churchyard and stopped the queen's execution, killing a number of our knights and wounding many more. This, we must all realize, cannot be allowed to go unanswered."

In the general hubbub that followed that statement, I glanced at Merlin, who frowned and then rubbed his eyes with his thumbs, steepling his fingers above his brow. If he was going to speak for prudence and caution, he was going to have a tough audience.

"As king, we cannot blink at treason when it comes to our attention. We cannot allow the authority and just decisions of our court to be undermined by rampaging knights. We cannot allow our vassals to make war upon us and sit idly by. Our response must be swift and it must be appropriate. I am told that Lancelot has withdrawn to his castle of Joyous Gard on our Kentish coast, there to await our response. This council is to decide what that response should be."

"War then!" Mordred was of course the first to speak. "Crush the traitor! Show the world that none can tweak Arthur's nose and get away with it!"

"Your Majesty," Merlin interposed as soon as he was able. "As your most senior adviser, I beg leave to speak." Arthur nodded to him, and the mage continued. "My lord, I have advised you on many occasions concerning wars you have fought against rebels in your own kingdom, against the Irish, against the Norsemen, against the Saxons, the Gauls, against the imperial armies of Rome itself. Those did much to consolidate your hegemony and to keep you in power. I think it can be agreed that I have never led you astray regarding

71

which wars were necessary and which were not; which wars would bring you honor and which would not. Hear me once more regarding this war with Lancelot: Your nephew Mordred calls for war, but if you look truly at the events that have broken the fellowship of your Table these past days, most of them can be laid at his own feet." Mordred jumped up as if insulted, but the king put a hand on his arm to calm him. It was a gesture that made me blink. It seemed a gesture of…what? Tenderness? Had Mordred weaseled his way into Arthur's sympathies at last? Or was the king merely trying to keep order in his council?

"Sir Lancelot has no wish to fight you," Merlin continued. "He will never attack you. His concern was for the queen, and if she is in any danger through your actions, he will fight to the death to save her—just as he would fight to the death to save you, my lord, if you yourself were in peril. You can have peace and maintain your honor as well if you receive concessions from him in compensation for his wrongs. This quarrel between the two of you has not only split the Table into factions, but has given every knight of that Table divided loyalties: They are torn inwardly, and we do not know how strongly they may commit to one side or another. My advice is that you send emissaries to him—I will volunteer to go myself, and I am sure my young colleague Sir Gildas, who was much in Lancelot's confidences and the queen's, will agree to serve as go-between. Hold off the full commitment of your armies for now, and let us see what diplomacy might accomplish."

I glanced about the table. The king seemed unmoved, but he was, as usual, maintaining a stoic demeanor throughout the proceedings. Ywain was nodding his head, his tawny mane bouncing as if he liked what he was hearing. Sir Gawain's countenance was dark, as if he was just barely holding his tongue out of courtesy but could explode at any moment. Mordred leaned back in his chair, sneering derisively as if he already knew what the outcome was going to be, and it didn't involve anything so peaceful as diplomacy.

But when I heard a soft "ahem" on my left side, I turned and realized that support for Merlin's plan was actually going to come from a completely unexpected source: from Morgan le Fay.

"Your Majesty," the king's sister began, choking the title out as if she still wasn't quite used to having to address this excrescence of a little brother, this accidental offspring of her dear mother and the brutish king Uther Pendragon who had raped her, as if he were her own sovereign. But overcoming that aversion, she continued. "Those around this table are not aware of what I came here to speak with you about several days ago. As you know, my husband Uriens' old kingdom was in Rheged of the Hen Ogledd, which you later renamed Gorre. I still maintain my own residence, a castle in that area, and fled here two weeks ago from marauding bands of Picts who were troubling the region. These barbarians think that you have turned your eyes to other things and are no longer interested in maintaining a force in that region, and they are ready to seize some of their old territories which you bereft them of in your early days. If you gather all your forces to make war on Lancelot at this time, you leave the whole north open for the Picts to plunder. For once this old charlatan is talking sense," she nodded grudgingly at Merlin. "I think you should do as he says."

I sat up hopefully. If Morgan was on our side, then her son Ywain, who already seemed to have agreed with Merlin, would certainly support us as well, and that meant we would have four voices for peace against only two—Mordred and Gawain—for war. With the majority on our side, it seemed to me that our voices would carry the day.

A foolish thought. I was not living in a democracy.

Sir Gawain had stood up, now dominating the table with his height, his flowing red hair, and his intense green eyes that pierced the heart of every person present.

"What the old charlatan has *failed* to mention," he began, addressing himself first to his aunt Morgan, "and what *nobody* at this table has dared to bring up," he continued, taking in the whole room with his gaze, "is my brother Gareth!" Tears now welled again in his eyes, but he controlled them—or perhaps they were driven away by his anger, for his next words had the force of a barely controlled rage behind them. "He was unarmed. He would make no martial show, in sympathy for the queen, and in deference to his idol, Lancelot.

And yet he, and my dear brother Gaheris as well, were cut down by Lancelot's own sword—or by one of his supporters, it amounts to the same thing." At this I saw Merlin purse his lips. "Whether it was deliberately done or whether it was done through an indiscriminate desire to kill anything in his path, Lancelot is responsible for these deaths and those of my son Lovell and my other brother Agravain, and while those may have been provoked, these two were innocent victims. And none was ever more innocent than Gareth.

"And so, Uncle, this is what *I* say," he turned his attention to the king. "I hereby vow to you, and swear by the True Cross of Him who harrowed Hell, that from this day forward I shall not cease in making war on Sir Lancelot until one of us lies dead. I demand that you prepare for war, Your Majesty, knowing that if you fail to do so you will lose my love and loyalty as well as my service. I have promised God Himself that I will pursue Sir Lancelot through all the corners of the earth until either I slay him or he slays me. And that is all that I have to say." And with that the Heir Apparent to Arthur's throne strode from the room and left us to pick up the pieces of the council he had just torn to shreds.

"Well," Morgan sighed after a few moments of silence. "I see I can still get a rise out of the boy." Merlin bit his bottom lip. He knew when more words were useless.

The derision on Mordred's face was undisguised as his eyes followed the oldest—and last—of his brothers out the door. I could see that he shared none of the grief Gawain suffered for his sudden and weighty loss and had only contempt for such strong emotions. Nevertheless he was pleased to see the council turning to his own desire. "Though he says it with great histrionics," he drawled at the king, "Gawain is right, Your Grace. Lancelot must be destroyed. The queen must be burnt."

Arthur could not suppress his bristling at Mordred's audacity, and, staring down at the table, growled in a low voice, "You'll forgive me if I do not display the same enthusiasm as you do, Nephew, for this task. But," he said more resignedly as he looked up and moved his sad brown eyes around the table, "no amount of reluctance can dismiss the necessity of our responding to Sir Gawain's ultimatum. With all the knights we have lost through these recent squabbles I cannot afford to be without Gawain's support in addition to Lancelot's, and still expect to wield power in what would be my kingdom in name only. Sir Ywain!" The king looked up at the Knight of the Lion.

"Your Majesty…I am at your service," Ywain responded bowing his tawny-maned head toward his uncle and making a conscious contrast with Sir Gawain's posture.

"Assemble the troops for war," the king demanded. "Let all the knights of the Table—all who remain—gather their own vassals and knights together, and then send word to all petty kings who owe me allegiance that they are to bring their full forces to Joyous Gard, where they are to join us in laying siege to Sir Lancelot's fortress. We will demand that he fight or we will starve him and his retinue out of that castle. Can you do that, Sir Ywain?"

"Yes, Your Majesty. I am on my way." And with that, Sir Ywain followed in Gawain's footsteps out of the building.

Morgan le Fay was still unsatisfied. "And what about the Picts, brother dear?" She asked, her expression nearly as cynical as her youngest nephew's on the other side of the table.

Arthur gave a slight shrug. "The Picts will have to wait until we have dealt with Lancelot." And with that he rose, waving the rest of us away. The council was clearly over, and war was now upon us. But Morgan did not move. She continued to sit in the same spot, and she followed the king out of the Council Chamber with her eyes, responding to Arthur's last comment under her breath. "And what if they don't want to wait?"

***

Merlin was walking thoughtfully, his hands behind his back and his eyes focused on his feet as we left the hall and started down the steps that led into the middle bailey of the castle yard. Obviously, he had something on his mind, and I wanted to know what it was, so I broke the silence. "Well, Old Man," I said. "That went pretty much as you predicted it would, didn't it?"

"It did," he said, not changing his posture any as we stepped onto the grass and he began making his way toward the front gate of the castle, planning, I assumed, to go back to his cave for the night.

"And what do we do now?" I asked. I was truly feeling at a loss without the steady hand of Sir Gareth to advise me. And frankly, I was beginning to worry about what was to become of my lady Rosemounde, who now, without the comfort and protection of the queen, might be expected to return to the household of her husband, a prospect that made my gorge rise and the back of my neck burn with anxiety. What *was* I to do? She was his lawful wife and joined to him for all eternity in the eyes of the Church, but he delighted in subjecting her to brutal, potentially lethal and certainly unreasonable torment, so that I feared for her safety if that reunion was forced upon her.

Merlin, however, was thinking about the more general situation. "We still have friends in the court, what's left of it," he answered. "Sir Ywain. Sir Palomides. We must team with them, urge restraint. A siege means fighting will be delayed, so long as Lancelot and his forces remain safely tucked away in Joyous Gard. And I have already been busy, sending word to someone who might be able to do some good, even with the king, if the hostilities can be delayed for some weeks."

"Oh?" I said, my face displaying my surprise. "Who on earth could that be?"

Merlin smirked a bit. It wasn't often he could keep a secret from me that I had absolutely no clue about. But he had me this time. "You'll find out when the time is ripe, *if* we can delay the time long enough for it to *be* ripe. But there is something else, potentially more important than this. I could not mention it in the war council because I have absolutely no proof yet, or even any certainty as to what it means, but there *may* be evidence that could curb Gawain's motive for revenge against Lancelot."

"What?" I cried. "You suspect that Gawain is laying the blame on the wrong shoulders?"

"I examined the wounds on Gareth and Gaheris, and listen, Gildas: They had both been stabbed in the back—not by swords but by knives at short range, by someone on the ground, not on horseback. Gareth,

76

it is true, had that great head wound, but the knife wound came first. I suspect he was hacked with a sword when he was already down, to disguise the true death wound. There would certainly have been no need for the knife in the back if the head wound had come first."

"Then..." the full weight of Merlin's comments struck me. "Someone on the ground, not on horseback, killed Gareth and Gaheris. Lancelot was not responsible at all!"

"God's eyelids, that's exactly what I'm saying, boy!" The old necromancer was warming to his theme now, and began gesticulating with his hands as we walked under the barbican. "But there is more: I looked at the other fallen knights, and in general their injuries were consistent with swords or lances inflicting wounds from horseback. Except for two knights: Sir Tor and Sir Aglovale. They were untouched by wounds from above...*but* both of them had their throats cut. Again, someone on the ground, someone hiding among the loyal knights of the Round Table, was responsible for those two knights' murders."

"Then if we can find out who killed those four knights, most importantly Sir Gareth, we can change Gawain's mind and stop this war before it starts!"

"And we need to start now, and hope that the siege will last long enough for us to solve this mystery!" Merlin concluded, as we made our way north of the castle toward his cave on Lady Lake. It seemed I'd be spending the night at Merlin's place again.

CHAPTER SEVEN

JOYOUS GARD

"**L**ancelot! Traitor! Coward! Come out of there and fight me like a man, instead of cringing behind those walls like the foul vermin you are!" Sir Gawain, seated atop his magnificent black destrier Gringolet, bellowed in fury at the unresponsive walls of Lancelot's castle. In his ire, his complexion was as ruddy as his flowing red locks, as crimson as the red-dyed leather that formed his horse's harness. He held his shining helmet under his left arm, and his shield, with its red pentangle on a green background, was over his right shoulder. The fine chain mail hauberk that covered his torso jangled as he shook with rage and frustration, just as it had every morning for the past month since Arthur had begun this siege. Gawain had issued his challenge at each sunrise, and had received no answer but silence for all his pains. It seemed that Lancelot's way of dealing with the siege was to ignore it.

Sir Lancelot's great castle of Joyous Gard had been granted him by the king when the Great Knight was younger than I was now. When Lancelot was eighteen years old, Arthur had promised his new knight that the ruined castle standing on this spot on the Kentish coast would be his if he could rid it of the group of outlaws and disgraced knights who held it at that time. In his zeal, the brash Sir Lancelot had attacked the walls of what was then called Dolorous Gard, climbed the rubble of the collapsed west wall and taken on all comers when the inhabitants resisted him. Once he had killed or chased off all of the castle's wicked inhabitants, he had changed its name to Joyous

Gard and had begun the project of restoring the fortress to its original glory.

Lancelot set to work, hiring masons to rebuild the walls and reconstruct the castle's keep taller and stronger than it had been originally. He had caused the walls to be plastered and then had gilded sections of the battlements and the tops of the walls so that the castle shone in the orange light when you approached it at sunset. Having made its outside glorious and impenetrable, Lancelot restored the interior as well, sparing no expense in lining the chambers' inner walls with beautiful tapestries, painting the ceilings in bright colors, and supplying the rooms with luxurious chairs and beds and chests from all over Arthur's kingdom. The castle isn't there any more—after Lancelot went back over the Narrow Sea to Gaul, King Arthur ordered Joyous Gard razed to the ground. He didn't want to see one stone left on top of another. And so it is to this day. But at that time—well, you couldn't imagine a better place to sit out a siege.

Still, I thought Lancelot must be reaching the breaking point by now. Having had only a few days to supply the castle before rescuing the queen, Lancelot would have brought a small herd of cattle within the walls and must have stocked up many tuns of wine. His castle staff must have planted gardens within the environs as well. But I also knew he had at least forty knights, plus servants and women, within that fortress, and I calculated that even if they went to half rations they would be reaching the end of their supplies soon. The king had an army of several hundred warriors, and though Lancelot was worth a company of armed knights all by himself, he was far outnumbered on the field. Lancelot and Bors had allies, of course, in their native Gaul and Benwick, and must have sent word to them before the siege began, but no ships had yet appeared crossing that strait between Dover and Calais, and I could feel the tension straining both ways—Lancelot's men praying that reinforcements would arrive from Benwick before their food ran out, and Arthur's men hoping that they could force the surrender of Joyous Gard before Lancelot's allies could invade from the sea.

Merlin had been meeting with Arthur on a daily basis since the siege began and had advised him to build wheeled Helepolises—

movable siege towers by which his knights might scale the walls of Lancelot's fortress and capture it in pitched battle. He advised the use of trebuchets with great swinging arms that could hurl heavy projectiles at the walls and smash them back to rubble as Lancelot had found them, or to fling great burning brands into the castle and let the fire consume those gardens, those ceilings, those tapestries, and force the residents out of the walls and into the open fields where they must be cut down by Arthur's vastly superior numbers. But the truth was that the king had no real desire to engage Sir Lancelot in all-out battle. He did not want any more of his own knights risking their lives against his former great vassal, nor did he really want to destroy any of the good knights siding with Lancelot, knights who until recently had been part of Arthur's own Round Table. If Gawain could entice Lancelot to come out of the castle and face him in single combat, then perhaps this whole dispute could be settled with the least amount of bloodshed on either side.

And so the king kept putting off building those siege engines. As Merlin knew he would. But since Merlin was honor-bound to advise the king as best he could in this situation, he kept recommending that the king build them. Meanwhile Gawain kept hurling insults and challenges in Lancelot's direction each morning, as Lancelot had grown to expect. And Lancelot, who had no wish to harm Gawain any more than he already had, kept ignoring him. As Gawain knew he would.

***

The only way I could see out of this that wouldn't end in a bloodbath was if Merlin could actually prove that Sir Gareth and Sir Gaheris had been slain not by Lancelot but by someone on the ground of that cathedral lawn. But finding the actual culprit was not likely to prove easy in this situation.

It's not that Merlin hadn't been trying. When he wasn't at the king's side, and when I wasn't parading around in my barely-used chain-mail my father had sent me from Cornwall the previous Pentecost, and displaying the new coat of arms on my shield (an azure-blue background on which crouched a couchant gold dog, which looked remarkably like my borzoi hound Guinevere), we had been meeting in the evenings with various knights encamped in the siege around Joyous Gard. Often accompanied by Sir Palomides—like me still mourning the loss of his great friend Gareth—we would question knights who had been present in the churchyard when Lancelot had made his daring and deadly rescue of the queen. Where exactly had they been in the yard? How well could they see Guinevere? Where had they been looking when Lancelot arrived? Had they noticed who had been close to Gareth and Gaheris as they flanked the queen? Had anyone seen where Tor and Aglovale had been?

As might have been expected, the wild melee was remembered differently by everyone who had been there. Some said they had seen Sir Tor and Sir Aglovale close to the queen's party with Gareth and Gaheris before Lancelot had arrived. Some said no, they remembered seeing those two armed knights at the forefront of those resisting Lancelot's charge. Others said they had seen Pelleas next to Gareth, but others said no, Pelleas had received his wounds fighting off Sir Bors when he first rode in. Some said Sir Hectimere had been next to his old master Gaheris in the fray, but others saw him holding up Pelleas after the latter's wounding. Sir Geraint had been with Tor and Aglovale, one knight remembered, but others said no, he was with Mordred when the bastard trailed behind Gareth toward the queen's stake. So after weeks of questioning witnesses, we were no closer to the truth than we had been when the siege started.

Our interviewee this evening, for example, had been Sir Bedivere himself, who you might recall had led the procession toward he stake just ahead of the queen and her escort. What he had told us was that until the sound of Lancelot's horses had made him stop and turn around, he hadn't once looked back at Guinevere and the two Orkney brothers. But when the noise of the rescue party caused him to halt, he glanced back over his shoulder and remembered only seeing Ywain on Sir Gaheris's side, and Palomides himself on Gareth's, and no one else that registered in his memory, for his attention was quickly drawn to focus on Lancelot himself, high above the fracas on the ground and whacking away with his sword willy-nilly. Bedivere showed some undisguised resentment at the thought of Lancelot's slaughter of his fellow knights. He couldn't say whether he saw Tor or Aglovale fall, but thought he vaguely remembered Sir Geraint and Sir Hectimere in the same part of the field as those two sons of Pellinore. Merlin had thanked the venerable knight and shown him out of our pavilion, and now the three of us sat looking at each other wordlessly, until Sir Palomides said with a deadpan expression, "Well my money is on Ywain, because I'm reasonably sure *I'm* innocent."

That did break the tension somewhat, and I gave Palomides the obligatory chuckle, looking across at Merlin as I did so to see his face relax and his shoulders loosen. "This line of questioning really hasn't gotten us very far," I volunteered. "Do you think it's time we took another tack, Old Man?"

Merlin shrugged and put his arms out in a resigned gesture. "I'm open to suggestion," he said. After another moment he added, "All right let's try this. We know that Sir Gareth, Sir Gaheris, Sir Tor and Sir Aglovale were all killed by somebody who was among the crowd in the churchyard, on the ground and not on a horse like Sir Lancelot and his fellows. We've been going at this in the hope that somebody in that churchyard saw what happened and can give us the name of the culprit. We've been thinking only about the who in this equation. Perhaps what we need to do is go in a different direction and see whether we can determine the *why*. What possible *motive* would someone have for killing those four knights in particular?"

Sir Palomides scowled. "Yes, it would be helpful to know such a thing, but how are we to determine the why *before* we know the who? We have no one to question about it."

Merlin nodded and closed his eyes, conceding the point. "Precisely, my dear Palomides. We shall have to use that most rarely consulted aspect of human consciousness, the art of *logic*."

I looked at the Moorish knight and rolled my eyes, while he looked away and sniffed. And Merlin began: "So. Just what do we know about Sir Tor and Sir Aglovale? Tor first—he was one of the first of Arthur's knights, as I recall. Showed up sometime near the inception of the Round Table and took part in one of its first adventures.

"It was a noteworthy entrance, I remember. Arthur was just

appointing his first knights of the Table as part of the celebration of his marriage to Guinevere—when her father had given them that huge round table as a wedding gift and he was trying to figure out what to do with it—so Bedivere, Kay, Gawain, King Pellinore, and a few others were about to receive the honor. The whole court was gathered in pavilions, not unlike the ones we are in now, to celebrate the fine weather, when a man came to Camelot dressed like a simple peasant on the land, with a gray-brown beard and dark features, and kind of a hang-dog look about him. And with him came his wife— who, though poor and ill-clothed, was a fine-looking woman, I can tell you. She was middle-aged by then, and the years had creased her face, but it was clear to me she had been a beauty in her youth, before hard work and poverty had worn her down. The villein, a cowherd named Aries, had brought with him a lad of eighteen years who was quite tall and broad-shouldered, with gray eyes and blonde hair like his mother, and a dimpled chin that resembled neither of his parents.

"They begged an audience with the king, and, it being a great holiday, Arthur was willing to meet them. 'This is my son Tor,' the cowherd began. 'His greatest wish is to be a knight. I can't get him to do any work on the farm, because he spends all his time riding horses and jousting at fenceposts with broom handles. My other sons have no problems working on the land. They do whatever I tell them. But this one,' and at that he jerked his thumb at the tall young man, who grinned broadly at the king in response, 'this one won't hear of it.' At that the poor man glanced around to see if his wife was listening, and then spoke to the king in a low, conspiratorial whisper: 'His mother's gone and named him Tor—you know, after the pagan Viking's god of thunder it is, and she mollycoddles him and gives him airs. I figure maybe if he comes to your court and gets himself thrashed around a few times by some of the real knights here, it'll knock some sense into him and he'll be ready to come home and get to work. And if he doesn't come home—well, I'm shed of a useless mouth to feed, that's how I'll look at it.'

"Now the three of them had come in a cart, and I could look over to where they had parked the vehicle and see two of the couple's other sons who had ridden along and helped to drive the wagon. They were both dark-featured and had the same hang-dog expression as their father. I also noticed how King Pellinore—a tall broad-shouldered knight with a dimpled chin, had made his way behind this Aries' wife and seemed to be whispering covertly into her ear. I told Arthur privately what I had seen, and told him the boy was pretty obviously the by-blow of King Pellinore and that poor cowherd's wife, and if the boy had inherited any of his true father's skills he'd probably make a doughty knight. But don't let's say anything about it openly right now—we don't want to cause problems in that poor fellow's marriage.

"Just then, the feast was interrupted by a galloping white deer that came out of nowhere and ran through the glade where we were feasting, followed by a pack of hunting dogs, led by a white brachet close enough to take a bite out of the deer's leg. And the deer, in a kind of frenzy to get away, leaps over the table where wedding guests were feasting, and gets away, knocking down one of the knights who's there as a wedding guest—an ill-mannered churlish knight by the name of Abelleus. Well that fellow gets up, grabs the white brachet and takes off with it."

"Are you making this up right now?" I asked Merlin. "Because it's not that believable. Or all that interesting, for that matter."

Merlin glared down his nose at me while Palomides stifled a laugh. "It picks up," he said. "And God's whiskers no, I'm not making it up—everything I'm saying did happen this way. So, a lady comes riding into the clearing on a white palfrey, and she is crying because she wants her white dog back. But in the midst of her wailing, in rides another knight who grabs her and rides off with her. Everyone around the table was stunned momentarily at this outrageous interruption, until Arthur says something like, "Wow, I'm glad that's over. That woman's crying was really annoying.' He thinks it's all been a joke that somebody in the court has played on him for his wedding, but Kay, who was in charge of the festivities, soon sets him right on that score. Now embarrassed and insulted that somebody has had the audacity to disturb his wedding feast in this way, the young king sends his knights off to restore order in this mess. He tells King Pellinore, his hardiest warrior at that time, to go after the lady and bring her back from that knight who had grabbed her. Then he has another thought, and he calls his nephew Gawain and tells him to chase after that white deer and bring it back to contribute to the feast, which he wants to keep going for a couple more days.

"Then Arthur remembers his new applicant for knighthood, the young Tor. Well, it was a wedding celebration after all, and in the spirit of the holiday and the exuberance of his new venture of the Round Table, Arthur thought he'd give the boy a kind of audition. The lady had wanted her dog back, so Arthur tells Tor to go after the knight who had taken the brachet and get it back for the lady. That's his first knightly quest, he tells him. And the boy jumps to it."

"You know, this is a different side of you, Old Man," I told him. "I've never heard you tell a story this way—usually you're pontificating, interrogating, or working out a problem. But telling stories? That's not been your style."

"Well God's eyeteeth, boy, I'd be glad to have somebody else tell it, but I'm the only one who was there, so close your Cornish lip and let me finish!"

"Proceed! Proceed!" Sir Palomides said, rolling his right arm as if to signal Merlin to get on with the tale. "But I don't see where this is getting us."

"God's knuckles!" the mage cried, with no little impatience in his voice now. "Do you want to hear this or not? The young man was fitted out with some second-hand armor and a sword, shield, and lance, and given the loan of one of King Pellinore's horses, and off he went after this Abelleus character. Well along the way Tor met a dwarf who convinced him to joust with a couple of other knights— Sir Felut of Langduk and Sir Petipace of Winchelsee—who you remember Lancelot killed coming out of the queen's chamber. Tor defeated both of them, and sent them back to surrender to Arthur, who ultimately made them both knights of the Table. But I don't want to bore you with the details of those side adventures," and with that he looked pointedly at me and at Palomides. "But before long Tor found the boorish Sir Abelleus's pavilion, where he was camped several miles from Camelot and where his lady lounged with what she thought was her new pet dog.

"The sight of a knight in full armor pulling up beside her tent and demanding the dog of her, though, changed her mind fairly quickly. Tor was courteous enough, as I understand it, but he wasn't leaving there without that hound—it was a greyhound, as I recall, and weighed a good fifty pounds, but Tor bent down and lifted the brachet up, legs kicking and all, and rode off with her. As he left he could hear the lady screaming for Sir Abelleus that somebody had just made off with her new pet. It took Abelleus a few minutes to arm himself and mount his destrier, and so he came galloping full-speed after Tor. He caught the boy and the dog a mile or so from the clearing where Arthur and Guinevere were holding their wedding party. He demanded the dog back from the callow youth, told him he was going to bring that white brachet back to his lady either by itself or accompanied by Tor's head, his choice. And maybe another young knight would have been cowed, for Sir Abelleus was a skilled knight and gruff and strong, but Tor had pretty much been living for this day, and so he stood his ground.

"Abelleus was winded from his pursuit, and so was his horse, and Tor was strong and confident after unhorsing those other knights in the joust, and he knocked Abelleus from his saddle on their first pass, then jumped down and began to pummel him with his borrowed sword. He kept pressing Abelleus to yield, as his first two conquests had, but this knight was stubborn and kept saying he wasn't going to go back to his lady without that blasted dog. So Tor kept pounding the stubborn knight further and further into helplessness.

"Tor had just about reached the point of forcing the knight to surrender or die, when out of the woods came two of the new queen's ladies in waiting, accompanied by a couple of young pages from their household. It was Lady Anne and another lady, Gudrun of Cameliard, who is no longer with us, but at that time was in charge of Guinevere's household. Gudrun said that she had seen Abelleus at the feast and had recognized him when he stormed off with the dog. This recreant knight, she said, had killed her brother in a quarrel when they had faced each other in single combat. Abelleus had beaten down Gudrun's brother, she said, and refused to grant him mercy when he asked. When she herself had intervened and begged Abelleus on her knees to spare her brother, Abelleus had merely laughed at her and slaughtered Gudrun's kinsman, decapitating him before her eyes. So she demanded Abelleus's head in recompense, begging Tor for justice. Tor was unsure what to do, but Abelleus, who clearly was not one of your brighter comrades in arms, sneered at the lady Gudrun that her brother was a weakling, and then got up and tried to flee. That was enough for Tor, who split the cowardly knight's skull with a single sword stroke. So Gudrun and Anne reported when they all came back to the king's wedding feast. With the white dog in tow."

Sir Palomides shook his head. "And Arthur made him a knight of the Table after that? I mean, yes, he had accomplished his quest, but it was not an especially meaningful one, recovering a dog..."

"Well," Merlin explained, "he had defeated three other knights in the process..."

"But killed one without mercy," I reminded him.

"A knight who had himself killed unjustly, and had refused to yield," Merlin replied. "And that particular act made him a favorite of the queen for the sake of her lady Gudrun. Besides, as the son of Arthur's close ally King Pellinore, it was the politic thing to do. Oh, and God's elbows, I forgot to mention, of the three quests the king assigned that day on a whim, Tor's was the only completely successful one: His father Pellinore's quest ended with the rescue of the lady, whom he found being fought over by her cousin Meliot de Logres and that other knight who had snatched her, and now claimed her as a prize won by force of arms at Arthur's court. Pellinore killed the other knight and brought Meliot and the lady back to court, where she was reunited with her hound. And that was the first time I ever saw Nimue, for that was the lady's name. But that is another story."

I was a bit taken aback, for I had never heard the story of how Merlin met the lady he was doomed to love hopelessly for the rest of his life. I only said, "And this Meliot..."

"Is the same Sir Meliot who was also killed in Lancelot's escape from the queen's closet. Yes. The story keeps circling back, doesn't it? But I didn't mention that, in pursuing Nimue and her abductor, Pellinore had galloped by a lady who was kneeling at the side of the forest with her wounded lover in her arms, begging the king for help as he rode by. So intent was Pellinore on his goal, however, that he ignored her pleas, and as a result the young man died—and the lady subsequently killed herself in grief. As it turned out, that lady was Pellinore's own daughter, and the knight her espoused husband. He hadn't recognized them in his monomaniacal obsession with accomplishing his quest. Pellinore was never the same after that blow, I can tell you.

"And as for Sir Gawain, he had chased the deer with his own hounds, and they had run it down near another pavilion when a knight came out and killed several of the dogs. He wanted the white hart as a gift for his lady. Gawain, impetuous as always, and much younger then, was so angry at the knight for slaying his hounds that he beat him down and wouldn't show the knight any mercy, though he pleaded for it. The knight's lady threw herself before her paramour, and in his blind rage, Gawain accidentally killed the lady; he was unable to hold his hand as he swung it toward the beaten knight. It was that lady's body, not the deer's, that he brought back to Camelot, and Guinevere made him swear by all he held holy never to refuse mercy to anyone who asked it of him again, and to always devote himself to the protection of women. That has been his lifelong penance.

"So you see, Arthur could hardly make his nephew and King Pellinore knights of the Table when they had so seriously botched their quests, and ignore Tor, who was the only one who had successfully completed his own. And so Tor became Arthur's knight."

"And so he was," Sir Palomides responded noncommittally. "Your story is quirky, lord Merlin…though interesting enough in its own way," the Moor added diplomatically when Merlin's eyes flashed in his direction. "But what do we learn from it that will help us in this case?"

"Well," I ventured, "what strikes me most about this whole story is the fact that Sir Tor was the son of King Pellinore. I mean, I realize that he did not grow up in Pellinore's household, but still he must have identified with members of that clan. It seems odd that this murderer, whoever he was, would have reason to kill him along with two members of the house of Orkney, Pellinore's bitterest enemies. What motive could anyone have to kill the three of them together?"

"That is true if one looks at the facts of the story," Palomides mused. "But the contrasting motives in the story are also fascinating. Look now: Sir Gawain in this story showed himself to be irascible and vengeful; his reputation for courtesy and honor was gained subsequent to this first quest, and in response to it, as he has since striven to be the perfect knight in his courtesy toward ladies and his chivalry toward his fellow knights. But the same irascibility and vengefulness showed itself later in his ambush of Sir Lamorak, and has resurfaced now. It was always there, only suppressed by a great exercise of will on Gawain's part. Sir Tor, on the other hand, though just as young as Gawain at the time and ill-schooled to boot, conducted himself with far greater maturity and restraint, and a far clearer idea of justice. I think what we learn from this anecdote is how unjust Tor must have viewed the proceedings against the queen on that day of his own death."

"And therefore there may in fact be a connection between him and those two sons of Orkney who also perished," Merlin nodded in agreement. "They would all have lamented the queen's condemnation. What, then, do we know of Aglovale?"

"Other than the obvious?" I put in. "That Aglovale, too, was a son of King Pellinore, and so Tor's half-brother? All told, it was two sons of Lot and two of Pellinore that were murdered in that churchyard."

"Yes," Merlin said. "But Aglovale was always much closer to his gentle brother Percival than he was to Sir Lamorak, and you recall that he and Sir Percival together forswore their family's feud with the house of Orkney and refused to seek vengeance for their brother Lamorak's death."

"For whatever that was worth," I added. "There was no evidence, at the time, of who had killed Lamorak."

"But it was, and is, strongly suspected that Sir Gawain and his brothers had a part in it," Merlin reminded me. "Aglovale was a loyal knight of the Round Table and fought in Arthur's Saxon wars. Fought bravely, as I recall. But he had a notion that he wanted to visit Jerusalem, and to go looking for adventure, after things settled down a bit in Camelot. I know he spent some time in Saracen lands, and that he is known to have fathered a son with a Moorish princess."

"That is true," Sir Palomides said. "It is long ago now, probably a good twenty years. Sir Aglovale's adventures had led him southwest of the Fatimid Caliphate in Egypt where I and my brother sojourned, to the city of Njimi, in the land of the Sayfawa dynasty of the Kanem empire. It was there he found and fell in love with Banjuu, the beautiful princess of that place. For a time he served in her palace guard, since, as a knight of the Round Table, his martial prowess was much admired in that kingdom. Meanwhile he and the princess had consummated their love in secret, but Sir Agovale was burning with a desire to get to the Holy Land and visit the shrines there, and he left Banjuu, vowing to return one day if God preserved his life. What neither he nor Banjuu knew at the time was that she was pregnant with his child.

"Sir Aglovale finally reached Jerusalem, and it was while he was there that he met other pilgrims from Logres, who told him that King Arthur and his knights were in Gaul and moving toward Rome, intent on pushing Arthur's claim to the imperial crown. Aglovale could not be away from his king at such a time, and so he left the Holy Land and sailed to Italy on the first ship he could find. By the time that war was over, Sir Aglovale's loyalty to his lord Arthur bound him to the king's service by ties stronger than those that called him back to Njimi."

"But you say he had a son," I said. "How did he learn of the child's existence?"

"It was some thirteen years later," Merlin recalled. "The boy showed up one day from his remote country on that other side of the world. Must have been right before you arrived in Camelot from your own remote country of Cornwall." I gave the mage a withering look, but he continued unfazed. "His exotic origin was stamped clearly on his countenance: He was tall and handsome, and quite as darkly featured as Sir Palomides himself."

"Indeed he was," the knight agreed. "Sir Safer and I welcomed him immediately and inquired after his parentage and his reason for coming. The answer to both questions was the same: Sir Aglovale. His name was Morien, the boy said, and his mother, the princess, had been disinherited of her rightful lands. In desperation, she had finally told the boy of his true parentage and had sent him on the long journey to Logres to seek his father. He had come to find Sir Aglovale and bring him back to Kanem.

"As luck would have it. Sir Aglovale was away from Camelot at the time, but Sir Lancelot and Sir Gawain were so taken with the boy's story that they promised to ride with him to find his father. They were pretty sure he had gone to visit his younger brother Percival in Galis, and rode with the boy in that direction. I understand they found a few adventures along the way, and that Gawain and Lancelot were impressed by Morien's skills at arms—he'd clearly inherited some of his father's physical attributes. I have heard that when he was introduced to his father, and Sir Aglovale realized for the first time that he had left his beloved Banjuu with child, that he had missed the boy's entire childhood, and that his former paramour was now disinherited and destitute, he could not keep the tears from his eyes."

"So I understand," Merlin said. "But to make a long story short, as I think it's time we did, Aglovale did return to his lady's Moorish kingdom, and with his son Morien and the rest of the princess's remaining supporters was able to put that lady back on her throne. And he married her, legitimizing Morien as heir to her throne. I understand, though, that the lady was to have a second child by Sir Aglovale, but that she died in childbirth, and it was said that the couple's new daughter did not survive either. Sir Aglovale, bowed down by grief, could no longer bear to stay in the land where he had lost his beloved Banjuu, and so he left his son Morien to rule Njimi and made his way back to Logres and to his place at Arthur's Table."

"Returning," added Sir Palomides, "just in time to introduce his brother Perceval to the court. So you see, Aglovale held no enmity toward Sir Lancelot, who had helped him find his son and had knighted his close brother Perceval. For that matter, nor would he have had any reason to dislike Gawain, despite Sir Lamorak's ambush, since Gawain too befriended him and his son Morien—and since, with Perceval, he had forsworn revenge. So, my friends, where does all of that leave us?"

"It leaves us confused," I answered. "We've essentially just gone over every conceivable reason why these two knights could not have been the target of any particular faction at the court—not of those supporting Sir Lancelot, nor of those supporting Sir Gawain. Just as, I might add, I can conceive of no logical reason why anyone would have wanted to kill Sir Gaheris or, particularly, Sir Gareth."

"But somebody did," said Palomides, shaking his head.

"And unless we can figure out who, and why, this civil war will continue, and mark my words, it will destroy the Round Table," Merlin added glumly.

Just at that point a cry began to sound through the besieging army. Riders had entered the camp, important ones, who had clearly been pushing themselves to reach their destination with all deliberate speed—they had ridden late into the evening, arriving even after the last rays of the sun had faded over the western horizon. We stood at the entrance to Merlin's pavilion and looked out as a number of men were bustling about at various tasks. Merlin stopped one of these men—it was Symkin, the groom charged with caring for the horses of the new guests, one of which he was leading now to stable and fodder—and asked him who had arrived.

"Papal legate they tells me, sir," Symkin said. "Some proclamation from the Pope himself, as I understands it, me Lords." And with that he rushed on.

"The Pope?" Sir Palomides was shaking his head. "What do you suppose that is about?"

But I was looking at Merlin, who had breathed a sigh of relief and had thrown back his shoulders with a smug look on his face. "*You* know something about this, don't you Old Man?"

"Well, I told you I had another iron in the fire, didn't I?" He answered, the left side of his mouth curling slightly upwards. "God's shinbones, everything is about to change!"

CHAPTER EIGHT
RECONCILIATION, OF A SORT

"**M**y Lord and most revered Majesty, according to your command and that of his Holiness the Pope, I have brought back to you Her Royal Highness, Queen Guinevere, as right and justice require. If there be any man here, be he knight or squire or yeoman or clerk, save only yourself, King Arthur, who would dare to claim that she is anything other than absolutely pure and true and devoted to you as her lord and sovereign, then I swear on my honor as a Knight of the Round Table that such a man will answer to me: I, Sir Lancelot du Lac, will make it good upon his body that she is faithful to you.

"Your Majesty, I know that you have listened to liars who have sought to drive a wedge between you and me. Many is the time in years past that I have pleased you by coming between the queen and the dangers she faced: When she was falsely accused of murder by Sir Mador de la Porte it was I who stepped in to defend her good name. When she was accused of treason by that blowhard Sir Meliagaunt, I again proved that she was innocent of his charges. I could only believe that it would please you again on this last occasion if I stepped in to save her from the penal fire. And so I did, and kept her living and intact for you, my Lord.

"But these tale-mongers, Sir Agravain and Sir Mordred, sought, as I say, to cut the bonds that held our friendship, and meant to have caught me in your lady's chamber. On the night in question, I affirm that I was summoned to the queen, for what purpose I do not know,

93

for just as I had entered her chamber, we were accosted by that band of knights, calling me traitor and adulterer, and I was forced to fight my way out. But all was false, Your Grace, that you were told. I now return the queen to your custody. Guard and love her well. And I say again, I will prove my lady the queen's innocence on any man who challenges the truth of my words."

Such were the unmitigated, bald-faced lies with which Sir Lancelot returned the queen to her husband, thereby ending the siege of Joyous Gard and fulfilling the letter of the Pope's command, if not its spirit.

Merlin of course, had been hinting for weeks that he had some new trick up his sleeve that might alleviate the hostilities in Logres and may lead to a reconciliation between the king and queen, perhaps even between Gawain and Lancelot. Merlin was far from being a devotee of the Church, but he did have some old acquaintances among the higher-placed clergy in Logres, whom he had known since the early days of Arthur's reign, and one of these old colleagues was the Bishop of Rochester. Merlin had discovered some time ago that the bishop was sailing for Rome and would have an audience with Pope Honorius. Merlin had entreated the bishop to make it clear to the Pope just what the situation was in Camelot between the king and queen, and with the kingdom's greatest knight, and to implore the Pope to intervene to make peace. Merlin, no novice in the arena of politics, secular or ecclesiastic, knew that it would be in the Pope's best interests to intervene, since Arthur, as presumptive emperor, was the chief bulwark and defender of the Faith, and civil war in Camelot weakened all of Christian Europe. The bishop's return, with the pontiff's own legate, could mean only one thing: Pope Honorius was stepping in to take matters into his own hands.

"I greet you, Arthur, King of Logres," began the sealed papal bull, which the legate had delivered to the king. "Lord of Scotland, Wales, Ireland, Scandinavia, Brittany and Gaul, acknowledged Emperor of the Holy Roman Empire, and I charge you as the heir of Saint Peter himself, head of Christ's Holy Church on earth, and by the authority of the Donation of the Emperor Constantine the rightful authority over all imperial Christian lands, that you pardon the much-maligned Queen Guinevere, and accept her back as your loving wife and queen;

and furthermore that you no longer use her supposed treason as a motive to make war on your vassal Sir Lancelot. I charge you this on pain of interdiction for your entire land of Logres. And I further implore you to find a way to make peace with Sir Lancelot, and end this internecine war within the realms of Christendom."

Now I didn't have a clue at the time what "interdiction" meant, but the king was clearly aware, and took the threat pretty seriously. Even Sir Gawain was sobered by the threat, and advised the king to do as the Pope ordered. "I have nothing against the queen, my Lord," he told Arthur. "And never supported her sentence to begin with. So I can have no objection to her return. My quarrel is with Lancelot. Exclusively."

And so negotiations began immediately, with the Bishop acting as go-between from the king's pavilion to Joyous Gard itself. It remained to be seen whether Lancelot was willing to give the queen up. He must have assurances, he argued, that Guinevere would be completely safe if she returned to Arthur's hands. The king was more than willing to swear any oath that he would allow no harm to come to his reconciled queen. And so it was agreed.

"Well," I said to Merlin in the small pavilion I shared with him among the siege army, after three days of negotiations had finally given us our truce. "Whatever this 'interdiction' is, it seems to have put a scare into our leaders, wouldn't you say? I mean, first Arthur condemns the queen to death by fire, and the next thing you know he's taking her back as if nothing happened. It's like the Pope waved a magic wand, and presto! We're all friends again."

"Interdiction is basically a kind of ecclesiastical blackmail," Merlin told me. "The bishop or prelate has something he wants a lord or, in this case, a king to do, and if the lord doesn't want to do it, the prelate places his lands under interdict until he gives in. And interdict is a prohibition, and what your Church does is withholds or prohibits religious services in a land that's under interdict."

"So the Church says no divine services until you do what we say?"

"That's pretty much the case. No services, no sacraments, no Christian burials. What you said about 'magic' kind of applies here. If you believe that those sacraments are a kind of magical rite that guarantees you your ticket to a Christian heaven, then you're going to be pretty upset if your land is under interdict."

"I take it you're not as averse to an interdict as the king and Gawain are," I said, knowing Merlin's skeptical views concerning most things spiritual.

"Oh, don't get me wrong. I'm perfectly happy this pontiff used whatever ammunition he had. It worked, and I was counting on that. Sometimes you just have to use what works, if it's the only way to achieve the right outcome."

"Are you sure this is the right outcome?" I asked. "Will there be a lasting peace if Lancelot returns to Camelot with the queen?"

"There will be peace. And I do believe that, if we can solve this mystery of the deaths of Sir Gareth and the others, we can assure the kingdom of peace for the foreseeable future."

***

This morning, five days after the arrival of the Papal Legate and the Bishop of Rochester, the king had assembled his major advisors before his royal pavilion to await the delivery of his errant queen from the man who had rescued her from the king's own death sentence. Arthur sat in a small portable chair he used as a traveling throne. He had no robes of state here in the field of battle, but wore only a simple, long blue woolen tunic, though one that sported a lining of vair at the sleeves. Over this he wore a surcoat bearing his renowned heraldic device of the three crowns. Nor did he have a crown of state, but only a small gold circlet that he wore as the emblem of his office. Sir Gawain stood at his right hand in full armor, while Merlin occupied the position at the king's left, as his chief advisor. Behind Gawain stood Sir Ywain, and next to him Sir Mordred, now by default one of the king's chief retainers by virtue of his being one of Arthur's only surviving nephews.

Against all expectations, the other person standing with the king, at Merlin's side, was yours truly. Arthur had reasoned that of all the knights present at this siege, the one that Guinevere would almost certainly feel most comfortable with must be her former page and confidante. And so it would be my assignment to see to the queen's needs and to escort her back to Camelot after she was returned to her husband.

Thus I witnessed first-hand the approach of the Great Knight and his sovereign Lady. The two of them issued from the opened gates of Joyous Gard on horseback, dressed in pure white samite garments, and followed by ten mounted knights in full armor and bearing their coats of arms. These were led by Sir Bors on the left, directly behind Sir Lancelot, and Sir Ector on the right, following the queen. When the party arrived before King Arthur, Sir Lancelot dismounted and helped Guinevere from her saddle, taking her by the hand and leading her to the king, into whose right hand he placed the right hand of the queen. Tears streaked down Guinevere's cheeks as she stepped to the side of Arthur, whose own eyes were glistening. And that was when Lancelot issued that unmitigated bundle of untruths proclaiming the queen's innocence and his own willingness to fight anybody who dared to suggest that what he spoke was not one hundred per cent gospel. Ah, chivalry.

Not that I was anywhere near as cynical as Mordred, whom I could sense straining and sputtering behind the king's portable throne. For him, all truth and honor was a sham, a veneer to hide the darker motives of greed and lust and cruelty that, being his own deepest motives, he ascribed to everyone else in the court, including his own father, the king. Nor could he have been much pleased by Lancelot's undisguised loathing of him, and the Great Knight's reference to him as a tale-monger, a liar and a coward, but to challenge Lancelot at that moment was, he knew, nothing short of suicide, and he was not about to be goaded into rashness by Lancelot's insulting words, not when his carefully-forged schemes were finally nearing fruition. But that came later. At this point, Lancelot's rhetoric went unchallenged.

And who is to say, really, whether Lancelot's characterization of events was not in a certain sense more faithful to the ultimate integrity of the truth than the facts it was intended to interpret. For Guinevere, and Lancelot as well, were always faithful to Arthur as king. And Arthur would have been the first to admit his failings as a husband, since such a role must always have been secondary and dependent upon his role as king. As for Guinevere's role as queen, her performance was impeccable in any formal or state occasion, save only in the one function most of the court saw as paramount: She had no children. That she was barren was manifest both by the fact that Arthur had sired a child upon his half-sister Margause, producing the bastard Mordred; and the twenty-five years she had been Lancelot's paramour without a hint of pregnancy from that quarter (though Lancelot himself had fathered a child, Sir Galahad, with Elaine of Corbenic). Neither of these things, of course, was common knowledge, but it was clear that, through no fault of her own, Guinevere was never able to conceive an heir to the throne of Logres—not even a semi-legitimate one from the loins of her noble lover. But even this was no serious impediment to the smooth running of the kingdom, for everyone was satisfied with Gawain as heir apparent, and so Lancelot's assertion that the queen was beyond fault was perfectly true in the sense that, if the stability of the kingdom was necessary for peace and justice to thrive in what otherwise could have been a brutish and dangerous world for all of Arthur's glorious empire, Guinevere's fidelity to that idea was a more important truth than the relatively minor fact of her fidelity to her husband's bed. And that was the truth that everyone present was willing to embrace, with the seal of the Pope's approval giving a pious air to the whole procedure.

But if I thought that perhaps this crisis was over, and that things in Logres might return to a kind of shaky peace, I hadn't figured on the depth and intensity of Sir Gawain's despair. Peace was the last thing on his mind. And it was Gawain who broke the silence that followed Sir Lancelot's challenge.

"As for the queen, she is welcome back and, for me, should be accorded all her former titles and honors. I have no quarrel with the queen. But as for you, Sir Lancelot du Lac, I hold you a recreant knight and I will never, never be reconciled with you, no, nor any of your kin," and with that he glared with lowered brows toward Bors and Ector. "You are directly responsible for the deaths of my son and three of my brothers. I do not blame you much for Agravain, for he deliberately sought trouble and found it, to his great loss. But

I cannot believe that Sir Lovell threatened you so greatly that you needed to kill him. Yet even if that were so, what of Sir Gaheris and Sir Gareth, who were unarmed and merely escorting the queen under protest? I say that they were treacherously slain, and slain by you or by someone under your command in that skirmish on the cathedral lawn. And this I cannot forgive. While I live, I cannot and will not excuse this outrage. I will avenge my brother Gareth's murder or I will join him in death. Honor demands it. I can do no more now."

A cold late November breeze blowing across the narrow sea tousled the Great Knight's wavy brown hair, and I saw his sky-blue eyes glaze over with tears, though those tears were certainly not a response to the weather. "My lord Gawain," he answered, with a genuine tenderness in his voice. "Of all men in the kingdom, save for the king himself, I would not have offended you. Not for fear of your sword arm, though I admit that is substantial," and with that Lancelot smiled modestly, and Gawain reddened a bit, knowing that the Great Knight was being generous, since nothing could match his own prowess. "But because I have always valued your friendship—and showed, I think, a true friendship for you when I rescued you from some predicaments you'd got yourself into..." And now Gawain blushed even more deeply, recognizing the truth of Lancelot's claim and the debt he owed Lancelot for saving his life. "But even more than that," the Great Knight continued, "I regret the death of Sir Gareth, whom I loved more dearly than even my own kinsmen. More dearly than I loved my own son Galahad. I was the one who knighted him. I was the one who sponsored him for his seat at the Round Table. And I know he loved me better than any knight aside from his own brothers," and with that his voice cracked. The tears he had been holding back began to streak down his cheeks toward his block-like jaw. "I did not see him, nor Sir Gaheris, and I do not know how they were killed but I accept the responsibility, for I know if I had not led the rescue of the queen, they would not have died. So let me make this offer: In penance for their deaths, I will set off today, barefoot and in the hairshirt that I wore in the quest for the Grail, and walk from here to Caerleon. And every ten miles I will found a religious house, of whatever order you choose, donating all my treasure to

99

this end: that each house will daily sing and pray for the souls for Sir Gareth and Sir Gaheris. And this, my Lord Gawain, would, I think, do their souls far more good than this war of vengeance you propose to wage against me and my kindred. What do you say, Sir Gawain? Your Majesty?"

The king, astounded, I think, at the outrageous generosity of Lancelot's offer, bent his head down, and had begun to nod it as if in agreement. And I'm certain that for his own part, he would have been more than willing to accept the Great Knight's offer. But he had not figured on the intensity of Gawain's passion. Moved by Lancelot's proposal, but adamant in his resolve, Gawain shot back in a voice cracking with grief:

"I cannot speak for my uncle, but I can tell you that if he accepts this offer then he has forfeited my support forever. I can never forgive Gareth's loss. The queen is returned, the Pope has had his way, and we are under truce right now. But I give you fifteen days to leave the country. Go into Gaul or whatever hole you choose to hide in, but after these two weeks I will follow, and find you, and you shall meet me in battle, and there will be an end to this torment. Gareth shall have company in his grave—either you or me. And I care not greatly which of us it is." And with that Gawain turned and left the meeting.

I looked toward Merlin, but he only sighed and shrugged his slumping shoulders. We had found no evidence to clear Lancelot of Gareth's murder. All we had was the knowledge that he and Gaheris were struck from behind by someone on the ground. At least from Gawain's viewpoint, that someone could just as easily have been one of Lancelot's men as what we were thinking—someone from the king's forces.

And that was where it ended. The queen was returned, but reconciliation with Lancelot was out of the question, so long as Arthur was held hostage by Gawain's monomaniacal need for revenge. A chagrined Lancelot made his way slowly back into Joyous Gard, there to plan the debarkation of his army within the next fortnight, and Gawain took his leave of the king in order to begin plans for an invasion of Gaul and Benwick in order to reignite the war with Lancelot on the Great Knight's own native soil.

That being the case, the king turned his mind to practical matters. If he and Sir Gawain were going to be adventuring over the Narrow Sea with the bulk of his knights, it was vital that some trustworthy vassal be appointed to hold Camelot as the king's steward to ensure the continued smooth running of the kingdom. Logres could not remain undefended for weeks or months—however long the king and his army would be out of the country. The king's guard was still at the castle, but the crown needed a strong and decisive advocate at the reins of the kingdom for the duration of Arthur's absence. Normally, Gawain would have been the obvious choice, but Gawain was leading this war against Lancelot. Therefore, the king turned to his next oldest nephew, Sir Ywain.

The Knight of the Lion's round face colored, growing darker than the tawny mane and beard that fringed his countenance, and he stammered, not wishing to disappoint his uncle, but unwilling to take on the responsibility Arthur proffered. "My…my Lord, or, I mean, Your Highness, I'm humbled, really, I mean, grateful for the confidence you show in me to offer to appoint me your royal regent while you prosecute this war. But truly, if I assess my own strengths honestly, I have to admit that I have a head better put to use in fighting than in governing, don't you think?"

"Nonsense, Ywain," the king answered. "You are honest, true, and practical. What better qualities can there be in a regent?"

Sir Ywain's mouth twisted up in a rather apologetic half-smile. "Would a practical person keep a full-grown lion as a pet?" He asked, rhetorically. "Besides, uncle, to be completely honest, I feel that I really must be at my kinsman's side in this battle. I believe the time will come when Gawain will need me in what I think will be his most trying hour. He has lost his closest brothers. I am all he has left."

I found that a remarkable comment, the more so in that no one else seemed to find it remarkable. Even Mordred himself, Gawain's one remaining brother—or half-brother—did not blink an eye when Ywain made his statement. But Sir Mordred was not, unfortunately, completely forgotten. For it was to him that the king turned next.

"Nephew!" the king addressed him, without the slightest trace of irony.

101

Sir Mordred, knowing what was coming, snapped to attention, his cynical face momentarily drained of acid. "Your Grace?" he answered, for all the world like a pure young cherub.

"Do you share in your cousin's demurrals, or are you willing to take up the assignment that your king and liege lord gives you?"

With a scarcely noticeable smirk of satisfaction, Mordred bowed his head, saying, "I am only too ready to take on any command that my liege lord places upon me, and am willing and eager to accept this role of Prince Regent in my king's absence."

Whether Arthur noted the deliberate promotion Mordred had given himself over and above the king's decree—that "Prince" addition to the title—he did not indicate. But he made his newly appointed proxy kneel before him and swear an oath on the cross-hilts of Excalibur that he would fairly and truly dispense justice and defend the realm in the king's absence, until such time as the returning sovereign should discharge him of his sacred duties. And Mordred swore this on his honor (of which I knew he had none) and all he held holy (which, as far as I knew, was nothing at all).

And that was how it turned out. The exchange was made. Lancelot was planning his retreat. Gawain and the king were planning their pursuit. And Mordred was to make his way back to Camelot, escorting a small contingent of his own closest advisors—Sir Pelleas, Sir Hectimere, and Sir Geraint, and their squires and accompanying foot soldiers—and the queen, with her own small entourage, which included exactly two members: her former page, Gawain's squire Peter, given leave by his current master to accompany his former mistress, for lack of other members of her household; and yours truly.

Such was Arthur's wish, and Guinevere's as well. Having been snatched from the fire in nothing but her light shift, the queen was bereft of her household and the company of her ladies in waiting— Lady Rosemunde, Lady Anne, Lady Mary, had all been holed up in the queen's apartments in Camelot during the course of this siege, and it would be more than a few days' ride back to the castle, during which Guinevere would have only the company and service of her two former pages for the duration of the trip. I braced myself for an outpouring of passion and distress, with not a little pique over the manner in which the men in her life had botched the entire situation. It did mean that I would not be at the coming battle that loomed between Arthur's army and Lancelot's. But for me that was just fine. My heart would never be in such a battle. Whatever the outcome, the victor could only be catastrophe.

Of course, I was loath to abandon Merlin in the middle of an investigation, especially one that seemed to be going nowhere and that therefore required my assistance even more than usual. But in fact Merlin seemed pleased by the arrangement. "I'll continue trying to put together evidence here in the king's camp," he told me, "while you see what you can nose out there among Mordred's cronies. If they know anything, you ought to be able to get something out of Hectimere, or perhaps young Pelleas. They seem to be honest enough. I'll try to get word to you soon, before the king is ready to sail. If we can learn who killed Gareth and Gaheris, we can stop this war before it starts, and maybe even save the Table."

***

It was not the most pleasant ride I've ever taken. Guinevere was cross that she had no change of dress with her but had to make the entire three-day's ride to Camelot in that white samite gown Lancelot had dressed her in for the exchange. She cursed the lack of foresight and Lancelot's theatrical desire to try to make the exchange an orchestrated event of high drama that all would remember forever. Thus the matching white outfits. But he was just heading back to the castle in his. She had to wear hers for days, as it worked out. And how easy is it to keep a white gown spotless while riding a horse through the woods for miles and miles? She rode glumly on a white palfrey, now spattered with mud, so that it matched her gown even more closely.

So there was a fairly constant tirade about the Great Knight's sartorial sense. But that was just bluster. I knew the queen. Something much deeper was bothering her, and she was masking it by the endless nitpicking about the dress. As long as she harped on that, she didn't have to talk, or think, about what was truly bothering her.

103

But on the second day of riding, her face growing more haggard all the time, she took an opportunity to unburden herself to me in private. She was, apparently, even hesitant to include Peter in her confidences, and for a time that afternoon Peter had trotted ahead of us to ride next to his old companion Sir Hectimere. This left me and Queen Guinevere to ride together last in the column moving through the great forest of Logres toward Camelot, with only two wagons of supplies, driven by some of the king's household servants, following us to bring up the rear of the procession.

That was when she finally turned to me, tears trickling down each pallid cheek. "Oh my Gildas," she sighed. "I can't keep up the charade any longer. You are the one person I can trust to keep my counsel and to never betray me. So it is to you I can show my true heart."

So that's where this was going. I knew from experience that a good deal that I would probably be better off not knowing was about to pour from the queen's lips, but I was used to that by now, and settled back into my saddle for a long siege.

"Your Highness knows me only too well," I murmured, inclining my head in her direction. "I am a tomb. What you whisper to me here in the green wood will never be heard by another living soul." I see you all are smiling at me. Yes, I am about to reveal her words to you, but they can harm no one any more, after so many years, and with all those involved sleeping soundly in their own tombs now, and I'm the only one left to whom any of this really matters anymore. So why not burden you with it?

"My life has ended," she told me then. "What you see before you is only an empty husk of flesh. My soul I have left in Joyous Gard. Oh, may it now be known only by that old name, Dolorous Gard, forevermore. For that is the name that fits it now. That is all I can call it ever again." And with that she broke off and wept, softly enough that only I and the trees could hear.

I waited. There was nothing I could say, and she did not expect me to answer. She expected me to listen.

"I have had my time," she finally continued, her voice stronger now. "I had the love of my life for twenty-five years. It was always a danger, always a secret. But didn't that make it more exciting after all?" She raised her eyebrow at me with something of the old spark at last. "Oh Gildas, he was the greatest of all knights. He was the most chivalrous. He was the most handsome. And he was the gentlest. And the kindest. You know it was *that* which first drew me to him. Not the rest of it. Those things were just the frills that came along.

"It was shortly after I had come to Camelot, and many of the young knights and ladies were out among the woods, gathering flowers and welcoming the May. Lancelot was among us, but had wandered off to be alone and sit beside the stream. He had just joined the table. He had been fostered, you know, in the household of the Lady of the Lake herself, and Arthur had welcomed him as the son and heir of his first great ally, King Ban of Benwick. Well, I had come upon him myself and saw him, through the woods, speaking with the boy Aglovale. Aglovale was the young son of King Pellinore, just arrived in Camelot. The lad was only about fifteen years old at the time, and still squire to his half-brother Sir Tor. But the boy was grieving. He was terribly homesick and had just learned that his mother had died back in Galis. He did not know whether to give up the idea of knighthood altogether and go back home to help raise his beloved younger brother Perceval, and he was weeping unashamedly— something he would never have felt he could do in front of the other knights. But Lancelot had found him there by the stream, had comforted the lad with a brotherly arm flung around his shoulder. You see, Gildas? Lancelot was understanding, compassionate, kind to the boy, and encouraged him to stay at Camelot, promising his friendship. And he always stayed a good friend to Aglovale, welcoming and even knighting the young Perceval when he arrived at court, even welcoming that Moorish child of Aglovale's, that boy Morien, when he came to find his father, taking on the young lad as he had his father at the same age.

"It was then that I knew I loved him, Gildas. Not when he performed all those great deeds on the jousting fields and in the tournaments. Oh, I was proud to be in love with the greatest knight. And it was good to feel confident that no one and nothing could possibly harm me as long as the incomparable Lancelot du Lac was my champion. But all that was secondary. It was his kindness that demanded my love.

That was his essence. And that is what made any charges that he was a traitor to Arthur absurd. His kindness made his love absolute, and he loved Arthur as much as he loved me. Oh Gildas, I am devastated that I shall never see him again."

I started, stunned by her conclusion. Surely she was simply being pessimistic, based on the current plight. But surely, I thought, all of this was temporary. Merlin, after all, was on the case, and would soon find a way to reconcile Gawain and Lancelot. And I told her so. "My Lady, please do not despair. This trouble between the king and Lancelot can be mended, I am certain. Listen, Merlin and I have found that Sir Gareth and Sir Gaheris were slain by someone on the ground, not by one of Lancelot's riders. We simply need to figure out who it was that actually killed Gareth, and prove it to Gawain, and all of this will stop. The Table will return to normal then, my Lady, and Lancelot will return to you."

The queen gave me a wistful smile and a half-mocking eyeroll. "Oh Gildas, you paint a bewitching picture, but it's made of patches of a dream. This breach will never be mended now. Do you think, even if things were to end peacefully, that Lancelot would ever be welcome in Camelot again? Do you think he would ever swoop in to carry me away again, in defiance of both the king and the Pope? The bow is bent. Lancelot and Gawain are in the sights. All we can do is flee from the shaft. I shall never see Sir Lancelot again in this life. All that is left for me is to try to aid my husband as best I can, if even he has any future now."

I knew better than to argue with Guinevere. We would just have to see how the solving of this mystery would affect the state of the war. But latching on to her last comment, I changed the subject, hoping to get her out of her distraught state of mind and into something more positive. "Well, undoubtedly you have your work ahead of you there," I said, nodding forward as if her new role was literally ahead of her on the path. "I'm sure the king is counting on you to be his eyes and ears in Camelot. He has put Sir Mordred in charge, purely, it seems to me, of necessity, but clearly he can have no trust in the bastard. He must be counting on you to use your influence to keep Mordred's ambitions in check, or to get word to him in Gaul if the bastard oversteps his bounds in any way."

She sighed, her mind drawn, at least for now, away from mourning the death of her love affair. "I will do what I can, dear Gildas. In this I fear you are only too right in your suspicions of Sir Mordred. I will have your help, and Peter's, and that of my ladies in waiting, but it will take constant vigilance on all our parts to anticipate and detect whatever schemes he concocts. Still, how much influence I will have with him remains to be seen."

And that was when a serious dread caught me somewhere in my chest and grabbed the back of my neck with an icy hand. "The lady Rosemounde!" I cried, as if awakened from a dream into a nightmare. "How safe will *she* be now?"

The queen frowned. It was clear she did not know herself what to promise. "He is regent. There is no changing that," she said. "But I am queen. What I say concerning the women in my train is still, or should be, within my province."

"But she is his wife," I pointed out, "and not merely one of your train. Without the king's authority on hand to back you up, can he not simply claim her from her place and take her to his household, to abuse her at will?"

"I grant that he can," the queen said grimly. "But whether he actually will do so depends on a number of things. He would have to trample on all my authority," she vowed.

"And he'd have to go through my sword," I swore for my own part, slapping my great sword Alsace where it hung against my thigh. But with that I heaved a sigh. "There is so little we can control," I lamented. "With someone so incompetent and, let's face it, completely self-seeking, who values neither the welfare nor the safety of the realm but only his own power and ego, what can we do?"

"Hope that Arthur finishes his fruitless war with Lancelot quickly, and returns to the throne while there is still a throne to return to," the queen muttered grimly. "What I can do I will do. It does not escape me that, were it not for my affair with Lancelot, these things would not have come to pass. That is over now, and we must build on the ruins."

I still believed these thoughts of hers were but her pessimism speaking, but a part of my mind had caught at something she had said earlier, and I chose this moment to address it, partly in the hope of deflecting this lugubrious conversation. "One thing, my lady, strikes me at your mention of Sir Aglovale. From what you say, he had significant personal reason to side with Sir Lancelot in his quarrel with Sir Gawain. As you walked toward the stake that fateful morning, you had Gaheris and Gareth walking beside you. But tell me, did you ever glance around, once the melee began? And if you did, did you notice whether Sir Aglovale had moved in close to Sir Gareth and Gaheris? Or perhaps was his brother Sir Tor nearby?"

Guinevere scowled at me, then raised her left eyebrow. "I was somewhat distracted at the time, my dear, what with the prospect of being burnt and all. And then with the pressing need to leap onto Lancelot's horse as he dragged me from the flames. Is this just idle curiosity or is there some kind of point to your random questioning?"

I bowed in deference, realizing that the queen could not have followed where my thoughts had been going, since she did not know all of the details. I provided them for her. "I apologize, my lady. Let me explain: I told you that Merlin and I were looking into the murders of Gareth and Gaheris, and the possibility that Lancelot was not responsible for the Orkney brothers' deaths. I mentioned that Gareth and Gaheris were struck down by someone on the ground, not on horseback. But you should know, as well, that Merlin also looked at the bodies of Sir Aglovale and Sir Tor in that bloody churchyard, and found that they, too, had been killed by someone on the ground—that they, in fact, had been murdered by someone who slit their throats from behind. These four are the only knights whose bodies had been found in that way, and whoever killed them must have assumed that, with all the other carnage of the day, no one would notice that these four knights had in fact been murdered and had not died in the battle."

The queen's face darkened as she followed my train of thought. "And you are asking me about their whereabouts because you think there may be some connection between those deaths. You want to know if they were near my guard at the time of the attack. What are you trying to suggest? That perhaps Aglovale and Tor tried to protect Gareth and Gaheris, and so were collateral damage for whoever murdered Gawain's brothers?"

I shrugged. "That," I conceded, "or its opposite: That Aglovale, loyal to Lancelot and wishing to support him in his mission, was convinced by some scheming traitor to turn against the king and, with his brother, kill Gareth and Gaheris treacherously. And that the two of them were subsequently dispatched by the same traitor who had seduced them in the first place."

The queen's lips came together in a pensive frown. "You talk around the point, Gildas, but I know what you are implying. You mean to suggest that ultimately it is Mordred who is behind all of this. That he somehow stirred up Aglovale and Tor to take up the ancient feud of the House of Pellinore against the House of Orkney, and to use the opportunity of the chaotic rescue, which everyone knew was coming, to take ultimate vengeance on the Orkneys by killing off their fairest sons, and at the same time to render Lancelot a service in helping his cause. And that Mordred himself then treacherously killed his instruments so that no one could lay the murders at his door."

"You put it more baldly than I might have, Your Grace, but essentially, that is just what I am suggesting. I admit that some of these suggestions may be far-fetched. Sir Aglovale and Sir Tor are—or were—honorable knights, and it is hard to imagine them taking part in such a scheme, especially considering the fact that they had both forsworn vengeance for Sir Lamorak's death. But Mordred is persuasive as the serpent in Eden when he wants to be. And Aglovale was committed to Lancelot's friendship. Think about it. Is anything in this scenario something the bastard is incapable of plotting or carrying out?"

"No," the queen admitted without hesitation. "He is certainly capable all right. And as I think of it, I can now recall seeing Sir Aglovale, at any rate, somewhere close behind me when Lancelot swept me up into his saddle. That much is more certain the clearer my memory becomes. But there is one flaw that I can see: Sir Mordred was nowhere near me, I am certain of it. He had fallen in behind us as we began the march toward the stake, but when I heard the hoofbeats of Lancelot's rescue party, and I turned to see what was coming, I remember seeing him fleeing back toward the cathedral, even as I recall Sir Aglovale coming toward us, along with several other knights whose faces are a blur to me now. But I know Sir Aglovale was among them. And I know that Mordred was disappearing in the other direction. And the next thing I knew I was in Lancelot's arms as he pulled me into Minuit's saddle."

I mused silently for a moment, finally responding, "I know that what you say must be true, because the scheming bully is also a coward, and it is precisely in his character that he would run from any possible confrontation with Lancelot. So perhaps my theory of the crime is not perfect. But I do think I have something. The question of Aglovale and his proximity to Gareth has got something to do with this mystery. I can only hope that Merlin is making progress with his own investigation, and perhaps we can compare theories before long and find the truth, before this pointless war proceeds any further."

The queen nodded her agreement, just as Peter held up his horse and waited for us to catch up to him. It was our cue to return to mundane conversation, as Peter told us that the procession was about to stop for the evening, and to rest before making our final push to Camelot the following day.

CHAPTER NINE

STRANGE BEDFELLOWS

Well, this was awkward.

It had taken the queen no more than a few hours to re-establish herself in her old quarters in the castle, with her ladies-in-waiting gathered around her in the inner chamber. Now Peter was standing guard in the outer chamber, beside the desk of Master Holly, her clerk, who seemed to have been simply waiting for her to return. At any rate the old man had expressed no surprise or wariness upon her arrival, but had merely bowed his head and taken up his quill at his desk, asking, "And will Your Highness need to dictate anything today?"

Mordred had simply ignored our party altogether, and had had a few words with John of Kent, a burly, red-bearded yeoman who served as his newly chosen Captain of the Guard, and with Roger the head cook and Taber, chief groom of the stables, as well as Father Gregory, acting priest of the royal chapel (in place of Ambrose, who'd gone with Arthur), to let them all know that he was now in charge and to register his preferences as to how he wanted the castle run.

So the queen was left to her own devices. Indeed, it seemed as if Mordred had completely forgotten her existence, as she and her household kept to their own part of the castle, and took their meals in the queen's own rooms, while he held court in the throne room and his supporters supped in the great hall. This shaky state of mutual disjunction persisted through the first few weeks of Mordred's regency: The *de facto* monarch of Camelot essentially ignored our existence, and we knew little of what he was doing on his isolated throne. It felt, however, with the castle fortified by soldiers loyal to the bastard, that we were less an isolated group of independent agents than prisoners in our own rooms. Christmastide came and went with little celebration in our quarters, and by the time it had passed into Lent we were becoming anxious to hear something, even a rumor, of what was happening in Gaul.

Thus it was a surprise, and a rather awkward one, when some three months after her return from Joyous Gard, the queen received an unlooked-for visitor in the form of the king's own sister, Morgan le Fay.

Gone were Morgan's cloak and robes of midnight black. Today she wore a rich violet gown of samite, with a narrow leather belt hanging almost to the floor before her, and sleeves that hung down nearly as far from each wrist. Over this she wore a blue silk wrap bordered with rabbit fur. Her long black hair, streaked here and there with gray, hung loose in copious waves across her shoulders—she scorned the convention that bound married women to cover their hair, and used her status as widow and queen (albeit of a petty kingdom) to go gloriously uncovered. As a sign of her rank, she wore a thin golden band around her brow, and her dark eyes flashed menacingly as, preceded by Master Holly, she entered through the curtain that separated the queen's outer from her inner chamber.

"Your Majesty," Master Holly stammered in his thin, reedy voice. "The royal sister begs an audience."

"Thanks, fellow, I will take it from here," Morgan said, dismissing the clerk without a backward glance. Guinevere, conscious of her position, did not rise but greeted the lady Morgan with a close-mouthed smile that did not reach to her eyes, and merely smoothed out her own simple green gown and waited for the king's sister to come to her. After a moment's hesitation, Morgan gave a huff and did just that, coming forward to stand before the queen, where she bent her head in the slightest bow and murmured, "Your Grace."

Guinevere acknowledged the grudging deference with a slightly broader smile, and said, "My lady Morgan, this is a surprise. Won't you be seated? We need not dwell on formalities here," and with that she nodded to the chair on her right side, the one that I had been occupying to that point, and I sprang up immediately to allow our visitor to seat herself, while I bounced back behind the queen's chair, where I could survey the entire circle of ladies in one glance.

As Lady Morgan settled herself comfortably in the seat I had vacated, Guinevere acted the gracious hostess as if nothing unusual were going on. "I'm not sure you are acquainted with all of my ladies," she began. "To your right there is Lady Anne, who has been with me the longest." Anne inclined her head slightly in greeting, a smile devoid of sincerity adorning her pretty face. "Next to her is Lady Barbara, and to *her* right is Lady Mary." The two teenagers nodded respectfully to the king's sister. "They are the youngest of my charges here. Next to Mary is the lady Alison, and then lady Vivien, another of my longer serving ladies, who came here from Gaul about the time Sir Bors and Sir Ector joined Lancelot here in the court."

"Ah, *bonjour*," Morgan began half-heartedly. "*Comment allez-vous?*"

"*Comme si, comme ça*," Lady Vivien answered cautiously. "*Et vous?*"

"*Ça va*," Morgan said, then continued with a little impatience. "And the last of the ladies, on your left, am I correct in assuming this is the wife of the current regent of the realm?"

At that Rosemounde snapped her head back and raised her eyebrows at the king's sister. I could see she suspected a note of disapproval in Lady Morgan's tone. Before she could speak, though, the queen stepped in. "Indeed," she cooed, "this is the lady Rosemounde, the legitimate heir of Duke Hoel of Brittany and now, as well, lady of Orkney, lawful wife of Sir Mordred. And my closest confidante." Guinevere added that last with an undercurrent of warning, determined to protect Lady Rosemounde from any presumptions Morgan may have brought with her.

Then, with a kind of lazy gesture toward the back of her chair, the queen added, "Sir Gildas of Cornwall, here at my back, I believe you already know."

"Yes, of course, I am acquainted with the boy," Morgan said with a marked lack of interest. I was a bit miffed—I was twenty years old by now, I reasoned. Hardly still a boy. Except, I suppose, by the standards of one just about old enough to be my grandmother. But I knew that nothing here had anything to do with me. Guinevere had tossed in my introduction as a means of deflecting Morgan's attention away from Rosemounde, on whom it had landed with an uncomfortable thud.

"But now that these niceties are behind us," the queen continued, "perhaps we can move directly to the question of why you are here. I daresay it must be a matter of some moment for you have come to me about it."

Morgan, far from seeming put out by the queen's dispensing with the formalities of court, set her jaw and nodded vigorously. "It is, Your Majesty, it definitely is. But I wonder if perhaps we could speak more privately? What I have to say is truly for your ears alone," and with that she flicked her eyes around the room, letting them rest for a significant time on the lady Rosemounde. It was clear to me that she did not know whom she could trust in the present circumstances, and if her concerns had to do with the king's bastard and his uncomfortable regency, then she might naturally be hesitant to speak in front of the bastard's own wife. It was certainly not common knowledge that Rosemounde was estranged from her husband, and that she clung to the queen like a drowning woman to a raft.

But Guinevere could see that if Morgan was truly going to open up to her, it would have to be in a room from which Rosemounde was absent. She knew as well as I did that trusting Morgan le Fay one hundred per-cent was probably a foolish policy, and so she made this offer: "If that is your desire, Lady Morgan, then let us retire into my private closet. I will bring with me only my advocate and bodyguard, Sir Gildas. He is privy to my most private thoughts, and will be my second pair of ears on this occasion."

After a few moments, the king's sister grimly nodded her assent and stood as the queen rose from her chair, to enter the tiny closet behind the heavy wooden door through which, such a comparatively short time ago, Sir Lancelot had cut down the dozen knights that had ambushed the queen and himself. I followed the two ladies into the room and closed the door behind us. The closet looked essentially as it had the last time I had seen it: the bed pushed against one wall, the others covered by floor-to-ceiling tapestries of the martyrdom of Saint Agnes, the martyrdom of Saint Ursula, and the queen's own favorite: Judith with the head of Holofernes. And above the fireplace—still an empty wall where the sword and shield that had proved Lancelot's salvation had formerly hung.

The queen sat on the bed and, to my surprise and her visitor's, invited the lady Morgan to sit beside her. Morgan sat, and immediately burst into a torrent of words.

"It's intolerable!" she began. "What was my idiot brother thinking, to leave the realm in the hands of that...that monster?"

The queen made no answer, but bowed her head in a gesture that could have meant accession or might have implied reticence. Clearly she wanted to see where the king's sister was going with this before tipping her own hand in any way.

"The bastard is a conniving, evil brute who only wants power and has no interest in actually governing this kingdom. Why, oh why, did Arthur not give this more serious consideration? Surely he might have found someone more worthy, more thoughtful, more benevolent?"

"He did offer the role to your own son," I blurted out, feeling a need to answer the lady and sensing no movement from Guinevere. "Ywain turned him down. Said he preferred to be at Gawain's side in his time of need."

This was clearly news to Morgan, who looked at me quizzically, as if she'd bitten into a sour grape. "Well, that's just like Yewey," she said at last. "Never thinking of himself, never letting ambition sway his thoughts. And yet he would have been so much better than this... this abomination."

"The king was looking to members of his own family, men that would have some natural authority by virtue of their relationship with himself," I offered. I felt exactly the way the lady Morgan did about Arthur's decision, but felt a certain loyalty to the king that urged me to defend his choice in the face of his sister's disapproval. But she jumped on my excuse with both feet.

"Exactly!" she cried. "He was looking for *men* from his own family. Why on earth didn't he think of his own *sister* for the regency? You think I haven't had experience ruling a kingdom in the name of its

115

king? Why, Uriens was nothing but a dotard those last years of his so-called reign! Why wouldn't Arthur appoint *me* to the post. Or," and with this she eased off her vehemence for a moment, "why not *you?*" And with that she gestured to the queen.

The queen was taken aback for a moment, but there was a flash in her eyes that suggested she had been wondering the same thing, at least about herself, but had simply been too much of a lady to bring the matter up. But in response to Lady Morgan's outburst, she wrinkled her brow in thought and then raised her left eyebrow as she answered: "You'll forgive me, I trust, for suggesting that in your case, the fact that in the past you have threatened the king's heir with beheading, and before that sought to place a minion of yours on the throne after conspiring to take my husband's life, may have given him some reservations about entrusting the realm to you in his absence, Lady Morgan."

The king's sister shrugged. "Water under the bridge," she muttered, waving the queen's suggestion away. "And besides, one might just as well say that he shrank from appointing you as his regent because he had just accepted you back from the knight that has been your lover for a quarter of a century. But these are trifles," Lady Morgan sniffed indignantly. "We both know that the true reason we as women are kept from real power is a built-in misogyny inherent in the patriarchy: This whole 'courtly love' ideal is nothing but a sugar-coated chain to keep us shackled to a pedestal. We can have no real power because we are professed to have the intangible power of love."

Now it was Guinevere's turn to shrug. Morgan's take on things was unorthodox, but it was hard to argue with it. For myself, I did not consider the queen's power intangible: Her ability to manipulate and to overawe the powerful men with whom she interacted daily was palpable to me, and I could easily imagine her doing so in an official capacity as regent. But it was certainly true that she *had* no official capacity, nor was she likely to in the future. But as for the power of love being intangible, my own heart and mind rebelled against the thought, being devoted as they were to pleasing the lady Rosemounde with my every breath. But I kept quiet at the time. No one in that room wanted to hear from me.

After a few moments in which Guinevere waited fruitlessly for Lady Morgan to continue, the queen let out a sigh, not without a bit of impatience, and said, "You're saying, then, that you have come to see me, what, in order to commiserate with me about not being regent of Logres?"

Lady Morgan waved that away as if the queen had got her all wrong. "No, no," she scoffed. "All I'm saying is this: Between the two of us, we are much more likely to represent the king's interests than that conniving stain on the Orkney name that currently occupies the throne room. And I think that, for the good of the kingdom, the two of us owe it to King Arthur to work together to limit the damage the little bastard can do until the king returns from his adventures in Gaul."

Now the queen's interest was definitely piqued. She leaned forward and spoke in earnest. "What do you mean? What exactly do you have in mind?"

"We work in secret," Morgan whispered. "We wait. We watch. We consider every move this Mordred makes and we consider every decision he reaches and every order he gives. We communicate regularly with one another to compare notes, and when anything seems amiss, we send word to Arthur immediately, wherever he is. In the meantime, we also infiltrate Mordred's court. We get close to his advisors, the captain of his guard, anyone who might give away his plans. We leave no stone unturned in finding out everything that is going on in this castle."

"Yes!" I cried, carried away by the lady's rhetoric.

Morgan paused, and the queen looked up at me with some amusement. "It seems," she said, "that my bodyguard favors your plan. And for that matter," she continued after a slight pause, "so do I. So how shall we proceed?"

"You keep your eyes and ears open. I will do the same. We can agree to meet here in your rooms once a week at this time, say on Fridays, if that will work for you."

The queen nodded, smiling. "My social calendar is not particularly full these days. I think that I can squeeze you in. But as for now, although we have been back in Camelot for some three months, the only observation I can make is that so far Mordred has made no request to see his wife or to be reunited with her. She has been under my care for some time, and with the king's support I have kept her from him. But law and Church would be on his side if he were to demand access to her. That he has not done so seems suspicious to me."

"Hmph," Morgan responded. "Either he is too preoccupied with something else to bother with his wife, or he wants to keep you pacified so that you do not turn publicly against him. But I agree, it's odd behavior. But his behavior in *my* report may a bit more direct. You may recall that before this business with Lancelot, I had come here to meet with my brother and warn him about the activity of the Picts along the Scottish border?"

"I heard something about that. The king seemed little concerned, as I recall."

"The king was preoccupied with other matters. His bastard, however, was apparently paying close attention. Because guess who I observed paying a visit to our bloody little regent this morning, as guests of state?"

The queen's jaw dropped. "Who? You mean…these pagans…"

"Precisely!" Morgan insisted. "A whole bloody delegation of blue-painted Picts ushered in to see Mordred in the throne room!"

"Picts?" I could not hold back at this revelation. "What on earth are they doing here? Mordred is negotiating with them? Is he making peace with them? That's so…so… statesmanlike!"

Morgan flicked her eyes up at me and curled her lip sardonically. "And wouldn't that be out of character? No, I don't think that's what's happening, my boy. It's a lot more likely he's making an alliance than making a peace treaty."

"An alliance against whom?" the queen asked—in her heart knowing the answer already.

"Exactly," Morgan said.

I didn't have to be told either. Mordred was trying to put together an army to wrest the throne away from his father. Why else would he be meeting with King Arthur's sworn enemies? "Well then we shouldn't wait!" I exclaimed. "The king should know of this right now, as soon as we can get word to him!"

"No," said the queen. "It is too soon. We need more substantial proof, and we also can guess only a small part of Mordred's plan. Another week of watching and listening is necessary, I think, just as the lady Morgan has suggested. Let us leave it at that," and with that she took Morgan by the hand in a gesture of unity. "We will meet again next Friday morning, and see what information we have then."

"Precisely," the king's sister answered. "We are partners in this, I and the queen. We will not allow this bastard's treason to stand." And with that, she herself stood. And when she looked down once more at Guinevere, she smiled darkly.

"Just to be clear: You do know I've always hated you, don't you my dear?"

"Of course, darling," Guinevere said as she touched Morgan's arm. "And be assured, the feeling is quite mutual. Bye-bye for now."

***

When the king's sister had left her rooms, the queen's ladies were naturally dying to know what the two women had talked about. Of course I let the queen tell them just precisely as much as she felt they should know: She told them that she and Lady Morgan had agreed to try to influence things in Mordred's court in a way that would promote the king's interests, which was true enough and, I thought, plenty. Some of those ladies, particularly the younger ones, were very loose-tongued, and you could never be sure what they were going to say and to whom they were going to say it.

But now it had come to that point in the day when, in the days before the current chaos, the queen liked to take up her embroidery. And so she was determined to take it up now, to simulate as best she could those more carefree days of the recent past, and the rest of the ladies prepared to do the same while listening to Lady Vivien read to them from an old book of romances, this one concerning King Horn and his defeat of the Saracen occupiers of his land with the help of a company of Irish knights. I thought I might go out into the bailey and give my great destrier Achilles a workout tilting at the

119

quintain, though my heart sank as I remembered how Achilles had been a gift from my master Sir Gareth on the day he sponsored me for knighthood in the Order of the Round Table. I wondered how he would feel about this war being fought in his name, between his favorite brother and his closest mentor—Lancelot, the knight who had sponsored *him* on the day of *his* knighting. And what would he have thought of his other brother, the despicable Mordred, being trusted with the regency in the king's absence? Sir Gareth had never trusted Mordred, had always believed him capable of anything. "I know you would be appalled," I whispered absently to the spirit of Sir Gareth that I unconsciously wished could still hear me wherever he might be. "Keep your eye on him, won't you, old Master?"

When I turned to leave I found myself staring straight into the smirking face of my lady Rosemounde. I gave a little start as I felt caught in those substantial, dark eyes. I often felt those eyes could see through me, but at the moment they were laughing at my embarrassment. "Are you reduced to talking to yourself now, Gildas of Cornwall?" she asked. "None of the present company to your taste?"

"No!" I answered. "I mean, yes, or, uh…the company is as pleasant as I could wish for, my lady, especially as you say, the present company," and I gave her a courteous bow. "But no, I was not talking to myself, I was…" and it struck me that I had no idea how to explain what exactly I was doing, but took a stab at it anyway. "I was having a…an imaginary conversation."

Up went her eyebrow and the corner of her mouth, and in the next moment Rosemounde was shaking her head. "Well, I think I shall imagine I didn't hear you say that," and she shrugged it off, but continued: "But tell me, Gildas, what did the queen and Morgan le Fay really talk about? I know you will tell me." She lowered her voice and a conspiratorial look came over her face, "because you can't resist my feminine wiles, and besides," she looked to her right and left in a pantomime of secrecy, "we can just tell anyone who asks that it was an imaginary conversation."

It was Rosemounde asking, and from her I had no secrets, so in a low voice I said, "It is essentially as the queen reported it, my lady. Only the two of them agreed that they did not trust your loving husband as far as they might be able to throw my horse Achilles, and they are determined to keep a close watch on him, and to report to the king at their first opportunity any suspicious acts Mordred engages in. They plan to get together once each week to share and compare what they have learned, especially with the king's interests in mind." I did not go so far as to tell Rosemounde anything about the Pictish delegation. That, it seemed to me, was the most important bit of information exchanged that morning, and I thought it might be best to keep that news as quiet as possible for now, until we could determine exactly what was going on between Mordred and those blue-painted heathen. Still, I cautioned Rosemounde, "but please, my lady, don't share anything I'm telling you with any of the queen's other ladies. Some of them, I know, are a bit more garrulous than I would like…"

No sooner had those words left my lips than a torrent of words assaulted us from behind. "Oh, Gildas I hope you aren't going to let Lady Rosemounde monopolize all of your time with us here, are you? It's really not fair, we hardly ever get to see any real knights any more since Lancelot's gone away and the king has chased him, and now they say they'll be gone for ever so long and we'll never get to see some of them again, but I know that you've just come back from Joyous Gard, haven't you, and so you must have spent a lot of time with Sir Thomas, isn't that true? And how is he, can you tell me? He hasn't been hurt or sick or anything like that, has he? Did he ever talk about me when you were together? What did he say about me? And did he give you any message to pass along to me? He must have…"

"Lady Mary!" I interrupted her, which was, I knew from experience, the only possible way to get a word in while Bedivere's niece was in the middle of one of her one-sided conversations. Still, as I looked into her flashing blue eyes that darted here and there as she spoke like a tiny bird flitting from branch to branch, I felt a stab of pain and sympathy in my heart remembering her poor sister, Lady Elizabeth—"Bessie" she'd called her—the young girl hand-picked by the queen herself to be my lawful wedded wife, and remembered again how that sweet, intelligent girl had suffered brutal murder the previous year in the episode of the queen's abduction. For Elizabeth's sake I would always be kind to Lady Mary. And I went on to answer her most fervent question.

"Thomas is doing well," I told her. "He, uh, mentioned you to me nearly every day." She smiled. (This was true. He would often tell me how peaceful his days were without Mary's constant yammering in his ears). "And," I added, glancing at her thin, blonde figure, "he talks often of your physical attributes." She blushed and hid her face momentarily in the nosegay she was carrying. (This much was true as well. I'd heard Thomas say more than once that his Mary was thin as a rake, but he expected her to fill out eventually, maybe by the time she was eighteen or so). "And yes, he does send you his love." And at that she jerked her head back and rolled her eyes in delight. This last was not absolutely true per se. But I knew Thomas would have done so if he'd thought of it and had the chance to speak to me before I'd left with the queen. The truth was that Mary was a vivacious young girl who was infatuated with anything new she looked at, and steady, practical Thomas was not quite sure what to do with her, now that it seemed he had caught her. Or that she had caught onto him like one blown about by the wind who latches onto a branch. I knew full well that he loved her, and that while he was momentarily thankful for the respite he was currently enjoying from her slightly frenetic personality, he looked forward eagerly to his return to what he hoped would be a slightly matured and slightly less turbulent Lady Mary.

The girl sighed. "It's *so* hard this way, to be left alone here in the castle." I caught myself before I made the comment that Lady Mary was hardly alone, surrounded as she was by the queen's gaggle of ladies, and Rosemounde lightly placed a hand on my forearm and raised her left eyebrow at me as a silent caution.

"I know just what you mean," Rosemounde answered. "Sometimes it can be lonelier in a crowd, as here among the queen's household," and she nodded toward the small group resuming their place in the circle of chairs and buzzing with gossip, "than being alone with your own thoughts, especially when you are missing someone so much."

"Oh it is, it is," Mary agreed, and pouted as she glanced again at the other ladies. "Especially around somebody like Lady Barbara, who's got her lover right here in the castle! She was so glad when Sir

122

Pelleas returned to court with Sir Mordred. I mean, she almost died when he was wounded in the churchyard when Lancelot rescued the queen, and then to have him go off again with the army was almost more than she could bear! But since he's been back she's been able to spend as much time with him as she can find, every moment she's not at the queen's beck and call, which is not all that often, to be sure, but it's a lot more time than I've gotten with Thomas! And you know, Pelleas tells her everything. How sweet it must be to have a lover so open and eager to share his thoughts with you. Why, he's even told her things I'm sure Sir Mordred would rather not hear of…"

I'd been letting Lady Mary's flood of words wash over me, but suddenly I was smacked to attention by the young girl's news. She had stopped talking (of her own accord) and looked at Rosemounde and me with a smug feline expression of having a secret and bursting to tell it. "And what exactly would that be?" Rosemounde beat me to the question.

"Well," Mary began, taking in a breath as if she expected this to be a long answer. "Barbara told *me* that Pelleas told *her* that he was having second thoughts about being on Mordred's side in this whole affair. He still wants to support the king, of course—he'd never go over to Lancelot's side or anything like that, for he's always been an ally of the house of Orkney, but Mordred, he says, can go too far, and he's especially unhappy about some of Mordred's other supporters, especially, and don't tell anybody else I told you this, but I mean especially Sir Geraint. Pelleas says *he's* not to be trusted at all, and he doesn't know for sure if he is working for Sir Mordred or for himself, but he's not at all happy about some of the things that he's seen Sir Geraint do since this war began. And not only that, but…"

Lady Anne had begun to clear her throat and to look in our direction, subtly gesturing to Rosemounde and Mary to stop the idle chatter and come to join the queen, for Lady Vivien was preparing to begin her reading for the afternoon. And with that Mary bobbed her head and said, "Well, that will have to wait, I guess. Must go join the queen. I'll talk to you later, Sir Gildas!" And she beamed up at me and was gone. Lady Rosemounde smirked, winked at me, and whispered, "Duty calls."

With that I turned and resumed my plan of charging the quintain with Achilles. But now I had something new to think about. If Sir Pelleas was discontent in Mordred's camp, then he was the perfect person for me to try to pump for information. Did he know who had killed Gareth and Gaheris? Was our search for the killer, and the truth that could end this civil war, so close? There was always an opportunity to isolate a particular knight. I just needed to work out how.

CHAPTER TEN

ON THE SCENT

My dog Guinevere was a borzoi, a kind of sight-hound related to the greyhounds currently so popular with hunters in Logres. But borzoi, a breed that had its origins, as I understood it, far in the east, on the snowy steppes of Russia, were furrier than greyhounds, and a little more independent—and, at least from what I'd observed, somewhat smarter too. The fact was I had named my girl after the queen because I was pretty sure she thought of herself as royalty, and thought of me as the serf who came around now and then to take her for a run. She was pushy, opinionated, dramatic, loyal, and brave; in short, she out-Guinevered Guinevere, and so that was the only name I ever considered for her.

And when I picked her up from the kennels the next morning, she came trotting out with a real purpose in her light step, and moaned at me a bit to let me know that it was about time, she hadn't had a good run in days and I'd better not let that happen again if I knew what was good for me. But when I held my hand out to her she pushed her head under it to be petted, then shoved her long nose under my arm, forcing me to give my full attention to stroking her and telling her what a good dog she was.

I was leading Achilles as well, but he stood patiently while I greeted Guinevere, an animal that he tolerated when she ran circles around him on the road or on the hunt, and whom he nuzzled occasionally when she lay down next to him at rest. Normally I'd have taken a smaller horse on a hunt, a lighter and swifter palfrey who would have been faster through the woods after the quarry. But Achilles needed the exercise, and my quarry today was going to be human, not venison. Hanging from Achilles' saddle were a small bag with a luncheon snack of bread, cheese and cold leg of lamb, and on the other side a crossbow with a supply of darts. Today we were joining William of Newcastle, Chief Huntsman of Camelot, who was off to track deer for dinner.

The kitchens of the great castle were supplied daily with livestock brought in from royal fields adjacent to Camelot. There were usually beef, pork, mutton, and a good deal of chicken available. Sometimes, particularly for fast days, this supply was supplemented by fish caught in the river that ran close by the castle. Trout and perch, pike and bream were pulled regularly from that river by kitchen lads charged with supplying dinner for Fridays. Still, particularly when Camelot was at its normal capacity, it was desirable, even necessary, to provide additional meat from the forests around the castle. This might be provided by hawking, as a number of nobles in Camelot had their own falcons and used them to hunt small game and birds, like rabbits or ducks. But hunting large game, mostly deer and the occasional wild boar, was the most reliable means of supplementing the typical diet of the folk in the castle, and finding that game was William of Newcastle's job.

With the castle as sparsely inhabited as it currently was, William's talents were needed only occasionally, though when the king and his knights were in attendance it was necessary to engage in a hunt nearly every day. William was joined in that sport by knights and squires from the castle, all of whom joined in at one time or another for the exercise and for the sake of their own dogs and horses. This morning, William was heading out for the first time in a week, and a few of the nobles in the castle had opted to go with him. I was one of them, dressed in a green tunic and hood and leather hunting boots. But I wasn't doing it for the love of the hunt, or even for the love of my dog. I was doing it because I had heard that Sir Pelleas was joining the hunt this morning, and after what Lady Mary had told me yesterday, I wanted a chance to talk to the knight known throughout Logres as "the Lover." If he was, as Mary had implied, disenchanted with Sir Mordred's leadership, then he may be willing to talk to me, and may even know something about the unsettling deaths of Gareth and Gaheris. In any case, it was worth a try.

I mounted Achilles there in the castle's middle bailey and, with Guinevere scampering about playfully around the great destrier's hooves, joined a small party of three other hunters—two squires and Sir Pelleas himself—in addition to William and his two apprentices. We moved off at an ambling pace behind William of Newcastle as he made his way under the barbican and over the castle's drawbridge, out to the forest to hunt.

I bided my time, waiting for the royal huntsman to determine where he was going to lead us. Guinevere had joined William where he had dismounted and was standing beside his own lymers or bloodhounds, who were sniffing about the trees just inside the edge of the forest. They seemed to have found something, and William bent down and examined the ground, then picked up the fumes the dogs had found and placed them in the ivory hunting horn that hung at his side. Then he looked carefully at the bushes nearby, checking to see whether a stag had rubbed off some part his velvet antlers in the branches. He spoke briefly with his pair of apprentices, Tom and Henry, then turned and came toward Sir Pelleas and me, as the ranking nobles on the hunt. He showed us the droppings he'd picked up in his horn, and said a fairly good-sized buck was moving off "in that direction," he waved vaguely into the woods, and that he thought if we left it to the dogs to track it, we should have bagged some venison before lunchtime. Pelleas and I concurred, and William mounted his horse and gave the dogs their head, and off we trotted.

I held back momentarily to bring up the rear, and Sir Pelleas, out of a kind of exaggerated sense of courtesy, waited to ride alongside me, as I anticipated he would. I wasn't absolutely sure how to go about this interview: I was pretty sure that Merlin would tell me that if I went straight into questions about Mordred and his machinations, I would scare Pelleas off and would never pin him down. I opted instead to take a circuitous route into Pelleas's confidence, and began with what I assumed was an innocuous question just to get him talking. It turned out to be one of my more epic miscalculations.

"So," I began, maybe with a little exaggerated affability, "Sir Pelleas 'the Lover,' eh? What's all that about? Where'd you get that nickname, huh? Quite a reputation with the ladies, then, is that it?"

But instead of the manly laugh and the faux-humble denial implying he was protecting the reputations of all those ladies whom he had bedded and left, all of which I had expected, Sir Pelleas gave me a furtive glance from the shadow of a face bowed in humiliation.

"Do you mock me, Gildas of Cornwall?" He shot back in a voice sounding less challenging than threatened. "What have you heard?"

Taken aback, I stammered, "I, uh…haven't heard anything at all. Which is why…why I asked the question. I don't know where the name came from, but," and now I tried to back off as quickly as I could, "but you don't have to tell me anything if you don't want to. Look, I was just making conversation…"

Sir Pelleas pulled his lips tight into a kind of resigned half-smile and, after a pause of a few seconds, he shrugged and said, "Not many in Camelot know the story. But I don't particularly trust those who do. I think perhaps I could trust you not to spread it around. If I tell you do you swear to keep my story to yourself?"

Again, this was all way more than I expected, and I was pretty sure it didn't have anything to do with what I really wanted to talk with Pelleas about. But I also figured if I could get him talking, maybe I could keep him talking, and I agreed, though I had to ask him, "But why do you feel like you can confide in me? Not that it's a bad idea, but do you really know me well enough to trust me with a story so very sensitive?"

Pelleas looked down, his eyes focused on some spot on the path before his horse's hooves. "Remember, Sir Gildas, we were both chosen as Queen's Knights, with the special duty to serve and protect the queen. I know that of all her knights, Guinevere had a special relationship with you."

"Oh," I responded modestly, "she had a soft spot in her heart for me because I had been her page, but that…"

"But that meant you knew her secrets. All of her secrets. I know that you were intimately acquainted with facts in the queen's life that she shared with no one else. You knew of her ongoing affair

128

with Sir Lancelot long before it was well known, long before that fateful night when Lancelot killed Sir Agravain and the other knights in the queen's boudoir. You knew and you kept the secret. It was the most explosive secret in all of Logres, but for you it was inviolable. I don't know that anyone else realizes the extent of your fidelity, young Gildas of Cornwall, but I for one am a great admirer of your loyalty and your courtesy. And that is why I know I can trust you. And why I will tell you my shameful secret."

This was getting to be more than I had bargained for, but if I was going to get Pelleas talking about anything to do with Mordred and his schemes, then I did need him to trust me, and I supposed this personal revelation, whatever it may be, was a step in that direction. I did not discourage his confession.

"This was several years ago, before I'd got it into my head to come to Camelot and pledge my sword to King Arthur. I come from Caithness you know, and my people came over there from Norway not many generations ago. Drove the Picts out of that part of Scotland and allied ourselves with King Lot and the house of Orkney. But that much you already knew. By the time I got old enough to start playing with real swords instead of toys, Lot had been defeated and Gawain and his brothers were pledged to Arthur's service. So fine, my loyalties were to them, and they were free to support anybody they wanted. But me, I stayed at the court of Orkney whether Gawain was there or in Camelot. And that court, while it's nothing like here, does have its own brand of chivalry. There's an annual tournament, you see, and when I was eighteen I entered myself in it. I'd got my own war horse, Leander, the year before—my father was not a poor man, he'd been a vassal of King Lot and had his own lands, and he'd been able to get me a horse and armor of reasonable quality. And I'd been practicing. I'd say I wasn't as skilled as I am now, with a few years of chivalry under my belt, but I was reasonably adept at arms, at least for those parts, and I ended up winning the tournament, unhorsing men twice my age with ease. And the prize of the tournament was a golden arm circlet made by Viking smiths generations ago, a prize provided by Sir Gawain himself, who had come back to Orkney to act as judge at the annual tournament."

"Well!" I said. "Congratulations! *I've* never even taken part in a tournament myself. I can't even imagine what it's like to win one. But how on earth is this a confession of your shame? I'm confused…"

Sir Pelleas closed his eyes, shaking his head. "Well no, that's not the humiliating part. It's what happened afterwards. You see I was in love at the time with a charming young maiden by the name of Ettarre. She was a beautiful lady of an aristocratic family, with long golden hair and flashing green eyes and a coy little mouth redder than coral, that smiled coquettishly at whoever she looked upon. She was rich as Croesus, and lived in a castle of her own not far from the seat of the Orkney clan. She attended the tournament, of course, as all the young noble ladies of the land did, and after Gawain had presented me with the gold band, I found her in the front row of the arena and, dismounting, knelt before her and offered her the circlet as a token of my love. She accepted it with a great show of courtesy, and placed it on her arm to show it off. I thought I'd won her heart. I mean, who wouldn't?"

"A logical assumption," I agreed.

"But that wasn't the case at all, as I learned all too soon. The following day I rode to her castle, only to find the doors shut against me and a churlish brute of a gatekeeper telling me to be on my way. Well, all right, I thought, she doesn't want to seem too easy. She's displaying the conventional courtly virtue of *daungeur*, wants to make me work harder before she lets her guard down and gives in. So I went home and composed a love song to sing to her the next day.

"Which I did. I stood beneath the small barbican over the main gate into her castle and sang of my love to her to the accompaniment of a small giterne. I'd had some training, you see, in the local cathedral school, learning a smattering of all the liberal arts from the priests there. A bit of Latin. Some mathematics. A smidgen of logic. And music—I was especially adept in music. But Ettarre was having none of it. Those doors remained closed to me, and that same oaf of a guard shouted at me to begone from his perch in the barbican. I returned the next day and again every day for a week, all with the same result. That, of course, is when people in the neighborhood started calling me 'Sir Pelleas, the Lover.' They might have qualified it with 'the unrequited lover,' because nothing I could do would move the beautiful but cold-hearted Ettarre."

"Well," I shrugged companionably. "That's unpleasant for you, sure, but it's certainly nothing to be ashamed about. Many a lover has been scorned by his beloved, even after she's taken expensive gifts from him, as your Ettarre had done. The secret's not to dwell on it. Nobody ever actually died of a broken heart, as Merlin is fond of saying. You pick yourself up and go on. That's just how love works, or doesn't work, in this fallen world of ours…" I was trying to keep the tone light. I did not, of course, believe a word I was saying, as I'm sure you know. I myself had been hopeless and lost the will to live when my own dear Rosemounde had been married to her beast of a husband. Even Merlin, far wiser and far, far older than I was, was crushed when he'd lost his beloved Nimue. But you can't say that to somebody in the throes of despair.

But I'd misinterpreted Pelleas's revelation. "It's not the rejected wooing that causes me shame," he was quick to assure me. "It's what happened afterward. Sir Gawain, who hadn't yet returned to Camelot, saw me moping around Orkney Castle one evening after another fruitless session of singing at Ettarre's gates, and asked me what the trouble was. 'You've just won the grand prize at a major tournament,' he says to me. 'What could possibly be getting you down?' And so I told him the whole story: He'd witnessed how at the tournament I'd given my prize to the beautiful Ettarre. He was surprised to learn how afterwards she had rejected my suit on a daily basis, and had done so without the courtesy of even a personal rejection.

"'The lady is entitled to accept or reject any lover she chooses,' Gawain cautioned me. And I understood that much. 'But,' he continued, 'after accepting your costly gift, courtesy would demand that she at least give you an honest rejection to your face, rather than have her underling cast you out like some peasant begging at her door.' And so with that Sir Gawain promised that he would go to visit Ettarre himself on my behalf. She could scarcely have her churl send off the prince of the territory unceremoniously as he had myself, and Gawain could at least bring me back an acknowledgment from the damsel's own mouth, either a definitive statement that she wanted

nothing more to do with me (in which case I hoped he would demand
back the golden circlet), or a hint that in fact she was displaying
the requisite *daungeur* that the courtly code demanded. If that was
the situation, Gawain was determined to plead my case with the
Lady Ettarre, to soften her toward my suit. And so we were agreed.
Gawain set off the next morning on his great horse Gringolet and
called at her gate. I followed him at a distance to see how he got on,
and when he presented himself at her gate, the guardsman opened
the portcullis immediately. I needn't tell you how excited I was. At
last I would have some kind of resolution to my love-sickness. It
might be a final rejection, of course, but I was prepared for that. At
least I would have some certainty."

With that Sir Pelleas stopped his reverie and stared ahead. The
dogs had not yet chased down their prey, and we were ambling
along behind the squires and the apprentices by at least a furlong or
two, so there was no chance that the others would hear what he said,
but he still seemed reluctant to continue. Finally he took a deep
breath and let it out with a sigh, saying, "Gawain did not come out
of the castle gate again for two days. He had the decency to blush
a bit when I confronted him to ask what had happened and told me
that for the lady's sake he really could not answer, but it was clear
to me what had happened. He had gone in to see her on my behalf,
but, impressed by Ettarre's beauty, he had ended up seducing her
himself. Or maybe it was the other way around. In any case he had
betrayed me and he had bedded her."

I nodded. It was not a great surprise. Gawain had acquired over
the years a reputation as a great seducer of women, while at the same
time forging a name as a great *protector* of women, and a paragon of
courtesy when it came to damsels in distress and the like. He had a
great respect and admiration for women, and both of these traits he was
known for stemmed from that same quality. But it was a quality that
had undercut Sir Pelleas in a way that had humiliated and devastated
him. That much was clear. Gawain had almost certainly not intended
to seduce Ettarre when he entered her castle, but most likely had put
up little resistance to the impulse once it had struck him.

"So now you know," he concluded. "I did not blame Ettarre so much. She did not *have* to choose me, just because I had given her an expensive gift. Though it was a bit disingenuous of her to have kept it. But Gawain—he was my liege lord, and he claimed to be my friend. And he had made me a promise. And he betrayed me. That I could not forgive, and I could not go on being his man. I left Orkney castle the next day and made my way to Camelot, where I pledged my fealty to King Arthur."

It was a story that explained a number of things about Sir Pelleas's motives. He despised betrayal, and no doubt saw in Lancelot's adultery with Guinevere a mirror image of his own betrayal, this time involving treason against his new lord. Furthermore, his pledge of fealty to the Orkney clan was now manifesting itself in his support of Sir Mordred, but it was obvious why he had not thrown his lot in with Sir Gawain's vendetta against Lancelot. But I was wondering whether that nascent loyalty to the house of Orkney might allow me to recruit him as an ally in trying to determine who had killed Gareth and Gaheris—two of the brothers who'd had nothing to do with his shaming at the hands of Gawain.

It seemed a good opening for me to steer the conversation toward Sir Pelleas's disenchantment with Sir Mordred, which Lady Mary had hinted at. I privately lamented Merlin's absence, since I was sure he'd find the perfect note to strike with this knight known as "the Lover." This thought gave me an idea. "You do now seem to have shaken off the disappointment of the lady Ettarre's rejection," I ventured. "You've found a new love in the queen's attendant, the lady Barbara, at least if one can believe the rumors. Isn't that so?"

Sir Pelleas bowed his head a bit and flashed a little half smile. "She is still a very young girl," he said, blushing a bit, though he was himself no more than twenty-three or so, I guessed. "And she certainly has been attentive to me, particularly after I'd received that wound in the cathedral yard from Lancelot's attack. But we've done little more than flirt a bit." He cleared his throat. "She is quite easy to talk to, though, I'll say that for her."

"So you aren't tongue tied and flustered when you're around her, then, as the poets suggest happens with the true lover in his lady's presence?"

Pelleas gave a short laugh and shook his head. "No, quite the opposite," he said. "It's easy and comfortable being with her. I'm not sure that isn't better, despite what the poets say, especially after my experience with the lady Ettarre."

"If only more lovers opened their hearts to the ladies they felt comfortable with, rather than to those who made them shake with humility, love would bring a lot more happiness than it does."

Pelleas gave me a genuine smile. "I've no doubt you're right there, Gildas of Cornwall. Maybe I should start thinking of the lady Barbara in a different way."

I returned his smile and gave him a slight nod. "And may you have joy of her, Pelleas of Caithness. How lucky it is for you that you are here now with Sir Mordred, since it gives you the opportunity to spend far more time with her than you'd be able to if you'd stayed in Arthur's ranks."

His face clouded for an instant. "Yes," he said a bit absently. "There is that, I suppose."

Pelleas's tone gave me the opening I'd been looking for and I pounced on it. "What?" I asked innocently. "Something about being with Mordred that's *not* to your liking?"

"I didn't say that," Pelleas quickly backpedaled. "Only…"

"Only what?" I encouraged him. "Is he not the friend you expected?"

"Mordred doesn't have friends," Pelleas confided, looking about as if making sure no one was listening. The squires were still well ahead of us, even farther ahead than before. "He has lackeys," he added in a low voice, barely audible over the sound of our horses' movements and breathing.

"Lackeys?" I echoed. "What do you mean?"

"He takes no advice nor admonition from anyone," Pelleas continued in the same low register. "He confides in no one, but expects absolute loyalty from everyone. Just yesterday, for instance, he told us to prepare for a delegation from Ireland that would be arriving any day. He'd decided, without taking counsel from any of his retainers, to negotiate a new treaty with the Irish, canceling their obligation to pay tribute. I told him that King Arthur would never approve such a treaty, and he told me that it was not Arthur these delegates would be dealing with but himself, and that I needed to listen more and to speak less."

I was appalled. Less at Mordred's manner to Pelleas than at this news of new negotiations with Ireland, a land the young King Arthur had beaten into submission with the help of my own King Mark, freeing Cornwall from Irish dominance and establishing Logres as the one real power in the region. Many Irish still hated Arthur. If Mordred was treating with them, it could only mean one thing: He was scheming to make them allies. But for what purpose? Coming on the heels of the suspicious Pictish negotiations just concluded, it looked ominous. Either Mordred was seeking support for his own elevation to heir apparent, displacing his brother Sir Gawain; or, even worse, he was plotting to depose King Arthur, and to be raised, by the strength of his foreign allies, to the throne itself.

The enormity of what Pelleas was revealing to me made my head spin, and I even teetered for a moment on Achilles' steady back. But I didn't want to give away my suspicions; Pelleas was still, after all, Mordred's man. "But why then do you stay with him?" I asked. "Are the others content to serve him in this fashion?"

"They are. They're all looking for something for themselves, as far as I can tell, and they're willing to toady up to Mordred, thinking he's going to divide up the spoils with them."

Spoils of what, I wondered, but quickly asked, "What about Geraint?" Now I had gotten to the question Lady Mary had dropped into my lap in the queen's chambers. "He is a petty king on his own account, isn't he? Is he content to serve Mordred in this demeaning way? What's he expect to get out of this?"

Pelleas gave a derisive snort. "Geraint? He's the worst of all. I expect he thinks he's going to end up sovereign king in his own land when Mordred's through. Anything for Mordred, is his motto. He's even brought all his retainers from his own country and stationed them in the neighborhood, quartering some in the castle and billeting some of them in houses in the city of Caerleon. At least three hundred of them, I've heard. Put them at Mordred's disposal, he has. Now why do you reckon he'll have done that?"

A generous interpretation would have been that Mordred, realizing the castle was in a relatively vulnerable position with Arthur's entire army in Gaul and only the royal guard to watch things here in Camelot, had asked for this army to keep the castle safe and to protect Arthur's realm. And frankly, defending the realm could actually also include making treaties with Picts and Irishmen to keep peace on the borders of Logres. But a voice in my head was warning me that the generous interpretation was not in fact the correct one, and that perhaps it was time to get word to the king that something suspicious was going on in Camelot.

I'd been hoping for a chance to bring up the subject of Gareth and Gaheris. Sir Pelleas was in a talkative mood, and this might be my best chance to discover something about the truth of their murders, if indeed Pelleas knew anything at all about them. But it was at just that moment that the hounds, apparently, had caught sight of the buck we'd been trailing and had begun to chase it through the woods. William of Newcastle sounded his horn and our horses began to gallop in pursuit of the horn and the barking dogs. Achilles was unused to running in a wooded area, and with my approval made his pursuit somewhat gingerly, and so it was that Sir Pelleas bounded well ahead of me on his palfrey.

Guinevere and the other hounds had surrounded the stag, who bolted from them in terror directly into the path of the hunters' mounts that were in hot pursuit. Finding no escape there, the deer spun about and galloped to the left where Guinevere, fastest of the hounds, leaped at him and bit his flanks, causing him to rear up in confusion, at which point a dart from William's crossbow caught the stag in its flank. The stunned beast stumbled and two more darts struck him down, then all the dogs were upon him, and his struggles ended. I hadn't got off a shot. But it wasn't the deer that was my real object today anyway.

Sir Pelleas and I stood beside our horses, breathing heavily after the exertion of the ride and the chase, and watching William and his apprentices begin to skin and dress our quarry and throw morsels of the deer to the dogs. As I watched Guinevere gobble her reward, I really wanted to resume our interrupted conversation about Sir

Mordred and Sir Geraint, but I couldn't see how to broach it with Pelleas now without arousing suspicion. And suddenly, to my great surprise, Pelleas plunged right in again as if he'd never paused. "If you talk to Geraint," he told me, "he's probably going to try to convince you to come over and join Mordred's cohort. He tries that with everybody. That's how I ended up here. But of course, I was easy to convert, what with my loyalty to the Orkneys but my feud with Gawain. But Geraint tries it with everybody. I remember even before the war with Lancelot, listening to him try to convince Sir Tor and Sir Aglovale to join us, using their enmity with Gawain and his other brothers as leverage—even though Mordred was a part of the ambush that killed their brother. That took some guts, I can tell you that."

I said nothing, but stood thunderstruck. The other shoe had just dropped.

CHAPTER ELEVEN

CRISIS

"**B**ut don't you see? If Sir Geraint was trying to solicit support for Mordred—for his claim to supplant Gawain as heir to the throne, or whatever he is aiming for—then that has to be connected to the deaths of Tor and Aglovale!"

"Mightn't you be jumping to conclusions, boy?" Morgan le Fay responded, a bit haughtily. "Why should they be connected?"

"Because," I began patiently, looking around the table at the faces of Queen Guinevere and Lady Rosemounde, to whose presence at these weekly meetings Morgan had finally agreed—at the queen's urging. Even though the sessions were held for the express purpose of exchanging information about Rosemounde's husband Sir Mordred, the king's sister had finally relented after Guinevere shared Rosemounde's history of abuse at Mordred's hands, and suggested the possibility that Rosemounde might understand Mordred better than the rest of us, the result of a shared intimacy no one else possessed.

"Because it explains their deaths. Geraint tried to recruit them, perhaps even tried to enlist them in the attacks on Sir Gareth and Sir Gaheris. And when Tor and Aglovale refused, Mordred killed them. Or had Geraint do it. They knew too much, and they could have given the conspiracy away if they were allowed to live after Gareth was killed."

"But that's all speculation," the queen said shaking her head.

"Maybe, but it makes sense. It's the first real evidence that suggests a link between their deaths and the Orkney brothers'. And it's all we have. We're certainly not going to find out from Sir Aglovale or Sir Tor what passed between them and Geraint."

"No, but you could ask Sir Geraint," Rosemounde spoke for the first time. I gave her a sidelong glance of disbelief. "Of course, if he's guilty of anything, he'll probably lie, but you're not going to find out what happened any other way. See what he says and then weigh it as evidence. What have you got to lose?"

I thought about that for a moment. "Well, if Mordred and his friends discover we're asking questions about Gareth's death, they may decide it is too dangerous to let us *keep* asking questions. They may feel their crimes are in danger of being revealed and try to silence us."

"What do you mean, *us*?" Guinevere asked. "*We're* just a group of ladies in here, doing our needlepoint and reading romances in verse. We don't know what *you're* doing, skulking about the castle asking all these questions."

"Oh, I see. Send me out as the bait and see if anybody snaps at me."

"Everyone knows that you and Merlin are always asking questions," Rosemounde said. "They expect it of you. At least they won't be surprised."

"Besides, you're reading an awful lot into Pelleas's comment," Guinevere cautioned. "You seem to have made up your mind that Mordred is behind Gareth's death and are looking for anything to support your suspicion, even without proof. Merlin would not approve."

I sighed. "I wish the old man were here now," I admitted. "I'm sure he'd know what to do, what questions to ask. But all right, I'll see if I can get Geraint talking and find out what he is willing to admit about Tor and Aglovale."

"Well, his men are certainly all over Camelot," Morgan spoke at last. "As your Sir Pelleas mentioned, hundreds of Geraint's knights have descended on the palace and seem well entrenched. If I didn't know better, I might suspect Camelot was being occupied by enemy forces in the absence of its king. But more disturbing than that is Pelleas's revelation that an Irish embassy is coming to Camelot. Let us think for a moment: If it is not diplomacy Mordred is seeking, then it is an unholy alliance. He has Geraint's warriors. He seems to have gained the Picts as allies. And now the Irish? If Mordred were planning a great coalition to make war upon King Arthur in order to wield absolute power in this land, he could not have done so with more aplomb."

Guinevere turned pale and looked at Morgan aghast. "You are quite right, Morgan. I had been choosing to believe that he would work more secretly, that he would connive some underhanded scheme. I was blind to the fact that he is building alliances of Arthur's enemies, and his only goal must be to seize power openly. Has the time come, then, to send word to the king? To warn him of this danger?"

Considering this, I shrugged and sighed. "Isn't this, too, all speculation? What Mordred is doing is suspicious, and we are all pretty sure what his ultimate goal is, but until Mordred actually shows his hand all we *have* is our suspicions."

"And if we wait until Mordred makes his intentions perfectly clear, is it then too late?" Rosemounde asked. "Would we even be *able* to get a message to Arthur?"

"But you know there's another problem," I stressed. "Arthur is locked in battle in Gaul even now against Lancelot at the behest of Sir Gawain. If he leaves that war, he loses Gawain's support. And without Gawain's support, he has only a small army of his own, since obviously he's already lost Lancelot's. Even if he wanted to come back to Logres now, he'd be coming back nearly bereft. What chance would he have?"

"He should be given the option," the queen insisted. "He should be told what is going on here and be given the chance to decide his response for himself. We cannot decide for him."

"Yes," Morgan agreed, but then added, "when we actually *know* what is going on. The youngsters' words of caution may be well advised for now. Let us meet again next week, after the boy has had a chance to talk with Geraint—if we do have more than suspicions about the murders of Gareth and Gaheris, that may help to assuage Gawain's lust for revenge, and bring him back here with the king.

And in another week we may see clearer signs of Mordred's true intentions."

The queen raised her eyebrows, looked at me and at Rosemounde, then sighed and nodded. "Another week, then. Who knows? By then even Lancelot himself might be persuaded to return to Logres at the head of an army…"

That seemed as likely to me as Mordred turning pilgrim and giving up the regency to walk barefoot to Jerusalem, but I held my tongue, bowed my way out of the queen's quarters, and walked out into the middle bailey, contemplating how I might be able to interview Sir Geraint without arousing too much animosity. But I was also thinking of other things. When I had spoken of Arthur coming bereft from Gaul I had seen a mental image of another figure—Mordred himself, sole survivor of the shipwreck that had drowned everyone else on the vessel that Arthur had placed him on as an infant, coming bereft to his mother's castle in Orkney. And I shivered with the recognition that all our worst deeds must in the end come full circle to crash around our heads.

***

If I had to do something unpleasant, I preferred to go ahead and get it over with. So the very next morning I rose from where I'd been sleeping, in the queen's outer chamber with Peter and Master Holly, and went off to find Sir Geraint and see what might be gleaned from a conversation with the knight who, according to Pelleas, was Mordred's own right-hand man.

I stopped first at the kitchen, to beg a slice of bread and cheese, with a slice of bacon and small beer from Roger, Camelot's chief cook. Roger was oddly somber as he obliged me, handing me my breakfast through an open window into the smoky kitchen. I looked at him with some concern. "All right, Roger?" I queried.

The old man shrugged. "Don't mind me," he said. "I'm thankful to have the likes of you about these days, Sir Gildas, don't think I'm not." Then his eyes rolled about the bailey, and glanced up on the castle walls, where, I now noticed, soldiers of Geraint's army could be seen milling about or on guard in the ramparts. "It's these other blokes, strangers with no history or appreciation of the place, that 'a been hanging about the castle. Them," now he bent closer and lowered his voice, "and the others—the Picts and the Irish and what not—that 'a been droppin' in here of late. It don't look like it's all above board, seems to me, Gildas."

I shrugged. "Army's all with King Arthur in Gaul and Benwick," I said. "Makes sense to have someone here guarding the place."

"Could be," Roger replied, unconvinced. "Still don't explain those Picts and such. What's Mordred up to, is what I want to know."

Yes, I thought, wouldn't we all like to know that? But I just shook my head to indicate my own lack of insight, and began to move on, munching on my breakfast. But I stopped abruptly, realizing that Roger might be just the person to help me find who I was looking for, since he kept track of who in the castle was where by knowing where and when people were eating. So I asked, "Speaking of Sir Geraint, do you have any idea where he is this morning? I need to talk to him about something rather important."

"Well, now to be right accurate, Gildas, we weren't talking about him at all, just thinking about him, I'd have to say. And truth to say I wasn't thinking about him in a real charitable way neither. But he was off early I think, heading with a few of this bunch," and with that he rolled his eyes about the walls of the castle again, "to the tilting grounds, to have a few goes at the quintain, I think."

That seemed reasonable, and it also fit into my own plans nicely, since I could run into Geraint at those practice grounds as if by accident and question him in a very casual manner. And so I was off immediately to the stables, where I figured Taber could tell me for sure if Sir Geraint had taken out his horse, and if so where I could pick up Achilles and be off to take a few passes at the quintain myself.

Taber met me at the stable door with the first smile I'd seen on his face in five years. I was wondering why but I didn't have to wait long. "Good to see a familiar face," he said. Which was also a pretty long speech for him. It seemed he was feeling the same kind of anxiety that Roger had expressed.

"Uh, thanks," I told him. "I've come to get Achilles, to get some exercise at the tilting yard. Anybody else gone there that you know of?" Casual, see?

Taber turned and nodded to one of his stable hands, who began to put his saddle and bridle on Achilles. Having heard that I was going off to tilt at the quintain, he was equipping Achilles with my jousting saddle, narrower than my usual riding saddle and sporting longer stirrups, with a high pommel in front that protected my groin from being wounded in a joust, and an elevated cantle in back that kept a jouster from being flipped backwards out of the saddle. As the young hand finished fixing the bridle, Taber finally answered me in his own laconic fashion. "Took Hectimere with 'im," he mumbled. "Maybe three or four of his own." And that was it. But it was fine. It was more than I usually heard from Taber. And his information was useful to me. If there were that many at the quintain, it meant that I'd have an easier chance getting Geraint talking while the others were focused on their tilting practice. I took Achilles by the reins and walked him toward the tilting yard.

The castle's practice lists were beyond the middle bailey on the far side of the keep. A large door there opened onto a narrow area some twenty yards wide by about a hundred yards long that lay between the inner wall of the castle and the outer, fortified and crenelated wall that loomed over the moat. A wooden dummy—the quintain—stood at the end of that hundred-yard run. I leaned in, peering through the gate to make sure there was no great war-horse bearing down on the quintain at that particular moment, and saw that it was safe to lead Achilles in. I walked him toward the end opposite the quintain, where five knights and three large destriers were already standing. One of the knights—it was Sir Hectimere—was mounted and in full armor, bearing a shield with a red (or gules) basilisk (the mythical reptilian beast that could reportedly strike you dead with its eyes). The creature was presented trippant, that is to say, one leg raised as if walking, on a field of gold. Hectimere's lance was couched and he was prepared to ride full tilt at the quintain. I sidled along the wall keeping Achilles close, though he had been here enough times to know when to stay out of the way. Hectimere galloped to the target, a dummy with a wooden shield hanging from a cross beam that swiveled on a pole, with a sandbag attached to the other end that swung about and struck the rider if he made a poor strike on the shield.

Which Hectimere did. His lance slid off the side of the mounted shield so that his horse actually ran into the shield as he sped past, and he barely escaped being knocked from his saddle as the sandbag swung around and struck him a glancing blow across his back. Nonchalantly stepping over to where Sir Geraint stood holding his own black destrier, I made a casual observation about Hectimere's tilt.

"Not the best I've seen him do," I commented. "Hectimere usually gets a solid hit in the center of the target. Maybe he took his eye off the quintain for an instant."

"Yes, he's a good lad with a lance, or close in with a sword or knife, for that matter. But he did slip up there, no denying it. Could have been your coming through the gate when you did," Geraint observed dryly. "Might have thrown off his concentration."

"Maybe," I acknowledged. I took the opportunity to observe Geraint. Like Hectimere, he was in full armor, and was leaning on his own shield, which displayed his own distinct coat of arms: a black eagle volant (that is, in profile in flight) on a field azure. Geraint's three retainers also wore armor, though they seemed to be sharing a single war horse today for purposes of attacking the quintain. "Madern, mount up and take a turn," he barked at one of the young men, and Madern sprang to life immediately.

"So, why the exercise in full armor today?" I asked Geraint, my eyes on the quintain rather than Geraint himself, as if I was indifferent to the answer. "It's like you're expecting some kind of real action soon. Is the castle in some danger?"

"You can never be too careful," Geraint answered, his own eyes on the quintain. I wondered how much he was concealing, and decided he was pretending to be indifferent even better than I was.

"No, I suppose you can't," I agreed. Then I thought I'd take a chance and, just to measure Geraint's reaction, I added, "especially when I hear that there are Picts and Irish envoys meeting with the regent in Arthur's own throne room."

If I thought I was going to get a rise out of Geraint with that, I was sorely mistaken. He merely turned to me and grinned. "Nothing *there* to be concerned about, Gildas. Those were peace envoys. Sir Mordred has shown great statesmanlike qualities in this. He's negotiating with these potential enemies and turning them into friends. This castle has nothing to fear from those quarters. Nor, I should add," and now his toothy grin became almost frightening and his cold blue eyes drilled into me, "is there anything to fear from the Saxons our regent has been in touch with."

"Saxons?" I repeated, shocked and not a little bewildered. "Mordred is in contact with Saxons as well?"

Geraint nodded, turning his face again to the quintain as his knight Madern made for it at full gallop while Hectimere ambled back on his own mount. "Yes," Geraint said. "He has been communicating with their kings, Hengest and Horsa, who are making a landing in Kent within the next few days and will be sending couriers here with their own messages. Soon every one of Arthur's enemies will be converted into friends."

I pursed my lips as Madern missed the quintain completely and actually rode into the dummy's shield with his own right shoulder, which made his horse rear back just long enough for Madern to be struck from behind by the swinging sandbag, and that sent him tumbling head over heels off the front of his horse. Geraint shook his head without comment as his other two retainers ran forward to catch the horse and to see that Madern was all right.

"Good thing he was wearing his helmet," I ventured, to no one in particular. But then I answered Geraint, "Friends of Arthur? Or friends of Mordred?"

Again he fixed me with that cold smile. "Isn't it all the same?" he asked innocently. Then his face became all seriousness and the smile faded. "Mordred is making many friends," he said. "I think you must see that, Gildas. The smarter of Arthur's knights recognize a rising star when they see one. I think that *you* are smart enough to recognize that it is Mordred's star that is currently in its ascension. Knights who care about their own futures have been seeking him out for the kinds of things his friendship can promise them."

"Is that so?" I answered carefully. "And what, if I may ask, has he promised you?"

Geraint shrugged and waved a hand, as if it was not worth talking about. "I have my own kingdom, what more can the regent give me? You know my lands—between Wales and your own home territory of Cornwall. Perhaps the future holds some lands in those territories that could come under my control..."

"King Mark rules in Cornwall," I reminded him. "He might have something to say about who holds his lands in vassalage."

"He might," Geraint acknowledged. "He might have more to say about it if he accepts Mordred's friendship."

"Wait, are you saying Mordred has been in contact with Mark?"

Geraint looked at me as if surprised. "Oh, who can say? I'm not privy to everything the regent does."

"And what about Wales?" I pressed. "What kinds of lands are you talking about there?"

"Well," Geraint drawled thoughtfully. "The lands belonging to the House of Pellinore have recently fallen back into the regent's hands..."

I flushed, thinking again of Tor and Aglovale. "You mean the king's hands, don't you?" I challenged him.

"Again," he said his dismissive smile coming back into his face. "Isn't it the same thing?"

"But Aglovale has a son, Morien," I remembered. "Known to both Gawain and Lancelot. Neither of those knights is likely to let those lands be given away to someone other than Aglovale's heir."

Geraint scoffed. "Lancelot will certainly have no say in the matter now. As for Gawain, I do not expect him to be in a position to care about this much longer, do you? Come Gildas, think about this. Mordred is the wave of the future." And with that he leaned forward and whispered to me: "Come and join with us, why don't you? I'm sure I can persuade the regent to accept your allegiance if you make a decision now."

It was my turn to smile. "The regent and I have something of a history," I answered him. "I am fairly certain that Mordred would rather crawl on his knees to meet your friendly Saxons at Dover than offer me a spot in his new order. But say, speaking of Sir Tor and Sir Aglovale, I understand you offered the two of them the same kind of enticements you're offering me here. What happened with them, if you don't mind my asking?" I didn't really care if he minded my asking. This interview was beginning to get on my nerves.

"Oh, them?" Geraint scoffed again. "They were too stupid to grab onto a good thing when it was placed in front of them and tied up in a bow."

"They turned you down flat," I confirmed. "So tell me," and now I figured I'd risk everything and just ask him outright, as Rosemounde had urged me to do. "Is that why they died?"

Geraint seemed only slightly taken aback as the full weight of what I was asking struck him. And then came the cold smile again. "That does seem likely, doesn't it?" was all he said. Then he turned to his men, who'd brought the hapless Sir Madern back with them, and began barking orders again. This interview was at an end.

***

The following Friday I sat again in the queen's chambers with Guinevere, Lady Rosemounde, and Morgan le Fay. What I had learned from Sir Geraint was crucial, I thought, and told them so.

"Saxons!" I told them. "Mordred has apparently been in contact with the Saxon tribes from across the Narrow Sea. You know they were one of Arthur's greatest foes in his early days, until he beat them soundly at the Battle of Mount Badon and made peace for a time. For Mordred to invite them back to Logres, now that the king is on the continent, fits with his other moves, to ally himself with the Picts and the Irish, also traditional enemies of Arthur's empire. I think the conclusion is inescapable. Mordred is building a power base to rival the king's own, either to force Arthur to name him his heir, or worse: to defeat the king in battle when he returns from Gaul and thereby seize the throne right now."

There were some pretty solemn faces that met my eyes when I had finished that little speech. The three women then glanced at one another and fidgeted with discomfort. "Unless," Rosemounde finally ventured, "his motives are what Geraint claims them to be: Mordred is trying to bring lasting peace to the empire by appeasing all of

Arthur's foes. Maybe to show the king how well he can govern, and in that way convince Arthur to name him heir. Isn't that possible?"

Now Guinevere and Morgan shifted again and looked at me to see what my reaction might be. "Logically that might be true," I answered Rosemounde. "I think it's beyond question that Mordred is making a play for the throne, one way or another. Geraint all but told me that when he tried to recruit me to Mordred's cause. But my lady Rosemounde: You have been married to the bastard. If anyone can know his motivations and his way of thinking, it must be you. Knowing Mordred as you do, do you really think his intentions are peaceful or honorable?"

It was Rosemounde's turn to fidget, and she looked down, not meeting my eyes. Finally she gave her head an almost imperceptible shake.

"There's more to it," I added. "Geraint hinted that Mordred's been in touch with King Mark of Cornwall as well."

"King Mark?" Guinevere exclaimed. "Why on earth would he contact Mark?"

I shrugged. "Mark is a petty king. Maybe Mordred is offering him free rein in his own lands if Mark supports him for the crown. Just what he seems to be offering Geraint."

"Let's not forget the Irish connection here," Morgan added with a canny squint of her eyes. "Under King Arthur, the Irish have been paying an annual tribute to Mark since the king's Irish war. If Mordred is wooing the Irish as allies, he has to give them something, and stopping the tribute if he becomes king is a good way to do it. But to do that, he needs to appease Mark somehow, or have him as a staunch enemy."

"And Cornish independence might be the way to do it," I conceded.

"But this is *still* all conjecture," the queen broke in, wringing her hands. "We don't have proof of anything. Is it enough to take to the king?"

"It must be," Morgan replied. "Even if it isn't all true, if we keep waiting while Saxons land in Kent and Irish in Wales, while the Picts come south through Gorre and occupy all of Northumberland, it will be too late to warn the king. He must return as soon as possible while there is still a Logres to return to!"

"And what of Gawain?" Guinevere asked. "Gawain is Arthur's most important vassal, and he is bent on this meaningless war with Lancelot. Arthur can't return unless Gawain comes with him."

I groaned. "I *know* Gareth and Gaheris were killed by somebody on the ground. Look, Geraint all but admitted to me that he killed Tor and Aglovale, and probably at Mordred's behest. If they killed those two, isn't it almost certain they killed Gareth and Gaheris too? Tell *that* to Gawain, and I'll bet he changes his tune."

Morgan fixed me with an intense stare. "'All but' admitting it to you is not the same as *actually* admitting it to you, and there's no evidence that the one pair of murders is related to the other," she insisted.

"No," Rosemounde agreed, "but we all seem to be assuming that Sir Gawain will only call off his vendetta if we can show him exactly who it is that's guilty of Gareth's murder. Why do we think that? If it can be proven to him that his brothers were killed by someone on the ground—and I believe you were sure that Merlin *could* do that—then isn't it likely that he'll call off this war, especially if he believes his uncle's crown is at stake?"

We all stared at her for a moment, speechless, when we realized how much sense she was making. "Of course!" Guinevere said. "Gawain will not balk at this when he knows the truth of what is happening here. And I think we dare not wait any more. Someone must be sent to the king to inform him of what steps his regent is taking, and what we suspect it means. Now whom shall we send?"

A few pairs of eyes slid in my direction, but I was having none of it. There was no way I was leaving Camelot and abandoning the queen and my lady Rosemounde to the whims of that bastard who held the regency. I quickly spoke up: "Peter is the ideal person. He's competent and trustworthy, and Mordred can have no suspicions of him—he has no history of dealing with him."

Guinevere nodded. "Agreed," she said. "Peter is the perfect choice."

"But he must carry the message in his head only," Morgan cautioned. "We want no written warnings to the king that can condemn him if he is captured by Mordred's guards, or lead them back to us. We must be seen as pure as the driven snow."

"I think that ship may have sailed for me," Guinevere sighed.

Rosemounde glanced at me and lowered her eyes. "Me too, I'm afraid," she added.

"Nonsense," Morgan scoffed. "If *I* can appear that way, I've no doubt *you* all can."

"Then it's settled," I said. "Let me call Peter in here right now. Let's send him off right away, as soon as he can get himself ready. I fear it's not a moment too soon."

And just as I said that, there was a knock on the queen's closet door, and Peter himself stepped in, looking unkempt and somewhat shaken. "Your Majesty!" He began in a quavering voice. "And your worships," he added courteously to me and the ladies. "I am sent to inform you that Lord Mordred commands your audience in the throne room."

"Commands?" the queen echoed with not a little haughtiness as she sat taller and straighter. "What gives him such authority..."

"My lady," Peter pleaded. "He says that he has received grave news from Benwick, concerning the king. He wants everyone in Camelot to attend him in the throne room so that he can acquaint us with this news."

We looked at one another wide-eyed, our muscles tensed. What was this news that called for so immediate an airing? Had we delayed our message too long?

***

High on a throne of royal state, which far outshone the wealth of Paris or of Rome, Mordred exalted sat. Having borrowed his father's throne room, he must have assumed it was only right for him to borrow the throne as well. He was dressed all in black samite, with a cloak lined with sable, and on his brow he had dared to put on one of Arthur's crowns—not his great heavy crown of state, but one of the gold bands the king wore on his travels. Still, the effect was the same. I felt the queen bristle when we entered the throne room and saw Mordred ensconced in that splendor. Beside the throne stood Sir Geraint on his right hand, and Sir Hectimere on his left. Behind, looking quite uncomfortable, stood William of Glastonbury, Bishop of the Cathedral of Saint David's in Caerleon. I wondered why on earth *he* was at this gathering, but I soon forgot that concern when I began to ponder something else: I searched the assembled crowd in vain for Sir Pelleas and questioned why he was absent from the party on the dais.

The throne itself was made of elaborately carved cherry wood gilded with gold leaf. On its dragon-shaped armrests now rested the arms of the bastard Mordred. It was Mordred whose skinny frame now leaned back on the three crowns that formed Arthur's coat of arms, and it was the bastard of Orkney who now sat beneath the dragon banner the king had borne into battle against King Lot and his other early foes. Around the other walls of the throne room were great tapestries depicting the most important victories of the king's reign: On the east wall was shown Arthur defeating King Lot, whose sons Gawain and Gareth and Agravain played such a momentous role in current events. On the west wall was Arthur's defeat of the Emperor Lucius, depicting Arthur and Gawain engaged in battle together against Rome, as they were now allied against Sir Lancelot. On the south wall, on either side of the great doors we had entered through, were two tapestries: one of Arthur winning the Battle of Mount Badon, where he was reputed to have single-handedly laid low nine hundred of the enemy; the other of Arthur, his mouth frozen in mid-battle cry, wielding his sword against the Irish King Rience, while in the background Merlin was shown enchanting the Giants' Ring in order to bring it to Logres and install it on Salisbury Plain, there to rechristen it Stonehenge. Seeing it again, I wondered what the old man was doing right now. I also wondered how Mordred's new allies, the Saxons and the Irish, had reacted to those tapestries when they saw them. Maybe Mordred had kept this door closed when they were in the castle.

The scope and majesty of the throne room was deliberately designed to cow visitors and to underscore the fact that they were in the presence of great power when they entered that room, and that design was quite effective, no matter who it was sitting on that throne. So when Mordred spoke there was absolute silence in the hall, and we all hung on his every word.

"Loyal subjects," he began in as authoritative a voice as he was able. And at that my brows immediately lowered, while I could feel the queen bristling on my right arm. "We have called you here on a matter of the greatest urgency and alarm." This was not beginning well. Murmurs, soft and indistinct began to ripple across the chamber. Rosemounde, on my left hand, gave me a quizzical glance and mouthed "we"? Was he talking about himself and his advisors? Or was the regent referring to himself in the *royal* "we," in which case he was committing treason even in his pronouns. But it was not long before we had far more serious things to ponder.

"Word has reached us just this morning," Mordred continued, "brought by a messenger sent from Gaul, from my uncle's army at the siege of Benwick. Rather than report it to you second-hand, we shall require our lieutenant Sir Geraint to read the letter aloud to you, just as it has been reported to us."

Definitely the royal "we."

Geraint stepped forward, to the front edge of the dais, and pulled from his sleeve a rolled shred of vellum, with a conspicuous seal hanging from its edge. Unrolling it, he struck a solemn pose, and read out its message in an exaggeratedly solemn voice:

> *From Bedivere, Marshall of the army of King Arthur Pendragon of Logres, lord of Scotland, Ireland, Norway, Gaul, and Rome, to all loyal subjects of the king now remaining in residence at the castle called Camelot, and in the royal city of Caerleon:*
>
> *Woeful greetings to you all. It is my sad duty to report to you that your beloved lord and master, monarch of the world, the incomparable King Arthur, is no more. As I write this, it is two days*

*since the king, in open battle with the forces of the
treacherous Sir Lancelot du Lac, was defeated and
slain on the field of battle by that same traitorous
knight. In the very same battle, the noble Sir
Gawain, the king's heir, was also slain, laid low by
the sword of Lancelot's closest partner in perfidy,
Sir Bors de Ganis. Their leaders thus fallen,
the king's army broke apart and fled in several
directions, while I and a few other loyal knights
regrouped in a village in Gaul which I dare not
name here, in case this message is intercepted. I
write you this that you may prepare yourselves: I
do not know whether Lancelot will stop now with
his most recent treason, or if he will compound his
outrage and dare to invade Logres itself.*

*Again I say, mourn as you must, but prepare! War
may be upon you!*

There were screams and gasps among the crowd as Geraint read
these words, and some of the ladies in the crowd swooned in shock
and despair. For the most part, though, the crowd in the chamber
stood in stunned silence, trying to comprehend the enormity of these
tidings. But among our small knot of onlookers near the rear of
the throne room, there was more than a little skepticism about the
contents of the letter. For myself, I could not imagine that, had any
of these reported disasters actually occurred, Merlin would not have
made certain that word had come to me and to the queen, with advice
or even instructions on what to do now. But we'd had nothing from
Merlin since we'd arrived back in Camelot.

I swallowed hard. Whatever was to follow this revelation did not
promise to be good news, at least not for the small group gathered
around me.

"You have heard this dire news, from the hand of the king's oldest
retainer, the trusty Sir Bedivere," Mordred began. "There is no
question of its authenticity." I had a whole lot of questions about its

authenticity, but there was no point in raising them there, in that den of vipers.

"Accordingly," the bastard continued, "We have three major pronouncements that we have decided upon based on this dreadful news. The first is this: The death of Sir Gawain means that we ourself are King Arthur's nearest kin, and as such we are unquestionably his heir and, hence, should now be the uncontested king of Logres, and emperor of all the Arthurian lands. This mantle of responsibility has fallen to us through our previous position as regent, appointed by King Arthur himself, and by virtue of our fa…uh, our uncle's death, as well as by acclamation by the chief peers of the realm currently residing in Camelot: Sir Geraint, Sir Hectimere, and Sir Pelleas."

Of course. Name his own stooges chief barons and then have them approve his promotion. That didn't look fishy at all, did it? From behind me I heard the indignant sputtering of Morgan le Fay, who was rasping, "Nearest kin? What kind of drivel is that! What about my Yewey?" And indeed, I was wondering myself how Mordred intended to deal with Sir Ywain, Arthur's oldest surviving *legitimate* male heir. Apparently by ignoring his existence, at least at this point. Nor did I suspect that his near slip in almost calling Arthur his "father" was actually a mistake on his part, but rather a subtle reminder of his actual relationship with the king.

"Second, we have taken steps already to ensure the safety and integrity of the realm. We firmly believe we are in imminent danger of invasion from Gaul, from the traitorous Lancelot and his minions like the criminal Bors and the toady Ector. Camelot itself, as you know, has already been fortified by troops from Sir Geraint's kingdom of Dumnonia. In addition, troops from our new allies, the kingdom of Ireland in the west and the nation of the Picts in the north, will be arriving soon to bolster our defenses around Caerleon. And finally, to ensure the safety of our shores from invasion over the Narrow Sea, we have enlisted our newest allies, the brave Saxon warriors from across the sea, and they are fortifying the area of Kent, from Dover southwest along the coast all the way to Portsmouth, in order to meet any challenge from that direction. So you can all sleep safely in your beds tonight, knowing that our land is well protected."

Protected by armies of our sworn enemies, I said to myself. Surely this had nothing to do with an imaginary invasion by Lancelot, but was rather insurance against a return to his own kingdom by the not-quite-dead king, in order to make him *actually* dead when he sought to come home.

"Third, and perhaps most important of all," Mordred continued, "we appoint the holiday of Beltane, three weeks from today, as the day of our official coronation. That is the traditional festival of renewal for the people of Logres, and we intend our reign to be a renewal for all our people. On that day, the celebration of the marriage of the earth itself, it was customary in ancient times for a new king to marry the land, in order to ensure fertility, restoration, abundance during his reign. For if the king is the light of the land and its true sun, what then is his queen but the land itself? Therefore we hereby announce this: On the first day of May, in three weeks' time, to underscore the validity of our reign and to guarantee its prosperity, we shall marry our late uncle's own queen, Guinevere, Princess of Cameliard and Majesty of Logres, which land she embodies in her person."

At that the room exploded with gasps of astonishment and cries of objection from all those who remembered the minor detail of his preexisting marriage to Lady Rosemounde of Brittany. When I glanced at Rosemounde her mouth was hanging open in astonishment, but Mordred raised his hands in a gesture of placation. "We are aware of the unusual nature of this step," the bastard continued. "But it is essential to secure the peace of our reign. And I have already discussed the matter with the bishop of Caerleon, and he has assured me that my current marriage to Duke Hoel's daughter, with whom I have not lived for nearly two years" (and this part he recited through clenched teeth, even forgetting to refer to himself with the royal pronoun), "can and should be annulled, in order to enable me to marry my uncle's widow without hindrance from the Church and to make it blessed in the eyes of God."

Well, that explained the bishop's presence on the dais, though he did not look particularly happy to be there. His head hung down, and his eyes looked from left to right as if he was looking for a hole to crawl into. I was fairly certain that his consent to Mordred's scheme was wrung from him at the point of a sword.

Just then a sudden cry from my right shocked me into attention. It was the queen. The cry was followed by a low moan, and her eyes rolled up in her head as she twisted slowly and fell senseless into my arms.

CHAPTER TWELVE
FLIGHT

With the prostrate Guinevere in my arms, I flew from that hall and made straight for the queen's chamber, with Morgan la Lay on my right and Lady Rosemounde on my left, and trailing the rest of the queen's entourage as we went. Morgan, the experienced healer, barked out commands as we went, asking for cool water and lavender to be brought if it could be found in the castle's infirmary. Peter dashed off immediately to try to find what he could. I couldn't help but notice, as we sought the refuge of that place, that Mordred had assigned two of the palace guard to trail after us, and they stood outside the curtain in the outer chamber, keeping tabs on anyone and anything that went in or out. As I shoved past the curtained outer chamber of the queen's quarters and into her inner closet, we could see there was just room enough there for me, Morgan, Rosemounde, Lady Anne and Master Holly. Rosemounde closed the heavy wooden door and while the other ladies congregated at the threshold, wringing their hands, I laid the queen's limp body down on the bed.

The moment her body touched the sheets the queen's eyes sprang open. "Are we alone?" she asked. I snorted. I had suspected all along her swoon was a ruse to get us out of that throne room as quickly as possible and to have an excuse to talk privately, and we needed to. And fast.

"We're alone," Morgan said. "But I don't know how long it will last. We must talk quickly."

"It is a certainty that Sir Lancelot did not kill the king," Guinevere began. "That is the truth we must start from."

"If anything Mordred claimed was true," I added, "it is certain that I would have had word from Merlin. So his claims are a ruse, and the armies he is gathering about him are to shore up his power against the king's return."

"The Saxons worry me most," Morgan mused. "They are stretched along the shore to prevent the king's making landfall in his own country. We must get word to Arthur as soon as we possibly can, but our messenger can't go through Kent or take ship at Portsmouth, where the king's ships will be under the Saxons' guard."

Master Holly, Guinevere's aged clerk and doorkeeper, pinched his wrinkled face together and shook his head. "This is a council at which you don't want to be disturbed," he said with the tact and composure of his profession. "I think I shall take my post at the entry to your chamber and try to make sure no one will surprise you in here." He turned, bent over, and tottered toward the door, but before he opened it he turned and added, "Just be sure you don't leave me out of your plans!" And with an almost invisible smile, he slipped out.

"But what is to become of the queen?" Lady Anne worried. "Mordred says he will marry her! How can that be? And why is he insisting on it?"

"Legitimacy," Morgan answered simply. "What he said is true. The people may have difficulty accepting him as king, but marriage to his uncle's queen, whom the people see as symbol of the fecundity of Arthur's reign, symbol of the land itself, that will go far in legitimizing him in the people's eyes."

"But when they find the king's still alive, it will backfire!" Lady Anne insisted.

"By then he will be fully established in authority," Morgan insisted. "Nothing to do about it then…"

"Well he seems to have dealt with his own situation decisively enough," I noted, moving on to the subject I was most keenly interested in. "He's had his marriage to my lady Rosemounde expunged, in which he's been aided and abetted by the bishop himself. What's to become of Rosemounde I want to know? Annulment or no annulment, I think she's in danger."

Rosemounde turned pale, and as I looked into her eyes she did seem frightened, though too stalwart to show it. But Morgan jumped in to agree.

"Her very existence is a slap in his face, and would undermine his plans to marry the queen, whatever that jellyfish of a bishop says," Morgan agreed. We've got to get her out of the bastard's reach. And speaking of threats to Mordred's status, what about my Yewey? Even if everybody believes Gawain is killed, there are those who know that Yewey is next in line, and will rally to him!"

"Which makes him a target," I said. "The messenger to Arthur must caution him as well—who knows but that Mordred may have sent an assassin to do him in. Else why would he not have claimed that Sir Ywain was murdered as well as Arthur and Gawain? What's one more lie?"

"He might have realized that Morgan would have had word of such a development immediately, and didn't want to be exposed as a liar that quickly," the queen guessed. "But as we consider who is in danger through the attribute of royal blood, let us not forget you yourself, my dear." And with that she nodded toward Morgan le Fay. "You are the king's sister. You have no small party of supporters of your own. You, too, may have a target on your back."

A more subdued Morgan frowned at the truth of this. "I must fly," she resolved grimly. Then, taking Rosemounde by the hands, added, "And you must fly too, you poor little thing."

"That's settled," the queen pronounced, then added, "As for me, I am certainly not going to stand idle and allow this forced marriage to happen. Listen to me: A queen cannot be wed without a sumptuous new bridal gown that will dazzle the court—and her attendants must be appropriately gowned as well. I shall insist that I and my ladies in waiting be conveyed to London, where the best clothiers in the realm shall attire us in garments fit for an empress. But when we get to London," now the queen's voice lowered, "I shall take residence in the White Tower, the Tower of London, where I know there is a small garrison still loyal to my husband. Once we are in that tower,

Mordred can besiege the place for months and never penetrate its defenses."

"But my lady, will Mordred trust you to leave Camelot?" Lady Anne asked.

"Of course not," I answered for her. "He will insist on an escort made up of his own men. But you must insist, Your Majesty, on members of the castle guard—not Sir Geraint's troops—to accompany you. Mordred will agree, but those men remain loyal to you and Arthur's reign. And you can convince them that the king is alive."

"But I know Mordred," Rosemounde warned. "He'll want that escort commanded by one of his close advisers."

I mulled that over for a moment and then cried out, "Pelleas! Insist that your escort be commanded by Sir Pelleas! He's one of your former 'Queen's Knights,' and so he has a history with you that you can exploit for purposes of this assignment. Mordred will see the sense in it, but Pelleas will not want anything to happen to you, and will certainly not want anything to happen to his lady Barbara, who will be with you. But most important," now it was my turn to lower my voice. "I've talked to Pelleas, and he's not at all sure that what's going on in Mordred's camp is for the good of the kingdom. He can be persuaded, and Your Grace, you are one of the great persuaders in my experience."

The queen gave a tight smile in spite of herself. But then she thought of something else. "Lady Rosemounde—Mordred is not likely to agree to your coming with me to London. Indeed, he may want to imprison you here, or worse, rather than let you out of his sight."

"We need to hide her," I insisted. "I don't know where, but there has to be somewhere Mordred's not likely to look. And we've got to sneak her out of the castle with your entourage when it leaves."

"The same is true of Morgan," Guinevere added. "There will be no need for her to come to London with me, in Mordred's mind, but she must get out of the castle as soon as possible."

At that point we were startled by a knock on the door to the queen's closet. We looked at one another, then I quietly cracked the door. It was Peter. He'd come with a large bowl of cold water and even some sprigs of lavender. Morgan sighed as he came in sheepishly, apologizing for being so long.

"I couldn't really find anything, then I thought to go to the kitchens. Roger and the folks down there were much concerned, Your Highness. They said to give you their best, and tell you if there was anything they could do for you, to just let them know. They seemed pretty upset by all they'd heard about what was going on with Mordred and all."

Now Rosemounde clapped her hands and smiled. "That's the answer!" she cried. "The kitchen! We just have to borrow some simple clothes from some of the cooks, and masquerade as members of the kitchen crew until your entourage gets ready to leave! You'll have to be victualed for the trip won't you? Morgan and I will bring the food, then stay in the wagon, hidden until we are away from the castle!"

I knew that would work, because I knew how much Roger resented Mordred's lordship over Camelot. But through all of this, though I knew my mind had to be on the queen's situation and on Arthur's sovereignty, worry for my lady Rosemounde's safety gnawed at the pit of my stomach, and sent tingling waves down the back of my neck.

"It works," Morgan said. "But once away from Camelot, I will not be going to London with you. For one thing, I think we will be more successful if we split up. You take your ladies to London, Your Highness, and I will make my way to my other old friendly nemesis, the Lady of the Lake. She may want to know what is happening, and perhaps she may have some part to play in all of this before it is finished. In any case, I believe she will shelter me as long as I am in danger from Mordred."

"Peter," I said, "I shall leave it up to you and to Master Holly to accompany the queen to London and fill the role of her clerk and personal page." Guinevere looked up at me in a way, I fancied, that suggested I was letting her down. But I averted my eyes and went on. "We have yet the matter of our message to Arthur to determine. Since ports in the southeast may be difficult or impossible to negotiate with the new Saxon presence there, I have one suggestion: Cornwall. That is my home, and I am best suited to make my way there and to take ship for Gaul. It may take a few more days going that way, but there will be no Saxon guards on the shore. I will go directly to King Mark."

"But I thought you told us King Mark had been approached by Mordred as well," the queen objected.

"Approached, yes, but Geraint told me Mark had not agreed to any terms. And trust me, King Mark owes his position to Arthur. He is not likely to approve of Mordred's killing him off. I think he will decide to help. At least he's a better bet than the Saxons. I will have to sneak out of the castle with your entourage as well, but once in the clear I must make my way westward rather than to London."

"So," the queen said, looking around and breathing easier. "That's settled."

"Not quite," my lady Rosemounde broke in. "My own case is somewhat delicate, we've all agreed." In the face of our nods she continued. "If I am to travel with the queen's train to London, it is possible that I may put the whole plan into jeopardy. If Mordred suspects you might be smuggling me away he might send troops after you."

The burning at the back of my neck had reached fever stage. "What Lady Morgan says is true," I began evenly. "It is better to scatter in different directions, to split up any posse sent to pursue us. Rosemounde should not be a part of your train, Your Majesty. She is quite right about that. Nor can she travel alone. She must come to Cornwall with me." I stated it calmly, as if it were the only possible solution, and for my pains I got a blank stare from Peter, raised eyebrows from Morgan, and lowered eyelids and a hint of a smirk from Rosemounde herself. The queen's blue eyes rolled back in her head so far I thought she might strain herself. But she only said, "Well, then, that's settled. Now..."

But what was to follow I never knew, for at that moment there was an urgent pounding on the door, and when Lady Anne cracked it a bit, Lady Mary's voice whispered a warning: "My Lady! Sir Geraint is in the outer chamber with a troop of guards, demanding that you come to Mordred in his own rooms. Master Holly is trying to stall them, but that can't be for long!"

"All right," Guinevere said calmly. "Rosemounde, Morgan, Gildas—you can't be seen. You all need to get into hiding as soon as possible, so as not to be prevented from escaping with us. Anne and Peter, you are with me. We shall meet this Geraint and demand to see the regent immediately, and I shall prevail upon him to allow me to take my ladies to London right away—tomorrow if possible—in order to be back before three weeks' time, since that is the day appointed for the wedding. It's to our advantage he set that date, for it excuses our haste! But as soon as I have left, you three must leave these rooms and hide amongst the kitchen crew. We can't afford to let you be imprisoned before we can carry you away! Come, Peter, Anne, we go now!"

***

It unfolded as the queen had called it. She demanded to see Mordred, which was what Geraint had come for in the first place, and once she had left the chamber, I led Morgan and Rosemounde through the outer chamber and down a back stairway out into the bailey, and along the shadows of the wall into the kitchen. It took only a moment to explain to Roger what was needed, and he was eager to assist them. Rosemounde and Morgan were outfitted in the drab tunics and linen coifs of kitchen wenches, and even Roger laughed at how radically the disguises changed their looks.

For myself, though, I decided to forego the kitchen disguise. I had a better idea. I stole my way to what had been Sir Gareth's rooms, which for friendship's sake he still had let me share with him even after my elevation to knighthood, there to fetch my sword Almace, my old master's own gift to me upon my elevation to knighthood, as well as my fine hauberk of chain mail—the gift of my father on the same occasion. A father I had not seen in seven years, but who had demonstrated his pride in his son's achieving the status of Round Table knight by working countless hours on this product of his trade as the premier armorer in Cornwall. I bundled the mail and the sword into a bedroll, tucked it under my arm, and made for the door as quietly as possible. There was no indication that Mordred was looking

163

for me, or had any notion that I was a danger to him, but the less I was seen the better. Out of sight, out of mind was my intention for the evening. With any luck, if the queen was able to convince Mordred to allow her to make a whirlwind trip to London, I would only have to stay hidden until the morning.

I made my way to the stables, where I knew we had another ally with Taber. And I uncovered the basics of our plot to him. I needed to be able to get Achilles out of the stables—and I wanted my dog Guinevere as well, who could be brought over secretly from the kennels. She was reliable as a hunter on the road, and as a watchdog if we were going to sleep in the open. And when the time came, when the queen sent orders to prepare horses for her and her ladies to ride, and, importantly, a wagon to carry supplies, I wanted Taber to send two additional palfreys out to tie behind the wagon, ostensibly to spell the wagon's horses on what was supposed to be a fast trip to London, but in reality to allow Lady Rosemounde and Morgan le Fay to split off from the queen's convoy and make their escapes on their own.

Taber was more than happy to help out when he heard the plan. And he went further: When word came to him, as it must, to prepare a convoy for the queen's journey, he would send his assistant Daniel with Achilles and my dog to hide outside the gates before they were closed for the evening by the watch. Daniel would wait overnight, ensuring that my own escape would not be noted by any of the guard. I could take Daniel's place as stable hand in the meantime, helping to hitch the horses to the wagon, then slip into the wagon just before the convoy left Camelot, to mount Achilles and flee toward Cornwall once we were out of sight of the barbican. I smiled and nodded in agreement, and the boy Daniel beamed at being able to put something over on the watch. And with a deep breath I settled in to wait there, out of sight in the stables, while Daniel fetched Guinevere from the kennels.

It was not long before word came through a messenger from Mordred himself that the stables were to make ready the following morning six palfreys for the queen and five of her ladies to ride to London, as well as a wagon for the transporting of food and other necessaries for the journey. Taber was also to prepare Sir Pelleas's great warhorse Leander, and sturdy mounts for four of the guard to accompany him as an escort for the queen's party. It was a small enough escort, almost an insult to the queen's status, but the point, I am sure, was to make the journey to London and back with all possible speed, and the smaller the convoy the easier that would be. I was fairly certain Mordred had probably objected to the wagon, since that would almost surely slow the progress down, but Guinevere must have convinced him of its desirability, thank goodness. I still had not worked out how to convince Sir Pelleas, when the time came, to allow Morgan and Rosemounde to escape, but I would deal with that when I had to. If necessary, I would hold him and his companions off long enough to allow the ladies to make the short run to the Lady of the Lake's palace, and allow the queen to plead ignorance of the ruse. But somehow I felt confident in Pelleas's good will.

At the word from the palace, Daniel bridled and saddled Achilles, took my bundle of sword and armor to load onto my destrier, and mounted the great horse himself. The hound Guinevere, happy for the diversion, cavorted about Achilles' hooves as Daniel made his way leisurely toward the open front gate and drawbridge. If any of the guard on duty, or Mordred's new commandeer John of Kent, recognized Achilles or wondered why he was being ridden out of the castle by a stable hand, they kept it to themselves, and Daniel slipped out and into the woods without a hitch. I let out the breath I had not realized I'd been holding as I watched them leave, then settled back into a bale of hay, Taber grinning at me with the four or five teeth he still possessed, and waited for dawn.

A few red rays of morning light were streaking into the narrow windows of the stable when I felt a gentle kick to my right thigh and opened my eyes to see Taber standing over me, his finger to his lips and a threadbare brown hood and tunic in his hand. I nodded with understanding, rolled over and sat up quickly, taking the clothes from him as he went back into the stables to begin leading out some of the horses to hitch to the queen's wagon. I slipped quickly into the tunic and hood, and hoped that none of the other stable hands, who were just now arriving, nor any of the guards, who were likely to watch our progress with the convoy, would notice that my leather shoes and fine hosen were probably not exactly the sort that one of the stable boys, even in Camelot, might be likely to wear. But I needn't have worried. I looked enough the part, dressed in that tunic, that no one giving me a casual glance would notice anything amiss, and nobody was interested enough in the mundane preparation of horses and wagons to give me more than a casual glance. And with my hood pulled up to keep my face mostly hidden, no one was going to recognize me as Sir Gildas of Cornwall, knight of the Round Table, unless he was specifically carrying out a search for such a person.

That, I think is where we got lucky. I did not fool myself into thinking that Mordred was not already calculating how he was going to deal with his enemies. Almost certainly he was already planning the imprisonment or even the deaths of Morgan, Rosemounde, and probably me as well. But he was too cautious to sweep us all up in the hours immediately after his coup. It was clear, from his orchestrated pronouncements the previous day, that he wanted his public image to appear clean and virtuous, at least for now. Therefore it simply wouldn't do if, immediately after claiming Arthur's throne, he made a move to assassinate Arthur's sister—or if, after casting his old wife off like an old shoe in order to marry his uncle's queen, he decided to immediately shut her up for good. As for me, I was known to be the queen's favorite, so eliminating me before he'd even tied the queen down by wedlock could not sit well with his new intended. So it was necessary for him to become a bit more entrenched in power before following through on his schemes to get rid of us for reasons of "national security." And that gave us a window to slip from his grasp if we took it now.

I saddled two gentle palfreys for the ladies' planned escape, and tied them to the back of the wagon which was now hitched to its team of draft horses. At that point, Roger, carrying three wineskins, came from the kitchen with two kitchen wenches sharing the burden of a small barrel of salted meat for the journey. The wenches kept their eyes fixed before their feet, finally placing the barrel into the cart. A sidelong glance at the two wenches was all I needed to recognize Lady Rosemounde and Morgan le Fay, and Roger made enough of a distraction talking to a couple of the guards standing about in the middle bailey that I doubted whether any of them noticed that the two wenches did not return with him to the kitchen. Both had crept stealthily into the wagon themselves and were lying out of sight on the floor. I stepped rather boldly onto the wagon and prepared to drive it out the gate behind the queen's ladies' horses.

The queen, dressed in travelling clothes of sturdy blue worsted, made her way from the middle bailey toward the horses gathered here before the gate. She was followed by the ladies Anne, Mary, Barbara, Vivien, and Alison. There was a somber pall over the ladies, who looked strait before them rather than chattering as they were wont to do. Even Lady Mary was quiet. The enormity of this adventure was clearly weighing them down. Peter had come behind the ladies, followed by Master Holly, and Peter proceeded to help the queen lift herself into the saddle of her white palfrey. As Master Holly climbed up beside me in the front of the wagon, Taber and one of the other grooms were helping the queen's ladies onto their mounts, and as they did so Sir Pelleas entered from my left, in full armor and carrying his shield bearing his simple coat of arms: on a field gules (or red), a dovetailed azure bend—the blue stripe bent from the upper left to the lower right of the shield and crenelated like a castle wall. His four guardsmen followed in a military march, the two in front carrying Pelleas's helmet and lance. I winced a bit, realizing that Sir Pelleas would be fully armed while I, even assuming I got to my horse before he tried to stop me, would have only my sword Alsace. But there was nothing to be done about that now. The success of our venture had never depended on my besting Pelleas and his quartet of guards in combat, but on our reasoning with him to make him our ally—or at least to convince him not to be our enemy.

I swallowed hard as Peter climbed into the wagon to sit atop one of the loaded barrels for the journey. I was glad to notice he was wearing a short sword at his side. His eyes glanced neither right nor left, and he kept his face blank, without sign of recognition toward me or toward the two ladies lying hidden under a blanket beneath his feet on the floor of the wagon. I fidgeted a bit as Pelleas and his men mounted and Pelleas moved his destrier Leander next to the queen, exchanged a few words with her, then looked back at the rest of us and called out, "All right, then, forward!" He began to lead us toward the open gate and drawbridge at a trot. He and the queen rode first, then the queen's ladies in pairs except Lady Mary, who rode alone just in front of the wagon. Two of the guards flanked ladies Barbara and Alison, who rode just ahead of Mary, while the other two guards flanked the wagon itself. I held my breath as we moved under the barbican, praying that no one in that tower over the gate noticed the two woman-shaped lumps under the blanket in my wagon. Then we were through the gate and over the drawbridge, moving into the woods north of the castle. I let out a sigh of relief and glanced over at Master Holly. He had his eyes closed and was blowing out his own long breath.

Now the horses had slowed to an ambling gait, much to the relief of the draft horses pulling the wagon, who would not have been able to keep pace with Pelleas the way he had started out. We had gone perhaps five or six furlongs when I began to look around in expectation: Daniel was to be waiting at the roadside with my horse and my dog just out of view of the castle, and in these woods this might be far enough. Pelleas would most certainly stop and demand an explanation once he came upon that sight, and I needed to be ready to spring into action—as did the women in the cart, who must hop up and mount those horses tied to the rear of the wagon quickly, while the guards were occupied with the groom in the road. "Be ready—it should be only a few more minutes," I whispered to my live cargo, knowing they could not see anything from where they were hidden, and would need me or Peter to cue them when it was time to move.

Then, as the birches and oaks seemed to crowd in on us from every direction, we turned a corner of the path and there, in the road waiting for us, stood a lithe long-haired hound next to great war horse on which sat a young livery stable boy. I saw Sir Pelleas's head snap back in astonishment when he saw what was waiting for him, and he raised a hand and called for the rest of us to halt. As the two guards on either side of the wagon trotted forward a bit to see what was going on, I turned back to where Morgan and

Rosemounde lay in the wagon and with an elaborate rolling motion of my arm signaled them to get up and mount those horses that trailed behind us.

They did not need to be told twice. With a speed and agility I never would have expected, Morgan le Fay stood in the wagon, pulled one of the trailing horses by the bridle toward her, and with a single graceful motion swung into the saddle and in fact, was galloping off before either of the guards had a chance to stop her. Rosemounde, a bit slower into the act, was forced to hold back while the king's sister made her escape from the back of the wagon. By the time Peter had helped Rosemounde climb into the saddle, one of the horsemen had ridden to her and grabbed the reins.

"Let her go!" I stood up and leaped down from the wagon, throwing the hood off so that they could see my face. It was Sir Pelleas, startled by the commotion in the rear of his convoy as much as by the unexpected horseman in the front, who asserted his authority now.

"No one move!" he cried, drawing the short sword from where it hung on his thigh. Then looking at me, he blinked. "Sir Gildas?" He asked, in a voice clouded by incredulity. He frowned, trying to get a grasp of the situation. "Why are you dressed that way, and driving a cart? And why is the lady Rosemounde dressed as a kitchen wench? Someone needs to explain…"

It was time for the queen to step in. "And I shall be happy to do so, Sir Pelleas," she began, bringing all focus back to herself—and while she spoke I began to make my way purposefully toward Achilles. "Lady Morgan has already fled, and I shall not tell you where. Lady Rosemounde, like Morgan, is almost certain to be a target of your master Mordred, and will be either imprisoned or murdered—you know it is true!" This last was spoken to squelch the beginnings of a protest Pelleas seemed about to make, and at the sound he shrugged and let it pass. "Rosemounde will also be fleeing, and Sir Gildas intends to accompany her, to ensure her safety, nor again will I tell you their destination!" I noticed that the queen had not mentioned that my ultimate destination was the side of King Arthur, where I intended to reveal to him the full extent of his bastard's treachery. Sir Pelleas might be somewhat sympathetic to our cause, but even he might balk at letting me out of the country for that purpose. Though I wondered if even he was aware that Arthur must still be alive, or whether he had believed Mordred's lies.

By now I had climbed onto Achilles' back, and Daniel had courteously drawn Almace from the satchel the horse carried and handed it to me so that, brandishing my own sword, I could effectively punctuate the queen's words. "What the queen says is true," I added. "I will take Lady Rosemounde to the safety she deserves, and I believe you are an honorable enough knight to look the other way as I do. If that is not the case, I am prepared to carry her away whoever tries to stop us," and with that I brandished Almace above my head and reared Achilles up on his hind legs, looking, I imagined, like a conquering hero and not a pretender dressed in the garb of a stable hand.

But I had not misjudged Sir Pelleas. He was not without honor, and had supported Sir Mordred's rise only because of his enmity with Sir Gawain. But he knew perfectly well that what the queen claimed was absolutely true, and that if he did not turn a blind eye, then the lady Rosemounde might soon very well be in Mordred's dungeon, if not in her grave. And so after a moment's thought, he sheathed his sword and nodded to me. "Take her then where you will, Gildas," he said, and added to his men, "Let them go." The four guards, who'd been tensed and waiting for orders as their queen and their commander sparred with each other over the fate of this knight and lady, breathed a sigh of relief and stood down.

With a nod to Pelleas and a wink of thanks to David, I trotted toward my lady Rosemounde, inclining my head toward the queen as I rode by. She closed her eyes and nodded in acknowledgment of my bow, and I felt a chill as I rode by her. Where I would see her again, and what the circumstances might be when that happened, I could not then imagine. I would always think of her as my sovereign lady, and my loyalty to her would never waver. Nor would I even consider leaving her now if it were not for the plight of my own beloved Rosemounde, and the danger to the kingdom. I could only pray that Sir Pelleas, who had proven to be an honorable knight here, would prove as honorable when the queen made her bid in London to find refuge in the tower.

I rode to Rosemounde's waiting horse, grasped it by the bridle and, with my borzoi hound scampering behind us, we made our way at a walking pace to cut through the woods, where we would pick up the road westward toward Cornwall.

And as we rode off, I could hear the queen's voice as she began her long, persuasive assault on Sir Pelleas's loyalty. "Do you know the White Tower in London, my lord Pelleas? Have you ever visited it? I can tell you it is one of the most imposing structures in all of Logres…"

CHAPTER THIRTEEN
CORNWALL

When I look back over the whole course of my life, as one is tempted to do when one reaches my age, I can say without hesitation that my happiest moments came to me in those five days I spent with Lady Rosemounde, riding through the forests of southwest Logres from Camelot to Tintagel, King Mark's impregnable castle on the Cornish coast where, some fifty years earlier, Uther Pendragon had sired the future Emperor of Christendom on an unwitting Duchess Ygraine of Cornwall.

Yes, it was certainly true that we pushed our mounts to the limits of their endurance in our urgency to get out of Mordred's sphere of influence and to bring word of his treachery to King Arthur with all possible speed. I was also distressed inwardly by apprehension over what to do with Rosemounde to ensure her safety. I was heading into a war zone, from which I expected to bring the king and his armies back to Logres and into a new war zone. There was no safety for her there, and no realistic possibility of my being able to defend her if Mordred decided to send a whole company of warriors after her. I might leave her at Tintagel, but frankly, despite my optimism in the queen's chamber, I wasn't one hundred percent certain of how I would be received by King Mark. He *had* been approached by Mordred's ambassadors, after all. What if I'd misjudged him? Or what if he was willing to surrender Rosemounde to Mordred's army if they besieged Tintagel?

A good option for Rosemounde might be to leave her in her father's duchy of Brittany, perhaps in the port of Saint-Malo with her brother Kaherdin. But would she be safe there? Would it not be the very first place Mordred was likely to look for her? And was not Duke Hoel certain to bring his forces to fight alongside his liege lord Arthur, thereby leaving his own castles weakened if Mordred sent a force against them? Was it not quite possible that Hoel was already with Arthur at the siege in Benwick? And even aside from all of that, my chief task must be to bring news of Mordred's *coup d'etat* to the king, and a stopover in Brittany could delay me by days. And every day that passed, Mordred was getting stronger, gathering more rebels to his cause.

Yet despite these troubling thoughts, I maintain that I regard those days on the road with Rosemounde as my soul's bliss, the closest I have come to Paradise in this life. Like our first parents in the blessedness of Eden, we spent our days in the beauty of God's created natural world, passing among the birches and oaks that crowded the narrow road, occasionally giving our horses a rest to pick the wood anemones and columbine, the cornflowers and daisies lining our path in order to make garlands for Rosemounde's hair. Among the deer, the rabbits, and the squirrels, alongside our own domesticated beasts, we felt at peace with all of creation in those hours, alone on the road heading westward.

Oh, yes, once in a while we passed other travelers, sometimes with suspicion or trepidation—anyone could be a group of bandits or, worse, allies of the bastard—but such encounters were rare, as there were few folk on this road just then in that part of the kingdom. All were converging at Camelot, or London, or the Kentish coast in anticipation of invasion. And so Mordred's eyes were elsewhere as we pushed west. And no, Guinevere did not have the same benevolent attitude toward nature that we did, being unable to resist a plump rabbit who might have the audacity to cross her path. She chased down at least one a day, a practice that at first annoyed Rosemounde, but she eventually accepted such behavior as inevitable in this fallen world. Nor did Rosemounde mind the addition of rabbit to our slim daily diet of bread, cheese, and dried meats we had managed to bring along.

Jay Ruud

But what gave me the most joy in those precious days was the way
we talked and laughed so easily, or sometimes rode in contented and
companionable silence like young lovers, which, in fact, we were.
Oh, you may wonder how we could possibly laugh and cavort in so
carefree a manner when all the world around us was coming apart
at the seams, but the fact is we were free. Her marriage had been
annulled. No husband, no father, could tell her what she could or
could not do with her life. No queen was there to assert her will over
us. I had responsibilities, we both did, and we were on our way to
fulfill those responsibilities, but on the road itself we were completely,
unabashedly free.

We sought whenever possible to avoid any towns that happened
to be on the road, particularly steering clear of inns, since we feared
any travelers might be on their way to Caerleon or even Camelot
itself, and could describe us to members of the guard or of Sir
Geraint's army if questioned. So we passed quickly through towns,
stopping only occasionally, perhaps, at a stable to buy a bucket of
oats for the horses, or we circled around the villages. But five days
on the road meant four nights, and avoiding towns meant sleeping
in the woods in the open. We were fortunate not to have any rain for
those four nights, for it seemed that God was indeed smiling on us,
making a gift of those few days, perhaps in recompense for what
was to come.

"I'll make up a bed for us here, near the fire," Rosemounde said
to me our first night on the road, after I'd roasted one of Guinevere's
rabbits over a small fire I'd built in a clearing not far off the path.
The horses were tethered to branches close by, and Guinevere was
stretched out asleep near the fire, gorged on those parts of the animal
that Rosemounde and I found less than appetizing.

At the phrase "for us" I felt my heart leap in my chest, and I began
to hyperventilate. Naturally I had hoped to share her bed on this trip,
given her new status as a free woman, and perhaps it had even been
in the back of my mind when I insisted on escorting her to safety
away from the castle. But to have her arrange so nonchalantly for
our sleeping accommodations, such as they were, without the need
for hinting or cajoling on my part, was the crown of my joy.

174

"Oh yes," I said. "That would be just…just perfect, I think. I mean…don't you?"

Rosemounde laughed out loud at my nervous reaction, and in the dim light of the fire I could see the left side of her mouth twist upward in her characteristic smirk as she removed the kitchen wench's smock she'd been wearing and hung it over a branch near her sleeping palfrey. To my surprise and delight, she was wearing nothing but a pair of hosen underneath. "Gildas of Cornwall," she said as she climbed between the blankets she had laid over a pile of leaves to make our bed. "You sound nervous as a young page, not the confident knight of the Round Table I know you to be. You act as if we've never done this before…"

"Well, to be fair, those other occasions were pretty brief, just a moment stolen from the everyday regimen of our lives," I answered, pulling off my own rough tunic and kicking off my own hosen as I slid between those blankets myself. "This promises a whole night together, with no husbands, no queens, no magicians, no Camelot talebearers looking over our shoulders. It's a much bigger test!"

She laughed at me again. She did that a lot. As she did so she rolled over onto her right side, saying, "Exactly. All the time in the world to get it right. Nothing for you to be nervous about at all." She sighed. "Or me either. Come spoon me for a bit, will you Gildas my love? And let us take our time, shall we?"

I curled my body against hers, feeling her naked back against the bare skin of my chest, and at that touch my flesh was aroused. I wasn't quite sure just how much time I would be able to take. I was still wearing the linen *braies* that reached to the middle of my thighs, and I undid the drawstring at my waist and pushed them down, pressing my lower body against hers as well, at which she let out a soft sigh. I clasped her closer and nuzzled her neck, the scent of her glowing skin rising with thrilling intimacy to my nostrils, and my left hand gently stroked her own left arm, then made its slow caress of her flank and hip. My breath was beginning to come in short quick gasps as I opened my mouth to whisper sweet flattering devotions into her ear.

And just at that point, like an arrow loosed deliberately amidst our bodies, the long sleek form of a thin, furry animal bolted onto the covers and burrowed its way between us. Stunned, I rolled onto my back, at which point Guinevere laid her head lovingly on my chest and looked up at me with adoring eyes, pushing her nose into my face and licking me on the lips.

Rosemounde's laughter tinkled like the rivulets of a clear flowing brook, and she cried out, "Somebody is jealous!"

My ardor cooled for the foreseeable future, I wiped my mouth with the back of my hand and sighed. "I love you, you know," I told her in answer.

There was a moment's pause. I don't remember whether I had ever before come right out and said that in so many words. Rosemounde seemed to be weighing her answer. Finally she said, "Are you talking to me or the dog?"

***

Well, I'm not going to go into the details of what happened later that night, or on the three successive nights while we traveled westward. That would be boorish, aside from being quite out of place here where we share these stories. I will say again that *there* was my bliss on this earth, and as I hope yet to see another kind of bliss sometime, somewhere beyond this thoroughfare of woe, I swear to you all that I shall never repent one moment of my time with her on that road, or at any other time for that matter.

Some might say I should have married the lady. How little they know of the situation. Had there been time, I'd have married her at the first opportunity. But there was no opportunity. Her father would have grudged in any case: How could the future duchess of Brittany be married to the lowest born of Arthur's knights, even if it was the knight who had saved her life? It doesn't matter, truly. In God's eyes we were married, and no priest or father could ever give that state more sanctity than did our own love. And that's all I have to say about that.

But I need to relate one other disturbing event from those otherwise delightful days on our way to Cornwall. It happened that first night, well past midnight, and in the depths of sleep. I dreamed I was back in Camelot, in the queen's outer chamber. Bright sunlight was coming in the room's only window, so bright that the figure coming toward me was shrouded in an aureole of bright light. As she drew nearer to me, I saw her as I had seen her on that last day: She wore a simple kirtle of blue linen, and over it a sleeveless white tunic, which she bound at the waist with a leather belt. Her light brown hair was uncovered, for she was an unmarried thirteen-year-old girl, and she tied it back with a long blue ribbon of the same shade as her kirtle. I wept when I saw the ribbon.

Lady Elizabeth of Winchester was the younger sister of Lady Mary and, like her sister, had been lady-in-waiting to the queen. They were the nieces of Sir Lucan the Butler and Sir Bedivere, the king's oldest knight and his marshal, and their father was Sir Lowell of Winchester, an impoverished knight who'd been married to Lucan and Bedivere's sister, and had become squire to Sir Gaheris. Though he wanted to remain faithful to the Orkney clan, his gratitude to Lancelot for his role in saving him from poverty led him to follow him to Benwick, though surely with some divided loyalties. The queen had taken the two girls on as part of her entourage as a favor to Bedivere, and had taken it upon herself to try to find husbands for the pair of them. It had been part of Guinevere's scheme to marry me off to the young Elizabeth: She knew, of course, of my passion for the lady Rosemounde, but knew as well that she could never be mine, and sought to give me a young wife who would be a good companion for me—and to give her a youthful husband who would be kind to her. As I would most certainly have been, despite her sometimes lugubrious affect, her unavoidable sarcasm and her occasional and outspoken flare-ups. She was insecure and wore a bevy of protective postures, but she was smart and funny and I could have loved her like a sister. If she hadn't been murdered.

She had died a year or so earlier, slain when she discovered how the renegade Sir Tirre had imprisoned Sir Lancelot. That blue ribbon had been the clue that led Merlin and me to discover her dying body. I groaned inwardly at the thought of that tragic consequence, just the first of the great misfortunes Lancelot's illicit love of the queen had brought down upon the peace of Camelot. Oh, would that it had been the last.

"Pay attention, will you Gildas? I really don't have much time," Lady Elizabeth said to me in the dream, though her voice sounded like it was coming to me from a great distance, or from a great depth. "I should be cold," she continued, "but my flesh is hot, so hot, I feel it burning like a great rage running through my blood!" With that her blue eyes blazed at me from within her soft, rounded features, and that light which had surrounded her seemed to swallow her up so that I could see her no more.

I fell to my knees in the dream and groped about blindly, and the other ladies in the queen's chamber surrounded me, asking what was the matter, and all I could say through my heaving sobs was, "I only want to know where she is! Just show me where she is!"

The next instant I was kneeling in the cart in which we had borne her murdered body back to Camelot. She lay in the bed of the cart, still and lifeless, while my tears fell onto her face. And it seemed that those tears revived her, for she opened her eyes and stared at me with orbs that suddenly turned black, and to my horror her face became as a skull, as her hand clutched my tunic and she cried out in a rasping voice, "I will not be buried! I will not be buried!"

And with a start I awoke. I sat upright in a cold sweat, my fists clenched and my jaw grinding with tension. But there were tears in my eyes, and I breathed heavily, vividly remembering the dream. It was, I reasoned now in the calm of my wakefulness, the sort of dream that Merlin and his Macrobius would have called an *oracular* vision, one in which a significant figure comes to you and tells you something important about things that are about to happen. Unless of course it was one of those things he called an *insomnium*, a nightmare caused by my anxiety about getting Rosemounde to safety. But if it wasn't that, if it was indeed a meaningful oracular vision, what exactly was Elizabeth trying to tell me in that dream? It didn't make any sense to me. She was burning? She would not be buried? It was beyond my power to understand. Perhaps, when I made it to Gaul and Arthur's camp, I could run it by Merlin. And at the thought of Merlin I froze. There was something in the dream that reminded me of something Merlin had said some time back. Something I couldn't quite put my finger on. Oh well, I thought. It will come back to me, no doubt. For now, though, I needed to sleep.

I settled down between the covers again, and I lay lightly against Lady Rosemounde, assuring myself that she was still there. But the dream had disturbed me too much. I had a restless night, and was groggy in the saddle the whole next day, haunted still by that last image of the lady Elizabeth, clutching me by the tunic and refusing to be buried.

***

On the morning of the fifth day since we'd set out from Camelot, Rosemounde and I crossed the River Tamar, which formed the border between Devon and Cornwall, just north of the town of Launceston. As we approached that town, we paused on the road outside of the Augustinian priory on the outskirts. We were a bit more than twenty miles due east of Tintagel, and we could make it to King Mark's castle in one more day of riding. But I decided to break our pattern and to stop in this town, the chief city of the area, because after pondering the dilemma for several days I had finally struck on an idea that I thought could guarantee Rosemounde's safety, if only she would agree to it. But before putting the plan into action, I felt compelled to don my armor, my fine chain mail hauberk that had remained rolled up in the bundle that Achilles bore on his back, behind my saddle. Rosemounde, puzzled at this humor of mine, asked whether the town was dangerous, since it seemed to require me to enter it fully armed.

Strapping on my scabbard from which hung the sheathed Almace, I shot her a quick half-smile. "One can never be too careful, especially when entering a strange town. We've avoided all towns and villages since we set out, but I think we are far enough from Camelot now to be beyond Mordred's immediate reach."

The land around Launceston was rolling, and on a steep hill overlooking the town was a stone castle with a strong rounded keep, a castle where King Mark kept a small garrison to protect the wealth of that town, which was not inconsiderable. Launceston was also the only town in all of Cornwall with a defensive wall around it, and as Rosemounde and I rode through the gate, a pair of guards watched us with no little curiosity—impressed, I could see in their eyes, by the richness of my finely-made hauberk. And, it must be said, by the beauty of the lady that accompanied me, despite her simple kitchen wench's garments.

"Do you have any idea where we are going?" Rosemounde whispered from behind my right side. I gazed back at her with that same closemouthed smile and nodded.

Riding through the main thoroughfare of the town, past the grand wooden structures that housed the guild hall and the local mint that produced copper coins for Arthur's realm from the regional mines in the vicinity (the chief reason for the town's castle and the defensive wall), the local townspeople stopped to stare at us. It wasn't that the town was unused to visitors—the regional market was housed in the castle and villagers and peasants from many miles around bought and sold there regularly. But a knight in full chain armor was not typical. Except, perhaps, on Armorers' Street.

I turned into this relatively short lane, where were several houses close to one another, some built of wood, some in the more recent waddle-and-daub style, and it was in front of one of these last that I stopped and dismounted, helping Rosemounde from her saddle and then tying the horses to a pole in front of the building that held a wooden sign in the shape of a helmet, indicating that we were at an armorer's shop. Guinevere gamboled around Rosemounde's skirts when she climbed down, having warmed to the lady deeply during the last few days of our journey. I told the dog to stay with the horses, and she more or less obeyed me, at least as much as a borzoi with a mind of her own was likely to.

Like most of the other houses on this street, this one had a ground floor that served as the shop itself, and a second story that projected outward from the ground floor, which was the living quarters for the master artisan whose shop this was. There were clanging metallic noises coming from behind the house, where I knew the forge was located.

"What *is* this place? Why are we stopping here?" Rosemounde demanded.

"You're about to find out," I answered playfully. "Come, we won't go in the shop. Come around back to the forge."

I held my head up and strode purposefully around the side of the house, with Rosemounde tagging behind, a puzzled expression on her face. We approached the charcoal forge, where two men in simple brown tunics and wearing heavy black aprons tied at the waist, their muscled arms glistening with sweat, bent over the fire, shaping small metal rings. The older man gave me a quick glance and looked back down, saying gruffly, "Be with you in half a moment, your honor, soon's I get this cooled."

But the younger man had looked up and, after a slight pause, gave out a short gasp, and dropped his tools, poking the older man in the ribs. The older man gave an exasperated sigh and muttered, "What's got into ya, Davey? You've almost made me ruin this piece." Then he looked up, his dark eyes flashing on my face for the first time. Then they widened, and quite suddenly glistened with tears, and his mouth spread out into a broad grin. He threw down his tools and spread his arms wide. But all he said was, "That's one first-class hauberk you've got on there, mate. Must have been a fine craftsman who fashioned that for you, I can see that!"

Myghal of Launceston, master craftsman and armorer for nearly all the richest knights in Cornwall, looked older than I remembered him. There were streaks of gray in his long black beard now, and wrinkles around his eyes where the skin had been tight before. There was even a bit of a paunch around his midsection. Business must be thriving, I thought, for he was eating well.

"Father," I said, opening my own arms. "It's been far too long." And I stepped forward, embracing him. He was still a good inch or two taller than me, and outweighed me by a good two stone, and his biceps were as big as my thighs, the product of hard manual labor performed daily for thirty years.

"Seven years, Gildas, my lad," he said quietly. "But I knew when I sent you off that I might be sending you out of my life for good and all. I had despaired of ever seeing you again in this life. I had your letters every Christmas, even though you knew I can't read, but I got one of the monks from the priory to read them out to me. And I had word sometimes, from knights who passed through. I knew you'd been squire to Sir Gareth. And of course you wrote me when you were to be knighted. Sent you that mail corslet. Thought it might come in handy!"

"Ha, I know you worked on this hauberk for years," I told him, feeling the fine mesh that was the envy of many, even knights of the Table.

"Ah," he looked down abashedly. "I kept hoping that one day you'd be elevated to that class, and I wanted to be ready with it when that happened!"

"He worked on it every spare minute he had!" interrupted his companion, whom I knew as his journeyman David of Frampton. David put out his hand to me, which I grasped in friendship. "He was so proud when we got the news of your knighthood he sat down and cried!" At that my father scoffed. "He did!" David persisted. "Sat right there on that bench and wept!" He pointed to the corner of the little wooden shelter that served as their forge.

"So David," I said, freeing my hand from his excited grip, "you're still putting up with this old windbag then?"

"Windbag is it?" my father said in mock annoyance. "Well perhaps I'll have no more to say to you then at all, and there'll be no fatted calf put on for *you*, my prodigal son!"

"I stay with him as long as he pays me," David answered, ignoring my father's bluster. "Just waiting for a better offer to come in from some better armorer..."

"Ach, you couldn't find a better armorer!" My father answered. "And if you did, he wouldn't have you! But now," the old man looked toward where Rosemounde stood behind my right shoulder, and I glanced back to see her left eyebrow raised almost to her hairline, her lips pursed, and her eyes looking at me expectantly. "Who is the lovely lass you've brought with you, and why are you being so rude in making her wait to be introduced?"

It was a mild rebuke and said with tongue in cheek, but I knew it was justified. I'd simply been so elated at seeing the old man again after so long that I could focus on nothing else. But now, remembering myself, I stepped back and said, "Lady Rosemounde, this is my father, the armorer Myghal of Launceston, with his journeyman armor-maker David of Frampton. And father, David, may I present Lady Rosemounde, heiress to Duke Hoel and future Duchess of Brittany."

Rosemounde smiled and inclined her head, but at the announcement David's mouth hung open as if he were a fish who'd swallowed a hook, and my father, after looking at her for a dazed moment or two, fell to his knees and bowed his head. "Your Grace," he murmured, stunned and apologetic, "forgive me. I did not realize—dressed as you are, you must understand. But we are at your service—both of us!" And at the hint, David fell to his knees as well, bowing as if it were the queen herself who'd paid them a visit.

I was taken aback at first, until I put myself in my father's place and remembered—remembered how far superior to me on the social ladder my lady stood, and how even I, now that I'd been knighted by the king and so ennobled, had thereby set a huge, unbridgeable gulf between my father and myself. Encounters with the highest tiers of the aristocracy were to me a part of my daily routine. For Myghal of Launceston, I realized, this was a once-in-a-lifetime meeting. In his profession, he dealt with folk of the knightly class, the lower echelon of the aristocracy like myself, quite often, but in a servile role. He'd never had one as a guest in his house, and now he had a duchess. Or as good as. Albeit one dressed like a kitchen maid.

Rosemounde had reddened slightly, but very deftly bade my father and David to rise, thanking them for their esteem and murmuring blessings on them, and I realized at that moment that she must be quite accustomed to this kind of adulation from all the lesser folk, whether villains, freemen, artisans, or yeomen. And with that knowledge I began to sweat, thinking that I had had the audacity to take her to my bed, and to think of her as my own true love.

"Your Ladyship...honors us with your, your visit," my father stammered after he had risen again to his feet. "Far more, I daresay, than we are worthy of. But please," now he wiped his hands on his apron and motioned toward the house. "Come into the house, and we really will put on the fatted calf, to celebrate your visit and the return of my son, that I feared was gone from me for good and all. You can tell us then, Gildas, how you come to be here, and why you are traveling with Her Ladyship, and how long you intend to stay…and why she is dressed like a peasant! Let me and David wash our hands, and we'll join you. But go in and see Nell, and she'll settle you in and put on some stew, begging your pardon, Ma'am. It's the best we have I'm afraid at present."

"It will be fine, I assure you," Rosemounde told him. "We've had a long ride and no great banquets on the way."

"Nell?" I inquired, raising my eyebrows. My father stopped for an instant on his way to the well. He looked over to me and then looked away a bit sheepishly. "I'd have let you know if I'd thought you were ever coming back," he said evasively, then plunged in all the way. "Nell and I have been living as man and wife for the past two years or so. She's David's sister, is how I met her. I thought about writing you once or twice, but then I can't write, and if I'd have had one of the monks write it for me they'd have…well, they'd have pressed me to marry her. But she doesn't want that, And neither do I."

Rosemounde smirked at me as she loved to do, and I shrugged. "It's fine," I said. "Nell, eh?" I repeated as I steered Rosemounde toward the house, through the shop and upstairs to the living quarters. My own mother had died a few years after I had moved on to Camelot, so I had never seen this house without her. She had died in childbirth, bringing my baby sister into the world. A sister I never knew, for the poor infant had followed her mother to the grave the very next day. I knew that my father must have mourned her, must have grieved over her for years as far as I knew, and I felt pangs of remorse for neglecting my home all that while, but news had come slowly from Cornwall to Camelot. All the time I'd known my father he had never been interested in another woman, and I had somehow assumed that even after her death he would have felt he was being disloyal. But since her passing, after he'd secured me a place as page in Guinevere's household, and he'd been without even my poor companionship for some years, it seems he'd allowed himself to bend this far, to find himself Nell. But not to marry her. For him, I knew it would feel like adultery if he received the blessing of the Church on his new liaison.

Nell of Frampton looked me up and down with suspicious, squinting eyes as I came through her door. She was thin, wiry, with straight black hair highlighted in gray, barely visible under the two-inch wide linen filet that circled her brow and connected to her barbette, the narrow band that fastened her headwear below her chin. Her simple homespun tunic was gray and, like the men of the house, she wore a sturdy apron. Her eyes were dark and penetrating, and her face was thin with a beak-like nose. Still, she would have been comely if her expression was not so unwelcoming.

I did not recall ever seeing her before, but she certainly knew who I was. "So," she said in an accusatory tone. "You come back here after seven years, dragging your wench with you, and what? You expect to be welcomed like your father's heir? You think you'll step right into this living he has made without ever having to work a day in the forge like my brother has for all these years? I say go back where you came from, we don't need you here, nor your kitchen slut!"

Not the welcome I thought to receive in my father's house. And Rosemounde looked at me with eyebrows raised and eyes bulging wide at the characterization she'd been given by this virago at the door. I bowed my head for a moment, trying to imagine how best to respond to this tirade, when Rosemounde herself stepped in.

"Sir Gildas is on his way to join King Arthur and his army in Gaul," she said sweetly. "So your concerns are unfounded, you will be happy to learn. As for me, I am currently traveling under his protection. My name is Lady Rosemounde of Brittany, where my father is Duke of that country and I am his heir. We would be grateful for your hospitality, Madam. Your husband has just invited us to join you for a repast after our long ride from Camelot."

Nell's dark eyes, which had been squinting at me with distrust, now widened with shock, and with the realization that she had just called a future duchess a wench and a slut. Her face had turned a bright scarlet, like the robes of a cardinal of the Church, and she sputtered and stammered as she tried to find a way to take back her unfortunate outburst. Finally she fell to her knees like her brother and mate, and managed to blurt out, "Forgive me, your Ladyship, I...I did not understand...I did not...your clothing..."

185

Rosemounde smiled benevolently, if a bit self-satisfied, and explained, "I am traveling in secret, concealed from some who would do me harm. That is why Sir Gildas rides with me."

"Forgive me, dear Lady," Nell repeated, her head bowed, unable even to look Rosemounde in the face.

I could only enjoy the woman's embarrassment for so long before feeling sorry for her. She was, after all, my father's common-law wife. "Nell," I said softly, "I can understand that you would resent my coming home after all these years to claim my father's business and cut out your brother, who has worked for him faithfully for more than a dozen years. But I left here because I hated the trade of armor-making and couldn't get far enough away from it." I was only exaggerating a little bit. "I will be leaving after we share this meal, for I need to reach King Mark today if possible. But I do hope that you might avoid jumping to conclusions, at least about me, without talking to me first."

But me she wasn't really listening to, to tell you the truth. Nell's gaze was now pretty exclusively focused on the lady Rosemounde, and she was watching her every move as if with a blink of her eye Rosemounde had the power to take away from her all that Nell held dear. Rosemounde smiled benevolently and reached out to touch Nell's head as the woman bowed it in her direction. "Now, Nell," she said in kindly tones, "I harbor no ill will toward you. We can forget your outburst, or pass it off as the choler of a moment. Rise now and let us have something to eat, if we may. We are near famished after our long ride here."

Nell's face lit up at the words, and at the same time my father's deep baritone surprised us from behind as he came through the door into the kitchen. "You do right to pay homage to a great lady, Nell, and you honor our house in doing so. But now let's get up and give the travelers a meal, shall we? It's many a league between here and Camelot, and it's been dry these past few days as well. David's feeding and watering your fine horses—and your rather pushy dog as well." I laughed. It hadn't taken him long to recognize Guinevere's essential character.

"I have a pot of goat stew boiling over the fire just now," Nell

186

said, her head bobbing little bows continually in what I thought of as annoying regularity but which the bemused Rosemounde accepted with the grace of a great lady, which in fact she was. "It's awfully simple for the likes of you, I'm sure, but it's hearty and it'll put meat on your bones!" With that a bit of an embarrassed flinch moved quickly across her face as she realized she might have misspoken, and she backtracked, saying, "Not that your ladyship is thin or scrawny or anything like that…"

"It's fine, I assure you. Goat stew sounds delightful," Rosemounde said, seating herself on a bench at the small table that took up much space in the kitchen. Nell seemed about to swoon with happiness as she dished up our plates from the pot over the fire. I got out of my mail hauberk and set it aside with Almace in the corner of the room. By now David had entered, carrying glasses of small beer from the pantry behind the kitchen, and the five of us settled down to my first meal with my father in seven years.

They wanted to hear all the news of the court: Though that world was completely foreign to them, things happened there that affected their lives, for good or ill—more often the latter—and to have the news straight from someone directly involved, rather than from third- and fourth- hand rumors, was a unique amusement for them. But I'm afraid what we had to tell them proved to be more disturbing than pleasurable. They knew that Arthur and Lancelot had fallen out and that the king was now in Gaul with his army. And they knew that Sir Mordred was acting as regent. But when we broke it to them that Mordred had read a letter purported to be from Benwick, to the effect that King Arthur and Sir Gawain had been slain, and that Mordred had proclaimed himself king, the three of them were dumbfounded.

I quickly assured them that we were certain none of that was true, and that Mordred had contrived the story to usurp the throne, at which they were greatly alarmed. If civil war was coming, they were at the mercy of any marauding bands of soldiers that might come this way. They could only hope that King Mark was able to keep Cornwall out of the paths of any roving armies. I suggested that the fighting that occurred was likely to be in Kent or along the southeast coast, where the king was likely to land, and then perhaps as far inland as Camelot, but was not likely to threaten Cornwall, at least as far as I could see.

"But," I told them, sopping up the last of the gravy from my goat stew with a crust of barley bread, "there are some ramifications of Mordred's treason that are affecting us personally. That is, Lady Rosemounde and me. I've already told you that I am on my way to bring news of Mordred's treachery to the King in Gaul. I have to go this long way around because Mordred's Saxon allies are watching the coast from Kent to Portsmouth. I'm counting on King Mark to give me safe passage on a ship of his own to set sail from Cornwall. But that brings us to Lady Rosemounde." With that I looked across the table to her and saw the puzzled look on her face. She raised her eyebrows at me quizzically and tilted her head, trying to guess what it was I was about to say. I had not run this idea by her first, and I hoped she would think about it before shutting it down.

"Lady Rosemounde, you should know, was married to Sir Mordred prior to his appointment as regent." At that all three listeners looked shocked, and a gasp escaped from Nell. "Her father Duke Hoel had married her to the king's nephew to cement the alliance of Logres and Brittany. But Mordred has renounced her, persuaded the bishop to annul the marriage, and proclaimed his intention of marrying Queen Guinevere." Audible cries of sympathy came from my audience, particularly from Nell, who now was hanging on my every word. "This is the reason why the lady has accompanied me here. We have good reason to believe that Mordred will not be content with having cast her off, but may intend now to imprison her or even to murder her to ensure that there is no legitimate challenge to his marriage to Queen Guinevere."

"Well, if King Arthur is still alive, I would think that would be a legitimate challenge," my father ventured, logically.

"Of course," I answered, holding my palms up in assent. "But it will be weeks before the king can mount an invasion, and by then the marriage will be a *fait accompli*. Mordred is counting on the common people to rally round his cause once he has legally wed the queen. When it is an established fact, the populace will not quibble about niceties."

"And you are expecting to take the lady Rosemounde to safety with her family in Brittany, then?" David asked.

"Well," I began, looking at Rosemounde, who smirked at me and tilted her head as if to say, *is* that what you're doing? "In my opinion, that would be the very first place Mordred would think to look for her. If he has assassins seeking her, they are quite certain to be heading toward Brittany even as we speak. No, I've thought of Brittany and ruled it out."

"Where then?" Nell asked with some panic in her voice. "Where can she be safe?"

"My thought was," I began, then paused, looking around the table with some uncertainty, "that she might stay here."

***

A whole lot of silence greeted that announcement, as faces around the table registered disbelief, and stared at one another with dropping jaws. Rosemounde herself looked honestly dumbfounded—a look that I'd never really seen on her face before. Usually she had a knowing, even ironic look, whatever was unfolding before her. But this she hadn't seen coming. Not at all.

The lady Rosemounde was the first to speak. "And I'm just hearing about this now? It didn't occur to you to let me in on your plans for me sometime, oh, I don't know, when we were on the road alone together for five days?" Yes, there was a bit of a chill in her voice at that point.

"My lady," I replied quietly, my eyes focused at the bowl in front of me on the table. "I wanted to get here and see the place first, and I wanted to be sure that you had had a chance to see it for yourself, before making the proposal. I assure you, I will follow your wishes in this affair whatever they are, no matter what you decide. But I repeat, I think it would be a mistake to leave you with your family, for the reasons I have already mentioned. Nor do I think leaving you in the court of King Mark is the solution: I have yet to know Mark's allegiances in this current power game, nor is it certain that Mordred would have no spies in his court. The only other option is to bring you to King Arthur's camp in Benwick, but that would take you directly into an active battlefield, where I despair of keeping you safe."

Rosemounde's face did not change expression but remained stony. Eventually she did nod, though, as if acknowledging the truth of my various assessments. "And this house?" she asked calmly.

"Nobody knows you here," I began. "Dressed as you are, no one in this city will suspect that you are anything but what you appear to be: a common kitchen wench. Perhaps it can be given out that you are another sister of David and Nell's. Or perhaps even David's own mistress," and with that I know I reddened, and Rosemounde, a bit more like herself, rolled her eyes. "But no one would ever think to look for you here, if Mordred has sent any spies or assassins after you. You should be safe and undetected until this war ends, and I come back for you."

Lady Rosemounde thought for a moment, then raised her eyes to mine and announced, "You've thought it all out, haven't you Gildas? I have to admit, I did think that you were planning to carry me to Gaul with you, and I had confidence that even there you would keep me safe. At any rate, I had no desire to be severed from you, and would have taken the chance of staying with you wherever you were bound. But it seems you care more for my safety than my presence, and this solution is the most sensible, given that desire." That chill had not yet melted from her voice.

"But we have not heard from your father or his friends as to how *they* feel about this sudden proposal of yours. What say you Myghal of Launceston? David? Nell? Are you willing to share your house with me, to be my protection in this plight I find myself in?"

I caught some worried looks on the faces of David and my father, but Nell spoke up immediately. "Our house is your house, Lady Rosemounde!" she proclaimed. "You are gracious and kind and good humored, and I feel you are family. And I have needed another woman in this house for years. Please stay—you do us honor with your presence!"

My father cleared his throat. "What Nell says is certainly true—we have no reason to resent your staying with us, Lady Rosemounde. But Gildas," he turned to me, "this house is not a fortress. We have no way of defending the lady—or ourselves—should soldiers from the regent's guard come knocking on our door."

"It puts us all at risk," David shrugged in agreement.

"Have I been sharing a roof with a couple of bloody capons?" Nell cut in, her voice climbing up a notch. "The lady needs a hiding place, not a castle. We're the best hiding place in sight. If soldiers come, we'll spirit her away somewhere. For now, she's going to stay, and that's that."

The two men looked at each other, shrugged again and nodded. "We'll keep her as safe as we can," my father said. "And now, Gildas, from what you've said, I know you are in a hurry to leave. It is good to see you, even for this short time. I hope you'll be able to visit with us longer when this war has been concluded."

I had stressed my need to reach Tintagel yet that day if I could possibly push my horse to that extent, and my father was resigned to that necessity. I stood up and embraced him, fighting back tears. "I will return," I said. "I will be back for the lady Rosemounde in any case, whatever the outcome of this coming battle. And I intend," I whispered for his ears only, "to marry her when I do. So please keep her safe, as if she were your own daughter."

He nodded with a close-mouthed smile, his eyes sparkling. Meanwhile Nell had begun to clean up the leavings of the meal, and when Rosemounde moved to help her, Nell waved her off and told her, "Not now, my lady. It's time to take leave of your man now. We'll leave you in peace for that."

Rosemounde held onto my right arm and walked me down the steps and out the front door of the house, as David quietly moved out to load my armor and sword onto Achilles, whom he fitted again into his saddle. As we stood outside the door, Guinevere bounded up and stood on her hind legs, flailing her paws at Rosemounde, whom she had decided was her new best friend during these past days.

"Down, girl," I said half-heartedly, and then I had a thought. It was a vivid memory of Guinevere running down a side road toward a suspicious manor house, risking everything to protect the young Lady Elizabeth, whom she had grown to love. "My lady," I decided. "You must keep Guinevere here with you."

"But she'll miss you and Achilles so much..." Rosemounde protested.

"She's attached to you now," I said, "and she is fiercely protective. She will not let any harm come to you if she can possibly prevent it. Besides, I would worry about her on a battlefield. There are too many, ways for harm to come to her. She is safer here with you, and you are safer with her. Please, keep her with my love."

Rosemounde laughed, that open laugh that sounded like the tinkle of crystals. "That is just what I'll do," she said. "Whenever I look at her I will see the embodiment of your love."

"Then keep her always at your side! My lady," I sighed heavily, knowing the time had come, "one kiss, I beg you, before I go." And with that I took her in my arms and pressed my lips to her soft mouth with the utmost tenderness. Then unexpectedly she shot her tongue quickly into my mouth and then broke away, laughing again. "And there will be plenty more where that came from, once you return. So see that you do! And quickly too!"

"I will be back," I vowed. "And when I do, I'm never going to leave you again."

"Never?" she asked, raising her eyebrows skeptically.

"No. When I hold you again, I'll hold you forever," I promised, grasping her small, thin fingers in my hand as a last farewell. "Hmmph," I murmured, looking down at the tiny hand. "Little bundle of twigs."

And with that I turned and mounted Achilles as David held his bridle for me, and we trotted off, leaving our two ladies standing at the door of my father's house, watching us go. Guinevere whimpered pathetically. I gritted my teeth and set my face toward Tintagel.

***

"Sir Gildas of Cornwall, I remember you from Arthur's court, what, some three years ago was it? It was right after the lamentable deaths of my wife and nephew, as I recall, and you were with the lord Merlin, were you not? Involved in that business of investigating the murders of my Isolde and Sir Tristram. I suppose I owe you thanks for finding

192

the killers and proving my own innocence to those backstabbers who would have blamed me for their deaths. Though the loss of the Lady Brangwain in that case was a hard blow for me. I can't thank you for that."

"Yes my lord," I answered, and then, "er, I mean, no my lord. That is, I'm sorry for all your losses, sir. It was a grievous time. But I am here on the business of King Arthur himself at this time, and I wonder," I looked around the crowded throne room to which I had been ushered by one of King Mark's guards after the king had agreed to see me immediately when I arrived at his castle. "I wonder if it would be possible to see you in private? The news I bear is for your own ears only." Mark looked at me with suspicion. Luckily, he had remembered me and associated me with the court, or he would have had me waiting indefinitely before giving me audience. But to ask for a private audience? That was a bold step, and there were a good twenty other knights and ladies in the room who had business with the king today.

King Mark, wearing an ornamental crown of state on his gray locks, and looking most regal in a blue samite tunic, covered by a woolen cloak in royal purple with a sable lining, sniffed and looked to his right and left. There his guards stood at attention in full armor, leaning on their spears. I knew what was going through his head. He was weighing his curiosity about my message, and the opportunity to do Arthur some good service and so please his king, against showing off in front of his courtiers by snubbing the king's messenger and thereby pleasing the regent. He decided first to stall and feel me out before making his decision.

"Word has just reached us from the court at Camelot," he began, "from the hand of the regent himself, that King Arthur and Sir Gawain have both been slain, and further, that all of Logres is in danger of invasion by French forces led by the traitor Sir Lancelot. Yet you say that you come on the king's business. How am I to interpret that, Sir Gildas of Cornwall?"

Devil take diplomacy, I thought. Let the rest of Mark's court hear. If Mordred had a spy here, let him know that his master's secret was out, and he wasn't fooling anyone. "You may interpret it to mean that the regent is a liar and a usurper, that he is fortifying the country against his rightful king, and that anyone who holds with the bastard Mordred is as great a coward and traitor as his master."

There was a shocked silence that greeted my outburst, and every eye in the throne room looked toward King Mark for a cue as to how they should react to these charges. Mark was looking at me open-mouthed, but there was an amused glint in his eyes that told me my words had not fallen on unsympathetic ears.

"Yes," Mark said thoughtfully, stroking his well-trimmed beard. "Perhaps you're right, Sir Gildas. I think we really should speak in private. Let's step into my private chamber. Guards, come stand outside the door while we hold council within." And with that Mark took my arm in friendly fashion and steered me through a door frame in the east wall of the throne room, then pushed closed a large wooden door that effectively shut out all the noise from the outside. The room was fairly small, perhaps fifteen by twenty feet, but with a high ceiling and a side window above our heads that let a good deal of light into the room. On the wall opposite the door hung a large, richly-woven tapestry that depicted a hunt for a unicorn, with the beast finally trapped, its head in the lap of a long-haired white-clad virgin. The tapestry's subject matter surprised me, for Mark had never struck me as someone with a romantic streak. Yet in a set of wooden shelves against the west wall lay several manuscripts that appeared to be romances rather than books of law or devotion. The rest of the closet was sparsely furnished, with two simple wooden chairs and a wood desk, piled with loose parchments and on which stood a quill and inkstand.

Mark sat in one of the chairs with a heavy sigh, lifting the crown from his head and setting it on the desk. "That thing gets awfully heavy after a while," he confided, motioning me to sit in the other chair. I did so gingerly, taken aback by the informality and the unheard of condescension that invited me to be seated in the presence of a king.

Mark was about King Arthur's age, just a few years younger, though he seemed older: He was more bent by his age, less powerfully built, grayer in the beard and the temples. Still, he had the bearing of a king, and commanded respect. Like Arthur, he had weathered the adultery of a queen, the betrayal of a chief knight, and the ignominy of being a royal cuckold, and had come out on the other side of all that with his kingdom and his crown intact. But those trials had left their mark, and his pale grey eyes never lost their burdened look.

"Well, Gildas, judging from the tone of your message, you are surely wise to deliver it in private," Mark began. "There is almost certainly at least one member of my court that would see to it that anything overheard between us would be straightaway communicated to the regent's ears."

I couldn't help a modest smile at that, and given the unwonted familiarity of Mark's manner ventured to say, "As you yourself used to have spies in Arthur's court, my Lord?"

"Ah," he said, unoffended at the jibe. "You refer to the Lady Elaine, in the queen's chamber, I suppose. Yes," he admitted, pushing his long hair back on his head, enjoying its freedom from the crown's constraint. "That is how the game is played, I'm afraid. But tell me now, what is this message you say you have?"

The moment had come, and I swallowed hard and looked Mark steadily in the eyes. "It is not a true message but rather a request. I have escaped from Camelot with the sole purpose of bringing news to King Arthur in Gaul regarding Mordred's activities in his absence. Someone needs to get word to the king that Mordred has usurped the crown, is organizing an army of the king's greatest enemies for the purpose of making war upon him, and plans to force the supposedly widowed queen to marry him to legitimize his rule. And that he has fortified the coast from Kent to Portsmouth with a Saxon army to prevent the king from landing his forces on his own soil."

Mark nodded. "Some of this I was aware of myself," he admitted, "though I was not aware of his plans for the queen, nor of his occupying the southeast coast against invasion."

"I've come to you," I continued, now reaching the essence of my request, "since I cannot go directly to Gaul through Kent or the south coast, to ask you for a ship that will take me to Arthur's army in Benwick so I may deliver my news to him there. I lay this before you, knowing that if you are a true vassal of the king you will help me with this. If you have been bought by the bastard Mordred, then my quest is doomed." And that being said, I left it in his hands.

Now it was King Mark's turn to let a smile flicker across his face. He squinted his eyes as if in deep thought and pulled absently on his right ear lobe. "So I take it by your innuendo that you're aware of Mordred's approaching me to ally myself with his cause. You're wondering how tempted I am by his offer." After a long pause during which he studied my features, he let out a scornful "Pah! And he sends that little weasel Sir Geraint to make the offer? What does he take me for? Geraint would like nothing better than to expand his kingdom by stealing a part of mine, so how am I to trust him? And I am to allow his new Irish allies access to my ports, and let them march across my land, when they have been paying me tribute for all these years? How do you think that would work? Not to mention becoming friends with the damned Picts and the Saxons, by all that's holy! Those people have been at our throats since I was a boy, and they are not going to change now. I may be isolated here, with the Irish to my west, Geraint to my north, and Mordred and his Saxons to my east, but by God, Arthur gave me this land, and I intend to hold it for him against any pissant Geraints or Mordreds who come along."

Sighing with relief, I left my chair and knelt before this man who I now acknowledged to be king of my homeland. "My liege," I said, "you've given me some hope, a light in this darkness. When can I take ship for Gaul?"

Mark turned to his desk and began writing immediately. "I have three ships in port here at Tintagel right now, and one of them I'm putting at your disposal. I'm writing out orders which I will verbally give to one of my guards outside. You and he can go directly from here to the harbor and board that ship to be off with the tide. I'm ordering the captain and the crew to make themselves available to King Arthur as well when they arrive, to help him as he plans the invasion of Logres to topple that bastard from the throne. The king needs to hear your message without any further delay. You're leaving Cornwall today."

CHAPTER FOURTEEN
A MYSTERY SOLVED

"**G**od's snowy white beard, boy, you've certainly taken your own sweet time getting here. Much has happened since you left on your cozy assignment at the court!" Merlin was first to greet me as I rode into King Arthur's encampment at the siege of Benwick Castle just after dawn. A small party of Mark's troops were marching here after me from where our cog had docked in the harbor, but since they were marching on foot and I had brought Achilles (who seemed more than ready to leave that rocking boat behind), I took the opportunity to gallop into camp and bring Arthur the news from Camelot as quickly as I could. It was now two full weeks since I had left Caerleon, and I knew that every day Mordred was getting stronger as his new allies gathered to make war on their sovereign lord.

"Well, I haven't exactly been idle all this time myself, Old Man," I told him, dismounting and grasping him by the hand. One of Arthur's grooms came up to take my horse from me and lead him to a long row of stalls that had been erected for the duration of the siege, and I walked with Merlin among that city of colorful tents to his own pavilion to confer with him, telling him that I wanted his counsel right away, but that I must see the king as soon as possible.

"It's early and he's had a fitful night," the mage told me. "You won't be able to get near him for some time yet. Take a moment to sit with me and we'll catch up on the news. What's happening in Camelot?"

And I proceeded to tell him, first about Mordred's alliances with the Picts, the Irish and the Saxons, and the blockade of the coast of Logres facing Gaul. Then about the bastard's lying revelation of the death of Arthur and Gawain, at which Merlin's eyes grew wide in surprise and horror. Then about his rejection of Rosemounde and his intention to marry the queen, at which the old man gasped audibly. Finally, I told him of the queen's escape to London and her plan to take refuge in the White Tower there, about Morgan's escape to the palace of the Lady of the Lake, and of my own whisking of Lady Rosemounde into Cornwall, though I hesitated even with Merlin to reveal where exactly I had left her.

"Don't tell me where she is," Merlin said, holding out his hand. "Even here in Arthur's camp, there could be some secretly loyal to the bastard. Keep her whereabouts to yourself, and there is no chance of revealing them to the wrong ears. As to the rest of it, the sooner we get this news to the king, the sooner he can make arrangements to invade Logres, if he can. Gawain must still be convinced, but I'll tell you about that in a moment. But speaking of Gawain, what about the other task? Were you able to make any headway in this mystery of the murders of Sir Gareth and Sir Gaheris? You had access, I suppose, to the most likely suspects in this villainy—Mordred himself and his sycophants. Did you learn anything, or were you too distracted by these other plots and intrigues?"

"Well, I had made some progress before we had to flee from the court, but I don't have any proof."

"Proof is a luxury right now," the mage shrugged. "Strong suspicion may be enough. What have you got?"

I proceeded to tell him about my conversation with Sir Geraint, and his blatant suggestion that Sir Tor and Sir Aglovale were killed because they refused to join Mordred's conspiracy. "Either Geraint murdered them himself, or he knows who did, and it was almost certainly Mordred who would have given the order. And if that's the case, then it seems not too much of a leap to say that the same killer also did for Sir Gareth and Sir Gaheris. It's just too much of a coincidence to think there were two murderers stalking different sets of victims at the same time!"

Merlin leaned back his head and lowered his substantial eyebrows in thought, stroking his beard at the same time. "Not too much of a coincidence if the one was aware of the other, both perhaps set in motion by the same master plan—or even, perhaps, if the one sought to cover his own crime by making it appear to have been committed by the same hand. There are too many variables that we haven't solved yet."

"But we have, as you say, a deep suspicion!" I reminded him. "So here is what it looks like to me: Geraint gets the order from Mordred, and so he kills Gareth and Gaheris, stabbing them in the back unseen, and he has one of his own knights, or one of the other knights of the Table who's declared for Mordred, do away with Tor and Aglovale in secret at the same time, cutting their throats from behind, and all of it camouflaged by Lancelot's cavalry charge to rescue the queen."

A page came to the opening of Merlin's pavilion, asking if we wanted anything to break our fast. The cooks were serving white bread with fish, either herring or cod, along with some of the local wine. I was famished from days at sea, and Merlin nodded, so the boy dashed off to bring us our meals, and Merlin finally opened up to me.

"You'll learn this soon enough, but I need to tell you the most important thing that's happened here: Sir Gawain lies wounded in his tent, his head bloodied by a great blow from Lancelot just five days ago."

"What? But this is terrible news. Then our investigation of these murders has been in vain—and so is everything we've done in trying to stop Mordred. If Gawain is gone, the bastard will inherit the throne in any case! What a catastrophe this is! How could Lancelot have added this to his catalogue of offenses?"

Merlin closed his eyes and raised his hands. "How many conclusions are you going to jump to in a single reaction, you Cornish blockhead?"

"Well," I said, taken aback. "How...what...isn't it as I've said?"

"Not a bit of it," the mage declared. "Look, for one thing, even if Gawain were to die from his wounds, which does not seem to be likely right now, then Sir Ywain is next in line for the throne, as Arthur's next eldest nephew. Mordred, whatever you and I may think he is, is officially the king's nephew, and in this is outranked by Ywain. And for another, our investigation continues, because Gawain still must be convinced to leave his mad quest for vengeance and support the king in his return to Logres to take back his throne. And I have more to tell you about that, too. And as for Lancelot, he could easily have killed Gawain, and the battle was solely at Gawain's insistence, as I'm sure you realize. So, at least three conclusions firmly jumped to."

He broke off because the page had reappeared with a tray of bread, cheese and fish, along with some watered wine to break our fast. As he set it before us, Merlin lowered his brows at me, impatient at the interruption, and I looked around the pavilion and said, "I like what you've done with the place. Did you bring your chess set along?"

When the page had finally left, I burst out, "That's all well and good, but Ywain is next in line only in the abstract. Right now Mordred is *de facto* king of Logres."

"All the more reason for us to have a name to bring to Gawain—with at least enough confidence to give him a face-saving excuse to give up this obsession, which even he now must realize is insanity. Now listen: This duel between Gawain and Lancelot gave me an opportunity to talk to someone I've wanted to get to since this whole investigation started."

"You mean Lancelot himself?" I stopped, surprised, between bites of bread and cheese.

"No, no," Merlin shook his head as if I'd made a ridiculous suggestion. "Lancelot doesn't know anything. All he remembers is that he came crashing in on his great war horse, striking blindly on all sides in order to make his way to the queen, whom he lifted into his saddle and rode off to Joyous Gard. He very well could have killed *anybody* in his way, even the king himself, without recognizing them. Which is why he was so willing to take the blame when Gawain accused him, and why he offered to do extreme penance and to pay enormous compensation for the deaths of Gareth and Gaheris. No, we have all of Lancelot's evidence we're going to get.

The person I wanted to talk to was your old friend Robin Kempe."

"Robin?" I responded, puzzled, interrupting my gulp of wine. "What on earth could you learn from him? He wasn't even there at the queen's rescue."

"Exactly, because he had fled the castle well before that day, to join Lancelot at Joyous Gard. You remember that Robin had been arrested by Mordred after Lancelot's escape from the queen's chamber, because he had opened the gate and drawbridge to allow Lancelot and his fellows to get out of the castle."

"Of course," I said, "but how does that make him such a valuable witness?"

"He was questioned for hours," Merlin said quietly. "And in a private cell. Questioned by Mordred and by his minions, who were trying to get him to incriminate Lancelot and anyone else that might be close to him or the queen."

"Well, I suppose that's true, but how does that help? It was still *before* the murders."

"God's fat lips boy, *motive*! What was Mordred's state of mind leading up to the rescue of Guinevere, which he knew had to come? What was Geraint's? Motive, boy!" With that he crossed his arms and smiled broadly. "Means, motive, and opportunity, I've told you a hundred times, are the three things a killer must have. Every knight on the ground in the churchyard that day had the means—the weapons they were carrying, being prepared for an armed encounter with Lancelot's knights. And they had the opportunity: In the chaos of that onslaught, anybody could have killed anybody else. But who had the motive to kill Gareth and Gaheris, as well as Tor and Aglovale? If Mordred or one of his crew was behind this, as we suspect, what was their state of mind just *before* the rescue in the churchyard? I knew they had been trying to get information out of Robin, but I wanted to know what kind of information they may have betrayed to Robin in that questioning. And when Robin arrived as one of the guard who accompanied Sir Bors when he came to this camp to meet with Arthur and arrange the details of Lancelot's single combat with Gawain, I was able to take the opportunity, with Bors' permission, to speak with Robin in private for a brief time. And I think it was worthwhile."

"Mordred opened up to Robin, did he, and said 'I'm just longing to kill my big brothers, because what did they ever do for me?'"

The old man rolled his eyes as if much put upon and reached out to cuff the side of my head. "I've missed you, you Cornish dunce. But your inane drolleries are still not amusing. No, Mordred did not say much. According to Robin, he was pretty laconic with his interrogation, asking only brief questions about facts—when did Lancelot leave, what did he say, that sort of thing. But each of Mordred's advisers came in and had a crack at questioning him, he says. As for Pelleas, he tended to be mainly diffident, and his questions were vague. He apologized, Robin says, for holding him like a common criminal, and asked him generally what kind of relationship he had with Lancelot, with the queen, with Mordred. Geraint, he says, let down his guard a lot more."

"I wonder," I said. "When I talked to him, he gave a lot away, but I didn't think it was unguarded. I mean, he dropped a lot of hints about how I ought to join Mordred's side. I don't think he knew about my history with the bastard. But he also implied that people who turned down Mordred's offer of friendship weren't likely to live long. And he hinted that's what happened to Tor and Aglovale. And that was no slip. It was a warning."

"That fits with what Robin said about him," Merlin said, nodding. "Robin says that, after Mordred and Pelleas didn't get anywhere with him with their simple questions, Geraint came in and tried to bribe him, wanted to know just how many sovereigns of gold it might take to restore Robin's memory and loosen his tongue. Robin says Geraint talked at length about how rich he was going to get from Mordred's rise to power: Sovereignty in his own kingdom of Dumnonia, he said, and the bastard's blessing to gobble up neighboring counties and add them to his own realm. But spurn Mordred's offer? That was not a healthy thing to do, Geraint suggested."

"Exactly the kind of thing he said to me!" I agreed. "That sounds like motive to me—at least motive for killing Tor and Aglovale. We don't know, but if Geraint and his reprobate keeper felt like Gareth and Gaheris were refusing to cooperate as well, why balk at killing them at the same time? I'm willing to go to Gawain and tell him

Geraint is the killer. It's enough to go on to stop this war and turn the army back towards Logres."

"I admit Geraint is a likely enough suspect," Merlin answered, holding up his hands. "We don't know whether he had someone else do the murders or carried them out himself at Mordred's bidding. Yet it may be enough as the 'strong suspicion' that we bring to Gawain. But wait. There was yet another interrogator in Robin's cell. The one who actually was in charge of Robin's imprisonment, and who produced him before the king that day, you remember?"

"Sir Hectimere, yes. The youngest of them all."

"And the most vigorous interrogator, so Robin says," Merlin agreed. "If Geraint tried to win Robin over by bribery, then Hectimere tried to *threaten* him into giving up his secrets. Geraint's threats were veiled and hinted, Robin says, but Hectimere's were vivid and bloody, rising, he says, even to a kind of frenzy at times."

"Frenzy?" I murmured. "Hectimere?" The young man had always seemed so reticent, often unsure of himself. A sensitive lad, I'd always thought, when he was Gaheris's squire.

"Of course, the captors were limited in what they could do to Robin there in the cell, because the men on duty were soldiers of the King's Guard, and Robin was their commander, or had been at any rate. They were not going to allow the use of torture or beatings. But Robin says that Hectimere was most affected by the idea of Lancelot's bedding the queen. He seemed obsessed with seeing it as a re-creation of Sir Lamorak's bedding of Queen Margause in Orkney. Robin says he kept raving about how Lamorak had polluted the fair sweet flesh of the lady Margause and deserved to be hunted down and slain by the Orkney brothers, just as Lancelot deserved to be slain for his defiling of the fair Queen Guinevere. He was consumed, Robin claims, by the thought of the queen's body—Queen Margause, that is, but he was making the connection with Guinevere as well. Anyone who helped or excused Lancelot deserved what Lamorak got, and what all his supporters deserved: death without quarter."

I felt the blood run from my face, and my knees felt like water. This was the revelation I had needed to put all the pieces I'd gathered in Camelot together. "Of course!" I said. "Sir Gareth told me that

Hectimere had been with Gaheris when he'd caught his mother in bed with Lamorak. He was just a young squire at the time, and I'm sure it was a sight he never forgot: the queen's enticing body there in the bed, being sullied by the lust of that beastly Lamorak—for that's the way Gaheris must have talked about him. If Lamorak deserved to die, then why not his kinsmen as well? Mordred and Geraint had no use for them anymore, so why not let Hectimere avenge the honor of Queen Margause on Tor and Aglovale, Lamorak's hapless brothers? And something Geraint said to me as well—Hectimere was very skillful in a close fight, with sword or *knife*. Tor and Aglovale had their throats slit by a dagger."

Merlin nodded. "It does seem to come together. Remember when we interviewed witnesses after the battle in the churchyard? Most of them contradicted one another, but you remember that Sir Bedivere told us he thought he had seen Hectimere and Geraint close by Tor and Aglovale when Lancelot burst on the scene?"

"This is a close as we may get to proof," I suggested, leaping to my feet. "There's certainly enough here to take to Sir Gawain. It's more than a strong suspicion—it's real evidence."

"I wonder," Merlin said. "There is evidence here, it is true, that Hectimere had means, motive, and opportunity to kill the brothers of Sir Lamorak. But to truly convince Gawain, we probably need something to connect him to the deaths of Sir Gareth and Sir Gaheris as well. It won't be enough to simply say that we know one killer was there on the ground, who *may* have been responsible for all four deaths."

I sank down again to the tent floor, deflated. "Oh, damn. You may be right. And why would Hectimere kill his own former master? Wouldn't he be loyal to the Orkneys in general, as much as he would be to their mother specifically?"

"God's elbows, of course I'm right. But that's the right question to ask. Listen: The young, impressionable Hectimere was smitten with the naked beauty of Queen Margause—she was quite beautiful, you know, beautiful enough to have seduced the young King Arthur himself—and he witnessed his master Gaheris beheading that great beauty before his own tender eyes. Perhaps he suppressed that great resentment for years, until he finally saw his chance to avenge her on her slayer there in the churchyard, his bloodlust having been piqued by the murders of the sons of Pellinore."

"And Gareth?" I wondered. "Are we supposed to assume that he was simply in the wrong place at the wrong time?"

Merlin hung his head and grimaced. "I fear, if what we are imagining is in fact what happened, our friend Sir Gareth was merely collateral damage in this bloodbath."

At that my heart sank all the way into my stomach, which felt like it wanted to rise into my throat. My good master Gareth, the very best of men that I believe I have ever known, murdered simply because he was standing next to his matricide brother. It was almost more than I could bear, and I wanted to howl with grief and anger, but I didn't want to alarm the warriors outside the tent, gathered in the already tense situation of that siege, so I merely sobbed quietly into my hands, while Merlin, uncharacteristically, patted my shoulder in sympathy.

"Well," the old man said at length. "We have enough, I think, to convince Sir Gawain that his furious vengeance against Sir Lancelot is unwarranted. Someone on the ground, probably Sir Hectimere, used Lancelot's bloody onslaught as cover for his own darker deeds of murder, and it was he, not Lancelot, who struck down Sir Gaheris and…the good Sir Gareth. Are you finished with breakfast? It's time we took this to Gawain's tent. The sooner we remove his objections, the sooner we can convince the king to mount an invasion of his own land."

"And drive the bloody Saxons back into the sea," I muttered, still smarting from what we had concluded here this morning. I took one last bite at a piece of herring and rose to leave. But just as we had reached the tent opening, I froze and slapped myself on the forehead. I had just recalled something that had lain dormant in my mind for months.

"'The look that kills strikes from behind!'" I cried out.

Merlin sputtered and looked at me as if I had just spoken in Icelandic. "What on earth are you blithering on about, you numbskull?"

"That 'vision' of yours, the one you had when you got that spell in your cave, just before this business of Lancelot and the queen was discovered. Don't you remember?"

"I never remember those things," he scoffed. "What did I say?"

"You said 'The maiden rises again! The look that kills strikes from behind.'"

"And your point is…?"

"Hectimere," I said, as if it were self-evident. "His coat of arms! I saw it when I was watching him in the tilting yard at Camelot. He bears on his shield the crest of a basilisk, trippant on a field of gold."

"The basilisk," Merlin said, pulling thoughtfully on his beard. "A creature whose very look can strike one dead. A device he adopted, I'd wager, in reference to his own sight of Margause with Lamorak, a sight that resulted, in his imagination, in her being killed by her own son. In Hectimere's mind, his was literally a look that killed. And indeed, Tor and Aglovale, at least, were struck from behind. It's as if my mind knew the answer to this riddle before the riddle was ever posed. But what of the first part of the vision? Who is the maiden who rises again?"

"That I haven't thought about yet," I answered him. "But it seems we have more than our speculations to point to Hectimere as the slayer. We also have your own vaunted psychic powers!" At that Merlin rolled his eyes. "But what I don't understand is this: Always, in the past, you did not have these prophetic visions until we were well into a case, and you explained them as your mind working on the problem somewhere beneath your conscious thoughts, and then presenting the solution to you in cryptic fragments, as in a dream."

"A *somnium*," Merlin corrected me.

"But if that's the case, how could your mind possibly present you with the answer before we had even begun looking for it?"

Merlin raised his eyebrows and pressed his lips together in thought, and then, shrugging, pushed me out of the tent. "Oh well," he said. "Who knows how these things work? Let's go see Sir Gawain."

***

Sir Gawain's pavilion was a tall, colorful affair near the center of the camp and just next to that of the king, whom we were to visit at the conclusion of our interview with his nephew. A great red pentangle decorated the green panel next to the tent's opening—Gawain's famous coat of arms, symbolizing the strength in his five fingers, the keenness of his five senses, his following the five great courtly virtues (that is, generosity, courtesy, compassion, Christian love and purity of thought), and his faith in the five wounds of Christ and the five joys of the Virgin.

Of course, we knew that Gawain was at this point an invalid, unable to rise from his cot as a result of his ill-conceived duel with Sir Lancelot. And Merlin was of the opinion that unless we could sway Gawain from his monomaniacal focus on vengeance, the lord of Orkney would linger here until he felt strong enough to rise, to exercise, and to challenge Lancelot again. And that he would do this over and over if it came to that until he was dead. Everyone knew he could not beat Lancelot. Gawain himself knew he could not beat Lancelot. But Gawain's life had been shattered irreparably when Gareth died, and his mind and faith had nothing left to lean upon. But he must still be Gawain and dying at the hand of the Great Knight was a more honorable suicide than other alternatives.

At the door of the tent, to my delighted surprise, Sir Palomides and Sir Ywain stood guard. Palomides was exuberant in his greeting. "Gildas, my *bon ami*, what a delight it is to see you! You've come with news from Camelot perhaps? How fares the queen?"

"And has my worthless cousin made a hash of the kingdom yet as regent?" Sir Ywain asked, though his joking manner vanished quickly when he saw my face blanch and I looked to Merlin in a kind of panic. The old Necromancer answered for me:

"There are, indeed, some grave concerns regarding Sir Mordred's conduct as regent of the realm," Merlin said. "The queen, however, remains safe for now, to the best of our knowledge. Young Gildas has not yet had his audience with the king, and so cannot be any more specific in his report at the moment, even with you, Arthur's most trusted vassals. We may be able to reveal more to Sir Gawain, as first in line to the throne, if he is well enough to receive visitors."

Palomides looked shocked, and turned to stare at Ywain, whose face had become grim, even angry. "I should have known. Let a bloody villain like Mordred near the throne and he's bound to show his true colors—and his are red as blood and black as sin. Blast! Now I could kick myself for begging off when Arthur offered me the post. If Mordred brings shame to the throne then it's me as has to take the blame." The Knight of the Lion kicked the dirt and growled in his throat.

"No, no," I told Ywain soothingly. "Mordred is a villain, and he would have been causing trouble here instead of there if you yourself had taken the regent's office." Though to be brutally honest, I had to admit to myself that Ywain was absolutely right. With Ywain in charge at Camelot, the bastard would not have had the power or the opportunity to unleash the havoc he had done.

"But, er...to answer your question," Sir Palomides said, "the prince would certainly be feeling up to receiving you, Lord Merlin, and you as well, Sir Gildas, knowing you have come straight here from the regent's court. Though he may still be sleeping right now."

Merlin was a bit impatient, but I saw no reason to rush my interview with the king now that I was here and must unburden myself sometime this morning in any case. Right now I wanted to hear a little more about exactly how Gawain's life had been so nearly lost.

"My news can certainly wait half an hour," I assured Sir Palomides. "Let's sit over here around the fire, if we may, and you can tell me what has occurred here. Before I left Joyous Gard with the queen, Lancelot was steadfastly refusing to meet Gawain in single combat. When did that change?"

Sir Palomides pursed his lips thoughtfully for a moment, before he finally said, "Do you know the parable of the persistent widow, in Luke's gospel?"

"I, uh, think I remember something about it," I told the newly converted Moor, whose knowledge of Latin made him far more conversant in the scriptures than I.

"Then you remember in the story that the judge fears neither God nor man, but the widow so persistently appeals to him for justice that finally he just gives in. He doesn't do it because God has commanded that as a true judge he should dispense justice. He doesn't do it

208

because he wants the respect of those over whom he holds office. He does it because the widow is so bloody persistent that he just wants some peace. I suppose after months of Gawain nagging him every single day, calling him coward and traitor and all the rest, Lancelot finally just felt he wanted some peace."

"Either that," said Ywain, now coming slowly out of his ill humor, "or Bors and Ector and the others wore him down from the inside, telling him that he just couldn't go on this way, having Gawain shame him every day before Arthur's troops and his own. His honor was at stake. At least I'm fairly certain that's what Bors would have told him."

"Yes," Palomides conceded. "It may have been so. Or both together. At any rate, one day last week, Lancelot accepted Gawain's challenge. He didn't do it by shouting down from the castle wall, but much more formally and, I must say, courteously. He sent Sir Bors into our camp with a small entourage and carrying a flag of truce."

"Yes," I said. "So Merlin said. He was able to converse with Robin Kempe during that visit, I understand."

"Indeed," the mage agreed. "And as I recall, you were able to catch up with an old friend of your own, were you not, Palomides?"

"So I was," Palomides smiled his broad grin. "The king's former butler, Sir Lucan."

"I'd have popped him a good one on the top of his sneaky head, if it was me," said Ywain. "I mean, skipping out to join the enemy without so much as a 'by your leave.'"

Palomides waved Sir Ywain's suggested away, "No, no, it wasn't like that at all. I knew how devoted Lucan was to Sir Lancelot, because of his part in trying to help his niece Elizabeth. He was doing well. He takes comfort in knowing that his other niece, the lady Mary, is safe with the queen. Yet he still mourns his little Elizabeth. He told me, though, that he knows Sir Bedivere is even more devastated by Elizabeth's loss. Bedivere, he says, has never gotten over the shock. But that's neither here nor there, I'm getting off track in my story."

"So you are," Ywain said. "Get to it then or I'll tell it myself."

"It was negotiated," Palomides continued, looking askance at Ywain and preempting the Knight of the Lion's attempt to upstage

209

him, "that the following day at terce, Lancelot would ride out from his castle attended only by Sir Bors as his squire, and before the castle walls he would meet Sir Gawain in mortal combat, in a space marked out by boundaries one hundred yards long and twenty yards wide—long enough for a tilt on horseback. The king's army were free to witness the event from outside the marked-out boundary, and Sir Lancelot's from the walls of the castle. There would be no official referee, but the battle was to last until one of the combatants would yield to the other—or until one of them had been killed. And so it was arranged. And so it transpired.

"At terce last Wednesday morning, Sir Gawain rode into the marked-off tilting ground before the castle gate, in armor *cap-à-pie* and proudly riding his faithful pure-white Gringolet, his familiar red pentangle on his bright green shield and on his surcoat, and called up to the walls of the castle as he had every day since Gareth's death: 'Traitor knight! Come out and fight!' But this time he had an answer: The castle's portcullis opened and its drawbridge came down across the moat, and out rode a fully-armed Lancelot, mounted on his great black destrier Minuit, his golden fleur-de-lys shining on the azure field of his shield and on the blue background of his surcoat.

"Bors followed Lancelot out the gate, carrying two spare lances for the Great Knight, and without a word the two of them rode to the west end of the field—you see, Lancelot was giving Gawain the advantage, since in his initial charge Sir Gawain would have the sun at his back. Gawain rode to the other end, with Ywain here acting has his squire, carrying extra lances of his own."

Ywain nodded. "So I did, though truth to tell, I feared Gawain would never get beyond his first lance. I assumed Lancelot would knock him out of the saddle on his first pass."

"Which did not happen," Palomides continued, unwilling to give up the thread of the story. "Gawain used all his skill in that first pass, and in fact struck Lancelot a decent blow on his shield. But Sir Lancelot was unfazed, and had given Gawain a buffet as well, a blow strong enough to stagger him in the saddle, but Gringolet galloped on, and Gawain was able to right himself, and so reached the other end of the field still upright.

"And there, hoping to seize the advantage and take Lancelot by surprise, Gawain turned Gringolet about quickly and, spurring his steed on to full speed, bore down on Lancelot before he'd had time to ready himself. But Lancelot could not be shaken. He turned to see Gawain already in mid-charge, leaned forward and met the onslaught with his own best strength, though Minuit was only at half speed. Gawain, this time, had been charging into the sun, and that is what confounded his attack. The morning sunlight, glancing off Lancelot's helm, blinded Gawain momentarily, and his lance slid harmlessly off Lancelot's shield. But he had run directly into the Great Knight's own lance, and his own momentum flipped him forward off his horse and into the dirt."

"So is that where it ended? Lancelot gave him a blow to the head from horseback and stopped the fight?"

"Never!" Ywain broke in. "We're talking about Lancelot here, not some run-of-the mill bully. Sure, Lamorak would have probably done that. Even Tristram most likely. But this is Lancelot, the paragon of chivalry, right? The knight whose touch healed Sir Urry. Is he going to take advantage of a fallen enemy?"

"He is not," Palomides continued. "The fall stunned Sir Gawain, for sure, and he'd have been helpless had Lancelot taken his advantage then and there. But instead, what does he do? He dismounts, so as to ensure he and Gawain are on equal footing again. And he doesn't simply wait until Gawain recovers himself and stands on his own. He *helps* Sir Gawain to his feet, lets him pause to get his breath and shake the cobwebs out of his head, which has got to be ringing from that fall, I'm sure. And then he makes sure that Gawain is recovered enough to draw his sword and handle it. And he makes sure Gawain has picked up his shield, which naturally had flown out of his fist when he took that fall. Now Gawain looks at Lancelot, and he's got tears in his eyes over the Great Knight's great courtesy…"

"Literally!" Sir Ywain interjected. "I was there on the field—I could see the glistening in his eyes!"

"But he shakes it off and gets into a fighting position and says, 'Enough, Traitor Knight! Have at you now, I challenge you to the utterance!' And with a sigh, Lancelot draws his sword and takes a defensive posture. Gawain lays on with stroke after stroke on Lancelot's shield, while Lancelot keeps fending him off and returning perhaps one blow for every two from Gawain. But against all odds, Gawain did not wear down; rather, he kept getting stronger, and kept redoubling his blows at Lancelot's head, which the Great Knight kept taking the brunt of on his shield. And this went on, I do not exaggerate, from terce all the way to sext, with Gawain—fueled by anger and grief—carrying his attack to his utmost power, so that by sext, Lancelot was barely able to hold Gawain off."

"You know," Ywain interjected, "they say that Gawain has always had the special power to increase his strength as the sun rises in the sky, so that when the sun is at its height, then Gawain's power is at its greatest strength. But as the sun begins to sink, so does Sir Gawain's vigor. And it certainly began to decline after sext that day."

Merlin's face remained blank and he tried very hard not to roll his eyes as he muttered between his teeth, "Or, we could say that Gawain's fury kept him keen to wreak harm on Lancelot until he'd completely exhausted himself."

"For whatever reason," Palomides continued diplomatically, "Gawain's strength was spent by sext, and Lancelot now had his way with Sir Gawain. He strode forward against Gawain, landing stroke after stroke on shield, helmet, and shoulder, until Gawain sank to his knees, and Lancelot landed one last blow to Gawain's head so powerful that it dented his helmet and cracked Gawain's skull. Blood poured from the wound down Gawain's brow, and he slumped forward, the weight of his armor causing his arms and chest to drag him toward the earth. Lancelot put up his sword and stepped back."

"The battle, it was agreed, was to be to the utterance," Ywain reminded us. "One of the combatants had to yield to the other or be killed. Lancelot stepped back, thinking Gawain had no choice but to yield. But if he expected to get that satisfaction from Gawain, he would be standing there still."

Sir Palomides cleared his throat. He had a different perspective. "Gawain was badly beaten," he said. "The wound on his head could have been mortal. He is only now, five days later, just out of immediate danger of death, and the doctors have cautiously said that he may live to ride and carry a sword again. Lancelot could have killed him then and there, and ended this war. But he merely stood back impassively as Gawain shouted at him, 'What are you waiting for? Finish it now!' Thus pleaded with Lancelot to end his life."

"He begged for Lancelot to stop his pain," Sir Ywain said quietly.

"And Lancelot?" I asked.

"Lancelot listened to Gawain's pleas for a few more moments, then he sheathed his sword, remounted his horse, and rode back into Benwick Castle, followed by Bors. And the gates were closed. Lancelot had never spoken a word. The battle was over."

There was silence for a few breaths, and then Ywain made one last addition to the story. "And Gawain was taken straight from the field to his pavilion, and he has lain unmoving here ever since. That's five days. And he's taking nothing but occasional sips of cold water and a bite or two of bread each day. The leech that was here this morning had high hopes for his complete recovery from his wounds, but Gawain seems indifferent as to whether he lives or dies, and insists that if he *does* recover, he will challenge Lancelot again, and will do so until one of them is dead."

"Stubborn Orkney pride," Merlin muttered.

"Not pride," Ywain said quietly. "Despair. Sir Gawain has nothing more to live for."

I grunted at that. "Well," I suggested, "it may be that we have brought him just what he needs: a reason to live."

"And what would that be?" Sir Palomides asked.

"A chance to restore the honor of the Orkney name," Merlin said. "Let us go in to see him."

***

Sir Gawain lay in the dim shadows of his pavilion, alone save for a small page who crouched near the doorway, and looked up at us with curious eyes as we stepped into the tent. The king's nephew was lost in a pile of costly furs, though it was certainly warm enough in Benwick, as we moved into spring and the lusty month of May. But Gawain shivered occasionally and drew the furs around him as if it were mid-winter. He was clearly far from well, despite his doctors' optimism, and his face looked gray in those shadows. His head was swathed in a wide white bandage stained with blood, and although his breath was coming in puffs and gasps, he kept his eyes closed as if he were asleep. But he had seen us enter and addressed us with a voice that rasped like long unused hinges.

"Old Necromancer, what have you come to torment me with now? Are you going to say 'I told you so' about my fight with Lancelot? And you, Gildas of Cornwall. Returned from Camelot are you? I suppose you've brought news to the king about what's going on there?"

"I have, my lord, and serious business it is, too," I told him, though Merlin grabbed my shoulder and gave it a squeeze to stop my tongue. I understood that he, as usual, wanted to take the lead in this confrontation.

"Well go tell it to the king, then. Why bother me with it? I don't care what trouble my brother Mordred has gotten himself into on the regent's throne. My only task is to exact vengeance from Lancelot. Now go, and stop disturbing my rest." With that Gawain rolled slightly under his furs to turn away from us.

"My lord," Merlin began. "We wanted to look in on you to see whether you were healing as well as your leeches say. Young Gildas was not present to witness your adventure in single combat with Lancelot," at that word Gawain gave a snort, "and expressed the desire to see for himself whether we could have hope of your recovery, and we both wanted to renew our devotion to you as heir apparent to the throne of Logres. Do you lack for anything, lord, that we might do to help you?"

At that Sir Gawain rolled back toward us, opening his green eyes and gazing up at the mage with a quizzical expression. "What are you playing at, Old Man?" he asked. "You've done nothing the past month but chide me for my obsession with making Lancelot pay for my brothers' deaths. Now that I have fought him and been beaten, you speak me fair? Out with it. Tell me what you really want."

"My lord Gawain," Merlin replied. "You would hear no advice from me about revenge being a hollow, fruitless pursuit, and you

insisted on going ahead with your vendetta. Very well, I shall make
no more arguments on that subject. But if you are bent on continuing
with this obsession I am here to argue that it is in fact misplaced."

Gawain's eyes opened wide in surprise. "What do you mean
misplaced? Lancelot killed my brothers, and so I will kill Lancelot."

"If I may point out what is perhaps obvious, my lord, it is far more
likely that he will kill you. But that is not what I am here to talk
about. I am here to tell you that you are mistaken about Lancelot. It
was not he who killed Gareth and Gaheris."

"What trickery is this, Old Man? Everyone in that churchyard
witnessed it. Lancelot charged in, and when the dust had settled my
brothers were dead."

"Gareth and Gaheris were killed by somebody on the ground, not
on horseback," I blurted out. When Gawain's eyes widened and he
stared at me as if I must be a raving lunatic, I added, "We examined
the bodies afterward. The wounds were not inflicted from above."

When Gawain's skeptical eyes turned back to Merlin, the old man
continued in the same vein. "It's true, my lord. I examined both bodies
closely. They were stabbed in the back. True, they were hacked with
swords later, to make it appear they had been killed that way, but
they were already dead, but through treachery, not the swordplay
of Lancelot's charge. What's more, we found that King Pellinore's
sons, Sir Tor and Sir Aglovale, were slain in a similar manner, killed
from behind by someone on the ground. The four murders seem to
be related."

"And we believe we know now who the killer was," I was quick
to add. And with that, Merlin launched into a long explanation of
the case we had put together against Sir Hectimere, and Gawain,
astounded by this new development, listened to the whole story
without interrupting. When we had finished, he grunted.

"So if I'm to believe you," he said his weak voice barely above
a whisper, "then it's Hectimere I should be challenging to single
combat now, and not Lancelot at all? So I've put my life on the line
for nothing here?"

Merlin, somewhat surprised by Gawain's reaction, scowled down
at Gawain, not knowing what to expect next. "Indeed," he answered

somewhat cautiously, "that is certainly one way to look at it. In any case, the vendetta against Lancelot seems misplaced now, I should think, in the light of this new evidence. In fact, it may even be your own brother Mordred who is behind all of this, if Hectimere was acting on his behalf."

"Now let me tell you this, Old Man," Gawain said, closing his eyes. "Hectimere or no Hectimere, Mordred or no Mordred, Sir Lancelot did, without question, kill my brother Agravain, as well as my beloved son Lovell. And if the whole truth be told, no one on the field that day would have had the opportunity to slay Sir Gareth and Sir Gaheris had it not been for the melee caused by Sir Lancelot's brutal charge into that churchyard to rescue the queen. So no, I do not forgive Lancelot. And I would still rather die at his hand than go back to Camelot and try to carry on bereft of every human relationship that sustained me."

"I daresay your devoted cousin Sir Ywain would be sorry to hear that," I broke in curtly. "But you say nothing concerning the possibility of your brother Mordred's involvement in this affair. And he's also the one that got Agravain and Lovell slain when they unwisely tried to hold Sir Lancelot at bay."

"Mordred is ignoble, there is no doubt," Gawain had to concede. "But he is no fratricide, of that I am certain. Nor was his the hand that slew my son, or my dear, dear Gareth. No, the honor of the Orkney family will not be satisfied until I bring down the Great Knight." Gawain's rasping voice choked on his tears.

"You may revise your opinion of your remaining brother when you hear the news that Sir Gildas has brought to the king from Camelot," Merlin resumed his argument.

Gawain closed his eyes again in mute frustration. "What's the boy done now?" He asked quietly.

"Mordred has spent his time as regent making alliances with all of the enemies of Logres: with the Picts, the Irish, and the Saxons especially," I told him. "He has amassed a mighty army with his new allies, whose sole purpose is to dethrone the king. But he hasn't even had the decency to wait until Arthur is defeated to claim the throne in his own right. He's let it be known by public proclamation that he was assuming the kingship himself, giving as his justification to the court the lie that Arthur has been killed in battle with Sir Lancelot—and furthermore that you, Your Grace, as heir apparent, have been killed as well. To top it off, he has disavowed his marriage to Lady Rosemounde, repudiating her, and is trying to marry Guinevere, as Arthur's 'widow,' to further legitimize his claim to the throne."

Gawain's mouth hung open for a moment, then he closed it and his eyes once more, clutched the furs around him and turned away. After a moment he choked out his pronouncement: "Surely the king's only recourse now is to take his army back to Logres at his earliest opportunity. I…shall not attempt to hold him here any longer. You may tell him, when you bring him this news, that I shall not hold him to his vow to support my vendetta against Lancelot. Now go and leave me to myself."

CHAPTER FIFTEEN

INVASION

"I've just woken from a terrible dream," King Arthur told us as we entered his tent. "Indeed, the most disturbing dream I have ever dreamt." He was haggard and wan, and his skin looked greyer than his hair in the dim light inside his pavilion. The pallet on which he'd slept looked as if a stampeding herd of wild horses had trampled it into chaos.

"Restless night, Your Majesty?" Merlin asked unnecessarily. There were two young pages in the king's tent, standing by the inner door, and one of these had a pitcher of wine he was bringing to a small table next to the bed. This one gave Merlin a cross-eyed look as if to say "You don't know the half of it" in response to the old man's question.

"Can you tell us the matter of the dream, Your Highness?" I asked as the king ran his hands through his tangled hair and shook his head as if to knock the dust and cobwebs from his brain. Then suddenly his eyes lit up as he finally recognized who I was. "Gildas! What... when did you arrive? You have messages from the queen? Or from Mordred? Are there things in Camelot that require my attention? My God, this nightmare remains in my head and makes me fear to ask..."

"Tell us your dream, my Lord," Merlin cajoled. "It is better to let the dawn shine on these night terrors, the better to disperse them, before settling down to face the practical realities of the day. What was there in this dream that caused you alarm, Your Grace?"

Now the king drew the back of his hand over his eyes as if dazed.

Clearly he was still groggy from sleep, and I realized Merlin had been right to wait before bringing him this news of mine. He'd had a restless night, though it seemed that the sleep he'd had this morning had brought him no rest. "Trying to recall…" he muttered. "It was a ship. I was on a ship, trying to steer it through a great storm. There was thunder and lightning all about—and the queen was at my side. At least I believed it was Guinevere. But…now I recall…the ship ran aground on the rocks, and I thought that I had sunk her, and the queen was nearly washed away by the waves. I called for her but she could not hear me over the thunder and the howling of the storm. Then I saw her rise from the waves and return to the deck of the ship—only it was no longer her. Her hair had changed from fair to black, and her face was the face of my sister Margause."

"Gawain's mother?" I said. "Could the dream have been about Sir Gawain, then?" But Merlin glared at me and hissed, "Quiet, boy!"

If the king had heard me, he showed no sign of it. He only continued his reverie: "She shoved me aside, so that I fell to the deck, and she began steering the ship wildly, so that I was sure she was going to sink her—in fact, deliberately intended to sink her. When I came up behind her to try to wrest the wheel from her hand once more, she turned on me with a face twisted with hatred and evil, and in her hand she held a long knife, with which she began to stab at me, landing blow after blow until I was bleeding from every part of my body. I knew I was going to die, and that the ship would be wrecked, and with my last breath I shouted out to her, asking 'Why? Why?' and she answered me with a cackle, as if she were demon-possessed or a bloody witch, and only said, 'You know why!'"

The king paused and sat at the small table, taking the wine in a silver goblet, and drank it down with a shaking hand. After a few moments, Merlin inclined his head toward him and asked, "And what do you think this dream means, my lord?"

Arthur gave a bitter laugh and looked up at him. "You tell me! You're the necromancer aren't you? Don't you have some special talent for such things?"

Merlin gave a tight, close-mouthed smile, and began with a learned observation. "This is no mere nightmare, my liege. It is surely a

219

meaningful dream, of the sort that the philosopher Macrobius would call a *somnium*—a dream whose meaning is shrouded in symbols and needs to be interpreted. The ship, I would venture to say, no doubt represents the kingdom of Logres, which you and the queen have endeavored to rule wisely and benevolently, to steer it safely we might say, for many years."

The king looked up, then shrugged as if to say that much was obvious. He took another drink of wine and commented, "I hope you can see more in it than that, Old Man. What message is God trying to send me with this *somnium* as you call it?"

Merlin lowered his brows a bit and said, "The dream has meaning I'm sure, Your Majesty, but I cannot say that it is prophetic. Its meaning, I think, has more to do with your own fears and forebodings. Why do you think your sister Margause has black hair in the dream?"

"Yes!" I couldn't help adding. "She was fair haired and blue-eyed, was she not? Just like my dear master Sir Gareth?"

"Indeed she was," Arthur agreed. "But her black hair made her look more like…" and then his face fell in a moment of realization.

"More like her other son, Sir Mordred," Merlin said quietly. "To whom you have given control of the kingdom. And whom, as this dream should tell you, you fear will destroy the realm, and you with it."

The king slumped in his chair and shook his head from side to side, not in disagreement but in a kind of helpless judgment on his own actions, which he now feared had been foolish. "I thought to give him responsibility in the hope that he would prove himself worthy. I felt…responsible."

As well he should, I thought. "You know why," Margause had said to him in the dream. Of course he knew why Mordred would try to destroy him. He had set the child Mordred adrift in a boat, along with the other babes who'd been born around the bastard's birthday. And all had died but Mordred. His unsuccessful attempt to murder his own child had failed and had now come back to haunt him. Why else had the dream taken place on a boat? Of course he'd been young and had listened to unscrupulous advisers, but some sins you just don't get to excuse yourself from. Still, this was no time to chide the king for past transgressions. I spoke up but not about any of that. "What about the queen?" I asked. "In the dream, she is lost at sea and replaced by Mordred's mother. Does this mean that you fear she is in danger from your regent?"

Arthur stiffened, then rose from the chair to look me full in the face. "Fear for the queen has been nagging at the back of my mind for weeks. But as you might recall," now his voice was gaining in power and confidence and he was truly becoming the king again, "that was the reason I sent *you* along with her, Sir Gildas of Cornwall. I think it is time that you stop holding back and tell me just why it is you have come here, and what precisely is going on in Camelot."

Indeed, the time had come for me to unbuckle my burden. I could only hope that Arthur would have the good sense to separate the message from the messenger. But I was never happier to have Merlin with me.

"Your Imperial Highness," I began, "your dream indeed may be called prophetic—or as my lord Merlin would rather say, your fears are well founded." The king's eyes narrowed and he sat up as if knowing he was about to receive a blow and was determined not to flinch when it landed. "The bastard Mordred has usurped your authority and has declared himself to be king of Logres."

Arthur's head snapped back and he looked up in anger. His open hand slapped the table in front of him, making the wine goblet quiver as if in trepidation. "Outrageous!" he bellowed. "How can he possibly justify such a claim? And why would any of the people follow him?"

"Because," I said, bowing my head and instinctively backing away a bit from the king's vehemence, "he has produced forged letters that purport to claim that you, Your Highness, have been slain in Benwick by Lancelot's armies—and that Sir Gawain has perished a well. And he has rallied the people to arm themselves and to fortify the southern coast in preparation for a likely invasion from Gaul—an invasion, he warns, by Lancelot and his host."

The king let out a frustrated cry and rose from his seat, then put his hands on his hips and began to pace around the tent, shaking his head in exasperation. "Fortify the coasts! He wants my own people to block my return to my throne! But how can he expect to carry

221

this off? When the people see that it is their rightful king returning, they will abandon their defenses, and rally to join me as I march on Camelot to bring Mordred to justice!"

I glanced toward Merlin, who tilted his head in the direction of the pacing monarch and raised the tangled mass of his eyebrows as if to say, "Hit him again, he hasn't got it yet."

"My lord," I continued. "Your own Britons are only a small part of Mordred's assembled army. Knights under Sir Geraint's banner have been used to fortify the castle itself, and beyond that…well, Mordred began making alliances with your former enemies the moment he assumed the reins of government. He has made agreements with the Picts, with the Irish, and with the Saxons to support his rule in exchange for their own independence, and armies of your foes have by now gathered into a significant force to be arrayed against you when you return to Logres. Indeed, my Lord, it is an army of Saxons that now defends the shores of Kent and Sussex."

The king reddened. He slumped back into his chair and stared glumly at me. After a moment, he said, "Gildas, you've done me and the queen many services in the past. But the news you have brought me this day may be the worst service ever done to me. If I were a less chivalrous king, I would have the tongue cut out of your mouth, as no doubt my father Uther Pendragon would have done."

Now Merlin stepped in to save me further embarrassment. "God's earlobes, Arthur, you can't blame the boy for bringing you the truth about what your own recklessness has brought upon you! Whose lust was it that begot the sniveling little brat, Mordred, in the first place? Who tried to cover up his mistake by having the boy killed? Who was it allowed your nephew's obsession with revenge to tear a breach in the Round Table and alienate you from your greatest supporter in Sir Lancelot? And who allowed the distraction of this battle to cloud your judgment in putting your greatest enemy on your own throne? Not Gildas, my king, not he. Look at your own figure in a glass if you want to see who has brought you to this pass."

Rest assured, there was only one man alive who could ever talk to King Arthur in this manner and expect to live, and that was my lord Merlin. And even he had better not try it more than once. But this was the time for it, and Arthur himself recognized the truth in the mage's words. He stood up, his jaw thrust out, and glared at the old necromancer with ill-concealed fury. "And who is it, then, who must undo all of this madness, and lance the boil of the kingdom I have made into a desert? Boy!" he called to the page who had brought the wine. "Bring me Excalibur! The time is come for me to gird on my sword and address my troops. We will end this charade, this spurious war with Lancelot. We must prepare for a full-scale invasion of Logres. We will need ships, and we will need to rally our allies here. Sir Gawain may resist, and some of my army will want to stay with him. But I shall carry out this invasion with any who will follow me!" He looked from me to Merlin and then back again. "Even if the only ones who follow are the two of you!" He smiled wanly and said, "Sir Gildas, I spoke discourteously to you, but only because I was impotent to lash out at those who have truly harmed me: Sir Mordred and...myself. I trust you will pardon me, and I thank you for your pains in bringing me this news. It occurs to me now that you may have been at some risk to escape Logres and find me!"

"Yes, Your Grace," I shrugged modestly. "There was some danger involved. And my lord," I paused again, since there was still one bit of news I had not delivered, "I escaped with Queen Guinevere. For you must know, Your Highness, that Mordred has determined, the better to bolster his claim on the throne, to marry himself to the queen. He has convinced the people that she is a widow, and he has cast off his own wife, Lady Rosemounde. But the queen escaped with me and has fled to the Tower of London. Your sister Morgan has also fled, to the Lady of the Lake. And I have bestowed Rosemounde to a place of safety in Cornwall. And I have come, through the aid of your faithful vassal King Mark, to bring you all this news."

The king actually grinned at this last revelation. "So there's fight in the old girl yet, eh?" He said and laughed. "Guinevere has gone to the Tower—our dear Mordred will have to waste half his army besieging her there! Good show, my queen, good show."

"Indeed my liege, the queen has shown her true colors in this case," I said. "And she ought to be safe, at least for the near future. The question is, my Lord, what will you do now?"

Arthur scowled in thought and then ran his right hand over his face. "We must move as quickly as we can, but we must be prudent as well. There are three things, as I see it, that must be considered carefully before we make any moves at all: First, Sir Gawain must be persuaded to give up this ill-conceived war on Lancelot and be convinced to lend his full support to this endeavor. Secondly, we must gather as many supporters as we can to our cause—if Mordred has the allies you say he has, we will be badly outnumbered if we try to storm the beaches of Logres with the force we now have. And we can't very well ask Lancelot to join us."

I saw Merlin's eyebrows rise meaningfully at that point, but he said nothing for the moment. And the king plunged ahead. "Third, we must have a strategy for the invasion. If the Saxons occupy the beaches in Kent, we must find another landing place where we can gain a better foothold on the beach before Mordred and his barbarians realize we have landed."

Merlin cleared his throat. "We have already met with Sir Gawain. He has been convinced to support you in this fight."

I cleared my throat in turn. "Well, what he said was he would not try to keep you here any longer and released you from any vow you made to support his war against Lancelot," I corrected Merlin, who glared at me from beneath eyebrows lowered like thunderclouds. "To be precise," I added, a bit chagrined.

"The fact is," Merlin continued, "my blabbermouth young numbskull of an assistant and I have been investigating the deaths of Gareth and Gaheris, as well as Sir Tor and Sir Aglovale, since the morning of their deaths, and we are convinced that all four of them were killed by someone on the ground, murdered from behind, and not struck down from above by anyone charging through on horseback..."

This assertion, taken for granted for some months now by Merlin and me, came as a complete surprise to the king, whose head jerked back and eyes bulged out at the revelation. "You...*what?*" he demanded. "What are you saying? Sir Lancelot is not responsible for Gareth's death after all? Why do you claim such a thing?"

"He and Gaheris were stabbed in the back by a small blade,"

Merlin said. "A dagger. The weapon of a coward who attacks without warning from behind."

"And we believe we know who the murderer is," I added. "The evidence points to Mordred's minion, Sir Hectimere!"

Merlin held out his hands to caution me. "At least we believe him to be responsible for the deaths of Tor and Aglovale. It seems likely that the murders of Gareth and Gaheris are connected."

Arthur's face grew stern and cold, and I saw the muscles of his jaw clench tightly. "So Mordred's scheme to seize the kingdom has been laid out at least that long, then. This puts a whole new light on things." He paused. "Gawain is with us, then?"

"Y…yes Your Grace," Merlin agreed tentatively. "He will join you in your fight against Mordred."

"But who else will?" Arthur asked as he began to pace the tent again. "Sir Gildas, you say the southeast beaches are all fortified by Saxon armies, yet you yourself were able to cross here from the Cornish coast. Does that seem a feasible place to land an army, would you say?"

"King Mark still holds the shores of Cornwall, Your Majesty, and he remains loyal to you. If you land an army there, he will lend a good portion of his own troops to bolster your own forces, I am certain of it, my Lord."

"Yes, that's good, Gildas. It's difficult to know, especially from this distance, which of my vassals are true and which may have gone over to the usurper."

"What of Duke Hoel, Your Highness?" Merlin recommended. "He has always been a true supporter of yours."

The king frowned in thought. "Of course, Mordred was his son-in-law, so there is an oath of allegiance there. But since Mordred has abandoned his wife, he may have an even greater desire to punish the usurper for breaking his own marriage oath!"

"And the Bretons have ships, my Lord. Send to Brittany, to Saint-Malo, and Duke Hoel will surely send enough ships to transport your whole army, and a large force of his own to help our cause."

Arthur pursed his lips. "I shall issue orders immediately to have these steps carried out. We really have no time to lose, as it will take at least a few weeks to gather troops here and to set sail, and at least another week of forced marches to bring an army toward Camelot. I must call a meeting of my senior advisers—you of course, Lord Merlin, and Ywain and Palomides, Kay and Bedivere, Gawain of course if he can be moved. They must know all these developments, and perhaps they can contribute ideas of their own to help us make our plans. But we must begin this process quickly."

With his head bowed slightly, as if he meant to bring up an unwelcome subject, Merlin stepped forward. "My liege," he began, "I think it might be worth reconsidering Sir Lancelot. Knowing his great courtesy, and his longtime devotion to you and…and to the queen, there is at least a possibility that he would march with your army as an ally…"

"Out of the question," Arthur waved off the possibility. "He has betrayed me with my wife. He has killed my knights. He has besmirched my honor!" And Arthur's voice grew higher with this last point, manifesting clearly which of these things hurt him the most. Then in a calmer voice, he added, "And I have made war upon him, and besieged him. Twice. And taken the queen back from him, at the Pope's urging. And allowed my nephew to berate him and challenge him daily, and to do battle with him with the avowed purpose of killing him. And if all of that isn't enough," the king continued, stifling Merlin's last attempt to slip in one more word in Lancelot's favor before Arthur dismissed us from his presence, "if I sue to Lancelot, Gawain will desert me, with all his supporters. No, Lord Merlin, I am going to alert my guard that they are to convene an assembly of my closest advisers to meet today at none. In the meantime, you are to compose messages that can be sent to King Mark in Cornwall and Duke Hoel in Brittany. Now you may leave us."

And on that note of finality, Merlin and I exited the king's pavilion to make our way back to Merlin's, and to a supply of ink and parchment. "God's bloody wounds," Merlin fumed as he stomped at my side through the camp. "Without Lancelot we will lose this war. It is that simple."

***

Despite Merlin's gloomy pronouncement, I felt some degree of hope over the next several days as the siege camp began to bustle into activity. Arthur's other senior advisers had little more to offer, but most were happy to abandon this futile war on Lancelot and rededicate themselves to a true cause, the cause of restoring Arthur to his rightful throne and putting down the usurper. Even Gawain was ready to turn his sword to nobler work, despite the fact that it involved defeating his own brother. Mordred was a brother, in Gawain's view, who only brought shame upon the Orkney name, and would be better brought low—though he was not eager to see the bastard, the last bounty of his mother's womb, extinguished, having borne the loss of every one of his other siblings.

The only one in the camp who objected to abandoning the siege of Benwick was, strangely enough, Sir Bedivere, who argued that Mordred could wait, that the chief blot on the honor of Camelot was the continued existence of the traitor and adulterer, Sir Lancelot. All Arthur's legacy, he said, would be stained by this knight who had been his chief supporter. Nothing anyone could say could change Sir Bedivere's mind, nor did he ever alter his opinion the entire time we prepared to sail for Logres.

Duke Hoel had responded to the king's request with incredible speed. Just three weeks from the time Arthur had sent his swiftest messenger to Brittany, an armada arrived off Benwick, led by Kaherdin, the duke's natural son and my lady Rosemounde's half-brother, who had been commander of the garrison at Saint-Malo. The fleet consisted of some forty cog vessels, each roughly fifty feet long and twenty-five feet wide. These were single-masted vessels, clinker-built from oak planks. Each ship had a five-member crew, and ten of the ships brought another fifteen Breton soldiers apiece; thus in all Hoel had sent Arthur one hundred and fifty soldiers in addition to two hundred sailors to support his cause. The other thirty ships had room for another four hundred fifty—enough to take Arthur's entire army and attendants to the beaches of Cornwall. Half of the ships had a cargo of grain and other foodstuffs that the duke had provided to help with the feeding of the army as it traveled across the Narrow Sea into Logres, and the cargo areas of the other ships were empty, so as to provide room for Arthur's knights to bring their great war horses back to Logres: They would, of course, be needed when Arthur finally faced Mordred in the field. And that was important. I wasn't about to leave Achilles there at Benwick castle.

As for the messenger sent to Cornwall, who had returned to Mark's kingdom on the very ship that had brought me to Benwick, we had no way of knowing whether he had reached Tintagel. Thus we did not know whether to expect word back from Mark or not, the state of things in Logres being far more up in the air than those in Brittany. But the chief decision that must be made now that the fleet had arrived was where to land the army on Cornwall's shores. From anywhere in Mark's kingdom it would be at least a five-day march to the neighborhood of Camelot, where we must assume Mordred intended to make his stand. The king wanted to do battle at his soonest opportunity, so as to engage with only those forces Mordred had currently at his disposal. Any lengthy delay would allow the bastard to seek further reinforcements from Ireland, from Scotland, or from Saxony, so Arthur's best hope was to strike now, to land his army in Cornwall and to gather additional supporters to his invading force from the countryside of southwest Logres as he marched toward Camelot.

By the time Duke Hoel's armada had landed, Sir Gawain was enough recovered to take light exercise, walking about the camp and meeting in Arthur's pavilion with Merlin and the king's other advisers, and to pore with them over a map of Logres' southern shore and debate the merits and drawbacks of every inlet along the Cornish coast. Finally the decision was made to steer for Plymouth, whose large natural harbor provided plenty of room for the entire fleet to land easily, and, while technically in Devon on the border of Mark's kingdom, it was by virtue of that location closest to Camelot itself, and so would provide the army with the quickest route to the battlefield. And the sailing time would be shorter as well. Plymouth was some 175 nautical miles from Benwick. Of course, everything depended on the winds, but if we had a favorable breeze we could make a good six knots, and that meant we could be in Plymouth in just two days.

That meant that, once we sailed, we could be facing Mordred on the field of battle in just over a week from the time we broke camp. All told that would make it something like two months from the time I'd left Camelot. Mordred could not have had time to gather huge additional numbers under his banner. Nor was it likely that he could be aware that I had been able to win through and warn the king, or that the king would have been flexible enough to have moved so swiftly. Nor could he possibly suspect where I had bestowed Lady Rosemounde. I could only hope that the forces he had accumulated before our escape would not be overwhelming in the face of the king's invasion.

Merlin was quite happy these days being busied with the details of planning the invasion and determining just who was going to make the voyage on which ships and how the cargo and the horses were going to be stored in the fleet, and so I was happy to leave him to it, and on the eve of the day set for our departure, I spent a bit of time catching up with my old friend and rival squire, Sir Thomas.

Thomas had his own pavilion, while I was lodging with Merlin, and so I met him in his tent and he ordered us some bread, newly baked from the grain brought on Duke Hoel's ships; one of the large codfish that had been caught earlier that day in the Narrow Sea; and the dregs of a barrel of local red Argences wine he and Palomides had purchased earlier in the siege from a nearby abbey that was, frankly, not the best I've had. But that was all right. This was likely to be the last chance we had to carouse a bit before committing ourselves to the sea journey, the long march, and the battle for Logres, which, it must be admitted, we would not be certain of surviving, though we were keeping that thought well buried in the cacophony of detritus that occupied our minds in that turbulent time.

"And the lady Rosemounde," Thomas probed, chewing on an overdone piece of cod and fixing me with his clear blue eyes. "What have you done with her to keep her safe in this turmoil that Mordred's created with his rejection of his wife and pursuit of the queen? I know that must have been a great concern for you…"

"The number one concern from the moment I heard it," I confided to him. "If he could cast her off like that, he could kill her without a thought. I had to get her out of Camelot, and away from the queen, because the first place the bastard would look for her would be at Guinevere's side. I've got her safe somewhere that Mordred will never think to look for her. And I haven't told a soul so don't expect me to tell you, no matter how much of this lousy wine you ply me with." And with that I took a long swallow of the vile stuff.

"Not asking!" Thomas held up his hand and shook his head so vigorously that his sandy hair—not so close-cropped as he usually kept it, there being few barbers at the siege of Benwick—flapped from side to side.

"Good," I replied, "because if I did tell you, I'd have to kill you. Nobody, I mean nobody, is going to get at Rosemounde if I can help it."

"What about the queen? She's safe too, I hear?"

"Locked up tight in the Tower of London, as far as I know," I replied, biting off a hunk of that fresh-baked white wastel bread. "Mmm," I said appreciatively. "That's good bread. Almost makes up for the wine."

"Almost," Thomas agreed. Then he moved on to what I knew was the topic he'd been politely holding back as he'd dutifully queried me on the things closest to my own heart. "And what can you tell me about the lady Mary? Did she leave Camelot in the company of the queen as well?" He asked almost as if he was indifferent to the answer, casually chewing an apple for dessert and looking away, but furtively darting his eyes back at mine with a barely concealed intensity.

I reached out to hold his left forearm, the better to convince him that the pretense was unnecessary. "Your Mary is safe," I assured him. "She went off with the queen, in the company of Lady Anne and Vivien and the others. They are safe in the Tower, which is well-fortified and defended by guards loyal to the king. And...she sends her love." If I could say that for him, I could make it up for her as well. I had no doubt she would have done so given the opportunity.

Thomas nodded, his eyes glistening with tears of relief. "She's a lively girl," he said. "But since her sister's death—her sister's murder—I've been worrying about her more and more. She's up and down with her moods, sometimes chatty, sometimes morose. I...I suppose it will improve with time, as all things must."

I thought to myself that there was no telling whether things would ever improve or not, but I didn't want to depress him, so I kept that observation to myself. And he went on, "The rest of her family are all handling Elizabeth's death in their own way, I guess, and some better than others. Her uncle Lucan, of course, is with Lancelot, but as far as I can tell has taken it the most calmly and has come to grips with it by now. Her father, Sir Lowell, was certainly distraught at first, and then he had the death of his master Sir Gaheris to deal with as well, but he seems to have accepted it all as God's will, I guess."

Why any of us would ever care about a God whose will was to have our child and our master murdered I have never been able to understand, and it's not something I'd ever say, even here in this holy place, but if that kind of poppycock gives some people comfort, then let them have their fairy tale, I say. I won't put it down, at least where they can hear me.

"It's her uncle Bedivere we're all most worried about," Thomas continued. "There've been times he's seemed almost mad with grief. And he hasn't let it go at all. Why, did I tell you how I found him that morning after Lancelot led his cavalry charge into the churchyard to rescue the queen from burning?"

"No," I said with some interest. That black day had been the harbinger of so many subsequent calamities that one more just seemed appropriate at this point. "How *did* you find him?"

Thomas shook his head and closed his eyes as if calling up the vision as he had seen it that day. "He was wandering alone among the corpses in the churchyard. His face was haggard, and his eyes were staring ahead but didn't seem to be seeing anything. It was like he was in a trance, bewitched or dazed or some such thing."

"Shock, I suppose, at the carnage of that field. I was sick myself."

"But there was more than that. Bedivere was holding up his sword, and it was covered in blood."

"He must have had a good chance to fight off some of those knights of Lancelot's, didn't he?" I responded. "He was closest of all of us to the queen herself, wasn't he?"

"He was," Thomas nodded. "But I don't think that's what was on his mind. When I found him, I took some time to calm him, and took the sword gently out of his hands, but all he kept saying was 'My child! My niece! My Elizabeth! My child!' All of that in that foggy daze he was in."

I'd had enough wine by then to counter the sobering effects of that description, but it took a while. After a few moments' hesitation, I only lifted my mug higher and called out, "Here's to Sir Bedivere! May his dark moods cease, and may he return to the living!"

But I'd had enough for the night, and we had a long day tomorrow. I took my leave early of Sir Thomas, and what I took from that conversation was only the realization that all individuals respond to grief in ways unique to themselves. It was a truth I'm sure I had sensed before, but never in such graphic ways. And I went back to Merlin's tent not realizing how soon it would be that I would experience more at first hand the truth of that observation.

CHAPTER SIXTEEN
PAX MORDREDA

The first shower of arrows had rained down like shooting stars from above, glowing with fire aimed to ignite the sails of Arthur's armada and burn any ships they could catch. So as our Breton sailors scurried to beat out any flames that resulted from that rain of fire, or to strike their sails for safety's sake if they'd been spared the first onslaught, Arthur's knights were busy manning the boats that would act as landing craft to take us into the harbor. When we dropped into the water, ten to each boat, we began alternating between rowing and holding up shields against the second wave of arrows loosed at us as our small boats moved toward shore.

We had approached Plymouth harbor just before dawn on the third day of our crossing. The winds had not been helpful, but they had not slowed us down significantly. What we had not reckoned on was the fact that, in the time it had taken us to assemble our invasion force, Mordred had reinforced Plymouth with a small army of Irish knights, intending to fortify his border against the possible incursion of forces from Cornwall. It was better than facing a full coast guard of Saxons, but our dream of finding an undefended shore to land our army was shattered as soon as they'd seen us.

Still, we had the advantage of surprise to some extent, since the Irish forces were scurrying about on shore, putting a defense together on the fly. Their archers had clearly been the first to form a disciplined resistance, and their artillery, coming from behind a makeshift wall on the docks, was causing us no little difficulty as a force of their knights, carrying swords and shields, scrambled into small boats and began to row out to meet us, hoping to overturn our boats or turn them back and prevent our landing. Knights hacking at each other from unstable boats on the water made little sense to me, and I feared, clad in my mail as I was, that a capsized boat would mean death by drowning as the weight of my armor bore me to the bottom of the channel.

I was gratified when, after several minutes' rowing, another shower of arrows descended on the Irish boats, launched by our own archers from aboard the king's fleet. It made the hailstorm of arrows that I heard batter Thomas's shield as he held it over the two of us seem less horrific somehow—at least if I was going to die with an arrow through my eye, I could feel better because some Irish gentlemen would be sent to judgment in the same manner.

Some two hundred yards from shore, the first of our boats met the first of theirs, amid a downpour of shafts raining from both directions. Sir Palomides, who was in command of our boat, called out for us to have swords drawn and shields ready as we moved toward one of their vessels. I pulled in my oar and pulled out my sword. In the dim light of that bloody dawn I kissed Alsace's blade and prayed that I would not disgrace her nor my king. As the Irish craft drifted past close by my side of the boat, I managed to strike one of them on the helmet, while another, in the rear of their vessel, had the misguided inspiration to stand up in the boat in order to swing his sword more freely down at Palomides' skull. Sir Palomides was taken aback by the Irish knight's imprudent attack, but recovered quickly and, grabbing a long oar from within the boat, used it to push into the standing man's chest just as he had brought his sword back, and so tipped the knight over, who, whirling his limbs about wildly, managed to capsize his entire boat.

Thomas and I gave a cheer, and now, since we were past the line of Irish vessels, and since the arrows had abated, the Irish archers being wary of slaying their fellows in the melee, we grabbed our oars and rowed vigorously for the shore. Behind us, there was more hand-to-hand fighting between boats, but I could see that our own boats were mostly getting through the line of Irish defenders, for it seemed we outnumbered them by at least three to one. Still, it seemed we were taking some casualties. And I wasn't sure what was going to happen when our boat made it to land.

"Expect a flurry of arrows as we step from the boat to the shore," Sir Palomides called to the rest of us. "But there are at least three boats right behind us, so we will not have to take the brunt of their assault for long, and after they let loose a volley, they will fall back. At that point we rush forward and cut down as many as we can before they have a chance to re-form." That sounded simple enough. I only hoped that those three boats full of knights behind us would be charging immediately on our heels, or it would be a pretty short attack. I expected, too—rightly as it turned out—that a second line of fully-armed Irish knights was waiting above, who would move forward when he archers fell back. And if that weren't enough, the Irish knights in the small boats that by now had rowed through our own line of vessels, would certainly now be turning their boats around to chase our soldiers onto the shore. Thus we were likely to have a wall of knights before us and another enemy line landing behind us, so we would be hard pressed from both sides. I could see that we outnumbered them, but it would be a hard blow to pile up casualties upon landing and still expect to take on Mordred and his whole army in full pitched battle in another few days.

We struck the shore and Palomides leapt out nimbly as a cat, holding his sword in one hand and his shield before him in the other. The rest of us scrambled out as quickly as we could and formed a close knot of warriors behind an impenetrable shield wall as arrows poured against us. When the barrage of arrows abated, Palomides cried "Charge!" in a voice like Doomsday, and ahead we ran, swords held high, crying out "For Arthur and Logres!" and trampling the barrier the archers had been standing behind, cutting down anyone still standing in our path. To my relief, at least thirty more knights were charging behind us, and the archers were routed. But as I expected, a line of armed knights was standing before us as we reached the first buildings of the harbor.

At that point a horn blasted from the west, and as I twisted my head in that direction, there were dozens of voices shouting "Cornwall,

Arthur and King Mark!" A squadron of knights had landed from the Cornish side of the river and were swarming over the harbor, some forming on shore to reinforce the knights now landing and to defend against the Irish knights now chasing them in their boats, and some coming in our direction, to help us overwhelm that line of stalwart Irishmen waiting to meet our challenge.

I hit my first knight a solid crack on his shield as we crashed into that enemy line, then parried his own swipe with one of my own. We exchanged several more blows until, reinforced by two Cornish soldiers, I had their help in making him yield, and we disarmed him as the battle now seemed to be winding down. The Irish defenders were either cut down, run off, or forced to surrender. We'd had a battle to get ashore, but it had been short and successful, and as I looked around, I saw all of Arthur's army being ferried to land. We'd taken the beach.

And we had done it without many casualties. As I surveyed the field I saw only a few of our own knights nursing minor wounds, with another four or five lying prostrate on the ground. Only a couple of these were not moving at all. Then I gasped. One of these, lying off to my right where he'd been engaged in mortal combat with one of the Irish knights in the line, was still holding a red shield with a gold pentangle. It was Sir Gawain.

***

Gawain's face looked paler and more haggard, as he lay in his pavilion that evening, than he had a few weeks earlier when we'd first seen him recuperating from Lancelot's drubbing. That his predicament was more dire than it had been on that occasion was clear by the grim look on the doctor's face as he whispered to the king over at the side of the tent. I couldn't be sure that the king's nephew was even aware of the presence of the rest of us around his bed—Sir Ywain, Sir Palomides, Merlin and me. Thomas had been there as well, but he'd been sent scurrying by the leech to fetch Father Ambrose, Camelot's chapel priest who'd come along on the king's Benwick adventure. And sending for the priest could only mean one thing:

By the anguished look on Arthur's face that one thing was what the doctor was now whispering into his ear.

The veteran knight's head was bandaged once more, and the blood seeping through was copious. For the past half hour Gawain had been moving in and out of consciousness. But now, surprisingly, he seemed to rally, and called out to everyone present, "Bring me some parchment and a pen and ink! Do it now, for I know I haven't got much time!"

We all looked at one another in puzzlement, and as we did Father Ambrose burst into the tent, followed more cautiously by Thomas. Ambrose was carrying a crucifix, his prayer book, and a leather kit that contained, I assumed, a vial of holy water, one of olive oil for extreme unction, and a pyx containing the consecrated host for the viaticum. But before he drew near to Gawain's bed, the wounded knight warned him off.

"Not yet, priest! I want parchment, pen and ink first!"

The king stood staring down at him for a moment, then in frustration reeled about, ordering, "Someone fetch writing tools..."

"Wait!" Merlin cried out from behind me, and reaching into an inner pocket of his long cape he pulled out a rolled piece of parchment, a quill pen, and a stoppered inkhorn. When we all looked at him with astonishment, he simply shrugged and said, "Would you think I of all people would go *anywhere* unprepared to write something down?"

Father Ambrose set down his other items and took the parchment, quill, and inkhorn from Merlin, then knelt facing Gawain while Sir Ywain stepped forward to hold up his shield, to give his cousin a hard, level surface on which to write. But when Gawain took the pen from Father Ambrose, his hand shook so violently he was unable to write, and he let out a curse so violent that the priest had to employ all his clerical tact not to call down God's judgment on the knight. Instead, Ambrose gently took the quill from Gawain and murmured, "If you will deign to dictate, my lord, I shall endeavor to write this document for you."

At that the knight closed his eyes and sighed, with a kind of relief it seemed to me, and said in a voice that had begun to quiver like his hands, "Let it be so. I thank you, father. Now please write as I say:

Composed this 17th day of June, on the bank of Plymouth Sound:
Gawain, Prince of Orkney, to Sir Lancelot du Lac, Lord of Benwick."

There were several raised eyebrows at that, and Father Ambrose
himself froze for an instant, as the king cried out, "Lancelot! At a
time like this? What are you thinking, Nephew?"

"Precisely at this time, Uncle!" Gawain rasped. "It will be now or
never, I'm afraid. Father, if you please, write this:

*"My lord Lancelot: The enmity between us has gone on far too
long, and I acknowledge the greater blame to be my own. Here before
God and a pavilion full of witnesses I forswear vengeance against
you on behalf of all the Orkney family, what is left of it at any rate.
Sir Agravain and my son brought about their own deaths by attacking
you, and I cannot blame you for them. More importantly, I hereby
declare that I no long hold you responsible for the deaths of Sir
Gareth and Sir Gaheris. The death of my beloved Gareth was a blow
that struck too near my heart for me to see a way past. I could see
only far enough to lash out, and so I thought, one way or another, that
I could find peace by hurling myself against your person.*

*"In his wisdom and irony, God has in the end granted that my
peace should indeed come through your hand. Know that the king
and his forces have gained a foothold on Logres once more, despite
the resistance of my bastard brother Mordred, whom I disown and
declare no longer a member of the Orkney clan. In storming the beach
at Plymouth, I received a powerful blow to the head from one of the
bastard's Irish allies, and by ill chance was injured once more on the
wound that you yourself gave me in single combat before Benwick.
This time, however, the wound promises to be mortal: The leeches
have all despaired and the priest even now presses to give me the last
rites. But I do not grieve. There is such honor in dying at the hand of
Sir Lancelot du Lac that I could not wish it otherwise."*

The lord of Orkney paused. His breath was becoming more and
more labored as he spoke, and Father Ambrose was indeed growing
more anxious with each sentence, though he dutifully recorded all
that Sir Gawain said. And Gawain, his eyes now closed, continued
with a voice even slower and softer than before.

"I beg you, courteous knight, pray for my soul, and I implore you,

for the love that was between us in the old days, that you will come to Logres once again and pay your respects at my tomb. You see now, My Lord, that there is no longer any reason for animosity between you and your sovereign lord, King Arthur." At that I glanced at the king and saw his jaw clench, and I knew that the king, for one, was not convinced that Sir Gawain's assessment of that relationship was completely accurate. But he said nothing and Gawain went on:

"The king," he dictated, *"stands in great need of your help. Sir Mordred has usurped the throne and surrounded himself with vast armies of Saxons, Picts and Irishmen. Further, the queen herself is at risk, besieged in a tower by the bastard, who plans to force her to marry him. Return, Lancelot, and rescue your king and queen as you were wont to do in the days before Sir Agravain wrought all this grief and caused the Table to crack. For your courtesy's sake, My Lord, I require you to make this journey into Logres, and to see my tomb."*

Sir Gawain ceased, and spoke no more. Father Ambrose began quickly to anoint the knight with holy oil, and strove to place the host wafer on Gawain's barely responsive tongue. For myself, I had no doubt that Gawain's soul was heaven-bound: That letter had truly been his last confession, and he had unburdened his soul's heaviest weight.

Sir Gawain, who had been the heart and soul of Arthur's court, rash and courteous by turns, boisterous and loving with his family, dignified and confident with others, deferent to the point of adoration to his uncle, was no more. Arthur knelt before the corpse and wept without restraint. My own eyes were far from dry, and at my shoulder Merlin said quietly, "Farewell dear friend. So passes a noble soul."

***

Sir Gawain was interred early the following morning with far less pomp and circumstance than there would have been had he died at any other moment. But there could be no further delay in the march toward Camelot if the king was to have any hope of reaching Mordred before his entire army was assembled. Gawain's letter to Lancelot was entrusted to the captain of one of Duke Hoel's cogs, several of which Arthur sent back across the channel to Benwick, to provide the Great Knight passage if he desired to bring his support to the king's cause, as Gawain's dying words had implored.

Not that Arthur expected such an effort on Lancelot's part. He didn't speak of it, but there was no doubt in my mind that the king still felt betrayed by his greatest knight, and was skeptical of any help coming from that quarter. Nor did he feel Lancelot could possibly arrive on the shores of Logres in time to be of any assistance in this war with Mordred, which the king believed must be waged with all possible speed if he was to prevent the bastard from overrunning the country. And so the army marched speedily and deliberately from Plymouth Sound across the land toward Camelot.

We were joined by King Mark's forces who had swept into the Irish camp and helped make our landing successful, and there were some two hundred of them, bringing our ranks to approximately six hundred troops, minus the few casualties we had suffered on the beach, and as we had expected, our ranks were swelled as we marched through Logres and men loyal to the rightful king joined our march to battle. By the end of the first day's march, there were at least eight hundred of us. Of course, only a few hundred of those were battle-tested veterans, and we knew by word of mouth that Mordred very likely had an army of some two thousand at his disposal, assuming his Saxon and Pictish allies had rallied to him. And so it was that Merlin rode constantly by the king's side, and whenever Arthur would let him, regaled the king with arguments as to why he should put off this battle if he could, in order to give Lancelot time to arrive.

"He will come," Merlin promised. "Lancelot has always been loyal to your person. He will not desert you at this time of your greatest need."

"Our bond is long since broken," the king answered. Riding just behind them on Achilles on that second day of our trek along the narrow road through the woods en route to Caerleon, I could see Merlin stiffen with agitation at Arthur's stubbornness.

"The past months do not erase the former thirty years," the mage argued. "And how can he disregard Sir Gawain's dying request? He will come!"

"He would come for the queen," Arthur grumbled. "But it's already too late. Mordred must be faced down now, or the kingdom is lost."

Merlin pressed his mouth into a thin line and shook his head in frustration. "If we can negotiate a truce…"

"A truce? He will have nothing short of the kingdom. And he has that now. What do we have to bargain with?"

I was glad none of the rest of the army was hearing this, or their confidence might dissipate into the mist that surrounded our march. The king had sounded sure of his destiny when we had started this long hike. "The usurper has no legal ground to stand on," he had told the troops. "And God will protect the right. We march to the most righteous battle in the history of Logres, to the greatest victory of my reign, and to the glory of God's kingdom here on earth! Follow me!" And off we had gone. But there is a difference between what you say when you rally your troops for a march into battle, and what you say when you talk to your advisers about the reality of a situation. And the reality was that Mordred held the capital, held London and all the eastern side of the country, including the Dover coast, and would have at least a three-to-one advantage in troops when we did meet. What we did have were troops that were loyal, not simply bands of brigands intent on getting whatever they could out of the usurper. Sure, many of the men we were picking up were untrained, but they were enthusiastic for the cause. And the knights we brought were the greatest knights in the world. They were knights of the Round Table. As for Lancelot, he was invulnerable, a killing machine who would tip the advantage to our side no matter how many warriors Mordred could throw at us.

"All the more reason to sue for peace now," Merlin continued to make his case. "Mordred doesn't want to fight. The outcome of a battle is always uncertain, no matter what the odds. A signed treaty is a victory without a battle. He wants to be king. Let him be king— upon your death. Sign a paper making him your heir, not only to Logres but to all the lands you've conquered. As lawful heir he can wield significant power while you live, and expect to hold supreme executive power upon your death."

"Which he'll no doubt do everything he can to hasten, make

no mistake," the king answered. "Besides," he continued after a moment's pause. "You know that Sir Ywain is next in line for the throne. Do you think I want to disinherit my only remaining faithful nephew?"

It was a point with which I could certainly sympathize. Ywain was less extroverted, less eager to please, less boisterous, probably less intelligent than Gawain had been, but in his quiet way he was as faithful, and was less apt to spring impetuously into action without consideration. Men would follow him if it came to that. But Merlin saw things differently. "Now is not the time to make promises to Ywain," he reasoned. "It's Mordred who must be dealt with. And you know, in all honesty, that Sir Mordred is more than your sister's son."

The king glared at his oldest adviser. Some things you just didn't talk about. Even if you both knew what was being left unsaid. In this case, *especially* if you both knew what was unsaid. But Merlin forged on. "To hell with tact," he said; and the king muttered in response, "As if you've ever had any…"

"Acknowledge the bastard," Merlin finished. "It makes him your legitimate heir in any case, and that's what he feels he should be. Give him what he wants. And then wait for Lancelot."

Arthur's face had darkened like a thundercloud and I have no doubt his response would have set the old necromancer back on his heels, but at that very moment we heard galloping hoofbeats coming toward us at breakneck speed from up ahead on the narrow road, and as we looked up the horse burst into sight and then reared up as the rider pulled him to a sudden stop. It was a knight covered in mail and wearing a visored helmet, and from behind that visor I could hear a familiar voice crying, "My liege! Well met! I have news!" As his horse settled down, the knight flung up his helmet and, breathing heavily from the exertion of his mad ride, repeated, "I have news!"

I blinked several times and then laughed out loud. "Peter!" I cried, astonished. "Why…how are you here?" Then, with a jolt of realization, cried, "What's happened to the queen?"

"The queen is safe," Peter gasped out between long breaths. "She was in the Tower…"

"Yes, yes, we were told so," Arthur interrupted impatiently. "What are you saying? She has left the safety of that place? Where has she gone now?"

Peter held up a hand. He was still huffing slightly, but he wanted to allay any fears we might have had. "She has gone to a convent, with her ladies-in-waiting."

"Convent?" Merlin exclaimed. "What convent? And tell us, you bumbling numbwit, why she left the safety of the Tower!"

"She's at Amesbury Abbey in Wiltshire, just north of here. We got word overnight that you had landed and were making your way eastward, so she sent me to bring you word. Listen: When we first found our way to the Tower, the guard there welcomed Guinevere and vowed to defend her against the usurper. They remain loyal to you, Sire." The king nodded with some gratitude, but his eyes begged Peter to continue. "Sir Pelleas was surprised but didn't seem too upset by the developments. He and that small attachment of knights that guarded the queen's convoy on the way to London just camped outside in a kind of siege, but there was really nothing they could do. I suppose Pelleas sent word to Mordred about what the queen had done, and was waiting for reinforcements, but he didn't seem too eager to do anything about Her Majesty. I think he was just happy to be away from Camelot and Mordred, and stayed in London just to keep an eye on things. Then he got word that Mordred was sending a force of several hundred men, led by Sir Hectimere, to lay siege to the White Tower, and Pelleas offered to convey her to safety wherever she wished to go, if she chose to leave the Tower."

"And she chose the Abbey?" I asked, with no small surprise.

"Does she believe the bastard will respect the Church's sanctuary?" Arthur asked. "There's little chance of that. He doesn't care about man's laws or God's. He is a law unto himself."

Peter looked a little taken aback. He shook his head, frowning as if we had not understood. "It's not…she's not seeking sanctuary, my Lord. She is…she plans…to take the veil."

Well that news shut everybody up pretty quickly. After a long pause during which we all stared dumbly at Peter, Merlin found enough of his tongue to say, "You mean to tell us, boy, that she has determined to take vows? The whole poverty, chastity, and obedience thing?"

243

"Yes, well, Amesbury *is* a Benedictine house, my Lord," Peter answered, bowing his head a bit as if unnerved at the effect his news was having.

After another lengthy pause, the king broke the silence with a loud "Harumph," followed by a shake of his head and another outburst. "Well, I certainly didn't see that coming." Then he shrugged. "Of course, considering my relationship with her over the past several years, I can't say it will change my own life in any significant way." Then his eyes widened and he burst out with a laugh. "But this is going to be quite blow to Lancelot, if he *does* decide to come to Logres. In any case, it doesn't change our necessity to meet Mordred on the field. But tell us, Peter, does it look like she will be safe there? Will Mordred's men pursue her?"

Peter shrugged. "Sir Pelleas has actually vowed to defend her, and his small band joined the guard from the White Tower to escort the queen and her ladies to Amesbury, and to offer their protection to the abbey, should Mordred's troops besiege her there."

Merlin looked grave. "Mordred will not shrink from violating a convent, nor from ravishing the queen, even if she has taken vows. He recognizes no bounds of human decency, and the queen will still be valuable to him in the eyes of the commons, even in a forced marriage. We must hope that Pelleas can withstand Hectimere and his troops, unless we can deal with Mordred in time. But Sire, this gives us even greater incentive to negotiate with the bastard: We cannot spare the men to defend Amesbury *and* face Mordred in the field of battle."

King Arthur frowned and kicked his horse into a trot. "I must consider the options," he said. "Let me think now as I ride."

Merlin nodded, then looked toward me and Peter and winked. If Arthur said he would consider something, it nearly always meant that Merlin had won him over. There was hope that a battle might be avoided, for now. Besides, given what the king had just learned about Guinevere's plans, he would certainly need to let that news sink in before trying to get his mind around Merlin's proposed truce.

For myself, news of the queen's conversion was perhaps less of a shock than for the others. They could not see anything in the

244

queen's intent but the seemingly ironic vow of chastity. But I knew that Guinevere, if she could not have Lancelot, her only and true love, would far sooner live a life of celibacy than remain married. I also knew that, having been freed from Arthur's vengeance by the intercession of the Pope, the queen felt a stronger commitment to the Church than she had formerly shown. And finally, I knew that the queen regretted many of the choices she had made in the past, believing that a true marriage to the king was really no longer possible after so many axe blows to the root of that bond, and she might actually be seeking a divine forgiveness where she despaired of receiving a human one. I felt my own heart reach out to hers in sympathy. And I rejoiced that my own dear Rosemounde was no longer with the queen, and so was out of danger.

***

Now as you've probably gathered by this point, this is a story framed all round by dreams, and as things developed, Arthur might never have finally agreed to negotiate a truce if it hadn't been for the dream he had on the fifth night after we'd begun the march toward Camelot. That night we were camped at the bend in the river that flowed out of Lady Lake, which opened into the broad plain of Camlann, not five miles outside of Caerleon itself.

Sometime after midnight we heard a disturbance in Arthur's tent—I was sleeping, again, in Merlin's pavilion, close by the king's, and so I bolted up immediately and rushed without ceremony into the king's tent, fearing that perhaps a spy or assassin had made his way in. But that was not the case. Sir Kay and Sir Bedivere, who had been on guard before the tent entrance, were standing with two young pages around Arthur's bed while the king, sitting bolt upright with an astonished look on his face, suddenly managed to astonish the rest of us by bursting out with a hearty laugh. Sir Kay, scratching his greasy head, stretched his flabby lips into a grimace that bared his yellow, horse-like teeth, and asked, "Your Majesty? Uh...what is it that has disturbed your sleep? Something...amusing is it?"

"No, no," Arthur held up his hands. "Sorry I called out. It was

245

the dream I was having. What made me laugh was the joy I felt at seeing my nephew again…Sir Gawain. It was Gawain, come to me in a dream."

Merlin, of course, was well aware of how often people will dream of the newly deceased, as their minds work, sleeping and waking, to come to terms with their loss. But he also was always ready to turn any situation to his advantage, and he pressed the king for details about the dream.

"It was as I said," Arthur told us. "A joy to see him, for in the dream Gawain was in Heavenly Bliss, where he was borne up and surrounded by a host of ladies whom he had protected and assisted in all his years as Knight of the Round Table. For you remember, Kay, Bedivere, Merlin, you were all present at the origin of the Table, when in that first adventure Sir Gawain, with his usual rashness, accidentally beheaded that young maiden…"

Kay gave a groan at that. "Yes, Your Majesty, that was a great misfortune for a new-made knight. I wasn't sure he could ever recover from that…yet he did, and did marvelously well, did he not?"

"Indeed," the king agreed. "But it was because I had put that penance on him, that he would evermore be particularly devoted to aiding any maiden who found herself in difficulty. He seems to have enjoyed that penance, as it turned out. But yes, there he was in Paradise. I need have no concerns over his soul, despite the vengeance he sought against Lancelot…"

And despite, I thought to myself, the vengeance he exacted from Sir Lamorak. I wondered that the king could so conveniently forget that. But of course, it had never been proven against Gawain or his brothers. And so as far as the king knew, it had never happened. At least I was pretty sure that's the way he thought about it.

"And why, my Liege, do you think Sir Gawain appeared to you in this dream? Was it solely to set your mind at ease as to the dispensation of his immortal soul, or do you think he may have had an additional motive for speaking to you in this manner?"

"Another motive?" The king pondered, frowning with his head bowed, as if straining to recreate the dream in his mind. "Perhaps…I seem to remember him moving his lips, trying to speak to me."

"Aha!" The old Necromancer jumped on Arthur's lack of a sharply defined memory. "Trying to speak to you, trying to tell you tell you something that he, with his newly acquired immortal sight, can see but that you, bound in mortal weakness and blindness, cannot. What do you suppose this can be, Your Majesty?"

Arthur, accustomed as he was to Merlin's machinations, answered slowly, "I really can't say, Old Man. But I have a feeling you might have an opinion."

"Me?" the mage responded in affected sincerity. "I would not presume to know what is visible only to the immortals. But I do suggest that this dream of yours is what the revered old Roman scholar Macrobius would have called an oracular dream: Your nephew has appeared to you in order to bring you an important message. Now what might he want to tell you? Clearly, it must have something to do with this battle with his half-brother that you're on the verge of launching. Perhaps we could deduce something of the import of that warning if we consider what kinds of things were on Gawain's mind at the time of his death."

"As we are both well aware," the king said, closing his eyes as he tried to rein in his annoyance at Merlin's persistence, "Gawain's last words concerned Sir Lancelot..."

"Oh yes," Merlin replied as if just now recalling the deathbed scene. "He was exhorting Lancelot to come to Logres and support you in this war." He now fixed the king with a gaze that was absolutely serious. "Isn't it most certain, then, that Sir Gawain, who spent his life supporting and honoring your sovereignty, would, in this posthumous visionary appearance to you on the eve of battle, bring you warning that unless you wait for the support of your greatest single ally, Sir Lancelot, you will lose this battle?"

There was a short pause as the king glared at Merlin while the mage gazed back on Arthur with mock innocence. Then with an exasperated sigh Arthur threw up his arms and said, "All right, it seems heaven and earth demand my yielding on this point. Go on, Old Man, and negotiate your peace. Take Sir Kay and Sir Bedivere with you under a flag of truce into the bastard's camp. Make a treaty that secures the points we have talked about." Now committed to the process, Arthur took a moment to suggest a few things to be considered. "You might go so far as to allow Mordred to call himself king of Orkney, so he has the status of a petty king like Mark or Geraint or Bagdemagus. He may keep that title until he inherits. But I do have qualms about whether this treaty is honorable: If, as you seem to suggest, the intent is only to keep this truce until the arrival of Sir Lancelot, when we shall break the truce and attack Mordred, I find no honor in that. Lancelot's presence will secure our peace and safety, but we must enter into the treaty with the intention of keeping it."

Merlin, now at perhaps his most devious, gave a crooked smile and, inclining his head toward the king and preparing to take his leave to begin his preparations, answered, "My Lord, your heart can remain pure. We know with absolute certainty that Mordred is completely without honor, and will look for his first opportunity to break this treaty. That being the case, we will have stalled just long enough for Lancelot to shore us up and ensure our victory. And now, Sire, I beg leave to go back to my own pavilion and make ready to leave by dawn." Then, turning to Sir Kay and Sir Bedivere, he told them, "My Lords, if you would be so good as to meet me here before the king's pavilion immediately after the hour of prime, we will set out for the castle to negotiate with Mordred without further delay." And with that, the old necromancer left the tent, and, seeing no reason to outstay my own welcome, I followed close at his heels.

***

By vespers that evening the delegation had returned, after what they considered a successful negotiation with the bastard. Mordred must have known he had a significant advantage in numbers, but he also knew that battles were always chancy, and that even if he were to defeat Arthur in the field, the common people of Logres would see him as a usurper and that would make ruling them a thorny proposition. And so he agreed to discuss terms with Merlin and the others, but, knowing he was bargaining from a position of strength, made outrageous demands and refused to agree to anything less.

But as luck would have it, Mordred's demands meshed almost

perfectly with the concessions Arthur had already empowered Merlin to make, and so an agreement was drawn up that did four things: It named Mordred the lawful heir to Arthur's kingdom of Logres, and to all lands currently under the king's imperial sovereignty. Second, it bestowed on Mordred the title "King of Orkney," in which capacity he was also vassal to King Arthur and foremost among his knights of what was left of the Round Table. Third, it disinherited Sir Ywain and, while it stopped short of recognizing Mordred as Arthur's son and legitimate heir, it did use the term "closest kin" when describing Mordred's relationship with Arthur. And fourth, it laid before the combatants the obligation to swear an oath that there would be peace between the two parties, and their respective armies, from the moment the treaty was signed and witnessed and into perpetuity, unless one or both of the litigants violated the terms of the agreement.

I sat alone by the campfire before Merlin's tent that evening after the old man had returned from his summit with the bastard, going over these developments in my mind. Merlin himself was exhausted from a full day of negotiating with the usurper, and using all his strength to remain calm in the face of what I knew must have been constant snide or malevolent comments from Mordred's foul, arrogant discourse. And I was glad that even Mordred had not felt confident in demanding the king's acknowledgment of paternity—although in fact Arthur had been willing to do so! Nor, I was glad to know, had Mordred made any demands about the queen. To insist on his betrothal to Guinevere would have been, to say the least, far more than Arthur had been willing to swallow. I worried momentarily that Mordred's abandoning the demand for Guinevere might somehow affect his attitude toward the lady Rosemounde—might he be moved to demand her return?—but I shook off that thought as soon as it surfaced. The marriage had been annulled by the bishop himself. Mordred would have no legal status in demanding the return of his former wife, unless of course she was herself willing to return, and there was precious little chance of that.

And now, because of Merlin's diplomacy, it appeared that war would be averted for the time being, that Lancelot could be counted on to return from Benwick and to support the king in his conflict with his bastard, and that the queen and her ladies would be safe walled within their convent at Amesbury. It only remained for the two parties to sign the agreement. Time had been set for the following day at sext, around midday, when Arthur and Mordred would meet before both armies in the middle of the field of Camlann and set their seals to the peace treaty. And thus the crisis would be forestalled.

As I sat by myself in the quieting darkness, on that eve of what now promised *not* to be a battle, brooding over recent events as I stared into the fire, I was suddenly aware of something pressing insistently against my right shoulder from behind. Before I had begun to consciously consider that nudging, a long furry nose poked rambunctiously between my torso and my upper arm, till it protruded several inches below my shoulder, and thrust forward a pink tongue as if in greeting. I couldn't help but laugh as I reached up with my left hand to stroke the familiar nose, then leaned away just long enough to let her whole body cavort around me until I enfolded her in my arms and said, "Hello girl!" and, after a moment's reflection, added with some trepidation, "Where did you come from, Guinevere?" And then with real panic beginning to set in, "Where is Rosemounde? Shouldn't you be back in Cornwall with her?"

"She is not there," a voice I knew well came from the shadows behind me. I whirled in time to see the face of Myghal of Launceston emerging from the darkness, leading by the reins the palfrey I recognized as the one Rosemounde had ridden with me to Cornwall just a few months before. But the face looked haggard, and it did not bear the smile I might have expected to see when he greeted his only son.

"Father!" I cried, with surprise that was quickly elevating into fear. "Why…what are you…where is Lady Rosemounde? You say she is no longer there? You mean Launceston? She's left your house?" What I really meant, of course, was: How could you let her leave the safety of your house, when I told you of her danger?

He looked down, avoiding my eyes. Then he avoided the question. "Fellow up the line told me I'd find you here. Nice chap. Friendly. A knight, I guess. Name of Thomas. Friend o' yours?"

I closed my eyes in anger and frustration. "Yes," I muttered,

"Thomas is a friend. But you're not answering me. Where is Rosemounde? Why is she not at your house?"

He looked now up to the heavens, as if the answer to my desperate demand could be found in the stars. "She…would not stay," he said after some hesitation. "She came to me some five days ago, and insisted that she must leave my house. Nothing I could say could convince her to stay. And how could I force her? She was, after all, a duchess was she not? Finally she told me that she would go at once, and that if no one in the house could accompany her, she would go off by herself, with just the dog for company." He looked at the ground again. "And so I agreed to come with her." He shrugged. "What else could I do?"

Despite my anxiety, I gave a tight smile. "She can be stubborn when she wants to," I conceded. "But why was she so bent on leaving? Was she unhappy in your house?"

"Not a bit of it!" Myghal cried, offended, looking into my face for the first time. "She seemed happy as a sunbeam, always singing or whistling through the house. She even helped Nell with the housework. Of course, Nell was mortified at first. Couldn't stand the thought of a woman of such high blood visiting with us and having to pitch in with the chores. But when she could see as how the lady Rosemounde actually seemed to enjoy the little tasks, and felt like she was earning her keep, you see, she let it go. No, the lady was perfectly content with us. It was, well, it was when we heard the king was on his way back to reclaim his rightful place—we heard about the fleet coming the day before you all landed at Plymouth, you see— that she insisted she had to leave Launceston and come to find *you*. You were bound to be with the king, she said, and you'd be marching toward Camelot, and so she was going to take the road to the king's castle and find you there."

"But that's so reckless of her! Why leave her safe place and come straight into a war zone? What possessed her? And for God's sake, *where is she?*"

This last question I fairly shouted in my anxiety, but my father's eyes slid away again from looking directly into my eyes. He breathed in deeply and then let out a shaky, indecisive exhale. "It was about two weeks past, I reckon, when she first whispered about it with Nell. She'd been suspicious but uncertain before then, but by that day she felt she knew for sure."

"What? Knew what?"

"Knew that she was carrying your child." He said it with a flat expressionless voice, and I was caught between a sudden unlooked for bliss and a nagging, terrifying premonition. For there was no joy in his voice.

"My...my child?" I said, hardly able to form the words. "You're saying she is pregnant? With our baby?"

"Had to be yours," my father shrugged. "She told Nell she hadn't been with her own husband, or her former husband, for more than a year. Your child, son. My own grandchild." And with that his voice cracked, and my hopes were shattered. This was not going to end well.

Steeling myself as best I could, but unable to keep the quiver from my voice, I managed to ask, "The tone of your voice tells me the child is lost. What of the mother? Where have you left her?"

Tears welled up in his dark eyes and began streaming down his anguished face, and in the shadows and the red light of the fire he looked to me like a soul in the torments of hell. But he would not rush his story. "She wore her simple kitchen-maid's clothes on the road, so that we would be unremarkable to any passersby. We passed few folk coming the other way, but a number of riders were eastbound on the road, including, a few times, small armed knights. Mostly they took no notice, but at least once or twice I saw one of those soldiers look back at us. Maybe it was the horse that drew their attention. Maybe the dog, I don't know. And I suppose it was one of them reported us to somebody who knew what he was looking for."

My insides twisted into agonizing knots and a raging fire burned the back of my neck. I could barely speak and felt like I may lose consciousness, but I could not stand this death by a thousand cuts. "Out with it, man! What's happened to my Rosemounde?"

My father's voice quickened, but he still had trouble blurting it out. "Two nights ago...we slept in the open, one on either side of the fire. In the middle of the night I heard the dog bark and growl, then attack someone in the dark. Then she started to wail, and by then I had grabbed the sword I had been sleeping with and charged across the fire, but I was too late, Someone had stolen upon us in the night, found Lady Rosemounde where she slept and…and cut her throat where she lay….” His voice broke. Tears streamed from his eyes. He slumped forward, burying his face in his hands. These are clichés. But it is what people do. It's what my father did.

And what did I do? I think perhaps I went mad for some moments. I can't say. Even now, after more than forty years, I can see my father, hear his words, they were like burning brands into my soul and the scars remind me every day of the story. But I cannot remember what I did. I may have screamed a roaring inarticulate bellow. I may have tried to throw myself onto the fire. I may have fainted dead away. I may have thought it was just another of the bad dreams that seemed to frame this story from the beginning. I think all of those things went through my mind, but I know I did not speak. The deepest sorrows of the heart are inexpressible. I think I came to my senses while Guinevere was licking my hand and whining. I touched her head, soft as a silk robe, and felt it might be the last tenderness I would feel before the great black pit I saw before me swallowed me up. But my father had begun talking again.

“I tried to follow the murderer but he'd gotten clean away in the dark. The lady was already gone. I don't think she ever woke up. So she was at peace when she went, there's that at least. I took her next day to the nuns at Amesbury Abbey—we weren't far from that place when it happened. They told me they would take care of her, see that she found a resting place in holy ground. I'm sorry, son, that I couldn't protect her. Who'd a' thought that they'd a' been so cruel, so ruthless, as to do her that way? Why would they do it? She wasn't hurting anyone. Your dog, now, there's a loyal beast. But she couldn't save her neither. She did get hold of the villain that cut her, though—tore this blazon off him…” And with that Mighal held out to me a piece of torn cloth, and I took it from him mindlessly, glancing at it but too stunned for it to register. But in the back of my mind I could see that it was the torn shred of a surcoat, one that a knight would wear over his armor. So the murderer had been a

253

fully armed knight—coming perhaps from a campaign? Or going to one? Unconsciously my eyes focused on the cloth. They made out a strange kind of mythical reptilian beast, rendered in a bright red, and it was on a gold-colored cloth background. After a moment I realized I had seen this image before. But where? The creature looked like it was walking, with one foot raised as if about to step down. It had a beaked head, leathery wings and a long snake-like tail. It was…now I recalled…it was a basilisk. A "trippant basilisk gules on a field or" in heraldic terms. I was blinded with red rage for an instant. It was Sir Hectimere's shield. He had slit my angel's throat. "The same way he killed Aglovale and Tor," I muttered.

"What's that?" My father asked.

"Nothing. I know who did this, father. There can be no doubt." And now my rage had cooled as quickly as it had flared. I felt nothing at that moment but cold hatred. I knew that if Hectimere had done the deed, then it followed that Mordred was behind it. It was that simple. Hectimere, who had taken from me my only love and my unborn child. Mordred, who had extinguished the only shred of happiness I had found in this life. Mordred, who was about to sign a peace treaty with the king and to be named heir to Arthur's throne. And now my path was clear.

CHAPTER SEVENTEEN
MORTE D'ARTHUR

As previously agreed, Arthur and Mordred were to meet in the midst of Camlann field, between their assembled hosts, and accompanied by a dozen of their close supporters and advisers. Merlin, Kay, and Bedivere, the king's negotiating team, were at his side as he sat at the table, the better to interpret any legal points in the treaty whose meaning was not immediately accessible to the royal eye. Arthur's other nine chief retainers, including myself, were mounted in full armor behind the king and his group where they sat. In line with me were Ywain, Palomides, Thomas, Lord Kaherdin (leading Duke Hoel's Breton troops), Sir Culwhich (leading King Mark's Welsh troops), and four of Arthur's veteran Round Table Knights: the Greek knight Sir Cliges, the Red Knight Sir Perimones (whom Gareth had bested on his first quest), the Frankish knight Sir Claudin, and Sir Marrok—whose wife was supposed to have turned him into a werewolf, but that's another story, surely one that involves a kind of madness, something that morning I was quite ready to understand.

On the other side of the table, surrounded by Sir Geraint and the allied leaders of the Irish and the Saxon armies that supported him, Sir Mordred lounged, his villainous face twisted into a grotesque and unconvincing mask of sincerity that veiled a scarcely disguised gloating sneer, for he knew he had won everything he could have wanted with this treaty, and he knew that Arthur knew it too. And besides, he also knew that he had no intention of keeping any of the promises he was making, if to break them would at any time be to

255

his advantage. Smile now, villain, I thought. You will not survive the day.

***

Had I said that out loud?

I drew some comfort from the intimate closeness of my beloved Achilles, solid as a rock beneath me, who even now was stomping his right hoof on the ground, itching for action. I was mounted, I was armed—what was I waiting for? At least, that's what the horse seemed to be saying. And as my right hand held erect a fewtered and sharpened battle-ready lance, my left hand reached to touch the hilt of my precious sword Almace—like the horse, a gift of my lamented master Sir Gareth, for whom I mourned as much as any friend I'd lost in these barbarous times—any save one.

My night had been spent alternating between bouts of burning rage and of chilling grief, interrupted only occasionally by spells not of slumber but of exhaustion when my tears had worn me out to the point of unconsciousness. My two fathers, Myghal and Merlin, had taken turns trying to give me comfort or to talk me down from the madness that threatened to engulf me forever.

With the dawn, the time had come for Myghal to make his way back to his responsibilities in Cornwall, and with Merlin's blessing he took the palfrey that had been my lady Rosemounde's mount. Surely no one was going to miss it in the chaos of these days. Before he'd left, Myghal had given me a stern warning: Don't let vengeance take root and fester in my heart, he'd told me. And listen to what the lord Merlin was telling me.

And what exactly was it that Merlin was trying to get me to hear just then? Things from that morning run together in my brain like diverse vials of distinct poisons, all blending to create a great fiery cataclysm. But I recall Merlin holding Sir Gawain up to me as an example of the futility of vengeance. "In the end," he exhorted me, "it destroys all it touches, and produces nothing of value, not even satisfaction. God's bile, Gildas, no additional death can bring Lady Rosemounde back, nor can it possibly make her shade happy to become the bane of other souls. Especially if one of those souls is your own—Gawain sought release from his pain through his own death, but his death has brought only further suffering to the king and to Ywain and to all who knew him."

And I nodded and nodded and simulated a kind of calm that I did not feel. When that morning the king had commanded that I be at his back at the signing of the treaty, Merlin rolled his eyes and put his hands on my shoulders. "Listen!" He told me. "Do not do anything that will jeopardize the making of this peace! The king needs it, the country needs it. It means the downfall of all the king has worked for, all that *I* have worked for, if we do not have this truce and give Sir Lancelot time to cross the channel. You must govern your emotions now. You *must* keep your temper in check." He looked at me from under those tangled eyebrows, the dark eyes piercing into my deepest soul. And making no impression whatsoever.

What did Merlin know? He had lost his beloved Nimue to the love of another, and that had kept him in dark moods, holed up in his lonely cave, for longer than anyone could remember. Was he able to bridle his own emotions on demand? And Nimue was still alive. Let him receive the spur to passion that *I* had, and then see just how restrained the old necromancer could be.

Waiting astride Achilles in that row behind the king, aware of the thousand troops ranged behind me, and the three thousand assembled on the enemy side, my mind wandered back to those idyllic days I had spent with Rosemounde on the road to Cornwall so very recently, and for sadness and longing I nearly slid from my saddle into a pool at Achilles' feet. Then I remembered, with a sudden jolt, that haunting dream I had had on the road, that dream of the lamented Lady Elizabeth, come from her grave to tell me "I should be cold," but revealing instead that her flesh was hot: "So hot, I feel it burning like a great rage running through my blood!" And ultimately telling me she would not be buried, clutching at me and refusing to rest quietly in her grave. That dream, was it prophetic? Was Elizabeth in the dream a warning of the impending murder of my Rosemounde, the heat of her flesh the heat of my own rage, her refusal to be buried my own mind's refusal to bury Rosemounde peacefully?

Let Merlin pontificate at the king's table with his precious treaty, a treaty not worth the parchment on which it was written, for it was written only to be broken, either by Mordred or by Arthur's own forces. I would not be a party to such a treaty, drawn up under false pretenses. Mordred did not deserve to live another day in a world deprived of the lady Rosemounde, and as for me, I did not care to survive in such a world either. But Mordred must be made to suffer— along with that crawling, spineless worm, his sycophant Hectimere. I may not care to be a part of this world any longer, but I would see to it that this cold new world was cleansed of two vile monsters before I left it.

"Be on your guard," the king had told us all prior to our breaking camp and gathering at this neutral spot. "Mordred is a man without honor, and there may well be treachery afoot at this meeting. Watch closely the ranks of his army. If you see a sword raised, then they are preparing to attack. You must respond quickly and effectively."

I had also seen Mordred confer with his lieutenants upon his arrival at this open-air conference table, and by the motions of his hands I could read the concern that he, too, had about this meeting. He had no illusions about Arthur's followers: Chivalry was all well and good but capitulating to a foreign army was going to be distasteful in the extreme to Arthur and all his followers, no matter what kind of pacifist noise the old necromancer made about negotiations; everybody in Camlann field was walking on eggshells, knowing it would take only the tiniest spark to start a great conflagration.

And that's when I saw him. Mounted on his own black destrier, bearing a gold shield with a red basilisk in the line of knights behind Sir Mordred was the vile Sir Hectimere himself. Murderer of good knights and more recently, to my own and the world's great loss, of angelic ladies, that vile serpent sat oblivious to his own impending doom. I do not think that he even saw me. But I saw him. And I was primed to act. Achilles himself seemed restless with anticipation as well, and he began to scuff the earth eagerly with his front hoof. I remembered that Hectimere usually had a good go at the quintain, and, as Geraint had told me, he was a good fighter with a short sword, and he'd proven deft with a dagger as well. But I also remembered his poor showing at the quintain when I surprised him that day I had sought out Geraint to interrogate. Surprise him now, get the jump on him, and he won't soon recover. Letting my lance drop, I decided that he would not expect me to come down upon him on horseback first with my sword, and anticipated that my speed and surprise would win the day quickly. I drew Almace, brandished it, and then with a great, anguished cry of "You Viper!" I touched Achilles' flanks with my spurs and he shot forward like a bolt of lightning.

At the flash of my sword and the sound of my cry the entire field erupted in martial chaos. Knights on both sides drew weapons, lowered their visors, reared their horses, and cried out, barking orders to squires and foot-soldiers and archers all around. But I had one goal and kept fixed on it. I had only perhaps fifty yards to cross, from the inner guard behind Arthur to the line behind Mordred. I was tilting at full speed straight for Hectimere, on the heaviest and grandest war horse on the field, Sir Gareth's gift. Hectimere's jaw dropped for a moment, then, realizing what was happening, he fumbled with his visor, raised his heavy lance from its fewter and attempted to proffer it to meet my charge, giving his own horse a kick to start toward me.

But he wasn't quick enough. Achilles was bearing down on him too fast. He might have actually had a chance if he'd grabbed his sword instead of trying to proffer his long lance, but that attempt was his undoing. Bearing down on him at full tilt, I parried his lance easily so that it slid ineffectively off my shield on the left, and on my way past him I swung Almace with all my strength in a great swooping arc toward his head. It was a stroke so powerful it knocked the helmet from his head and toppled him from his mount onto the ground. I halted Achilles, rearing him up and turning him about, so that his hooves came down on Hectimere's squirming body. He never had a chance.

But I needed to make sure, and to tell him to his face that he was dying for Rosemounde. I slid down from Achilles' back and knelt beside Hectimere's prone figure. He was badly bruised and perhaps his ribs were broken, for he was breathing with some difficulty. "I yield," he gasped. "Your oath as a Knight of the Round Table requires you to spare a fallen enemy who appeals for mercy."

I have to admit *that* was rich. "As you gave mercy to Tor and Aglovale?" I responded. His eyes fell. It must have surprised him, my knowing that. "You slit their throats from behind, didn't you? But you're saying that I should be a better person than you? Well perhaps I have been. But now? There is no Round Table any more, I'm afraid. You and your friends have seen to that, so the oath isn't binding any more either, is it?"

Hectimere gave a hacking cough and spit out some blood, then weakly held up a hand and tried to excuse himself. "It was Mordred!" He protested. "He ordered me to kill Tor and Aglovale…"

"And the lady Rosemounde?" I shouted, now beside myself with frustrated rage. "Did he order that as well?"

That truly surprised him. He must have thought he'd gotten clean away with that murder. But he could think of nothing more to say. He knew I would brook no excuses. I knelt on his chest and put the point of Almace up under his chin.

"What I really can't understand," I told him, just before taking his life, "was your old master Gaheris. And Gareth? The best man of all knights…" and with that word I shoved the blade of my sword up through his neck and into his brain. If he had any excuses for Gareth, he could make them in Hell. But the astonished and puzzled look that came over his face when I mentioned Gareth and Gaheris stayed in my mind's eye. It was not the expression I expected to see on his dying face.

I had been in single combat before, and beaten my foe, but this was the first time I had ever taken the life of another human being. After the shock of the lady Rosemounde's death, following so hard upon the loss of my dearest friend and master Sir Gareth, I had expected to feel some release, some purging of my griefs, through vengeance on their murderer. But to my chagrin, I felt only a dull sickness. I heaved up what little I had taken for breakfast that morning as I groveled there in the dust while shouts of men and clashing of arms echoed all around me. Perhaps it was that strange, puzzled look on Hectimere's face that quelled the triumphant joy that should have swelled my breast. Perhaps it was the fact that I had slain only the minion, while the venomous spider at the center of this great web of evil still lived somewhere on this battlefield. There was one more piece of vermin I needed to exterminate: the bastard Mordred, who had masterminded everything. When I thought of him, I remembered his threat: He had vowed once to cut Rosemounde's throat before seeing her with me. And the bastard had done just that—and wiped out the unborn child of our love at the same time. The bastard could not live! Once more the red rage boiled in my entrails and I felt the berserker fulminate within me. I was on my feet again in seconds.

It was only then that I truly became aware of the pandemonium all around me. True, I had never been in the midst of a major pitched battle before, but even so I could swear the field of Camlann was a melee of a quite different order. Surely in a normal battle, there are battle leaders, *duces bellorum* as the old Roman Britons used to call them, who directed the armies, leaders who would command troops in organized tactics and strategies on the battlefield. But this was bloody chaos. Of course, no one had ranged their troops for actual battle. Neither side had come with a plan or positioned their armies strategically because both thought they were merely there to witness the signing of a peace treaty, so when my unsheathed sword had sparked the whole valley into sudden aggression, knights on both sides had simply begun to fight with whatever enemy was closest. All around me were swords, maces, and battleaxes clanging against armor, the cries and grunts of men straining as they battled for their lives, the moans and laments of men dying in their own gore and entrails. And everywhere, everywhere, horses kicking and dust flying. It looked to me like a great tumultuous and anarchic circle of Hell, and in self-defense I simply began to swing my sword from one side to the other, effectively wading through the blood of wounded knights but not engaging any individually for I had only one goal in mind: find Mordred before someone else had the honor—no, the *pleasure*—of killing him.

Time seemed to slow down as a mist began to settle over the plain, and I felt as if my limbs were moving through water. Enemy soldiers came toward me to engage me as I moved across the field, but I merely parried their swords or axes and passed by. There was only one man I wanted to find. I stopped and turned about quickly,

261

realizing that I could search the plain much faster on horseback, and I hoped that Achilles was unhurt and close enough to hear me call. I put my fingers to my mouth and gave a shrill whistle, hoping to be heard above the fray. And to my great delight, the mighty warhorse came galloping up to me out of the mist. I tried to heave myself into his saddle quickly, holding Almace in my left hand as I did, for there were foes wherever I looked. With one foot in the stirrup, I was accosted by a blue-painted Pict who came at me with a spear. I swung my sword in an arc downward to parry the spear, and knocked it away from my torso, but not quite far enough, as the point of it ran through my calf and into Achilles' flank.

At the prick Achilles bounded forward, carrying me with him as I swung my right leg over his saddle. We were both wounded, but not enough to stop us.

Now that the battle's first burst of rage had spent its frenzied energy on futile carnage, men were forming into companies to bring some martial order to the barbaric chaos. To my left as I rode I could see a group of Saxon warriors forming themselves into a shield wall. As through a nightmare I rode slowly through the mist, where shadows of my friends moved in and out of my vision like ghosts or phantasms in a waking dream.

Sir Palomides, leading a company of mounted knights, moved across my path toward that Saxon shield wall, hoping to crush the Saxon determination under the weight of irresistible shock warfare. Seeing me mounted, he motioned to me to join his armored barrage, but I had one goal here and this was not it. I shook him off, and shouted to him above the din of battle, "I'm hunting Mordred!" And that was enough. He nodded, knowing that the loss of their leader could in itself dismay and scatter the enemy. Then he held out his sword and called his followers to charge, and into the mist they disappeared at a thundering gallop.

For a time I moved unmolested among piles of corpses and among men still struggling in hand-to-hand combat. Bodies, living and dead, came in and out of the mist into my sight. At one point Achilles stepped cautiously over the body of a sandy-haired youth, and my stomach dropped. It very well could have been Thomas, though in truth the face was damaged and bloodied beyond recognition. But I could not stop. He was most certainly dead, and I could not be distracted from my self-imposed quest. Further on, amid the mad shouting and clanging metal of small bands of Irish soldiers in mortal struggle with some of Mark's Cornishmen, and on the field there, framed by grass crimsoned with his own lifeblood, lay Sir Kay, dead on his back with a lance through his midsection. His eyes were open and staring, his lips stretched into a grimace that bared his yellow teeth in a final twist of agony. He would boast no more. But he had died with his wounds in front, I would give him that.

As I pushed on, dozens of Irish hands reached up toward my legs, trying to pull me from the saddle to kill me and steal my horse. But as long as Achilles could still move I had no fear of such devices. My sword sang out, severing several hands from those groping arms, as the horse sped ahead unfazed. But I had not gone far from that encounter when a hand reached out of the gloam to hold Achilles by the bridle.

"Still mounted, are you?" rose up a familiar voice, and I looked down into the face of Sir Ywain, almost unrecognizable with his face bloodied and covered in dust. He had apparently lost his helmet somewhere, but his tawny mane and beard gave him away. "I'm leading this lot," and he nodded toward a group of shadows paused in the mist, "over against those knights of Sir Geraint's. They're putting up the strongest fight—probably because they've got a stake in it, being Britons of Logres after all. But I think we can break their resistance if we strike hard. Join us?"

At that I blanched. I hated to turn him down, but I had but one goal, and this wasn't it. "Mordred must be stopped," I told Ywain. "I'm going to do it. For Rosemounde, for Gareth, for Arthur and the queen. I won't be distracted from that."

Like Palomides, the Knight of the Lion seemed to understand. "Go after him," he said. "I believe you have it in you." But he paused again before he pushed on. "Wish my lion were here with me. Left him back with Lady Alundine in her castle. Do me a favor, Gildas," and now he looked into my eyes, more serious than I'd seen him in a long time. "If this battle is the end of me, as it has been the end of a number of our knights, and if you manage to survive, promise me you'll visit my lady Alundine, and tell her I died with her name on my lips." Then, looking down for a moment, he added, "and tell her to set the lion free." With that he was off, leading that group of shadows into the fray beyond the mist. It was the last I ever saw of him.

Achilles, I now realized, had been losing blood during the whole of this ride, since that Pict had wounded him, and the sight of that made me aware of the pain where the same spear had pierced my own leg. I thought that I could probably still stand on it if need be. I certainly would not let it impair me when I came face to face with the bastard, which I now felt, in my monomaniacal search for him, to be my destiny. It was no surprise when at last, after what seemed like another hour of riding through that infernal landscape of severed heads and limbs, pulped corpses and anguished cries, the mist cleared long enough for me to see, near a single tree on a small hillock some hundred yards ahead, two figures locked in single combat, battering one another with exhausted sword arms. From my vantage point I could see that both were bloodied, that both were at the end of their endurance, but that neither would give up. Three gold crowns on a red background could still be seen on the torn surcoat of the knight with his back to me—the king's coat of arms. The other could only be the king's bastard.

They were alone here, at the edge of the field of battle nearest the shore of the lake, engaged in the single combat that should in fact determine the outcome of the entire battle, if anyone else were there to witness it. The fact is, I was there, and there was only one way this combat was going to end. I would see to it. This was war, not chivalry, and Mordred must die. I spurred Achilles into a trot—all he was capable of now after his own loss of blood. I raised my sword and made my way toward Mordred as fast as I could. But as I rode, King Arthur fell to the ground before my eyes, wounded…could it be mortally? If it wasn't, I could see Mordred now lifting his sword to ensure that the king would never rise from this last collapse. With a final desperate scream as I pushed my horse up that hill, I bellowed "No!" as I saw Mordred's sword raised high over his head, ready to swing down.

At that moment there was a sudden great flash of light and a thunderous crash as the ground exploded directly behind the bastard, and I realized I was not the only one witnessing this battle. That blast could have come from only one source: Merlin. From the corner of my eye I could see the mage, toiling up the hill just to my left. "See to the king!" I shouted to him. "Leave the bastard to me!"

I glimpsed the old man reaching the king and taking his prostrate body into his arms as I pushed Achilles, huffing and puffing, up that slope and, just as the dazed Mordred, shaking himself into consciousness, was rising to his feet, charged the heavy horse straight through him, trampling the bastard back down again into the dust. Turning, I gave Achilles a quick touch with my spurs and he stopped, badly winded and weak from his wound.

I climbed down as quickly as I could manage, sword in hand, and limped to the prone body of that man I considered the prince of evil. He lay on his side, still breathing but battered and bloody. I kicked him over onto his back, then kicked the sword from his strengthless hand.

Mordred's eyes opened and focused on my face, then he scoffed and in a weak voice he said, "Not very chivalrous that, Sir Gildas of Cornwall, running me down with your horse. You didn't give me much of a chance."

"More of a chance than you gave Lady Rosemounde, you villain!" I stood over him, my sword Almace pointing directly at his exposed throat.

The bastard gave a subdued chuckle, then gurgled and spat out a mouthful of blood. Achilles' trampling must have broken his ribs, I guessed, and thus punctured his lungs. He could not live much longer. But still he talked, if only to torment me with his last breath. "Yes," he smiled, "I hear *she* didn't have much of a chance either. Hectimere can be quick and deadly with his knife. Served her right, though, the slut. Didn't I tell you I'd slit her throat before I let you have her?"

With that I gave him a hard and heavy kick in the ribs, a blow that elicited a scream of agony, followed by a spasm of coughing and a good deal of blood from his mouth. I heard Merlin murmuring

265

behind me, "There, there," but whether it was for my benefit or was spoken to Arthur, I did not know.

And still the bastard continued to laugh softly, painfully. "The pristine Sir Gildas, so chivalrous, so pure in his love. So easy for you, wasn't it? To do the right thing, to love the right way? Always had your father's love, didn't you? Made you that corselet you're wearing. Sacrificed everything to send you to Camelot. Even looked after your girlfriend when you went to war. Your father never tried to kill you when you were a baby, did he? Your father never denied you were his, or cut you off without inheritance? Did he? And yet look at you." Here he coughed again, and shuddered with the pain. "In the end you're no different from me. Ruthless."

"Bastard." I refrained from kicking him again only by a superhuman act of will. "You think harping on your father issues is going to play on my sympathy? You couldn't have made a worse move. Because of you I'll never be able to be a father to my own child! You killed my baby when you killed Rosemounde!"

His dying eyes flashed life once more. The news that Rosemounde had been with child when Hectimere slew her was news to him, and he welcomed it. "Then the devil is kind," he smiled up at me, "to have crowned my labors with such a sweet revenge."

I ignored his pathetic gloating. "And you cry about having no father—you who cared so little for your own brothers that you had Gareth and Gaheris killed!" I'd had enough of this and raised my sword.

But with that Mordred narrowed his eyes. "Gareth?" he questioned, his face contorting in pain. "But...I would never have hurt my brothers..."

But by now I'd have enough of his games and his lies. Or maybe I was just sick of seeing him suffer. I plunged Almace into his tender throat, and Mordred breathed no more.

My emotions seething from the bastard's taunts and his last words, I turned quickly to see how the king did. By now Merlin had been joined by another figure, who was kneeling before the king, his head bowed. It was Sir Bedivere.

Merlin, looking older and more tired than I had ever seen him—I was certain that one of his black moods was about to descend upon him—looked up at me with swollen, drooping eyes and said in a low, hoarse voice, "The king's wounds are many, and there is nothing I can do for him. He needs a skilled healer, or he'll die, and likely before the sun sets on this wicked day."

"His sister, Morgan—she is in the palace of the Lady of the Lake, just here! If I could ride to her palace and bring Morgan back, perhaps there is time..." but with that I collapsed onto the ground beside Sir Bedivere. My wounded leg had given out, and I could no longer stand. Looking at Achilles, who had himself lain down in the grass half a furlong away, I realized that the horse would be galloping nowhere else this day.

Then suddenly I was aware that the king was speaking, so low and so soft that he was barely audible. "Sir Bedivere!" he called to his oldest and most faithful knight. "Take my sword—take Excalibur." The knight, not understanding, began to shake his head. Whatever it was, he feared it signified the end. Arthur laid his hand upon Bedivere's shoulder. "Take it, I say, to the shore of Lady Lake, and heave it with all your might into the water, out into the middle of the water. Do it now, while there is time!"

"If...if that is your wish, my liege," Sir Bedivere stammered. Merlin helped him slip Excalibur, now in its scabbard, from the king's belt, and the knight stood up and began walking with it hesitantly toward the lakeshore.

The king lay back on Merlin's lap and the old mage, his back against the only tree in the vicinity, finally looked directly into my face with accusing eyes. "God's burning eyeballs, you Cornish dolt, didn't I tell you that your thirst for vengeance must be subjugated to the king's need for peace?"

Of course it had not escaped him that it was *my* sword, unsheathed, that had provided the spark that ignited this mortal battle. But his words were spoken without much vehemence. He was too tired, too overcome with melancholy, to scold me with as much passion as he no doubt felt I deserved. As for the king, I don't think he heard. He himself was in and out of consciousness. It was only me and Merlin.

"What would you have me do, old man?" I answered him, in

equally low but energetic tones. "There is no world for me without Rosemounde. For her sake I would sacrifice more than one kingdom. As for my child, what father could do less?"

Merlin sniffed. "And was this revenge of yours satisfactory?" He mocked with his piercing eyes. "Have you set the world aright? Are the souls of Lady Rosemounde and Fetus Gildas Junior satisfied now? Will they rest in peace, and will you *live* in peace? Your mind, Gildas, is it at peace now?"

I sighed. For my soul was in turmoil, more so than it had been before. Justice had been done! But I felt none the lighter for it. While Merlin waited for the answer that would not come, I peered after Sir Bedivere as he made his way to the shore of the lake, a few hundred yards distant. I saw him take Excalibur out of the scabbard and look admiringly at the blade and the bejeweled hilt, then place the sword down on shore, hiding it under some trees, and start on his way back. Curious behavior, I thought. Why would Bedivere fail to follow the king's wishes?

Merlin had lowered his voice to a harsh whisper, and as I watched Sir Bedivere return empty-handed from his task, I listened to more of the old necromancer's chiding. Then he sighed. "Perhaps it is a moot point after all. There was always only a slim chance that Lancelot would land in Logres with an army to sweep all before him. And Mordred could never be trusted in anything he did or said. It is likely he was planning some attack of his own at that treaty signing. Who can say?" Then flaring up again he concluded, "*No one* now, you Cornish blockhead! You've seen to that!"

Now Bedivere had reached us again, and bowed to the king, who, rousing himself from his stupor, met the faithful knight with an eager, "Well?"

"Well…what, Your Majesty?" Bedivere answered, clearly taken aback by the greeting.

"What did you see? What did you hear when you threw the sword into the lake?"

"I…saw nothing unusual, my liege. Just the…the sword splashing into the water…"

"Faithless villain!" the king snapped, shutting his eyes and shaking his head sorrowfully. "*Now* you decide to disobey my commands, *now* when it matters most? Go back to the lake and do what I tell you, for God's sake!"

Bedivere gave a quick bow and scurried back toward the shore, still moving uncertainly, as if measuring the significance of this symbolic action against the actual value, martial and otherwise, of Arthur's legendary sword. But as he was making his way back down toward the lake, the groaning step and heavy breathing of another knight could be heard, and I saw a shadowy figure emerging from the dispersing mist. His surcoat was in tatters, but he quickly removed his helmet and the exhausted face of Sir Palomides was revealed. "My liege!" He cried, falling to his knees at the sight of Arthur lying still in Merlin's lap. Then his quick glance took in the sprawled and bloody corpse of the usurper lying nearby, and the moor whistled in surprise, and noted in his low bass voice, "Then he is dead! The king and his traitorous nephew have killed each other, and so ends this sad story!"

I didn't bother to correct him. If that was the story Palomides wanted to tell, let him do so. He would, no doubt, compose verses to that effect, and why not let the story be told in that way? "The king lives," Merlin apprised him. "For now."

"But my friends," Palomides added, rising and taking in the rest of us, including Sir Bedivere now returning. "The Irish army is fled, and the Picts as well, after heavy losses. Even the Saxons have given up the field now that their ally Mordred has been slain. I don't know how many of Arthur's army still live. But the field, it seems, is ours." I raised my head and looked around. For as far as I could see through the dispersing mist, the field lay strewn with corpses. Here and there a riderless horse ambled, confused by the carnage. And on the far side of the plain, a few scavengers were beginning to rifle the bodies for valuables.

"It may be ours," I answered glumly. "But what are we going to do with it?"

By now Bedivere was back and reported to the king that his order was carried out. "And?" said the king with anticipation. "What then did you witness there?"

Bedivere only shrugged nervously, knowing there was something the king expected but having no clue what that might have been. "I saw nothing, My Lord…but the deep water and the wan waves."

"Traitor!" the king raged with such vehemence I thought his fragile body must burst apart with the effort of his cry. "Have I no faithful knights around me, even here at the last? Are you like one of these scavengers stripping the corpses, Bedivere, that you seek to steal my sword for the value of its pommel? Sir Palomides, can you carry out my last command?"

Sir Bedivere, abashed by the king's rebuke, held out his hand to Palomides and murmured, "I will take care of it," then ran, as best he could in his advanced years, down the slope to the lake and now, with all of us watching him, lifted Excalibur from where he had concealed it in the trees, and, holding it by the hilt in both hands, swung it upwards in a great arc and let it go, sailing the weapon end over end far out into the lake. You may believe this or not, it is your prerogative: But I can still see it as clearly as I saw it that day, more than forty years past. A thin arm, clothed in white samite, burst from under the waves and, reaching above the water, caught hold of the great sword before it plunged into the lake. Then, after brandishing the sword three times like a fencer stepping into a competition, it disappeared back into the water, pulling the sword under with it.

From the top of the hillock, we stared open-mouthed, until the king, with sudden urgency, croaked in a voice that weakened by the moment, "Help me down to the shore. I pray we are not already too late." And with that Sir Palomides lifted the king onto his back and began to make his way down to where Sir Bedivere still remained astounded.

From the other side of the lake, I could now make out a boat with a red and white sail, crossing with as much speed as it could muster to the shore toward which Palomides now bore the king. "From the Lady?" I asked, and Merlin nodded. "She is sending the barge to ferry the king to her palace on the Isle of Avalon."

"Where she once healed *your* wounds," I recalled, thinking back on how the nymph Nimue had rescued Merlin after Palomides' renegade squire had wounded him with an arrow.

270

"And where she now hopes to heal the king's injuries," the old man mused. "Or, failing that, prevent his progression towards death. Remember, if you will, how the Lady's realm lies beyond our notion of time: The king may lie there in his wounded state for years, while only a few moments will have passed in Avalon."

"Or so it is rumored," I responded skeptically. "Lord Merlin," I changed the subject. "My own wounded leg is hindering me. I know you are weakened yourself, but do you think I might be able to lean on you so that we can make our own way to the shore and see this enchanted boat?"

"Indeed," Merlin said, getting up and reaching his hand out to me as he did so. "Lean on me. God's gimpy knees, you've been doing so for years, why stop now?"

If the old man was going to joke with me, then perhaps he was not as angry with me as he had been. Or perhaps he simply did not want to quarrel then, at our last meeting. Of course, I didn't realize that's what this was. I did want to know what was going on with Bedivere, though. "Curious thing that, about Sir Bedivere," I wondered aloud. "Why would he try to keep the sword after Arthur told him to throw it? Doesn't make sense to me. I know he's no thief."

Merlin grunted as I leaned against him and we started our descent. "Confirms my suspicions," he said. "I knew it was something. Bedivere wanted the sword. He knew its reputation: That he who wields Excalibur cannot be defeated in battle. Magic sword, you see. Balderdash, of course. Just a bloody well-made sword is all. Yet it's what everyone thinks. But Bedivere wanted it because he thought he could kill Sir Lancelot with it."

I stopped and gaped at the mage in stunned silence. "Kill Lancelot? Sir Bedivere? What are you on about?"

"Oh yes," Merlin said, keeping up his slow pace and nodding sagely. "Hadn't you figured it out yet? It was Bedivere killed Sir Gareth and Gaheris. Surely you realize that."

Still I gaped. Only more so.

"Remember that enigmatic prophecy of mine? 'The maiden rises again! The look that kills strikes from behind.' We had determined that Hectimere, with the basilisk shield—the look that kills—was the

271

one who struck Tor and Aglovale from behind. But the maiden rising again? It's the dear Lady Elizabeth, Sir Bedivere's sorely grieved niece, the only maiden who has died, that rises again."

With a chill I remembered my own nightmare, in which the maiden herself had warned me, like an oracle, that she could not stay buried. "She rises," I mused. "From her grave?"

"Metaphorically, of course, you dolt. Don't you see it? Sir Bedivere could not keep her buried. Her death loomed perpetually before his eyes. His beloved niece. Slain when still only a child. Sir Tirre, who'd killed her, was gone. But his soul cried out for vengeance. Whom would he blame? Who was responsible for the girl's death? Who, indeed but Lancelot himself. Lancelot, who was needed to defend the queen in the lists but had irresponsibly disappeared. Lancelot, who had heedlessly gotten himself captured and imprisoned by a lunatic. Lancelot, who had to be sought by a host of others, including his ill-starred niece, who would have been nowhere near that evil dungeon if she hadn't been searching for the Great Knight, and been smart enough to figure out where he was. So it was Lancelot who needed to pay."

"But…but why Gareth and Gaheris? What had they to do with the lady Elizabeth's murder? They had no part in that business."

"No," Merlin acknowledged. "But Gareth was always Lancelot's greatest defender. He was defending Lancelot at the time, wasn't he? Protesting the queen's sentence by walking unarmed in her wake, just waiting for the rescue he knew was coming. And Gaheris would go along with him—he always did. Killing them would hurt Lancelot more than anything else Bedivere could imagine, except of course the queen's burning, which he knew Lancelot wasn't going to allow anyway. But think of it the way he did: Not only did killing Gareth pain Lancelot, making it look as if Lancelot had killed him himself would pain him more, and it would set Gawain and all of Arthur's shattered Table after him. Bedivere hoped that the death of Gareth would bring about the death of Lancelot. And the whole thing was so easy for him. Gaheris and Gareth were right behind him in the procession: All he needed to do was stab them quickly while their attention was focused on Lancelot and his riders. Then raise his sword and pretend to be fighting off the rescuers but in fact slashing down at the already-fallen Gareth and Gaheris so that it looked like they'd been slain from above."

"Thomas told me how they'd found Bedivere wandering on the field after the Queen's rescue, his sword bloodied, and babbling about his niece," I remembered and now, in a rush, I remembered the other hints we'd had: "Then Mordred was telling the truth, that he hadn't slain his own brothers. And Hectimere—no wonder he was confused when I charged him with Gareth's death. Oh lord, now I recall Sir Palomides mentioning how Sir Lucan worried about his brother's inordinate grief for Lady Elizabeth, and Bedivere's own reluctance to abandon the siege of Benwick Castle. I should have known."

"Of course you should," Merlin agreed. His voice was growing weak again as we neared the lakeshore and he tired of holding me up. "As long as Arthur besieged Lancelot, there was hope that the Great Knight could be vanquished. As long as Gawain, a more powerful knight than himself, sought his own vengeance on Lancelot, there was hope that Bedivere could enjoy the Great Knight's destruction vicariously. But now, at the end of the Table and of Arthur's reign itself, Bedivere must take vengeance himself if it is to be had at all, and to do that he must have Excalibur."

"But he's thrown Excalibur away now!" I added. "He's given up his desire for revenge?"

Merlin scoffed. "His loyalty to the king forced him to make that decision, but make no mistake. He will kill Lancelot if he is ever given the chance."

Glumly I muttered, "For the death of my master Gareth, he should be brought to justice! What shall we do?"

"Do?" Merlin looked at me bewildered. "For justice? The kingdom is no more. There is no court. There are no magistrates or judges handing down sentences in Logres, because there is no government after this battle. You've done your part in bringing that about. The axis of the world tips toward chaos. Perhaps Lancelot will come to restore order. Perhaps the king's closest living relative, his distant cousin Constantine in Cornwall, will try to rally supporters to some cause. Or perhaps the Saxons will come back after this and sweep into power themselves. Who knows? But there can be no bringing Bedivere to justice at this point. The only thing you can do is wreak your vengeance on him as you did upon Hectimere and Mordred, and call that justice if you will."

We had reached the shore, and with Bedivere, Palomides, and the king, watched as the barge approached. I could see clearly now that three women were aboard, all dressed in black mourning robes. The first was the Lady of the Lake herself, who commanded the barge and seemed intent on bringing the king aboard as quickly as possible. At her side was her chief lady-in-waiting, Merlin's own beloved Nimue, looking concerned not only for Arthur but for her own old ardent follower himself. And seated in the front of the boat, reaching out toward the king as if she could not reach him fast enough, was his half-sister Morgan le Fay.

"My brother," she said, weeping. "You've waited so long, I pray there is still time left to save you!"

Two men were rowing the boat onto the sandy shore and leaped out to assist Sir Palomides in taking the king's barely breathing form onto the barge. I recognized Sir Launfal, the king's former knight, now consort of the Lady, and Sir Florent, Arthur's own grand-nephew now wed to Merlin's beloved Nimue. Florent had never gotten on well with the king's sister, but I imagined that the ever-adaptable Morgan could adjust to that situation, at least until she had helped heal the king and felt safe in returning to her own castle. They placed the king into his sister's arms, and her pose reminded me of a pieta. The king, beyond speech now, blinked at me benevolently, and raised his head ever-so-slightly to Bedivere and Palomides.

But it was Merlin who surprised me. Slowly and carefully, as if it were expected of him, he stepped aboard the barge himself, as Nimue held out her hand to draw him in. "Old Man!" I cried. "What do you think you're doing?" I had assumed that the mage would remain with me, that I could continue to lean on him in the turmoil we would have to pass through in the wake of the fall of Logres. But Merlin had other ideas.

"My time in the world of men has come to an end, Gildas. My sole purpose was to support Arthur, the greatest king in Christendom. If along the way I was able to be of some service in helping a young Cornish blockhead to maturity, I'll count that among my triumphs as well. He passes now to Avalon, and I go with him. Who knows? If his wounds can be attended to, he may yet come again, and I shall return with him. But who knows when that will be, if it happens at all? Oh, God's eyelids, boy, don't be blubbering now!" For it must be admitted, tears were streaming unabashedly down my cheeks. The boat began to move away from us now, on its way to Avalon, and Merlin called out a final valediction: "Farewell Gildas! Remember what I've taught you! If you ever do see Lancelot or Guinevere again, remember me to them."

Now the boat drew farther and farther from the shore, and Bedivere wept, kneeling in the sand, for the loss of his master. And Sir Palomides began to intone in his sonorous bass an impromptu dirge, whose spontaneous words must, I thought at the time, echo down the long years whenever Arthur's name was invoked:

> *Oh King of Glory, from whose breast*
> *Salvation came to ease our woe,*
> *On earth you set us on the quest*
> *To forge Your kingdom here below.*
> *For which task our Arthur, Lord, You chose:*
> *From the great deep to the great deep he goes.*

After the boat had disappeared, I glanced down at the prostrate figure of Sir Bedivere, lost and grieving in the sand, and I thought of all the damage his thirst for vengeance had caused: the deaths of Gareth and Gaheris. The enmity of Lancelot and Gawain that had necessitated the siege of Benwick and sanctioned the installment of Mordred in the regency, and thus fomented his rebellion. Not to mention the mad desire of Gawain for revenge, that cracked the Round Table itself and culminated in Gawain's own death. Then I considered what my own avenging mania had caused—the deaths of Mordred and Hectimere, but in the same battle the deaths, I must now admit, of Thomas, of Ywain, of Kay, of every lost knight whose body lay rotting on Camlann field.

Then I closed my eyes and forswore vengeance for evermore. And I turned my back on Bedivere, and walked away, into the darkness and the uncertainty of the new world.

EPILOGUE
SAINT DUNSTAN'S ABBEY

The shadows had grown long in the infirmary, where even with the windows opened to let in the late afternoon breeze it had become close and stuffy as the young monks and novices gathered around the bed of their oldest brother. The aged monk cleared his throat, having completed his long tale even as the infirmarian was finishing his examination and was, with a grim and subtle gesture, pursing his lips and giving the prior an almost invisible shake of the head.

"There it is, Prior Stephen," Brother Gildas concluded. "Now you know. *I* was responsible for that disastrous Battle of Camlann. It was *my* sword that flashed and put an end to those peace negotiations. It was *my* thirst for revenge that led to the end of Arthur's reign, and to the deaths of all those good knights. I've carried the burden of that guilt with me for nearly five decades, and I've told those stories of Arthur and Merlin and the Knights of the Round Table again and again over the years, partly as a self-imposed penance, but I've never told this particular story before. Consider it my confession. And by the grim face of our brother infirmarian here, I suspect it may be my last confession, is that not so, Brother Aedwulf?"

Aedwulf, the most skilled healer at the abbey, gave Brother Gildas the same pursed-lip expression he had given the prior, and then nodded ever so slightly. Brother Gildas had been increasingly tired over the past several weeks, finding it more and more difficult to do even his cloister walks during prayers, and for the last few days, displaying a marked reluctance even to rise from his narrow bed in the morning. Then he had fallen during the office of matins the previous morning after a bout of dizziness and had been in and out of consciousness ever since. He had rallied this afternoon when his small knot of admirers had come to visit him, and had been inspired to tell them this last story of Camelot, which had energized him even more: He spoke almost manically, as if compelled to tell all before this last burst of energy waned forever. He knew there would be questions and so steeled himself to answer if he could.

He glanced first at the tall, thin Brother Nennius, always most interested of all the monks in the details of the story, as if trying to memorize them himself. "Sir Lancelot? Did he return to Logres? What did he do when he found the king gone and the Table destroyed?"

"Did he find Guinevere again, and were they reunited?" Curly-headed Brother Abelard wanted to know—as always, chiefly interested in the fates of lovers.

Brother Gildas closed his eyes and breathed deeply. With some effort he said, in a voice barely above a whisper, "Lancelot arrived, with Sir Bors and all of his allies, and when he found that Arthur was king no more, he made his way directly to Amesbury, to the queen. It was, as Arthur had predicted, quite a shock to him to find that the queen had taken the veil. She was done with court life and with power games, and her conscience would not let her ignore her own culpability in the deaths of all those good knights and the fall of the king. She would remain in the convent, she told him, to do penance for her past deeds. She hoped she could do no more harm from inside the cloister, and hoped to be able to do some good." The old monk paused for breath, then added, "She didn't say it, but I think she also liked the fact that there behind those convent walls, there were no men to tell her what to do any more. Most of her ladies-in-waiting stayed with her and became her fellow nuns. The young Lady Barbara, though, whose Pelleas had survived the war, chose to marry him and so left the queen's service. I think Lady Mary was the only other one that decided to make her way in the world rather than in the abbey."

By now Gildas was finding his second wind, and felt a need to talk, to unburden all he could. "The funny thing was that Lancelot, not to be outdone by the woman he'd worshipped for so many years, looked on the whole thing as a new opportunity and a challenge. If Guinevere was going to move on to holy living, by God, he was going to as well, and was going to do it better than she did! He had Bors to guide him, after all. Sir Bors would certainly have entered holy orders himself after the Grail quest, but he felt he had to come back to Camelot because Lancelot needed him. *Now* Lancelot needed Bors to show him how to live a holy life. They visited Gawain's grave, as the king's nephew had asked, and there Lancelot made a vow to withdraw from the world. He and Bors teamed with William, the old bishop of Caerleon, who was pretty much out of a job after the fall of Camelot, and the three of them set up their own little hermitage in the forest outside Caerleon, joined eventually by Bleoberis and Brandiles and Sir Urry, Sir Lucan and Sir Lowell, and they spent all their time in prayer, penance, and good works. When Lancelot finally died Bishop William even had a vision of him being borne straight to heaven, and it was the same day Sir Ector found them, after searching for them since Lancelot had left Benwick. Ector gave a stirring eulogy for his brother—I happened to have heard about it and attended the funeral—and he called Lancelot the 'most courteous knight that ever bore shield,' and 'the truest friend that ever mounted a horse' and 'the truest lover that ever loved a woman' and 'the kindest man that ever struck with a sword,' and other illogical but perfectly appropriate titles. It was a sad day for chivalry, and I wept again for its loss." Brother Gildas stopped again for breath.

"But how do you know all this?" asked Brother Balthazar, the young monk with the wing-like ears. "Where did *you* go after the battle, what did you do that you could know what Guinevere said to Lancelot when he visited her?"

Gildas smiled. "I had it straight from the queen herself," he said. "I rounded up Achilles before I left Camlann, and then I went to the tents and baggage and found my dog. And I went off into the wild. Lived off the land until Achilles was ready to carry me again, and my own wound was healed, and went first to the abbey at Amesbury. I needed to see where Rosemounde was buried, you see. After the first shock at seeing the little mound, which tore a hole in my heart, I was able to accept that she was really gone. It wasn't real to me until I saw that spot. It was a simple grave there among the nuns, but she was never haughty. She'd have been fine with that simple remembrance. And the queen told me she would make sure that the sisters prayed for Rosemounde's soul on a regular basis in perpetuity. If you can believe it. I knew that probably meant as long as Guinevere was alive, but that was all right. Rosemounde was an angel and I didn't think she needed their prayers. But I'm sure she would have appreciated them anyway.

"That's when the queen told me she had just had a visit from Lancelot, and what she told him. She looked me square in the eye as well, and reminded me that I had talked about a vocation myself at one time, especially after Rosemounde had married Mordred, and suggested I think about it some more. I told her I would definitely do that, but I wasn't ready then to forsake the world. I was feeling too guilty about what I'd done to Arthur and the murders I'd committed in the name of justice to think about turning to the Church."

"Sir B...B...Bedivere? Wh...what happened to him?" came a question from Brother Notker, nicknamed the Stammerer for obvious reasons. "And S...Sir P...P...Palomides, who you l...left there at the l...lake?"

The old monk rolled his eyes upward, searching his memories. "Bedivere," he answered, "never did make any attempt on Lancelot's life. Though he must have known the Great Knight had come back; there was a bit of a furor when his ships landed and his knights disembarked, and he did a virtual progress to Amesbury after assessing the situation. I don't think it was fear that held Bedivere back. I think the carnage of that wicked day at Camlann knocked his thirst for vengeance out of him, just as it had me. I do think he wandered about for awhile, but his brother and brother-in-law were with Lancelot, eventually, in his new religious community, and Bedivere wanted no part in that. So he had nowhere to go. I had heard that he went over the Narrow Sea and tried to find a lord who would take him on as a retainer somewhere in Gaul or Provence, but at his age that was unlikely. I never heard news of him again. But if I were to speculate, I'd say that faced with his losses and with his guilt over the sorrow he'd caused, he may have ended up taking his own life. Or at least taking part in some reckless skirmish or adventure and got himself killed.

"As for Palomides, I can be more specific. Like Bedivere, he had no desire to join Lancelot and Bors in their devotions: Yes, he'd been baptized, but his Moorish roots and his experience in the crusade would have made such a step distasteful to him So he, too, spent some time wandering from court to court, but with more success than Bedivere, because he was a younger and more puissant knight, but also because of his talent as a maker and singer of love songs. And I have no doubt that he also spread stories of Arthur's court through his songs: That's where the myth of Arthur and Mordred killing one another at Camlann came from.

"But Palomides didn't wander forever," Brother Gildas continued. "You might remember how Robin Kempe had been with Lancelot at Benwick, along with Alan of Winchester, as well as the dwarf Thorvald? Well that lot certainly had no intentions of turning monk with Lancelot, and given the anarchy of the times, they thought the best thing for them would be to go off and live off the land, as I had at first. They formed a little band in the woods of north Logres, and lived by hunting and, it must be admitted, a bit of roguery. Palomides eventually fell in with Robin and his band, and that's the last I heard of any of them." He paused, breathing hard once more. It seemed clear that he could not go on for much longer.

That's when the red-haired Brother Christopher, who had heard more of Gildas's stories than anyone else present except Prior Stephen himself, asked the final question: "And so what brought you here, Brother Gildas? How did you join the community here at St. Dunstan's?"

The old brother lay back, staring up at the ceiling, his strength was waning now. His listeners leaned in close as his voice dwindled. "Oh, I was a lone knight errant myself for a time. I did fulfill my promise to Ywain, and looked up lady Alundine, to tell her what had happened to him and pass along his last message. She was broken-hearted but grateful. And we let the lion loose together. I think she was a little relieved not to have it so close by all the time. For a time I served

281

in her castle guard, but after awhile I had the feeling that she was in the market for a new Lord of the Manor, and frankly I couldn't think about such things. The loss of Rosemounde had so bereft my soul that the thought of any other woman overwhelmed me with shame and grief. And so I left Alundine's service. For a time I served the King of North Wales, one of the petty kings that had been Arthur's allies in the old days. But I grew restless, and so Achilles, Guinevere and I offered our services to my old liege, King Mark, but that didn't last terribly long either. Oh, I didn't have any real complaints about Mark, but he sure wasn't Arthur. I decided to leave him as well, and considered heading north to look up Morgan le Fay at her castle in the old kingdom of Gorre. But I hadn't traveled far when I lost my dog Guinevere.

"She'd been my closest and constant companion for some six years by then, but I couldn't say how old she was when I first adopted her, so I can't say how old she was when she died. But I suppose it was a ripe old age for a borzoi. Her death triggered memories of all the others: not only Rosemounde but Merlin too and Gareth and Elizabeth and Colgrevaunce and my mother and everyone else who'd left me. I truly felt as if I'd lost my very last friend, and sat down on the road next to her bereft and weeping. It may have been my lowest point. And that's when I knew what I had to do. The world held nothing for me anymore. I could do as the queen had bid me. I could withdraw from this world that passes soon as flowers fair, and join a community that worked in its own small way for the physical and spiritual good of its members and to the extent possible the outside world. I would do penance for the evil I had wrought. I vowed to divest myself of all worldly goods and afterwards to offer myself as a novice at the first monastic house I could find.

"I took Guinevere to Camelot, where Arthur's cousin Constantine was trying to establish some sort of order in the region, and buried her in sight of the kennels where she'd been so happy in the past. I rode Achilles back to Launceston, and there I left him with my father Myghal, to use as he saw fit or to put out to pasture. And I left Myghal my sword Almace and my precious mail hauberk he had made me, for I had use for them no more. And wearing only a rough brown tunic and a walking stick, I started north. And reached this place. And here I stayed."

Brother Gildas seemed to choke on those last words, and with a sudden spasm his face stiffened, his eyes bulging. His temporary ebullience, which had lulled them all into insouciance, was spent, and the reality of his physical condition came home to them all. With that Brother Gildas closed his eyes and seemed to slip into an ultimate insentience. The infirmarian bent down quickly to listen for Gildas's breathing and feel his pulse, then looked with mild alarm at Prior Stephen, who began herding the young monks out of the room. He looked grim, and the novices had tears in their eyes as they passed back out into the cloister.

Prior Stephen knelt by the side of Brother Gildas's bed, taking from the pouch at his belt a stole that he placed over his shoulders, his prayer book, and his pyx, which contained the consecrated wafer for the administration of the viaticum. He spoke gently into Gildas's ear and, seeing a flicker in the dying brother's eyes, determined there was enough life there to allow him to receive the sacrament. Taking Gildas's long narrative of his sins as his final confession, Prior Stephen placed the consecrated host in Gildas's mouth, and noted there was enough life left to allow him to swallow what was put on his tongue. And with his last instant of consciousness, Brother Gildas reached inside his robe in order to clutch a faded piece of blue ribbon from the hair of a fifteen-year-old girl that he had carried next to his heart for some fifty winters.

Now, blinking away his own tears, Stephen took out the consecrated oil from his pouch and putting some on his thumb, placed the sign of the cross on Gildas's closed eyes as he recited the prayer:

"Per istam sanctan unctionem et suam piissimam misericordiam, indulgeat tibi Dominus quidquid per visum"

("Through this Holy Unction or oil, and through the great goodness of His mercy, may God pardon thee whatever sins thou hast committed by evil use of sight")

If Gildas heard any of this he did not react. It was merely background noise to him. He was completely caught up in a vision—or perhaps it was just one last dream—of a beautiful white light that lay before him, and of a long tunnel through which he seemed to be passing as he moved toward the light. All about him a host of faces and voices surrounded him on his passage through that long shaft.

On his left he saw Arthur and Gawain, Lancelot and Bors, smiling encouragingly as he moved by them. On his right stood his master Sir Gareth, and behind him Ywain, with Thomas and his old friend Colgrevaunce, and he imagined he heard Gareth saying, "We'll tell some fine stories now!" Again on his left, to his amazement, he saw Mordred, standing with Hectimere and with Sir Bedivere as well, and in their eyes forgiveness and a little bit of surprise that they were here at all. Then once more to his right, smiling reassuringly, stood his father Myghal and his long dead mother, who stood holding the baby sister he had never known.

Prior Stephen droned on, busily making signs of the cross over all the ports of Gildas's body through which sin might enter.

"Auditotum, odorátum, gustum et locutiónem, tactum, gressum deliquisti.

(Sight, hearing, smell, taste and speech, touch, ability to walk).

Meanwhile, on the other side, Gildas felt he was passing the queen, and with her the beloved Lady Elizabeth, gone too soon, and Guinevere seemed to whisper to him as he passed, "Welcome Gildas. You know you were often the only person I could stand."

Now, having nearly reached the light itself, Gildas passed, on his right hand, the figure of an old man seated at a small table, looking at him expectantly. "God's knuckles, you Cornish numbskull, what's taken you so long? White or black?"

But before he could answer, Gildas entered the light itself, and, as his eyes adjusted, he saw quite clearly the Lady Rosemounde, an eager borzoi lying expectantly at her feet, and in her arms a beautiful newborn girl child whose smile was the picture of her mother's signature smirk.

Rosemounde flashed her dark eyes at him. "Welcome, silly boy," she said. "What a long time you've been about it!"

CAST OF CHARACTERS

Aglovale de Galis: Eldest legitimate son of Sir Pellinore. A knight of the Round Table, Aglovale is killed during Sir Lancelot's rescue of the queen.

Agravain of Orkney: Sir Agravain is a nephew of King Arthur, one of the brothers of Gawain and Gareth. His accusations set in motion the events of the book.

Alan of Winchester: Alan of Winchester is a corporal in the king's guards, under the command of Robin Kempe. With Robin, he proves loyal to Sir Lancelot.

Alison: Lady Alison, one of the queen's newer ladies-in-waiting, is the petite, dark-haired daughter of an alderman from Bath.

Anne: Lady Anne is the longest-serving of Guinevere's ladies-in-waiting. She has a tendency to take charge when the queen is not around, and the other ladies tend to let her.

Arthur: King of Logres, holding sovereignty as well over Ireland, Scandinavia, Scotland, Wales, and Cornwall, Brittany, Normandy, and all of Gaul. And he is claimant to the emperor's throne in Rome. He is the son of Uther Pendragon and Ygraine, former Countess of Cornwall.

Ascamore: Sir Ascamore is a veteran knight of Arthur's Table, who joins Agravain and Mordred's plot to capture Lancelot and is killed when the Great Knight escapes.

Bagdemagus: King Bagdemagus is a petty king of the land of Gorre, one of Arthur's faithful vassals and a former knight of the Round Table.

Baldwin of Orkney: Sir Baldwin is the former squire of Sir Agravain, and has always been known for his surly temper. He is killed in the queen's chamber during Mordred's attempt to trap Sir Lancelot.

Barbara: Lady Barbara is another new lady-in-waiting to Queen Guinevere. She is a beautiful young teenaged girl, attracted to Sir Pelleas.

Bedivere: Sir Bedivere is one of Arthur's oldest knights, having been with him from the beginning of his reign. The recent death of his niece, Elizabeth, has disturbed him profoundly.

Bellias le Orgulous: A proud knight of the Outer Isles who is slain by Sir Lancelot during his rescue of the queen.

Blamor de Ganys: Sir Blamor is a knight of the Round Table and a close ally of Lancelot and Bors, from their own country.

Bleoberis: Sir Bleoberis is one of the knights of the Round Table closely allied to Lancelot and Bors.

Bors: Sir Bors de Ganis is Sir Lancelot's cousin and his closest companion. He is steady, logical, and true. He is also pious, and was one of the three chief Grail knights.

Brandiles: Sir Brandiles is a relatively obscure knight but one closely devoted to Sir Lancelot. He was one of the official Queen's Knights before joining Lancelot's party in the war against Arthur.

Breunor le Noir: Nicknamed (by Sir Kay) La Cote Male Tayle ("The Badly Tailored Coat"), Sir Breunor is a supporter of Sir Lancelot, and slips out of Camelot to join him after the queen is condemned to death.

Caradoc: Sir Caradoc is a petty king of Gwent, an older knight of Arthur's court who, devoted to Lancelot, secretly leaves Camelot after the queen is condemned to death.

Colgrevaunce: Sir Colgrevaunce was a close friend of Gildas, killed on the Grail quest.

Cursesalyne: Sir Cursesalyne is an otherwise obscure knight who takes part in the conspiracy of Mordred and Agravain to entrap Sir Lancelot in the queen's chamber. He is killed by Lancelot in the subsequent fight.

Degore: Sir Degore is a knight of the Round Table residing near Winchester. He is married to Lady Constance, a former lady-in-waiting to the queen who is also the daughter of King Bagdemagus. He takes part in the plot against Sir Lancelot in vengeance for the death of his brother-in-law, Sir Meliagaunt. He is one of the knights Lancelot kills in his escape.

Ector de Maris: Sir Ector is the brother of Sir Lancelot and the second son of King Ban of Benwick. He is, of course, a staunch ally of his brother.

Elizabeth: Lady Elizabeth was one of Queen Guinevere's youngest ladies-in-waiting. She was the thirteen-year-old niece of Sir Bedivere and Sir Lucan, daughter of Sir Lowell of Winchester, and sister of Lady Mary. Elizabeth was shy but outspoken and independent when roused, and the queen had been cultivating her as a potential wife for Gildas. She was killed in the previous novel, during the rescue of Sir Lancelot.

Ettarre: A beautiful lady of the Orkneys, who is the object of Sir Pelleas's affections.

Gaheris of Orkney: Sir Gaheris is son of King Lot of Orkney and Queen Margause—whom he is known to have beheaded when he

287

found her in bed with Sir Lamorak. Gaheris resembles his younger brother Sir Gareth in coloring, but not in temperament.

Galleron of Galway: Sir Galleron was a Scottish knight who originally was an enemy of Gawain's, but became a knight of the Table. In this book he joins his fellow Scots Agravain and Mordred in their plot against Lancelot, and is killed in the assault on Lancelot in the queen's chambers.

Gareth of Orkney: Sir Gareth is a knight of the Round Table and younger brother to Sir Gawain, Sir Gaheris, and Sir Agravain, and half-brother to Sir Mordred. He is son of King Lot of Orkney and Margause, the daughter of Ygraine and Duke Gorlois of Cornwall and so Arthur's half–sister, which makes him King Arthur's nephew. Gildas was formerly squire to Sir Gareth.

Gawain of Orkney: Sir Gawain is Arthur's nephew and heir apparent. He is son of King Lot of Orkney and Arthur's half-sister Margause, and the older brother of Sir Gareth, Sir Gaheris, Sir Agravain, and Mordred, and father of Lovell, his former squire.

Geraint of Dumnonia: Geraint is a young knight, but a petty king of that region of Logres called Dumnonia. He comes down in support of Sir Mordred in this story.

Gildas of Cornwall: Son of a Cornish armor-maker, formerly squire to Sir Gareth and page to Queen Guinevere, Sir Gildas of Cornwall is one of the newest knights of King Arthur's Round Table. Gildas narrates the story and is Merlin's assistant in his investigations. He is twenty years old at the beginning of this story, and remains in love with Lady Rosemounde, lady-in-waiting to the queen, who is married to the villainous Sir Mordred.

Griflet: Sir Griflet is a veteran knight of the Round Table, here killed during Lancelot's violent rescue of the queen.

Gromerson Erioure: Sir Gromerson Erioure is one of the knights convinced by Mordred to take part in the plot to corner Sir Lancelot in the queen's chamber, and is slain by Lancelot in the ensuing battle.

Guinevere: Queen of Logres, and married to King Arthur. Gildas was formerly a page in her household. She is the daughter of Leodegrance, king of Cameliard, an early ally of Arthur's. Her long-standing affair with Sir Lancelot, Arthur's chief knight, is a perilous secret in the court. She is fiercely protective of her lady-in-waiting, Rosemounde of Brittany and of her former page, Gildas of Cornwall.

Hectimere: Sir Gaheris's former squire, now a knight of the Round Table, who sides with Agravain in his dispute with his brothers.

Helyan le Blanc: A young knight who, devoted to his foster father Sir Bors, is fiercely loyal to him and to Sir Lancelot. He leaves Camelot in secret after the queen is condemned to death.

Hoel: Duke of Brittany, and Arthur's vassal and close ally from the beginning of his reign. He is the father of Lady Rosemounde.

Holly: Master Holly is Queen Guinevere's aged clerk and doorkeeper.

Kay: Sir Kay is King Arthur's seneschal, which means he is in charge of the king's household. He was Arthur's foster-brother when they were boys, and Arthur promised Kay's father Sir Ector that there would always be a place for Kay in his court. He tends to be something of a braggart and a bully, but his loyalty to the king is unquestionable.

Lady of the Lake: Queen of Faerie, a being of great mystical power. She is responsible for giving the sword Excalibur to King Arthur. She lives in an enchanted palace north of Camelot on a lake named for her. It was in this palace that Lancelot du Lac was raised.

Lamorak de Galis: Sir Lamorak was the son of King Pellinore, who killed King Lot and thus began a feud with the house of Orkney. Sir

Gaheris caught Sir Lamorak in bed with his mother Margause and let him escape, but Gawain, Gaheris, Mordred and Agravain killed Sir Lamorak later in ambush.

Lancelot: Sir Lancelot du Lac is the greatest knight of Arthur's table, and is the secret lover of Queen Guinevere. He is the son of King Ban of Benwick, and his close kinsmen—Sir Bors and Sir Ector—form a powerful bloc of Round Table knights.

Lavayne: Sir Lavayne is the son of Sir Bernard of Astolat, lord of Guildford, and is wholly devoted to Sir Lancelot.

Lot: King Lot of Orkney was an enemy of Arthur's who would not accept the fifteen-year old boy as king of Logres. With an alliance of other kings, he made war on Arthur to get him off the throne, but was ultimately defeated and killed (by King Pellinore). He was married to Arthur's half-sister Margause, and was the father of Gawain, Gaheris, Agravain, and Gareth.

Lovell of Orkney: Sir Gawain's second son, and his former squire. He is now a knight of the Round Table and at first a close ally of his father and uncles Gareth and Gaheris. Yet he is persuaded by Mordred to join the plot against Lancelot.

Lowell of Winchester: Sir Lowell was married to the sister of Sir Lucan and Sir Bedivere, and is the father of the Lady Mary, one of the queen's ladies in waiting. As this book opens he is squire to Sir Gaheris.

Lucan: Sir Lucan the Butler is, like his brother Sir Bedivere, one of King Arthur's earliest knights. He is uncle to Lady Mary and the murdered Lady Elizabeth. He makes the difficult choice to follow Sir Lancelot when he breaks from the king.

Mador de la Porte: Sir Mador de la Porte is an Irish knight who, in an earlier installment of this series (*Fatal Feast*) accused Queen

Guinevere of the murder of his cousin, Sir Patrise. He was later forced to retract his accusation after being beaten by Sir Lancelot in a trial by combat. Here, he is one of the knights killed in Mordred's attempt to capture Lancelot.

Margause: Mother of Gawain and his brothers, Margause was the wife of King Lot of Orkney and was one of Arthur's half-sisters, daughter of his mother Ygraine and Duke Gorlois of Cornwall. Her incestuous affair with her half-brother Arthur led to the conception of her youngest son, Mordred. Not known for her high moral standards, Margause was killed by her own son Sir Gaheris when he caught her in bed with Sir Lamorak.

Mary: Lady Mary of Winchester is one of the queen's ladies-in-waiting. She is thin, blonde, vain, and talkative. She is Sir Lucan's and Sir Bedivere's niece and the daughter of Sir Lowell of Winchester.

Meliagaunt: Kidnapper of Queen Guinevere in a previous story (*The Knight of the Cart*). Killed in that book by Lancelot in a trial by combat.

Meliot de Logres: A new knight who is cousin of Nimue, the Damsel of the Lake, and was once saved by Sir Lancelot. Yet he takes part in Agravain's assault on Lancelot and is killed by the Great Knight.

Melyon of the Mountain: Sir Melyon of the Mountain is an otherwise obscure knight who joins with Agravain and Mordred in their plot against Sir Lancelot, and dies in the battle in the queen's chamber.

Merlin: Arthur's chief adviser in his early days, Merlin helped Arthur solidify his realm, win the war against King Lot and his allies and the war with Ireland. Rumored to have magical powers and to be able to see the future, Merlin is essentially just a more logical and scientific thinker than most of his contemporaries. He is often called upon to solve the mysteries of Camelot.

Mordred: Sir Mordred is the youngest brother of Sir Gawain and Sir Gareth, the youngest child of Arthur's half-sister Margause. He is married to Gildas's beloved Rosemounde. He is also, secretly, the king's own bastard son.

Morgan le Fay: Former queen of Gorre and wife of King Uriens, Morgan is the half-sister of King Arthur, with whom she has a rather rocky history. She is also the mother of Sir Ywain, the Knight of the Lion.

Myghal of Launceston: Myghal is Gildas's father back in Cornwall, the armorer and creator of Gildas's magnificent mail hauberk.

Nell of Launceston: Common-law wife of Gildas's father in Cornwall.

Nimue: Lady-in-waiting to the Lady of the Lake, Nimue lives in the Lady's mystical palace and never ages. Her beauty enchanted Merlin, who remains in love with her though she has definitively rejected him.

Palomides: Sir Palomides is a Moorish knight who has joined the Round Table and become a Christian. He was Sir Tristram's great rival for the love of Isolde, and is known as a composer of love poems. He is a close friend of Sir Gareth and, by extension, Gildas. He is also one of the "Queen's Knights" who remains faithful to her in this tale.

Pelleas: Sir Pelleas is known as "the Lover." He is a Scottish knight whose loyalty to the house of Orkney convinces him to come down on the side of Sir Mordred as this story progresses.

Pellinore: King Pellinore was an early ally of King Arthur and killed King Lot in battle, thus kicking off the feud between his house and Lot's. His children include Sir Lamorak and Sir Perceval, as well as Sir Aglovale and Sir Tor.

Perceval de Galis: Sir Perceval was the youngest child of King Pellinore and one of the three Grail knights. After achieving the Grail he entered a monastery.

Peter: Peter is Queen Guinevere's former page, who is now Sir Gawain's new squire.

Petipace of Winchelsee: Sir Petipace was originally a knight defeated by Sir Tor, and as a result was sent to Camelot to pledge his loyalty to the king. Ultimately, he was raised to the Order of the Round Table. But here, he takes part in Mordred's assault on Lancelot in the queen's chamber and is killed by the Great Knight.

Priamus: Sir Priamus is a Tuscan knight loyal to King Arthur, who is killed during Lancelot's rescue of the queen.

Robin Kempe: Captain of the King's Guard and of the Royal Archers, Robin spends a good deal of time on guard in the barbican of Camelot, when he isn't training his archers. A friend of Gildas, he is imprisoned in this book after opening the front gate of Camelot to allow Sir Lancelot and his supporters to escape after the battle in the queen's chambers.

Roger: Roger is the chief cook of Camelot.

Rosemounde of Brittany: Lady Rosemounde, lady-in-waiting to Queen Guinevere, is the object of Gildas's deepest affections. She was married to Sir Mordred in Gildas's absence so that her father could make a valuable political alliance with King Arthur. She remains in that perilous marriage, but is protected by the queen as long as she remains in Camelot.

Taber: Taber is the chief stable hand at Camelot.

Thomas: Young sandy-haired former squire to Sir Ywain, Sir Thomas is now a knight of the Round Table and one of the Queen's Knights.

Because of their similar positions, Thomas has been one of Gildas of Cornwall's closer friends. Like his former master, he is a close ally of Gawain and of Gareth.

Thorvald: Thorvald is an old dwarf with a white beard, who formerly drove a cart in which prisoners rode who were being taken to places of punishment, but now makes a living as a merchant. He is devoted to Lancelot.

Tor: Sir Tor is the illegitimate son of King Pellinore, who becomes a knight of the Round Table, and is killed during Lancelot's rescue of the queen.

Tristram: Sir Tristram was nephew to King Mark of Cornwall, and in love with his uncle's queen, La Belle Isolde. He was murdered in Brittany prior to the events of this story.

Urry: Sir Urry is a Hungarian knight who, having been wounded in a tournament in Spain, was healed by Sir Lancelot, and so is devoted to him.

Vivien: Lady Vivien is one of Queen Guinevere's ladies-in-waiting. She is French by birth, has green eyes, and enjoys romances, poetry, and gossip.

William of Glastonbury: Bishop of the great cathedral of Saint David in Caerleon.

William of Newberry: Chief huntsman of the royal castle of Camelot.

Ywain: Sir Ywain, known as the "Knight of the Lion" because he often goes on adventures with his pet lion, is another nephew of King Arthur, the son of King Uriens and Morgan le Fay, Arthur's half-sister through his mother Ygraine.

ABOUT THE AUTHOR

Jay Ruud is a retired professor of medieval literature at the University of Central Arkansas. In addition to *Fatal Feast, The Knight's Riddle, The Bleak and Empty Sea, Lost in the Quagmire,* and *Knight of the Cart*—the first five books in his Merlin mystery series—he is the author of *"Many a Song and Many a Leccherous Lay": Tradition and Individuality in Chaucer's Lyric Poetry* (1992), the *Encyclopedia of Medieval Literature* (2006), *A Critical Companion to Dante* (2008), and *A Critical Companion to Tolkien* (2011). He taught at UCA for fourteen years, prior to which he was dean of the College of Arts and Sciences at Northern State University in South Dakota. He has a Ph.D. in Medieval Literature from the University of Wisconsin-Milwaukee.